PROLOGUE
GONE

I breathed in and out trying to calm myself, my chest tight and constricted. Looking down at my sister, I reached out with my mind for some hint of life in her. I had just learned of our ability to communicate telepathically hours before, but somehow in those short hours, I realized that we had always been able to communicate that way on some level. That is how I now knew she was dead.

You would think that the bullet holes in Selena's chest were the biggest clue, but they weren't. It was the silence... The inability to sense the presence of Selena was more proof to me of her death, than the physical evidence of bullet holes.

I turned and scanned the area around me. It didn't take a hunter or a tracker to see the signs on the ground of what had happened here. The walls of the gully where Selena now lay showed where she had slid down the steep bank then tried to hide behind a large rock. Other footprints were along the rim. The murderer had obviously come upon my sister, and the hiding spot became a dead-end trap. All that he had to do was point and shoot. He didn't even need to enter the gully.

There was still danger present, but I didn't care anymore. My twin sister meant the world to me, even though we were opposite in so many ways.

Slumping to the ground next to Selena, I was not shocked to feel that her hands were cold and growing stiff. I knew that they would be.

In some distant part of my brain, it amazed me that I had found Selena at all. Her hiding spot was located fifty miles out of the nearest town in a remote area that could only be accessed by traveling a series of dirt roads. Selena's body was nearly two miles from the nearest dirt road in a gully gouged out from the run off of melting snow. It was dry now.

I reached out with my mind again, desperate for the smallest spark of life from Selena's lifeless body.

Emptiness.

And yet, I did sense a distant presence, and warning bells went off in my head that whoever it was represented a dire danger to me personally. From my experience earlier that day, I was no match for that danger, but I no longer cared.

The loss of my sister crashed down on me at that instance. I began to brush loose dirt off of her. Whoever had killed her had begun to kick dirt onto her lifeless body, but probably gave it up realizing how impossible it was for anyone to find her in such a remote area. The killer had walked away leaving my sister exposed to the elements and whatever animals were in the area. The grief was overwhelming, and I laid my head on her shoulder and began to cry.

I don't know how long I lay there. One thing was for sure, life didn't seem worth living without my sister. She was my closest friend, the person who knew me the best. Selena was aware of my every weakness yet somehow loved me anyway.

I knew that I should begin to look for Selena's necklace with the crystal on it, the one our mother had given her, but I was too exhausted. Plus, there was that strange last message that I chalked up to Selena being in shock, because it made no sense to me. Step-by-step instructions of what to do about the dragon that I would find guarding the necklace.

I wasn't aware of any dragons in Oregon, so her message had me puzzled, despite my sadness. The shock of being hunted must have made her have a break from reality.

Somewhere along the way, the overwhelming tiredness from my grief and the terrifying events of the last two days overtook me and I dozed, my head still resting on my sister's shoulder. I dreamed of the events that had happened just the morning before today.

CHAPTER ONE

TWINS

"Good morning sunshine," I yelled mid-jump sailing across the room. My flight path was taking me to the empty side of Selena's bed. Very few people could guess that we were twins. Selena being a girl and me a boy was the first strike, but it didn't stop there.

Selena was athletically built, but small and thin with straight blonde hair. And surprisingly strong, almost alarmingly strong. I am not small nor am I thin, and truth be told, athletically awkward. My hair is brown and very wavy.

And the list goes on: I'm right-handed, she's left-handed. I can be unsure of myself while Selena exudes confidence. I am introspective and she is outgoing. Selena is smart as a whip, and I can spell whip...with the help of Google.

We weren't even interested in the same activities. I was more of a homebody, wherein Selena was always on the go. She would sometimes spend an entire summer off on some adventure, while I remained at home content to go to football camps and enjoy the great outdoors.

It is a matter of personal pride that when I bounce on Selena's bed, I can usually launch her several feet into the air and onto the carpeted floor. The "Wheaties" I ate for breakfast must have kicked in that morning because Selena literally flew off the bed, landing in a tangled heap on the floor. It could very well have been the greatest sister-launching of all time. Even though I was howling with laughter at how high I had catapulted Selena, I watched carefully because she was ferocious in our little brother-sister engagements. Any minute I expected her to explode off of the ground in full-frontal attack mode. Most people are a little intimidated by my size, but Selena never was. Besides, Selena knew my one weakness.

I have one fatal flaw that evens the playing field with regards to my sister, and it is a great source of shame. You see, I'm ticklish. And not just "kind of ticklish," or "a little ticklish," I'm the sort of ticklish that when I'm tickled, all my strength seems to disappear and I am left nearly defenseless, trying to ward off a finger to the ribs, knees, armpits, or worse, the feet.

Selena's greatest attack method was to wrap herself around one of my legs and start tickling my immobilized foot. No matter how hard I kicked or fought back, she would not let go. I would quickly and immediately concede to whatever her demands were to get her to stop the tickle torture, but today was different. I knew that I had launched Selena higher than ever before, but she is so tough that I expected that she'd just be angry that I had managed such a feat. Instead, she lay motionless on the floor in a heap. Knowing that she was faking it, I kept my distance.

"You're not fooling anyone," I said bravely from the safety of the bed. No movement came from the heap on the floor.

"Seriously, I don't believe you're hurt. You can stop faking now, Selena." A small amount of doubt was entering my mind. What if I had launched her too far? Maybe she had hit her head or something.

Still, she was mighty sly. She had to be faking.

"Whatever you do, don't laugh," I said trying to get a reaction out of her. I couldn't even detect her breathing. Maybe something had gone awry with my plan.

On edge, I moved a little closer trying to determine if she was breathing or not. Her body seemed unnaturally still and was crumpled in an odd way. More fear entered my mind and a little knot formed in my stomach. Maybe I had finally injured her. Still, there was a nagging thought that she was faking the whole thing, just reeling me in like a fat trout on a line.

What bothered me the most was that she was so motionless. Normally, Selena was a bundle of energy and couldn't stay still for more than a moment or two.

And then her foot twitched… unnaturally. A shot of fear ran through my spine. Determining that something was actually wrong, I knelt down next to her with the intent of trying to detect some movement in her chest to see if she was actually breathing. I sat for about ten seconds and saw absolutely no motion. Now I was scared.

"Selena, are you all rig…." I began.

Instantly, I found myself in an epic struggle with the Tasmanian Devil. Faster than I could believe, Selena went from motionless to a blur of angry energy, intent on my destruction. And remember, she knew my humiliating weakness.

Feinting towards my right leg, she then spun and shot for my left leg instead. Trying to jump back out of the way, I tripped on some blankets that had fallen to the floor and I found myself lying on my back with a she-tiger wrapped around my leg, removing my slipper and preparing for torture.

"Noooo! OK, ok, you win!" Better to concede early than endure the horrible torture.

"You're dead meat, Marcus Brent Harmon!" She pulled off the slipper and threw it across the room. "I was planning on sleeping in a little this morning, you moron!"

"Noooo! I give, I give," I shouted. "Please don't tickle me! I give up!"

"You're not getting off that easy, sonny-boy!" Using her fingernails, she raked the bottom of my foot from heel to toes.

"Nooooooooooo! Stop! Aaaahhh, seriously Selena stop! I give, I give!" I was desperate now.

"Dishes for the week?" she asked.

"What? For a week? No wa… aaaaay here, heeeee!" I shrieked. "Stop doing that! No, no, no! OK, ok! Dishes for the week! Just please let go!" I hollered, all shreds of dignity and manliness thrown out the window. I contemplated calling for Grandma, but she generally took Selena's side.

"Atta boy. I knew you could do it. By the way, Marcus, you squeal like a grade school girl," she said, releasing me from the torturous tickle grip.

"Shut up! I do not!" was my brilliant reply. It was difficult to come up with something clever when I had been humiliated by my sister who wasn't even half my size. Besides, I had no intentions of doing the dishes for a week. I would just deny it if Selena told Grandma that we had a new "arrangement" for doing the dishes.

"And what would Becky Newberry say if she knew that her big football stud was actually a girly-man?" Warning alarms began to go off. Selena was up to something.

"No worries," I responded. "Who do you think she'll believe? You or 'Marcus the Love Machine'?" I stretched the word love out for several seconds for emphasis.

Grabbing her phone off of her nightstand, Selena placed the ear-buds into her ears.

"Let me show you something," she said.

"More of that Whitney Houston crap," I asked while she played with some of the buttons on the phone. Selena was an old soul when it came to music, and I actually had a secret crush on Whitney Houston, but why muddy the waters?

Selena held the ear-buds out to me. After I had the ear-buds in place, Selena pushed play and I heard a familiar voice and saw myself in a desperate struggle with the she-devil. *"Nooooooooo! Stop! Aaaahhh, seriously Selena stop! I give, I give!"* She had recorded the whole fight, grade school girlie squeals and all. Somehow she knew an attack was coming and she had set me up to do her chores.

"You set me up!" I yelled. Selena quickly yanked the ear-buds off my head and ran to the bathroom, taking her phone with her. I followed as fast as I could, but found the door slammed in my face and locked.

"Give me the phone right now you little creep," my voice had panic in it.

"Dude, you're not even a challenge anymore. Like shooting carp in a barrel," she said from behind the door.

"You little weasel! You set me up! Somehow you knew what I was going to do and set me up!" I was tempted to bust through the door, but knew Grandma would likely shoot me if I did. With my size, I tended to go through more than my share of furniture.

I heard the sound of a drawer opening, then Selena's taunting voice. "Well, would you look at this? Your cell phone is in here with Becky's phone number. I wonder how it got in here? I might just give her a call and let her hear my favorite recording."

"She-Devil!" I yelled. "Give me back my phone!" I was getting desperate. It was not out of the realm of possibility that Selena would indeed call Becky and play the recording over the phone. I was in trouble.

"How about dishes for two days? Is that a deal," I asked.

"I bet Becky is going to be speed dial number one. Well, what do you know? She is!" Oh, man! She was going to do it. I could tell. It's a twin thing.

"Fine! You win! I'll do dishes for a week!" The thought of Becky hearing that recording was intolerable. I worked hard at my manly-man persona, and this would ruin things for certain if anyone at Mountain View High School found out about my non-manly deficiency.

"I want to hear you tell Grandma that you switched chores with me and that you'll be doing dishes for this week. You're not worming your way out of this one," Selena roared behind the bathroom door.

Plan one thwarted.

"Grandma, Selena and I will be switching chores for a while. Is that ok," I hollered down the stairs.

Grandma appeared around the corner and I swear she had a trace of a smile at the edges of her mouth. Grandma was short in stature and had graying hair that still had a touch of dark brown throughout.

"That's fine, Marcus. As long as they get done, I don't

care who does what. I'll be leaving for Seattle in a few minutes. I don't want to come home to a dirty house, you hear?" Grandma replied and started downstairs. There was no way that Grandma would come home to a dirty house. She was all the family Selena and I had, and we loved her more than anything.

"And don't plan on spending your evenings at Paul's house to get out of dishes, either," Selena said from behind the door.

Jeez! How did she do it? Plan Two thwarted. Typical of me, there was no Plan Three. Two plans were my limit. After that were just different forms of begging.

"When you complete washing dishes for a week, then I delete the recording. Maybe over time we'll forget what a girly-man you've become," said Selena.

I could hear the shower turn on, and I knew that this little episode was over and that I was destined for dishpan hands for a while. What had started as a lovely game of "Launch the Sister," had ended in a very horrible manner for the launcher instead of the launched.

I returned to my room and picked up my guitar. It's old, but it is my favorite possession. It's an Ovation six string guitar, and it seemed to fit my hands like it was a part of my body. Playing the Ovation was my way of relaxing and thinking. Selena once told me that she knew what I was thinking about just by what I played. When I'm contemplating something, I love playing what is in my head, freestyle. The music just seems to flow out of me. Sometimes Selena would listen then try to guess what I was thinking. I suspect that the times that she was wrong were faked so as to not freak me out. She was just too accurate sometimes.

While I was playing, I began to think about my little sister. We barely knew our parents, Franklin and Lorraine. They were both killed in a car accident while we were only five. Our parents had taken a night out together without us twins and had been killed by a drunk driver. Ironically, the driver lived while they did not. We were raised by our only surviving grandparents. Grandma Torrey and Grandpa Dan were my dad's parents. Grandpa Dan died of a heart attack several years before, leaving us alone with Grandma Torrey. Mom's parents had died before we were born. We knew very little of them, not even having a photo.

I wouldn't admit this to anyone, but Selena was the strong one out of the both of us. I think I relied more on her emotionally than she did me. She just seemed to know exactly what to tell me when I doubted myself, or when I got down. Lately, though, she has been extremely introspective and contemplative. When I would ask what was wrong, she would put on a different face and tell me that everything was fine. I might not have been as good at reading her mind as she was at reading mine, but I knew instinctively that this was a lie. Something was bugging her, big time. I admit I was kind of hurt that she wouldn't share with me what was going on.

Selena came into my room wearing a bathrobe and drying her hair with a towel. She sat at the end of my bed and listened to me play for a couple of seconds.

"Stop worrying about me, Marcus. I've just had something on my mind these last couple of weeks," she said.

"Maybe I was thinking about something else. Has that ever occurred to you?" I asked.

She snorted through her nose. It was a little habit she had gotten from our dad. "Yeah, right. I know you too well. You can't hide anything from me and you know it."

"Yeah, well, you can't hide anything..." I let the sentence die. Who was I fooling?

Selena laughed, both of us knowing how foolish that sentence sounded.

"Still, if there is something I can help you with? I could hit someone in the head for you." I said hopefully.

She seemed to waiver, but then shook her head. "Please trust me on this," she said, standing and giving me a big bear hug. Although we are as close as siblings could possibly be, we're not big into hugs or kisses or other physical displays of emotions. Selena's actions had caught me off guard. Worse, I was getting poked by the crystal that mom had given her that she always carried on a chain around her neck.

Selena looked up at me. "You know I love you, right?" she said after releasing me. "Please, Marcus, I need you to trust me."

CHAPTER TWO

ON THE CHASE

I was still a little bemused by the strange way Selena had acted. I was supposed to be heading into Portland to buy new football cleats, but I was convinced that I needed to stay and see that Selena was fine. She insisted that all was well, and that she needed some space. It took some convincing, but she finally got me out the door.

Living in Oregon is the greatest. We live in a small town on the outskirts of Portland called Mountain View. Although Mountain View is tiny, I wouldn't live anywhere else. The Columbia River is there during the summer for fishing, boating, and windsurfing. Mt. Hood is close enough for skiing and snowboarding during the winter. There is always something to do. Even though it was mid-July, the temperature was about eighty five degrees.

Daily doubles for football were just around the corner, and I was excited that morning to get a shot at playing varsity ball. I was big for being a junior in high school, but I was unfortunately equally as awkward. My strength and coordination hadn't quite caught up with my growth spurt, unlike Selena who was naturally athletic. Since our team was small, most of the starters played both offense and defense. I played center on offense and was a nose tackle on defense. I loved defense, but lacked the speed and agility needed to be effective. I had my eye on playing varsity center since it was vacated from last years' starting center who graduated.

This morning I was on the hunt for the perfect pair of cleats. We tend to get a little rain during the football season, so having traction is critical. I was looking forward to getting back at some of the Eastern Oregon teams that had come to our side of the state last season during the championships. I don't know what they feed those boys, but they were big, tough and strong. And ugly. They pretty well knocked us down and took our lunch money last year, but not this year. We had some pretty tough kids returning this year, and we would show them a thing or...

"Marcus, I need you now!"

I jumped so hard that I momentarily swerved into the oncoming lane. Fortunately, there was no traffic. The voice seemed to come from right inside the car, but there wasn't anyone else in the car. Immediately I reached for the radio dials thinking that it had something to do with the radio. The obvious answer came to me.

"Very funny, Selena. You can come out now." I said glancing in the rearview mirror certain that Selena would pop up with a huge grin. I reached behind the seat and felt around. Nothing. But she was small and sneaky.

"Marcus, I need you now!"

It was Selena's voice, right inside the car, but she didn't seem to be in the back of the car. Was she in the trunk? That seemed unlikely because she didn't like cramped spaces much. Immediately I pulled off the road to check the car, certain that Selena would be perched behind the seat with a huge grin on her face. To my confusion, I found nothing in the backseat. Reaching inside the car, I popped the trunk latch, and the trunk door came free. Looking inside the trunk, I spotted my gym bag and nothing else. I scratched my head in puzzlement.

Two tattooed bikers had also pulled over and were checking a map.

"Got a bee in your car or something," one asked with a grin on his face.

How was I going to answer this one? "No, I thought I heard something..." I began.

"Marcus...are you there?" came Selena's voice again. But

this time I was outside the car, and it still seemed like she was standing right next to me.

I looked hopefully over to the bikers who were staring back at me. "Did you just hear that," I asked.

"Hear what, man," the other biker asked. Both gave me a funny look. I began to feel silly.

"It was...a girl's voice," I said lamely.

"Dude...I'm speaking from experience. Lay off the hard drugs, man. They mess you up," said the first biker, and he didn't exactly use the word "mess."

"Marcus, please, I need you! Can you hear me?" came Selena's voice.

I began to hyperventilate and I leaned up against the car. The bikers seemed a little alarmed.

"Hey man," said biker two. "Are you feeling o.k.? You look a little shook up."

"What?" I asked. "What's going on?" I shook my head in disbelief. Maybe the shock of being tickled was finally taking its toll. Maybe now Selena would see how evil this tickling thing really was. It was affecting my mental health.

"Marcus, if you can hear me, I need you right now!" Again, the message came, but clearer and brighter, as if Selena were right there.

"Marcus, you're not imagining this!" I'm not sure whether I liked that or not. If this wasn't my imagination running amuck, then this was real. Looking at the bikers, I knew that they couldn't hear Selena, so it must be in my head.

"I need you right now! Please! This wasn't supposed to happen so soon!" Her "voice" was desperate.

My breathing was coming out in strange gasps. I shook my head again trying to clear it.

Our twin bond was good, but this had never happened to me before, hearing my sisters' voice in my head. She must have known it was possible to do, because here she was calling for help in this extraordinary manner.

"Marcus, I need you right now!" came Selena's voice. The

urgency wasn't so much in her voice as I could actually feel waves of fear that must have emanated from Selena.

"Selena, where are you? What...how are you doing this?" I asked again. The bikers looked at each other and then started to walk slowly towards me.

"Hey, it's going to be alright, ya hear? You just need to sleep this thing off, alright?" biker one said with what he probably thought was a comforting smile. He reminded me of one of the pirates straight from the Caribbean.

"Come home right now. Something is wrong and I need your help. Can you hear me?"

"Yes I can hear you!" I shouted. "What's...what's going on?"

"Marcus, can you hear me? They can't know that you're around," came a chilling response. *"Hurry, but when you get near home, you need to not be seen. Just follow my instructions. I hope you can hear me!"*

"What's going on?" I shouted even louder. Loud enough that it stopped the bikers in their tracks. Both looked at me with a great deal of alarm thinking that I was high on some wild drug. As quickly as I could, I jumped in the car and shifted to drive. I heard the bikers both yell something about being too messed up to drive, but I was already moving.

"If you hear me, please, please, Marcus, try to speak to me," came Selena's voice.

"I'm trying to speak..." I began to shout. I looked in the rearview mirror to see both bikers shouting and waving their hands in a vain effort to get me to stop. At least they would have an interesting story to tell at the end of their ride.

"Project your thoughts. Don't try talking with your mouth. You need to concentrate and focus your thoughts on me."

"Selena, I hear you! I'm coming home now!" I thought as loudly as I could.

"Please Marcus. Can you hear me? I need you to come to me."

Concentrating as fiercely as I could I thought in my

mind, "SELENA, I'M COMING HOME NOW!"

"There's something wrong! They somehow found us after all these years. Be careful when you come near the house. Please keep trying to speak to me. It takes practice, but we don't have much time."

Whatever I was doing or not doing, Selena wasn't able to hear my thoughts, but her thoughts were as if she were sitting right next to me holding a conversation in person. The fear from her was the only thing that kept me from freaking out about this new development in my life. It was almost like running from a hungry lion intent on eating you, and while you were running you suddenly grew a third leg. You don't have time to think about the third leg because you'll get eaten if you stop to contemplate. So, you keep running.

Gripping the steering wheel as tight as I could, I controlled my breathing and focused on one thought. *"SELENA!"*

"Marcus? Oh, Marcus I hear you! Please hurry! Are you on your way home?"

Focusing again as fiercely as I had last time, *"YES, I'M COMING. I'M JUST COMING INTO TOWN NOW."*

"Marcus, you need to listen. You can't be seen by the people in the house. They can't know about you."

"SELENA, WHAT'S GOING ON? I DON'T KNOW..." I began.

Selena's thoughts cut me short. *"I don't have time to explain. This is the worst possible thing that could happen! Park the car next to the laundry-mat and listen to me. You need to follow my directions without questioning me."*

"I'M GOING TO SNEAK INTO THE HOUSE AND TRY TO GET YOU OUT OF THERE!" was my reply.

"NO! Are you listening to me, Marcus? Don't you dare try something so so stupid! Everything, and I mean everything that mom and dad setup will be ruined if they know about you! Please! Don't do anything stupid! No matter what happens, you can't be discovered!"

What was she talking about? Was this really happening? I was hearing my sister's voice in my head -- and that voice was telling me that she was in danger, but that I shouldn't come to her, that somehow it was more important for me not to be discovered by whoever was in our house, and what did this have to do with mom and dad?

"Marcus. This is a really bad thing that is happening. I can't even begin to imagine how you are feeling right now. It took months for me to get used to mom's voice in my head even though we were children..."

"WHAT ARE YOU TALKING ABOUT, MOM'S VOICE IN YOUR HEAD? SELENA, PLEASE! WHAT IS GOING ON? I CAN'T EVEN THINK STRAIGHT..."

This was beginning to be too much for me. Instinctively I knew that I was hyperventilating. Darkness began to crash in on my vision. My mind said, "Tunnel vision," naming the ailment that I seemed to be going through.

"SOMETHING'S WRONG. I FEEL...I FEEL WOOZIE. I...."

I couldn't seem to catch my breath. My last thought was Selena's voice in my head.

Dimly I heard, *"Marcus! Marcus! What's happening? Don't leave me..."*

Coming to, I shook my head trying to clear my thoughts. What had just happened? How long had I been out? Surely, I had fallen asleep and dreamed some strange dream. I would wake up in my bed and marvel at the intensity and vividness of this insane dream and have a good laugh with Selena over the weirdness of this strange episode.

It was silent, and it didn't appear to be a dream because I was sitting in my parked car, right where I had stopped while talking with Selena using my newly discovered method of communicating. I reached out with my mind for Selena.

"SELENA, WHERE ARE YOU? ARE YOU STILL THERE. I SEEMED TO HAVE PASSED OUT FOR A SECOND."

No reply.

"SELENA, ARE YOU THERE? WHAT DO YOU WANT ME TO DO?" I asked with my mind.

Focusing all my attention on my sister, I called out with

all the force I could muster. *"SELENA!"*

One word flashed in my mind.

"Follow," was the word I heard, but it was weak. The closest way to describe it was almost like a radio station that was beginning to fade. Then a picture flashed in my head. In the image I saw the inside of Selena's car. Through the windshield, I saw a roadside sign that I immediately recognized. It was for Interstate 84 heading east towards the town of Hood River.

Selena must have been about thirty minutes ahead of me if she was on I 84. I tried again and again to communicate with Selena with my mind. Panic set in, because the only thing I knew for sure is that Selena was in trouble. My biggest fear was that I would lose contact with Selena and not know where to find her. I tried over and over, but no response came back. Perhaps this newly-found telepathy thing had a range limit. It made sense if it did. Rather than send me a message, Selena had sent me an image. Maybe it was easier to send one focused image than to communicate, when there were distances involved.

It seemed like only moments later when I realized I was going to pass the exact same sign that Selena sent as an image to my mind. Concentrating furiously, I focused on the sign and took a mental image of it. Not knowing how all this worked, I was concerned that I wasn't going to be able to do it right.

With the sign image fresh in my mind, I projected my thoughts towards Selena with every ounce of mental energy that I could. A moment passed, and I was about to try it again when an image flashed into my mind. It was from the inside of Selena's car, but what caught my attention was that I could see Selena's smiling face in the rearview mirror and she was giving me the thumbs up sign. She had gotten my message! Immediately, another image flashed to my mind. It was a roadside sign announcing that Hood River was only eleven miles away. I knew I was on the right track at least.

If you've ever traveled along the Columbia Gorge, you'll understand what I mean when I say you're in for a treat. Sheer cliffs covered with green vegetation align both sides of the Columbia River. As you drive down the highway, numerous waterfalls can be seen cascading over the cliffs, often several hundreds of feet.

The granddaddy of them all is Multnomah Falls. It is actually two falls, an upper and a lower falls. The upper falls drops water over five hundred and forty feet into a large basin of water. As the basin of water drains, it drops another sixty nine feet and runs into the Columbia River. The volume of water spilling over the falls is impressive. Even though I have driven past Multnomah Falls hundreds of times, I have never not felt a sense of awe at its grandeur and beauty – until today. I don't recall even giving it a single thought as I sped past the falls in search of my sister.

Moments after passing Multnomah Falls, Selena sent me another image. Through her windshield, I could see her taking the last Hood River exit. I knew this exit well because we often would come this way to camp with Grandma and Grandpa Harmon. Even though Grandpa had died, we still came here to go camping once a summer for about a week. When Selena wasn't away on her summer excursions, she would sometimes accompany us. We always went to the same campground, and it holds special memories for both Selena and I. Maybe that's where Selena was heading.

Glancing down at the speedometer, I realized I was flying at nearly ninety miles an hour. Slowing down to seventy five seemed like I was creeping along, but it was still ten miles over the posted speed limit. I needed to be stopped by the cops like I needed a hole in the head. What jolted me even more was that I saw that I only had an eighth of a tank of gas left! Focusing on the gas gauge, I sent a mental image to Selena.

She sent back an image of a gas station. Another image followed that showed her pointing at her watch. The signal was clear. Get gas, but hurry. I decided that I had enough fuel to make it to the Hood River exit where I could then gas up.

It seemed like an eternity before Hood River came into

are able to track me even on these backroads," she said.

"Selena," I said, *"let's just call the cops. This is crazy being in such a remote area with no help around. Seriously, what is going on?"*

I could feel the hesitation that Selena felt before answering my question.

"The cops can't help us. I don't have time to explain right now, but trust me, that would just create more problems than you can ever imagine."

"How could...." I began.

"Marcus, just shut up and listen. The danger is real, more real than I can explain right now. And now you're in real danger because I believe they know you are here, and they will use you to get to me."

"Who are these people, and why are they after you?" I asked.

"I don't have time to answer that right now, but you need to know that they are the same people who killed mom and dad."

Killed mom and dad? But they had died in a car accident. What was she talking about? This nightmare was getting worse.

I sat several moments pondering what Selena had just told me. I didn't know how to respond.

Finally I asked, *"What exactly do you mean?"* I was afraid of the answer.

Again I felt hesitation from Selena before she answered.

"Mom and dad were killed by people who wanted them dead. It wasn't a car accident that killed them," she said.

I sat in stunned silence. Black was now white, up was now down, in now out, and I didn't know what to do about any of this. To make matters worse, I began to wonder about the relationship with my sister. How come she knew all about this? Why was it that she knew things about my parents that I didn't? Why was she hiding all this from me for all this time? For the first time in my life, I realized that I really didn't know my sister, and that hurt more than getting a sucker punch to the face.

Selena must have sensed my feelings. Several moments went by while she allowed me to absorb the information that she just dumped on me.

"Marcus, are you still there?" she asked. There was timidness in her question. I think she had realized just how much information I was absorbing.

"Yeah," was my brief reply. I was still trying to make sense of everything that was happening to me at this time.

"If you don't hate me too much, I still need my big brother to help me out of this jam."

"Where are you?" I asked, *"you must be close because I can 'hear' you clearly."*

"I am very close, but it's best that you don't know my exact location," was her response.

"Why?" I asked.

She paused, *"Because if they find you, they will use you to get to me. Remember Marcus, these are the same people that killed our parents They will do anything, and I mean anything, to get what they want, and that includes torture and killing. I can't bear to see you hurt, even if it means that I'm captured."*

"Selena, this is ridiculous!" I shouted with my mind, *"if you're with me, at least I'd have a chance to protect you. As it is, I have no ability to protect you at all."*

I could tell that Selena was having a difficult time answering my questions. On one hand, she needed me to know certain things about the people that were chasing her. On the other hand, I could sense that she was hiding even bigger secrets from me.

"Marcus, you don't understand. There's nothing you can do to physically protect me from these people. They're not like the people you know. I wish I could explain it better, but I don't have time right now. This is literally a life-and-death matter. I'll explain everything if I get through this thing alive."

The reality of the situation became starkly apparent when Selena said, "if I get through this thing alive." Both of us sat for a moment of silence to let that sink in. I wanted to argue

CHAPTER THREE

MURDERED

Almost immediately after pulling on the road, I spotted the Mercedes. That the occupants of the car saw me was obvious in the way that the car quickly turned around and sped after me.

"Come to Papa," I said out loud.

The Mercedes quickly closed the gap. I could make out two figures sitting in the front seats.

"They're following me," I told Selena. *"You need to get away right now."*

"Just stay ahead of them, Marcus," Selena said back to me. *"And for heaven sakes, don't do anything stupid."*

Looking back at the Mercedes, it was obvious that they were following me. To make sure, I made several turns that made no logical sense. The Mercedes matched me turn for turn. Either they didn't care if they were being obvious, or they hadn't watched enough cop shows to realize they had tipped their hand.

"They're definitely following me," I said to Selena.

"Just keep to the plan and drive to a populated area," Selena replied. *"It will be only a couple minutes more before our telepathy will be out of range."* Again, she stressed, *"Marcus don't do anything stupid."*

"Oh, come on," I said, *"you know me."*

"Yeah, I do know you. Again, I'll say, don't do something stupid." Yep, Selena did know me. Doing something stupid was what I did best. It's a gift.

Driving the two-lane highway back to Hood River, I was

careful to stay out ahead of the Mercedes so they could not tell that someone else was driving the car. I made it a point to slouch down in my seat to appear that I was smaller. From a distance, no one should notice the switch. I kept a careful watch on my rearview mirror, making sure that the Mercedes was always behind me. I wanted them as far away from Selena as possible before they knew something was up.

On one particular straight stretch, I could see the car speeding to catch up. It was about a quarter mile back when the Mercedes did something I didn't expect. It quickly slowed down, flipped around, and sped back the opposite direction. It could only mean one thing. Somehow, they had discovered our trick and Selena was back in danger again.

Using my newly found telepathic powers, I sent an urgent message to Selena.

"Selena, are you okay?" I asked frantically.

There was no return reply. We must've traveled out of our telepathic range. Finding a wide spot in the world road, I quickly pulled off and turned around. For the second time this day, I sped towards my sister who was in trouble. My hope was to get within telepathic range so that I could warn Selena that she was again in danger.

Focusing intently, I sent a one-word message.

"Danger!"

What I didn't understand is how the folks of the Mercedes knew that they had been tricked. The only thing I could think of was that there was more than one car trying to find Selena. Somehow they found out our trick and signaled ahead to the people in the trailing car. My only thought was to get back to Selena. I tried to follow the black car, but after a couple turns, they had accelerated too far ahead for me to see where it had gone. I decided to return to the last-place that I had seen my sister. Perhaps then, we would be back in telepathic range

It seemed like hours, but it was only a few minutes before I was back to the campground where I switched cars with Selena. I quickly tried to contact her.

"Selena, you're in danger!" I could hear the urgency in my telepathic voice.

A very faint reply.

"I know," was her message.

I had stopped the car at the far end of the campground. It was more remote than the other sites, so there weren't any campers around. I wanted to be able to focus all my attention on contacting her.

Summoning up my focus I prepared to send another message. Movement in the rearview mirror caught my eye. An object was coming up on me fast. Sitting up, I turned around to see that it was actually a man running at my car at a tremendous speed. And when I say tremendous, what I mean is unearthly. I had never seen a man move that fast before. So shocking was the speed of the man that I could only stare in disbelief. It wasn't until the runner was about thirty yards away when I realized that I was the object the man was running towards, his eyes focused intently on me. It was that intensity in his eyes that brought me back to reality.

Fortunately, I had not turned off the car to contact Selena. I had merely let the car idle as I had sent my message. Dropping the car into drive I floored the accelerator. Almost immediately I felt an impact on the back of my car, the force of which caused the car to almost swerve out of control. Looking back into my rearview mirror, I couldn't see the man anymore. Movement in the passenger-side mirror caught my eye. The man had moved to the right side of the car, and although I was accelerating, he was keeping even with the fast-moving car.

Have you ever had a nightmare where you couldn't escape whatever was chasing you? That the thing that was chasing you seemed superhuman and whatever you did, it kept gaining on you? I was living that nightmare. Fear clutched my throat and I could feel the hairs on the back of my neck and arms stand up.

I was shocked to see the man crash into the side of my car on purpose. Using his shoulder like he was blocking for a running back, he rammed into the right rear part of my car. The jolt was like getting hit by another vehicle. Again, I almost lost control, the backend swerving crazily. Fortunately, I was able to gain control and accelerate. Who says that video games are useless? I made a mental note to thank the makers of "Gran Turismo."

In my rearview mirror, I could see the man following me start to fall behind. The speed and strength of the man shocked me. What I witnessed didn't seem humanly possible. I'm guessing that the man was about 5'10" and at best weighed about two hundred pounds. Perhaps a little larger than average, but nothing out of the ordinary. He shouldn't have been able to run that fast or strike my car with that kind of strength. I realized that my breathing was coming out in great gasps, my heart pounding as though it wanted to escape my chest.

As soon as the man realized that I had escaped, he immediately turned around and ran back in the opposite direction. I assumed that he was heading to where he had parked the car.

It finally sunk in the reason why Selena had been so forceful in warning me not to engage with the men and the Mercedes. How did she know that these men are so dangerous? Instead of getting answers, all I was getting was more questions.

"Selena?" I asked "are you there?"

"Yes," she replied. "I'm here."

"What's going on here?" I pleaded. "Why did a man of unearthly speed and strength just try to knock my car off the road, with his bare shoulder? More importantly, how do you know about these men and I don't?"

I could tell that Selena didn't know how to respond to my questions. The pause before her answer said it all.

"Marcus, I wish there was time to tell you everything, but as you might have guessed, I wasn't expecting this. Neither was I prepared for this," she said. "I'm just making it up as I go. We have to escape, Marcus. So much is riding on our survival."

"What....." I began.

"We don't have time. I can feel that they're closing in on me. It might be only a matter of moments before they catch up with me. Obviously, I'm no match for them physically. My best option is to get away," she said.

"What do you want me to do?" I asked.

"I just need to buy some time. Marcus, there is a safe place nearby for me to go to, but these men can't even know that it exists. If I can get to it, I will be safe. Totally safe. But I need you to run interference, if it's possible," she said.

Again, I asked, *"What do you want me to do?"*

I could tell she was thinking before she answered.

"I'm reasonably sure that they don't know my exact location. How they found out that it was you driving my car, I don't know. There must be two or more groups out to find me."

"I wonder if they think I know where you're at or where you're going?" I asked.

"I've been wondering that too," she said. *"Even if we get one group to follow you, that will give me a better chance to get away."*

She paused.

"Marcus, I hate to put you in danger, but it is imperative that I get away at all costs. I wish I could explain, but the explanation would take too long and I have a feeling that we have only minutes," she said.

I caught her meaning. When you're a twin, little nuances speak volumes. Selena was essentially telling me that her escape outweighed my safety. That whatever she was involved with was so important that she was willing to put me at risk. I could even feel the waves of emotion pouring out of Selena. Fear was paramount, but I also felt the love she had for me, and her sense of duty of doing what was required of her, even though I didn't understand what that was.

Although I was very confused about what was going on, I felt a wave of love wash over me for my twin sister. I felt that she was trying to do what was right, even though I didn't understand what it was that she was doing.

Placing all my faith in her, I said, *"Selena, I don't under-*

stand what's going on, but I trust you. Tell me what you need and I promise I'll die trying to help you to the best of my ability."

I could feel the waves of relief and gratitude emanating from Selena.

"Idiot," she said. It was a term of endearment, believe it or not. "Haven't you been listening? I want you to lead them away and then get away yourself moron. I just want you to be aware of the danger."

"Believe me, after seeing what that dude could do, I'm aware of the danger," I said. "Other than incredible strength and speed, is there anything else that I need to know about these men?"

Selena hesitated.

"I.... I don't think so. That doesn't mean that you can let your guard down. Some of this is new ground to me, too." That was good to know.

"Well," I said, "you're the one calling the shots. What do we need to do?"

I could almost hear Selena thinking out loud.

"I think we need to stay within communication range this time. It might be necessary to coordinate with each other. I need about twenty five minutes to get to my safe spot, but I can't take more than an hour. And no, I can't explain why it can't take more than an hour."

Why did that not surprise me?

"Okay, where do you need to get to?" I asked.

I knew the answer before she said it.

"I can't tell you where exactly, just trust me on this, okay?" she said. "Where are you now?"

"I went back to where we met to change cars," I replied. "Now I'm heading towards the convenience store where we used to buy bait to go fishing with Grandpa. Do you know which one I'm talking about?"

"Perfect!" was her reply. "We need to keep you away from remote areas. They're more likely to be cautious when there are people around. Pull into the parking lot and keep your eyes open for the Mercedes, or anything else that seems suspicious."

I don't know about Selena, but EVERYTHING seemed suspicious now.

The convenience store was also the only service station for miles around. If anyone needed gas, this is the only place to get some. I counted ten cars in the parking lot and at the gas pumps. Although small, the convenience store was open all night and I don't recall it ever being empty of customers. It was the only convenience store that serviced the several campgrounds located on the lake. I felt relatively safe in the presence of other people.

I decided to act like I was using the pay phone so that I could scan the area without looking suspicious. My mind wandered briefly as I marveled that pay phones had been a pretty standard way of communicating back in the day.

Glancing around, I noticed a blue Ford pickup truck with wood racks that had pulled off the road about a quarter-mile away. A man and a woman climbed out of the truck and rummaged in the back for something. They seem to me to be around the age of retirement. After a moment or so, I could see that they were loaded up with fishing gear, a small cooler, and a couple of those folding lawn chairs. It was obvious that they were just going to the lake to do some fishing.

"Dang, dude," I said to myself, "don't get fixated on something irrelevant to the situation at hand."

Ignoring the retired couple, I started scanning around trying to find something more suspicious than trout happy lovebirds.

There was no sign of the black Mercedes, and other than the pimple faced store clerk ogling a couple of teenage girls in shorts and T-shirts, no one else appeared to be suspicious. I also scanned the teenage girls closely, just to be safe. You can never be too careful when it comes to hot teenage girls wearing shorts and T-shirts. My visual scan led me to the conclusion that I just might like being assaulted by the brunette with curly hair and green eyes. Just to protect my little sister, of course. Always looking out for my little sister.

"I don't think they followed me. I don't see anyone that seems suspicious," I said to Selena.

"Right now, I'm sensing they're not quite as close as they were before," said Selena from her hiding spot. *"Whatever you did seemed to buy me some time."*

"So, you can feel whenever these people are around?" I asked.

"A little," she said. *"It's not exact, but like telepathy, the closer you get, the more accurate it is."*

A few more moments passed by as I scanned the area for anything suspicious.

"I think it's safe," said Selena. *"I'm on the move."*

"What do you want me to do?" I asked.

"Stay where you are right now. Keep in sight of other people at all times, and if you see anything suspicious, I need to know immediately. I'm pretty sure that we will be able to stay in contact with each other until I'm safe," she said.

Don't ask me how, but I knew that Selena was now on foot having ditched the car. Not wanting to distract her from finding her destination, I kept my new found telepathy quiet and let her move. Nothing around me appeared to be out of the ordinary, or in any way strange. Nobody even gave me a second glance. I began to feel a little silly about pretending to talk on the phone.

A tap on my back almost caused me to jump out of my skin. Quickly spinning around ready to kick my assailant in the kneecap, I came face-to-face with the brunette and her friend.

"Whoa there, tiger," said the brunette's friend. "Didn't mean to scare you like that."

There is nothing worse for a teenage boy than to be embarrassed in front of teenage girls. I quickly tried to recover.

"You didn't scare me. I'm actually a ninja, and I move that fast all the time," I said.

"Ninja? What are you talking about?" Selena asked.

That was just great. I had tried to talk to the girls using my new found telepathy. So, in essence, I had just been standing there gawking at them like a doofus.

"Uh...if you're not using the phone still, we could really use it," said the brunette with green eyes. "Our cell phones died."

I had forgotten that I was pretending to talk on the phone. I was just holding the phone in my hand while talking with Selena. Strike two for my doofusness in the eyes of the beautiful brunette and her friend.

"Right. Phone. You want to use the phone?" I asked. I could feel my face turning red. So now on top of everything else that happened that day, I could add humiliation in front of hot girls to that list.

Again Selena asked, *"What phone? Dude are you alright?"*

I had done it again. It is safe to say that I'm not a multi-tasker.

"Nothing. Forget about it." I answered aloud.

"Forget about what?" The brunette asked with a concerned look on her face.

Saying nothing, I just handed the phone to the hot brunette with green eyes and curly hair and walked off in shame, sure that if I opened my mouth again someone might institutionalize me. The sound of giggling followed me into the store.

More so to hide from further shaming myself than any need to go to the bathroom, I walked into the men's room, found an empty stall, and locked the door.

"Are you okay?" asked Selena. *"You're not in danger, are you?"* I could feel her concern.

"I'm only in danger of dying from humiliation," I replied. You can be darn sure that I made certain to communicate with Selena telepathically. All I needed was someone to hear me talk to myself in a bathroom stall to complete the demise of any manliness that I possessed.

"I guess that's a story I'll have to hear some other time," said Selena. *"Do you see anything suspicious?"*

"If you've ever been to a men's room, then you know that everything is suspicious looking," I said looking down at the

filthy floor.

"Oh, so you're hiding in shame. Let me guess, the girl was really hot." Trust Selena to further humiliate me, even when we are both facing mortal danger. And for crying out loud, how did she know it was a hot girl?

"For your information, there are two hot girls that I am hiding in shame from," I replied.

"That's my big brother," said Selena. *"Why humiliate yourself for just one girl when you can get a two-fer."*

Exiting the stall, I splashed cold water on my face, hoping that it would shock me awake and I would discover that this was all some sort of weird dream, brought on from eating a bad frozen burrito.

"Marcus, I think something's wrong," came Selena's urgent message. *"I think I might've been set up in a trap. I can sense that they're really close."* There was a frantic urgency in Selena's message.

"I'm coming!" I said as I sprinted out to my car. The bathroom door rebounded off the wall from the force of me hitting it at full speed. *"Where are you?"*

"It's too late," said Selena. *"Marcus, I need you to pay strict attention right now."*

Both the sound of her voice and the volumes of emotions pouring forth from Selena stopped me dead in my tracks.

I knew that I couldn't get to Selena in time.

Standing next to my car, I could feel Selena opening up her mind to me. She showed me her exact location and how to get to where she was at. Distinct landmarks were placed into my mind as to how to get to her.

"Marcus, it's imperative…for you to find my body," she said.

A sob escaped my throat because I knew beyond a shadow of doubt that I would never see Selena alive again.

"Did you hear that Marcus?" she asked.

"Yes," was all I could manage. My eyes blurred with tears, but I still saw the images sent to me from Selena in my mind's eye.

"Find my body, but more importantly... and I mean this Marcus, find Mom's Crystal necklace. If you love me, you'll find the necklace and keep it safe for the rest of your life," was Selena's final message to me.

I was about to question why the necklace was so important to Selena when a new image was sent to me. I knew I was looking through my sister's eyes in real time. I saw what she was seeing.

She appeared to be lying on the ground, beside a large rock, in a gully gouged out from the runoff of melting snow. Her focus changed, and I could see a man standing on the edge of the gully. In his hand was a gun. The gun was extended, and I could see the face of the man as he sighted the pistol at Selena. It was the same man who nearly chased down my car on foot, then nearly ran me off the road by slamming into my car with his body.

It was then that Selena quickly sent me strict instructions about the dragon.

Without a trace of remorse showing on the face of the gunmen, I saw the gun flare. Once, twice and the connection between us began to fade. One last frantic image was sent to me before blackness.

....

I don't know how long I stood there. Selena was gone. I knew that beyond a shadow of a doubt. I was so shocked by the profound aloneness that I just stood, leaning against my car for a very long period of time.

I heard soft footsteps come up behind me. I didn't care that the footsteps could mean danger for me.

"Hey there, Tiger," said the brunette. "Is something wrong?"

I lifted my head and looked at the girls. The anguish I felt must have shown on my face.

The brunette stepped towards me. "Whatever it is, it will

be all right."

"You're wrong," I said, "nothing will ever be all right again."

The brunette seemed to be about to say something else when a man stepped out of an RV.

"Let's load up, girls," he said, speaking to the brunette and her friend.

"Okay Dad," replied the brunette "we'll be right there."

Then to her friend, "Go ahead. I'll just be a minute."

"See ya around, Tiger," said the friend as she walked off.

I just stood there. There was nothing I could really say, the grief was too great.

Slowly, the brunette walked towards me. Placing her hand softly on my arm, she stood on her tiptoes and gave me a kiss on the cheek. Without saying a word, she walked back to the RV. Turning, she gave me a wave and disappeared into the vehicle.

I did not know what to think about the brunette, but I was very grateful for her kindness. I still pictured her face as she turned around to wave. Her eyes were brimming with tears as if she could feel my pain.

I watched as the RV drove off. In the distance I saw the same retired couple lugging the same fishing gear and loading it into their pickup. Most likely the fish weren't biting, but the bugs were.

I opened the car door and sat down. I was dreading what I had to do next. I knew I had to go find Selena's body. For whatever reason, she also wanted me to find mom's crystal. It was vital to her that I find the crystal and keep it secure. In the final moments of her death, the safety of the crystal had been her last conscious thought. That last memory she sent me was of the location of the crystal. She had hid it nearly a mile away from where she was killed. I had no idea what the significance of the crystal was, but I suspected that perhaps the crystal was the reason for Selena's death. And then there was that thing about the dragon...

Starting the car engine, I dropped it into reverse, and backed out of my parking space. Purposefully, I pulled out of the parking lot and headed in the opposite direction of where Selena had hid the crystal. Frequently I checked my rearview mirror to see if anyone saw me. The only vehicle I saw was the retired couple heading home at a leisurely pace. Two random turns later and their vehicles were no longer in sight.

Because of the telepathy, Selena was able to send very specific directions. I hoped against hope that when I found her, she might only be wounded, but the reality was that I knew. I knew she was dead.

It took nearly a half-hour to find where Selena had parked her car. From her car, I knew it would be a short amount of time before I found her body. However, without the specific directions that Selena had sent me, her body might never have been found because of its remote location. Standing by the passenger door I scanned the hillside looking for a lightning struck a tree. This was my first landmark. It took several minutes to hike to the base of the tree where I was able to spot my second landmark, the large round boulder. Reaching the boulder, I took a large breath and prepared myself for finding Selena.

Stepping around the boulder I was able to see down into a gully. At the bottom of the gully was a large rock. Selena's body lay next to the rock.

CHAPTER FOUR

DRAGON

I awoke with a start. Sitting up, I realized that I had re-lived the events of the day through my dreams. Immediately I was aware that I was in great danger. Before I had fallen asleep, I had felt something ominous in the distance, but now I knew that it was decidedly closer. I had not intended to fall asleep, and I needed to fulfill my promise to Selena by finding the crystal.

I learned from Selena's last message that the crystal was only a short distance away, but hidden in such a way that only specific directions would lead to the crystal. A burning curios-ity came upon me. It was obvious now that the crystal played a pivotal role in the events of the day. It had been Selena's dying wish that I find the crystal. Why was the crystal so important, and why didn't I know about its importance? That I had been kept intentionally in the dark was very obvious. Not only was I saddened at the loss of my sister, but I was extremely hurt that she kept the secret from me.

Next to the gully where Selena had been killed was a hillside of shale. You've probably seen shale before. Shale is a sedimentary rock formed from mud or clay. Shale is fairly brit-tle and will break along its parallel layering to form rocks that are amazingly flat. If you've ever seen an area where shale is abundant, you would know how difficult it would be to distin-guish between one rock from another. Selena had hid the crys-tal under one specific rock among thousands. The shale slide covered almost two football field sizes of the hillside. About halfway up the shale hillside was a gigantic stump. Selena was too smart to hide the crystal right next to the stump, but it was a good landmark.

Getting to the stump was more problematic than I anticipated. The shale proved to be unstable, and I frequently found myself sliding back several feet. It felt like I was taking five steps forward and sliding six feet back. Eventually though, I reached the stump. On the uphill side of the stump, I stopped and took a breather. Searching around, I spotted what I needed. About fifteen feet from the stump were some shale pieces with unusual coloration. It was easy to distinguish various layers within shale rocks. One of these rocks had been strategically placed so that one of the corners of the rock pointed me in the exact direction. By aligning myself with the corner of the rock, all I had to do was to pace off twenty steps. Upon pacing the twenty steps, I was able to locate the specific shale rock where the necklace was hidden. It was an unusual rock because it was almost perfectly oval. The other shale rock pieces were more angular, so I was able to recognize it immediately.

Lifting the rock revealed a leather pouch with the necklace inside of it. I stared at the crystal, trying to understand its importance. I couldn't fathom why it would be important to anyone, yet my sister died because of the crystal, of that I was sure.

I was so intent on the crystal, that the impact caught me off guard. I immediately thought the blow was from the man that had slammed his body into my car. The hit had knocked me to the ground, and knowing that my life was now in danger, I jumped up quickly to try and defend myself. To my amazement, there was no one around. I quickly reached for the crystal, and was again knocked to the ground with greater force. Again, I searched the hillside looking for my assailant. And again, there was no one around.

It was then that I remembered Selena's instructions about the dragon. You need to look at it from my angle. I had thought that Selena's last instructions about the dragon had come from being in shock. Surely those were not instructions from a rational mind. The last time I had checked, there were no dragons in Oregon.

Recalling the instructions, I reached out to the dragon with my mind. To my amazement, I felt an immediate connection to the dragon even though I couldn't see it.

"*Come, Vesuvius,*" I said telepathically, feeling foolish.

With a loud whoosh, and to my utter surprise, there sat a dragon as large as a grown elephant directly in front of me. It was dark blue and was staring intently at me with emerald green eyes. Reaching slowly for the crystal, I picked it up and as per Selena's instructions. An ominous rumble issued from the dragon when I handled the crystal.

Holding the crystal eye level to the dragon, I again reached out with my mind.

"*Vesuvius, ludo callae proctoe,*" I said, hoping desperately that I remembered Selena's instructions precisely.

At first, I thought I had said what Selena told me to say incorrectly because the dragon sat motionless, staring even more intently at me.

The sound emanating from the dragon started as a low rumble, then began to build and build. Selena had instructed me to hold the crystal eye level to the dragon without moving. The dragon, still issuing the rumble that continued to crescendo, took two steps forward and stretched out its neck until his nose was touching the crystal. Gently taking the crystal in its lips, it carefully sat the crystal on the ground. The rumble had become as loud as a freight train. Taking a step back, the dragon opened its jaws. Instinctively, I took a step backwards. Blue flame shot from the dragon's maw and encompassed the crystal. The heat from the dragon's fire turned the crystal bright white. After several moments, there was a sharp cracking sound as the dragon closed its jaws, cutting off the flame.

The dragon seemed momentarily confused as it stared down the crystal. Then, raising its ferocious face to the sky, let out a terrible bellow. And even though this was the first encounter I have ever had with a dragon, I sensed that this was a bellow of sadness and rage.

It then gathered itself, gave me one last look, and shot into the sky moving at a terrific rate of speed. I was surprised at the silent stealth that such a large animal could manage, answering why it was able to surprise me at our first encounter.

Having retrieved the crystal, the biggest concern I now had was to get back to Selena's body and contact the authorities.

Starting down the hill, I became aware of the very real and strange sensation that I was being hunted and that I was in danger. Furthermore, I was acutely aware that the danger was very close. I immediately halted my descent and crouched down. With the new found telepathy, I didn't for a minute doubt these feelings. Without turning my head, I scanned the area with my eyes. The sweep revealed nothing out of the ordinary, but I trusted my feelings.

The shale hillside I was on offered me absolutely no cover. An observer could easily spot me against the hillside. Risking that my movement might attract attention, I decided to quickly get off the mountain side and into the tree line where there would be more cover for me to hide.

I was nearly off the mountain when I spotted movement. Instantly I froze. About two hundred yards away, I spotted the elderly couple. Both stood facing me, and it was obvious that they had seen me. And what was even more obvious to me was that I knew without doubt that they were the source of the danger. There was another sensation also. There seemed to be an evil aura that surrounded them, something I was inherently afraid of. This feeling really spooked me.

To my right was the tree line with some brushy undergrowth. I felt as if I could get into the undergrowth, I would stand a better chance of getting away or finding a place to hide. With a burst of energy from the adrenaline being dumped into my bloodstream, I shot off into the foliage. My best hope was to get as deep as possible into the forest, lose my pursuers, then get to safety.

Unfortunately, the dense underbrush began to thin out. I needed a hiding spot fast. I took a quick glance behind me to see if they were coming, and although I didn't see anything, I knew that they were very close. This surprised me because I'm fairly fast for my size, and I just assumed that I would be able to outdistance the elderly couple quickly.

I spotted a decent hiding place. It was a clump of bushes densely packed together. Worming my way into the center of the bushes, I found an open space where I could squat down. The brush was so thick that I could only see a few feet around me. I was confident that I couldn't be seen by someone who wasn't even ten feet away.

Almost immediately I could hear the sounds of my pursuers. A shot of fear raced up my spine. The elderly couple should not have been able to get this close so quickly. I figured that my speed and conditioning would allow me to get away from the couple, yet they were very, very near.

Having sprinted through the forest getaway, I was breathing heavily trying to catch my breath. I was afraid the noise from my breathing would attract attention, so I tried to breathe quietly. A bug crawled up my pant leg, but to move was to die, so I remained motionless.

Several minutes passed by and I didn't hear anything. I was tempted to stand up, get my bearings and head back to the car, but it just didn't feel right. The nagging feeling that danger was near was as strong as ever, so I remained silent.

I just about jumped out my skin hearing a female voice speak. She must've only been a few feet away. She spoke softly. Had I been further away I might have not heard her voice at all. I couldn't understand what she was saying.

From further away a male voice answered, also speaking softly. I also realized why I didn't understand what they're saying. It wasn't just because they're speaking softly, they were also speaking in a different language. A language I couldn't identify, but that sounded Eastern European to my untrained ear.

From time to time I heard movement around me. It chilled me to the bone to hear footsteps directly behind me. There was a desperate need in me to turn around to see what was happening, but to do that and be heard, was to die.

It was obvious that they were still in search of the crystal. My first thought was to bury the crystal right next to me. That way, if caught, the crystal wouldn't be on me, but I loathed doing that because it was Selena's last desperate communication for me to keep the crystal safe.

Moving with exaggerated carefulness, I opened the leather pouch and removed the crystal necklace. I was fairly certain it was the crystal and not the gold necklace chain that was important. Holding the crystal in my hand, I again wondered at the importance of the gem.

Knowing it would be uncomfortable, there was only one solution I could come upon to keep the crystal safe.

Popping the crystal in my mouth, I swallowed. Because of its texture and size, I almost gagged and spit it back up, but exerting all my willpower, I was able to force it down. I returned the necklace chain back to the pouch. This I buried under a rock next to where I was sitting.

Five minutes passed by, then ten minutes, and finally when I judged an hour had passed, slowly began to rise up from my hiding spot. Nothing.

I carefully scanned the area around me. There was nobody around me. There remained a feeling of danger, but I thought it might be more dangerous for me to stay hidden in one area. It wasn't just one group looking for the crystal. The individuals in the Mercedes and also the retired couple were the ones that were known for sure, but there could have been more. If they all mobilized to the same area it would only be a matter of time before it was caught.

Maybe it sounds foolish, but I determined to take Selena's body with me. I couldn't stand the thought of leaving her alone. As quickly and quietly as possible, I began to backtrack towards where Selena's body was.

Just as I was about to reach the gully, I spotted the older lady. It was obvious that she had anticipated that I would return to Selena. She was casually sitting on a stump, just waiting for me to show up. She was medium build, with dark brown hair streaked with gray. I would judge her to be between sixty and seventy years old. Everything about her screamed "ordinary," until you looked at her brown eyes. Her eyes showed both hardness and cruelty. The smile that was on her face was neither pleasant nor beautiful.

In a heavily accented voice, she said, "I knew you'd come back for your dead sister. My husband thought you would head back to the car, but I figured out your weakness."

"What do you want with me?" I asked.

She stood up. The motion was surprisingly swift and graceful. Nothing about her movement suggested that she was even a little bit hampered by age. On the contrary, her movements suggested great athleticism and strength.

Walking slowly towards me she said, "I think you know what I want. You can either give me the crystal and I will make your death quick, or I can take the crystal from you forcefully. You won't like it if I have to take it from you." I could tell from the look on her face that she would enjoy taking the crystal from me forcefully.

"I don't know what you're talking about," I said.

She tilted her head and examined me like she would examine a bug about ready to get squished. A cruel smile turned up the corners of her mouth. "You have chosen unwisely," she said as she crouched into an athletic stance in advance towards me.

I wasn't about to underestimate the woman in front of me. Too many weird things had happened for me to take anything lightly, including fighting a seventy year old woman barehanded.

The cruel smile on her face broadened when I also dropped to an athletic stance and prepared for battle.

Moving with incredible balance, speed, and agility, the

woman began the circle. I could immediately tell that she was quicker and faster than me. With lightning speed, she darted in and landed a punch to my face. The force of the blow shocked me. The blow had stood me up and forced me to take several steps backwards. Before I could catch my balance, another blow to my belly knocked the wind out of me. I dropped to one knee trying to catch my breath. I was absolutely shocked and horrified at the strength and agility of the woman.

Rather than come in for the kill, the woman stood back several feet, enjoying watching me try to catch my breath. That I was shocked and frightened excited her.

"Give me the crystal and I will make it all end right now," she said.

As soon as I gathered enough breath, I said, "I don't have the crystal. Whoever killed Selena must have taken the crystal."

Before I could even stand up, the woman darted in and kicked me in the ribs. The sickening sound that accompanied the blow told me that she broke my ribs before the pain set in. When the pain did come, it was so intense that I couldn't help but let out a choking moan. My obvious pain made the woman laugh out loud, her face contorting with evil mirth.

With me on the ground, seriously injured, I could not put up an effective defense against the woman's violent attacks. Time and time again she would dart in, land several blows with either her fist or foot, then dart away. It occurred to me that she didn't want me to grab her. Perhaps that was a way for me to nullify her speed and quickness.

Pretending that I was more hurt than I really was, I let my movements slow. I wanted to appear in a very weakened state. Truth be told, I didn't have to act that much. Each blow from the lady had exacted a terrible toll on my body. Sensing that I was hurt, the lady began to take less and less care of getting out of my reach.

After a flurry of blows which I had failed to defend against, the lady stood over me with her hands on her hips. Her face was flushed with excitement and a cruel smile lingered at the corner of her lips.

"Tell me," she asked, "how does it feel to know that you're about to die? To know that you totally failed your sister? To know that your life is worthless?"

I didn't answer. Summoning all my strength I waited for her last blow. After studying my battered face for a moment, she stepped towards me. She brought back her leg, I could tell that she intended to end my life with one last kick.

Rather than roll away to avoid the kick, I rolled into the kick and grabbed the leg she was balancing on. Even off balance, she was able to land a solid kick to my thigh. The pain was tremendous, but to let go was to die. Blows from her fists rained down on my head and shoulders. Summoning the last of my strength, I pulled her legs out from under her, toppling her over onto the ground. As quick as I could, I jumped on her before she could get up. With an enraged snarl she began to pound me with her fists. Grabbing her wrists, I managed to get control over her somewhat. Using my superior size and weight, I was able to keep her immobilized on the ground. Her strength was incredible. I was a strong young man nearing my physical prime, and it was all I could do to keep hold of her wrists.

Just when I thought that I had gained the upper hand, I felt a hand seize me on the back of my neck, and then I was violently thrown aside. And when I say violently thrown aside, I mean I was physically lifted and thrown through the air, landing in a bloody bruised heap.

Standing over me was the woman's husband. Behind him were two men, one of which was Selena's killer. Both of those men held guns.

In a language I didn't recognize, the man appeared to bark an order at the woman. She quickly jumped up and joined the men with the guns. She appeared to be ashamed and a little scared in front of the man I assumed was her husband.

The man studied me for a moment. "Where's the crystal?" he asked.

"I don't have it," I managed to choke out.

With as much effort as one might use on an infant, he quickly immobilized me and gave me a pat down in search of the crystal.

"Hey, now," I said, "you could at least buy a guy dinner before we get to the romance."

He wasn't amused. I, on the other hand, thought it was pretty good, considering the circumstances.

"You are of no importance to us without the crystal," he said. Snapping his fingers at one of the men, he then turned his back to me, collected his wife and walked off. The man stepped forward, raised his gun. I closed my eyes. I was too weak and damaged to fight.

With a rush of wind and a bellow that I now recognized, I opened my eyes to see the dragon slam into the man with the gun. He fell, his neck snapped with the head hanging at an unnatural angle. The dragon looked over at me, the emerald eyes burning, then rushed into the woods moving with incredible quickness. Shots were fired, but moments later screams confirmed that the shots had been ineffective.

From what I heard, the three remaining attackers must have separated, because screams could be heard from different parts of the forest. It sounded like they weren't much of a match against the dragon. I wasn't sorry for them.

I heard rustling nearby. A very bloody elderly woman stood over me with a gun pointed at my chest. The gun flared once, and I felt the impact of the bullet.

Instantly, the dragon appeared. With a scream, the lady fired the gun at the dragon. It didn't even faze the dragon one bit. With unearthly quickness, the dragon lashed his tail out at the woman who fell headless at my feet.

My last conscious thought was that I had been killed by the same people who had killed my sister.

CHAPTER FIVE

AFTERMATH

I awoke one very sick dude. I remembered being shot, but surprisingly it was my ribs that hurt more. Every breath drawn in caused me agony. Deep breaths brought on fits of coughing. Coughing brought up blood from my lungs. I suspected that my broken ribs may have punctured a lung.

My entire shirt felt damp, and when I looked down I could see that it was covered with blood. A raging thirst seized me. I figured it was from the loss of blood, but I was too weak to move.

Looking around me, I found myself in close proximity to where Selena was. Although she was about one hundred yards away, it might as well have been one hundred miles. There was no way to get to her. I was overcome with despair, realizing how badly I had failed my sister.

I faded in and out of consciousness until I was aware that I heard voices. Movement in the bushes caught my attention, but my vision was so fuzzy I was unable to make out who it was.

My first thought was that my tormentors had come back, but then I remembered the dragon and figured there was no way they could have survived its attacks.

Four blurry figures appeared. I wasn't able to focus in on their faces. I had been struck in the head many times, so there was most likely a concussion to go along with all my other injuries. That elderly lady had really worked me over.

One of the figures knelt down beside me.

"How are you doing there, Tiger?" was the question

from the blurry figure.

I tried to answer, but my strength ebbed away and I faded into blackness. Several times I awoke to find myself being carried by someone. I was only lucid for a couple seconds at a time. Selena's body was being carried by a stranger, only it wasn't a stranger. It was the beautiful brunette from the convenience store. She was carrying Selena as if she didn't weigh any more than a small child. Remarkably, the brunette had been crying. Why she was crying, I didn't know.

I don't know how long I was carried. I recall waking once to find that it was dark and my body had been laid next to a blazing campfire. I tried to sit up, but didn't have the energy and every slight move caused me more agony than I thought possible.

"You mustn't move," said a man. I recognize the man as being the father of the brunette. He had blood stains on his shoulders. He must've been the person who carried me.

"Here," he said, "drink this. I imagine you're dying of thirst right now."

Lifting a water bottle to my mouth, he poured a little bit past my parched lips.

"I know you're thirsty, but you need to take little sips at a time. If you drink too much, it may make you sick to your stomach and you might vomit. We need to keep you as hydrated as possible," said the man.

"Who.... who are you?" I squawked through parched lips.

"A friend," was his only reply.

I faded in and out for what must've been most of the night. Raging thirst would wake me every couple of hours.

When daylight came, the beautiful brunette knelt down beside me.

"How are you doing?" she asked.

"Still thirsty," I replied.

She lifted the water bottle to my lips again.

"You're going to be all right," she said. "The authorities have been contacted and they will be here in the next ten minutes. Unfortunately, we can't stay around to meet them."

"What's going on?" I asked.

She thought about that for a second.

"There is no quick answer to that question," she said.

I was getting mighty tired of being left in the dark. I had lost my sister, been beat up, shot, and then left for dead and nobody would tell me why. And then on top of everything else, there was a dragon of all things.

"Well, Tiger," said the beautiful brunette, "we've got to be going. For what it's worth, we don't believe that you'll be in any kind of danger, even if they do find out that you're still alive. They were after Selena. You just got in their way."

She looked over at Selena and her eyes moistened. I got the distinct impression that this girl had known Selena. Quickly she knelt down next to me. Softly, she kissed me on the cheek then stood.

"You may have a hard time explaining some of the more... incredible aspects of the story to the authorities. You might want to leave those parts out, to save yourself some grief. Just sayin...." she said, and then she was gone. The short exchange tired me out and I quickly went to sleep, or just plain passed out.

A hand on my neck woke me up. I feebly grabbed the unknown assailant's wrist and tried to pull away.

"Relax buddy. We're just checking to see if you have a pulse." An Oregon state trooper was kneeling beside me. Another trooper was searching the surrounding area.

"You look like you're in pretty rough shape," said the trooper, "where do you hurt the most?"

"My ribs," I said. "Need a drink." My broken ribs caused me to take short shallow breaths. The last thing I want to do is start coughing.

"You have a bullet wound in your chest. Do you want to tell me about that?" asked the trooper. He was gingerly looking over me to see what other injuries I might have sustained.

The brunette's warning about what I said to the authorities ran through my mind. Who would believe me if I rambled on about discovering telepathy, men and women with super strength and agility, a crystal, and a freaking dragon?

The best thing was to take time to think through what I was going to say.

"Water please," I asked.

The brunette and the man had left several water bottles next to me. The trooper unscrewed the lid of one of the bottles then held the bottle to my lips. The water was cool and delicious. Drinking gallons of water would not have been enough. The trooper was of the same opinion as the mystery man that carried me here.

"Careful there, son. Just a little water at a time is what you need."

I knew the trooper wanted to question me, but I needed to buy time to concoct a story that made sense. "Winging it" just seemed unwise, so I pretended to pass out. In truth, I was so tired I just closed my eyes and fell asleep.

……………………..

The next couple of days were a blur. The bullet had grazed one of my lungs, but missed the heart by fractions of an inch. A minor concussion was sustained on top of everything else. Because of the concussion, I felt like I was floating around in a cloud. I was also bruised from head to toe from the beating I had received from the older couple.

Grandma had rushed back from her visit with her sister. She was grieving mightily for Selena. At the same time, she was trying to stay upbeat and positive for my sake.

Police detectives interviewed me several times. As you can imagine, they were confused and suspicious about the details of my attack.

I had told them that Selena and I had decided to take a one-day trip to Mt. Hood for a hike. While on the hike, we were attacked and Selena was killed. I told him that I had fought back, but had been outnumbered, and had been shot by the same person who shot Selena.

"So why take two cars?" asked the detective.

"After the hike, Selena and I had different plans. It was just easier to take separate cars," I replied.

"What were your separate plans?"

"Selena wanted to go straight home after the hike. I thought it would be cool to drive up to Timberline Lodge for dinner. With two cars, we could both do what we wanted to," was the explanation.

The most puzzling thing to the detectives was who had carried us out of the woods.

"You're a big guy, Marcus. We found where you had fought and then got shot. Not too far away is where your sister was killed. Who moved you to the place where you were found?" The detective asked.

"I wish I could help you there, but I had lost consciousness after being shot. The first thing I remember is the police officer that found me," I said.

"You were spotted at the convenience store. Nobody remembers seeing Selena."

"I had stopped there along the way. I met up with Selena later. It wasn't too long after that we were attacked and Selena was killed." I replied.

The detectives were very suspicious of my story. They kept coming back to who had attacked us and who had found us and carried us out, then mysteriously disappeared.

"Why would somebody save your life but run off before the authorities got there?" was one variation of the same question that I had been asked at least twenty times.

My standard answer was, "As I told you before, I was unconscious after being shot. I don't remember who carried us out."

An unexpected question just about ruined my explanation.

"Why did you swallow your sister's crystal?" Asked the

detective. In his hand was an x-ray of my stomach. Selena's crystal's unmistakable on the x-ray photo. In his other hand the detective held up the crystal.

"I....uh... swallowed it because I thought they were going to rob us," I said.

"We tested the crystal. The crystal is quartz. Why go out of the way for what amounts to maybe ten dollars," was the question.

"It's a keepsake. It was something my mother owned before she died. She gave it to Selena as a gift. The necklace is one of Selena's prized treasures. She wouldn't give it up for anything."

The detective shook his head.

"I got to tell you, Marcus," said the detective, "there's just something about the story that is not adding up. Something tells me that you are hiding something. What I want to know is why you feel the need to hide something from us." The detective's gray eyes seemed to drill a hole right through me.

CHAPTER SIX

SCHOOL

"Good morning, Marcus. How are you feeling?" It was two weeks later and I was home at Grandma Torrey's.

"I'm fine, Grandma. Really, it doesn't hurt nearly as bad as it did." The doctor had been correct. My ribs did hurt more than my bullet wound. Every time I took a breath, my ribs rebelled. Taking short, shallow breaths was the only way I could cope. Little by little I was doing better physically and I was anxious to be up and about.

The talk with Grandma Torrey had been difficult. She listened without interrupting me throughout the whole story. Grandma and Selena had been so close. Tears streamed down her face as I told her what happened. If she noticed any gaps in my story, she didn't seem to want to push. She was happy that I had survived, but I could tell that she was hurting very badly from Selena being gone.

"I'm so sorry that this happened," I said for the thousandth time.

"Marcus, it's not your fault. Those men are to blame. Anyone who attacks someone as harmless as Selena are very, very evil people, and it's not your fault that she is dead."

"But if I only..." I began.

"Stop it!" she said with a forcefulness that surprised me. "You did what you thought was the right thing to do. This is all water under the bridge. There's no way you could have known what those men had in mind. If you had given up, well, then I would have been angry with you."

After Grandma left my room, I reached under my shirt

and pulled out the crystal. While I was in my surgery from being shot, an x-ray showed the necklace in my stomach. My doctor had decided to remove it as a precaution, rather than let it pass through my system, uh naturally, shall we say.

I had removed the crystal from the chain and placed it on a larger chain to fit around my larger sized neck. I kept the original chain on my desktop.

I gazed at the crystal, looking at its many facets and thought of my sister. It seemed eerily silent after having her speak directly to my mind, even if it were only for those two days.

Many of my friends and teammates had stopped by to talk with me, but nothing they said could cheer me up. I sunk deeper and deeper into utter sadness. School was starting in a week, and although the doctor had OK'd me for going to school that first week, I was dreading going back. I didn't want to face the questions and looks. Mostly I didn't want to face the world without Selena.

Grandma came back in. "Coach Mendez called again. He spoke with your doctor and in a couple of weeks you can maybe start playing football again," she said. "Doesn't that sound good?"

"I won't be playing football this year."

"Marcus, this sadness will pass. You have to trust me on that. Right now, it seems horrible, but in time you'll move on. Selena wouldn't have wanted for us to be sad all the time. We honor Selena's life by remembering the good things, not the few ugly last moments of her life."

Grandma Torrey might be ready to move on, but all I really wanted was a cruel and horrible death to several people that I didn't even really know. It was all I thought about, avenging my sister. There wasn't a whole lot I could do about it in the condition I was in, though.

Agent Larry Robbins wasn't making things any easier, either. He believed all the important stuff, but still told me repeatedly that there was something that I wasn't telling him. It was almost a daily ritual now, him calling me to confirm some small detail. "Something just doesn't add up here," he had said over and over.

He could ask me from here to eternity; I vowed to never tell anyone about the telepathy that Selena and I had experienced those two days.

I was really dreading school. Enough so that I even went online to find out what it would take to be homeschooled. Having fun with my friends and doing day-to-day things like school seemed to be in the distant past. Grandma Torrey had other ideas about what I needed and was adamant that I attend school instead of running away.

The day before school started, I went to see our family doctor, hoping that she would tell me that I needed some more rest before going back to school. Sadly, this wasn't to be so.

"Kids heal fast," Doctor Rodriguez told my Grandma. "His bullet wound is really healing well, and his ribs are mending better than expected. Remarkably, actually. You must be taking good care of him." Doctor Rodriguez pulled the stethoscope out of her ears and started lightly kneading my ribs. This would have been agonizing several days ago, but wasn't too bad now. I cursed my good fortune at healing so well. I should have faked being more hurt, but the idea occurred to me too late to do anything about it now.

"Well Marcus, I wouldn't want you to play football for a couple of weeks, and I'll write you a note to get out of P.E. for a while. Otherwise, you're doing pretty good. Why don't you step outside and I'll talk with Grandma for a minute." I knew that they would be talking about my mental health.

On the way home we stopped and bought school supplies. Grandma was trying to keep the mood light and tried to keep a happy face. She was fairly successful until she looked into the cart and realized that she had been putting two of everything in the cart. Tears sprang to her eyes and we hurriedly put half of everything back on the shelves and then quickly went through the checkout stand.

Morning started badly. Paul and Brent, my two best friends, decided to come over to the house so that we could all go to school together. I know that they were trying to be supportive, but I really wanted to be alone more than anything else.

"Dude we're really going to miss you on the O-line for the game against Humbolt on Friday. Andrew is a good kid, but he's no "Mad Marcus." Paul said, punching me lightly on the shoulder. I hadn't gotten around to telling them that I didn't want to play football at all.

"Yeah, but you can still be on the field with us, you know. Your presence will be a real boost to the team," said Brent.

Paul and Brent were almost two peas in a pod. Both muscular and athletically built, they were fearsome football players. The three of us had had big plans on walking on at Oregon State University and playing college ball. Well, those two might walk on to Oregon State, but I knew I was too awkward.

Normally, we would be cutting up and laughing, but my presence was kind of a downer on anything remotely funny.

"Hey, man. We're here for ya, you know," said Brent.

"Yeah, dude. All you gotta do is ask if you need something," added Paul.

They were trying hard to connect with me. "Yeah, guys, I know. It's just that… you know, bad stuff happened and I'm not even close to being over it."

Entering the school was even more traumatic than I had thought. Even though people were trying to be supportive, they were just making things worse. I became more and more withdrawn throughout the day. Both teachers and students offered their condolences, and as well-meaning as it was, it became unbearable.

The worst was my girlfriend, Becky Newsome. I had been pretty successful at not getting cornered by her the days and weeks after Selena's death, but now that I was at school, she was constantly at my side. Becky was a sweet girl, but I needed space and I began to contemplate how to break up with her.

I mentioned this to Brent. "I don't know, Marcus. You're not yourself right now, you know? Why don't you give it a couple of days before you go and do something like that."

Brent was probably right, but I was beyond listening to reason.

"She's a real sweet girl. It might be good to have Becky around to, you know, have a shoulder to cry on," Brent said.

Normally when my friends said someone was a "sweet girl," it meant that she wasn't good looking, but that wasn't true with Becky. She was very sweet, and drop-dead gorgeous to boot. She reminded me of Selena, and that was the real reason I wanted to break up with her. As sweet and as kind as Becky was, I couldn't bear the thought of being reminded of Selena because of their similarities. It would just be easier to break up with her and deal with the pain alone.

I spent most of the day avoiding Becky, which was pretty difficult because Paul, Brent and Becky were good friends, too. We joked that Becky had become the "fourth mus-keteer." Actually, she was the fifth musketeer because Selena had been the fourth.

After the last bell rang and the school day was over, I skipped going to my locker and went straight to my car. I just wanted out of there in the worst possible way. Despite feeling better, I was pretty tired from a full day of school.

Before I could shut my door, Becky came running up.

"Marcus, wait up. Aren't you going to drive me home?" she asked.

"Sure," I replied mechanically. This would be as good a time as ever to break things off. Normally I would have felt horrified of the prospect of hurting someone, but I was pretty numb to anyone's feelings but my own.

When we reached her house, she leaned over for a kiss. Pulling away I said, "Becky, we need to talk."

Not reading the signals right, she thought I probably

wanted to "spill my guts" and lean on her for emotional support. She scooted over closer and said, "I will always be here for you, Marcus," she said in a low tone.

"Yeah, well, about that. With everything that has happened to me these last couple of weeks, I need some space, you know? So, maybe it's best if we don't see each other for a while." The blunt approach was all I could come up with. I wasn't in the mood to try to be tactful.

Whatever Becky was expecting me to say, that wasn't it. "What...what do you mean?" she asked, her eyes wide.

All the pain, sorry, emotion came to the surface. "I just want to be left alone! Can't anyone understand that?" I realized too late that I was shouting. Becky pulled away and was looking at me with fear and confusion. I knew that I was taking all my anger out on Becky, but I couldn't seem to stop myself.

"I, I..." she began then the tears began to flow.

And then, the famous line, "It's not you, Becky, it's me. I need to be alone."

Without another word, Becky grabbed her backpack and opened the car door. She didn't even bother with a backwards glance as she slammed the car door and went inside her house. Rather than being upset, I felt strangely free. One less complication in my life.

When I got home, I went straight to my bedroom. I glanced over at my guitar. It hadn't been touched since Selena's death. Somehow the guitar reminded me most of Selena. I remembered how remarkable it had seemed that Selena had been able to guess what I was thinking about while I was playing. I wondered if I would ever play the guitar again.

I don't know what it's like at other schools, but at Mountain View, teachers took a perverse pleasure in assigning homework the very first day. I was a good student, but struggled with certain subjects. Selena, of course, breezed through every class without bothering to study much.

English and history were my worst subjects. I couldn't seem to wrap my head around certain aspects of both those subjects. But math and science, now that was different. I loved that concrete nature of both of these subjects. Everything seemed black and white with math and science. If you follow the equation properly, you get the right answer. Black and white, right and wrong. English and history seemed more nebulous. Selena loved history and English. Whenever she had any time to herself, her nose would be buried in a book.

Mr. Cornwall was my English teacher this year. Selena had taken an advanced literature class with him last year and loved every minute of it. "He really challenged my thinking," she had said. I wasn't as enthused as Selena about Mr. Cornwall. Right off the bat he had given us a reading assignment. Swell. Reading. Just what I wanted after such a rotten day of school. On top of that, he assigned us a portion of an epic poem by Shakespeare. It wasn't very long, but he also wanted us to come prepared to discuss what we thought it meant.

A decision was made to play the, "my sister died and I didn't feel up to studying last night" card and parked myself in front of the Playstation for the rest of the evening.

During the night, I had a vivid dream. I must be a pretty deep sleeper because I don't usually remember dreams, but the dream that night was different.

It was a strange dream because so very little happened in it. I had simply reached down and opened my guitar case. I wanted to pick it up, but I couldn't control my body very well. My body seemed foreign and awkward. I tried a few other things like trying to move my legs, but that seemed even more awkward. My fingers felt like I had no dexterity.

And that was the extent of my dream. When I awoke, I lay on my bed a little bemused. It was such a weird dream. Turning over on my side, I looked over at my guitar. The case was open! It was the same as my dream!

I shook my head to try to get the remaining cobwebs out. This was weird. I had never slept walked before in my life.

"Great, now I'm turning into a basket case and thrashing about in my sleep." I thought. At least I knew why my dream was so vivid. I had actually reached down and opened my guitar case during the night.

....

Word must have gotten around that I had broken up with Becky before I got to school.   My grandpa had a favorite joke:

What are the three most efficient methods of communication?

1)   Telephone
2)   Television
3)   Tell a woman.

Becky had obviously told her friends that I had broken up with her. They all sat together in a group outside of junior hall. They knew that I had to pass by them to get to my locker. Becky was in the center, her eyes red and puffy. Several of the girls were sitting around her patting her hand and consoling her.

I tried to avoid eye contact, but Becky called out, "Hi Marcus!"

"Uh, hi Becky." I turned the corner and hurried to my locker.

Behind me I could hear Becky begin to sob. "What did I do wrong?" she asked the girls around her. "Nothing girlfriend, he's just in denial about the whole thing."

Denial?

Paul and Brent were waiting at my locker.

"So, dude. You let her go, huh?" asked Brent.

"Yeah, well, I don't need complications right now, I guess," I said.

"It's all over school that you two broke up," Paul said. "I guess you need some space, huh?"

"I think it's a mistake. Becky can help you through this. You need friends in times like this," Brent said.

"Thank you, Dr. Freud," I said. "I happen to think it's a

good choice for me right now."

"Just don't hurt her, O.K?" Brent said.

"Having someone break up with you isn't the worst thing that can happen to a person," I said pointedly.

Brent turned red. "Hey, man. You know that's not what I meant."

"Yeah, well, this was my decision and I think it was the right thing to do."

I was glad that Becky was a sophomore because that meant that we didn't have any classes together. One less thing to be bothered with during class at least. But that all changed with fourth period -- Mr. Cornwall's class. I walked in and there sat Becky with two of her friends. Mr. Cornwall would occasionally allow sophomores into his junior English class if they were more advanced. Unfortunately, Becky was one of those students.

She had positioned herself in the middle of the room so that I would only be a couple of chairs away no matter where I sat. I took a place behind her, off to her right side. She would then have to turn around to see me. Becky's chin dropped to her chest and her shoulders began to shake. For the love of Mike! That's just what I wanted, a crying ex-girlfriend in my class! What a pain this was turning out to be. Why couldn't women just let things go without all the drama?

To make matters worse, Mr. Cornwall decided to forgo a discussion about Shakespeare's poem. Instead, he wanted everyone to do a little writing assignment in class. I had hoped to hide the fact that I hadn't done any work on the poem, but that wasn't going to be.

"Friends," I hated when he addressed us that way. "Take a couple of minutes to jot down your thoughts on what the reading meant. After that we'll call on a couple of volunteers to share their thoughts."

I hadn't even read the verses yet. Like I said, it wasn't very long, but I just wasn't interested in even reading it last night. Taking out the assignment, I read through the verses for the first time. The verses were taken from Shakespeare's Poem, "The Rape of Lucrece." Now there was a bright title to make my day better.

> 'What win I, if I gain the thing I seek?
> A dream, a breath, a froth of fleeting joy –
> Who buys a minute's mirth to wail a week?
> Or sells eternity to get a toy?
> For one sweet grape, who would the vine destroy?
> Or what fond beggar, but to touch the crown,
> would with the scepter straight be stricken down?'

The verses seemed unfathomable the first time I read them through. Why did everyone make such a big deal over Shakespeare anyhow?

I read it through again and looked down at the empty spot on my paper where I was supposed to jot down my thoughts. Nothing was coming to me. I leaned back and closed my eyes, hoping that it appeared that I was deep in contemplation. Of course, it backfired on me.

"Mr. Harmon, illuminate us if you please, on what you think these verses mean," asked Mr. Cornwall from the front of the class.

Crud. Now what?

Looking down at the verses, I began to panic.

Cause and effect. A thought came. Not bad. I was a little surprised I had come up with that.

"Cause and effect," I said out loud.

"Good analysis," said Mr. Cornwall. "Do you care to elaborate?"

Not really. No. I didn't care to elaborate, but thanks for asking.

We should gauge our actions against the outcome, came another thought. Again, not bad.

"We should gauge our actions against the outcome," I said.

"Very good, Mr. Harmon. You obviously put some thought into the homework. I thank you." Mr. Cornwall gave me a little bow. Man, he must have gotten beat up every day as a kid.

Becky had turned around when I had answered the question. She was staring at me intently when I said, "cause and effect," and "gauging our actions against the outcome." The look in her eyes said, "you big fat hypocrite!"

Mr. Cornwall went on with his lecture as I quickly jotted down what I had just said on my homework paper. I was afraid that I would forget what I said if I left it until the end of class.

Exiting class was an ordeal because Becky's friends were waiting for her to come out. She had left the room first, and I found myself having to squeeze through a crowd of angry women. I couldn't help but compare them to a flock of sheep all grouped together. Angry sheep. Didn't they understand that I had just lost my sister? I just wanted a little slack.

I started walking toward my locker when Becky called out to me.

"My mom can't come to pick me up, would you mind giving me a ride home?" she asked hopefully.

I snapped. "Can't you get it through your mind? We're through! Done! Finished! You got that?"

Hot poker glares were sent in my direction from the rest of the "flock." Whatever. I stomped off while the "flock" bleated and did whatever flocks do when a wolf is around.

Brent and Paul were waiting for me by my locker.

"You might give the girl a break, you know," said Brent. "She's not a bad kid and all."

"Yeah, well, I don't feel like having a clingy girlfriend right now."

"You can still be friendly, though. No harm in that." said Paul.

"I don't want to string her along. It's pretty well done for good," I said.

"Dude, just be her friend, then. You can at least be nice to her," said Paul.

Why was everybody up in my business? "Why don't

you guys back off? Geez! Can't a guy just have some space?" I stormed off. I could feel the stares from my two best friends as I walked away. I had put them in a strange position. They were my friends, but they were also friends with Becky. They were in the middle and I could tell they didn't like it a bit.

Becky was waiting for me by my car. Not again! Why couldn't she just leave me alone?

"Marcus, why won't you talk with me?" she asked pitifully.

"Because I want everyone to leave me alone! What's wrong with you people?" I shouted. Several students and teachers looked over at us, obviously hearing my outburst.

I jumped in my car and the tires screamed in protest as I pulled out of the parking lot and raced home. My room seemed to be the only place that I could truly be alone. Without saying anything to Grandma Torrey, I took the stairs three steps at a time to the top floor. Slamming the door, I threw myself on my bed and covered my face with my pillow. Anything for some solitude.

After a while, Grandma Torrey knocked on the door.

"Yeah," was all I said.

A moment or two of silence. "Can I come in?"

"Sure Grandma."

She sat on the edge of my bed. "I'm worried about you, Marcus. Is everything OK?"

Pulling the pillow off of my face I said, "Everyone is smothering me. I just want to be left alone, but no one will give me any space."

"Do you think that people are purposefully trying to hurt you?" asked grandma.

"No, it's just that they don't know when to back off."

"Advice from an old woman: Don't drive your friends away. You'll need them someday and they won't be there if you drive them away. By the way, that nice girl called. Becky, right? She said to tell you she's sorry, even though she doesn't know what she did wrong." She stood and left the room, closing the door after her.

CHAPTER SEVEN

BECKY'S REVENGE

I was able to finish my homework quickly that night. Most of the homework had been fairly light, so I was able to get through it. Also, I was finding a clarity of mind when it came to my more difficult classes. Concepts that had previously made little sense were more clear and I was able to concentrate better on them. The death of Selena must have made me more focused or something.

I had felt better physically that second day of school. I could tell that my body was healing pretty good. It would only be a short time until I was well enough for some light football practice, but I had no plans of playing football. I didn't have a lot of plans for anything, as a matter of fact.

All I wanted was to avenge my sister, but I was powerless to do anything. Agent Robbins had said that they were doing everything they could to find my sister's killers, but they had little success at anything. As far as I could tell, they had hit a dead end. They still pumped me for additional information, but I had little to add.

My dreams that night were confusing. I was having problems controlling my own body movements again. Nothing worked like it was supposed to. I was trying to do something with my arms, but I didn't know what. I was swinging at something, but missing. Part of the problem was that I was swinging with my left hand, and I was right-handed. Selena was left-handed of course but….

WHACK! I slapped myself in the face! And not a "pattycake" slap either, but a full-on whack that rang my bell. I sat up in bed thinking I had just dreamed the whole thing, except my face was burning where I had slapped myself. It was the left side of my face that was on fire, and my left hand was also stinging. So I had slapped myself in the face with my left hand. Weird.

I was cracking up for sure. Maybe I should think seriously about seeing a shrink of something. Looking around the room, just to make sure that no one else was there playing a horrible prank on me, I spotted my guitar case still sitting beside my bed where it usually was. But the case was open again just like the night before. I knew that it had been closed before I had gone to bed. Now it was open.

"You're going nutso, Marcus my boy," I said out loud.

Sitting up in bed, I felt for the crystal around my neck. I didn't take it off for anything, even to shower. It was something that connected me to Selena.

"I wish you were still here," I said out loud. "You at least would help me through this."

Or at least tell you that you're being an idiot, came a thought. Great, now even my thoughts were turning against me.

With my mind still confused at my weird dreaming habits of late, I tried to fall back to sleep. I was having a difficult time of it because I was afraid of having those weird dreams again. Somewhere along the way, I drifted off into troubled slumber.

Apparently, the weirdness wasn't over for the night.

I awoke sucking my thumb. Sucking my thumb? Seriously? I yanked my thumb out of my mouth and stared at it like it was an alien. Freaky! My thumb was all wrinkled and pruney like I had been swimming for hours. Why on earth would I start sucking my thumb? I dried off my thumb on my blanket.

"What is wrong with me?" I asked out loud. "I never even sucked my thumb as a kid."

And when I thought that sucking my thumb was the

weirdest thing that had ever happened to me, I felt the wetness.

I HAD WET THE BED! I was a sixteen year-old junior in high school and I had wet the bed! Humiliated, even though no one else knew, or would ever know, I began to clean up. My mind was reeling.

I had wet the bed. I couldn't get the thought out of my head. "Are you KIDDING me?" I said out loud to myself. I stepped out of my wet underwear, wrapped them in my wet sheet, slipped on my robe, and hurried down to the basement where the washing machine was. Fortunately, there was nothing in the washing machine and I was able to get everything in and washing before Grandma could ask questions.

Running back upstairs, I hurriedly climbed into the shower. I felt small twinges in my ribs, and the exit wound from the bullet in my back hurt. Otherwise, I felt pretty good. I just had to be careful turning certain ways.

My little accident was going to put me a little late getting to school. At Mountain View High School, if you're late to first period, you have to go to noon detention, unless you have a note. It was the school's way of making sure people were on time for first period. Since I would rather eat worms than tell my grandma the reason I was running late, I decided to take the detention. I would just say that I slept in.

Getting to school late did have one benefit. I didn't have to face Becky and her flock of girls. Everyone was in class already. Going to my locker, I found a note had been slipped through the ventilation slots. By the perfume smell that emanated from the note, I knew who had written it before even opening it.

"*Dear Marcus,*

I don't know why you're so mad at me. What did I do to make you hate me?

Please meet me at lunch so that we can talk.

Love,

Becky."

Was this never going to end? I grabbed my books for Math and hurried to class. On the way it occurred to me that since I was going to noon detention, I could avoid talking with Becky like she wanted. I actually felt relieved to go to detention. They made the students eat plain cheese sandwiches from the cafeteria if you got detention. They also made students sit in complete silence. Another bonus! I wouldn't have to endure anyone bugging me about Selena, or Becky for that matter.

Opening the door to math, I made a point to catch Mr. Carter's eye.

"Sorry." I said.

I wanted to make sure that he knew I was late to class. Mr. Carter was a stickler about tardiness. He would send me to detention, even though I was one of his favorite students. Mr. Carter nodded in my direction and walked over to his computer where he updated the attendance. I sat back, content that I had successfully avoided Becky today. She couldn't be mad because I had an ironclad excuse as to why I couldn't meet her at lunch.

I purposefully made it a point to let Becky enter Mr. Cornwall's class first so that I could let her sit down then choose a seat away from her. Sitting down several seats away from Becky, I settled in, ready for class.

Coward, came a thought. Whatever.

Gratefully Cornwall's class went by quickly. We were starting to read Shakespeare's, "The Taming of the Shrew." I was able to turn my brain off while students each took a turn to read out loud. Reading was fairly harmless and I didn't mind taking my turn to stand and read. My eyes started to feel heavy listening to student's voices as they droned on. I was glad lunch was coming up. I could run home and grab a sandwich....crud. I forgot about noon detention.

Just before the end of class, an aide came in and handed a note to Mr. Cornwall. I knew the note had the names of people who were tardy and had received noon detention. Just as expected, Mr. Cornwall read the names off. "Alan, Jaimie, Cynthia, Marcus, report to the auditorium for noon detention today." I could see Becky look up at the ceiling then shake her head. She knew that her little discussion with me had been thwarted. Detention was going to be a life-saver.

Walking into the auditorium, I looked around to see if I knew anyone. There were familiar faces, but none of my friends were here. I took a seat next to a freshman football player who I knew casually. I didn't know why he was out for football. He was small and thin, and as I recall, was constantly getting knocked down during practice. He didn't get much playing time even in scrimmages. He was an easy kid to forget. But still, he was the most familiar face so I sat down next to him. He seemed delighted that I was there.

"What's up Marcus?" Dang. I had forgotten his name.

"Doing good. You?" I asked racking my brain for his name.

"Pretty good. Hey, when do you get to come back and play football? The team isn't the same without you man," the freshman said.

"It might be awhile. Bullet wounds and cracked ribs don't mend fast. I have to watch out for my health, you know?" I said. The wounded card was the easiest to play. No one needed to know that I was a fast healer.

"Yeah, I'm sorry for your loss," said the freshman.

"Thanks," I said. Then to divert the discussion away from me I asked, "What are you in detention for?"

"Oh, uh...you know, I was late for class this morning," he said.

"Me too." then added, "It's such a stupid rule."

"You got that right, man." The freshman was trying hard to act casual. He was one of those kids who never really fit in with anyone. That he was brilliant made even some of the teacher's avoid him, whatever his name was.

"OK noon detention people, silent time has started. Marcus, you're new to our usual crowd here. Could you please help pass around the sack lunches?" Mr. Larson was an ex-marine built like a small tank. He was also the linebacker coach. People naturally did exactly as Mr. Larson asked. Even the adults. Especially the football players.

"Yes, sir," I said.

I passed the sack lunches around as Mr. Larson checked and re-checked his list to make sure that he had all of his juvenile delinquents accounted for. He seemed puzzled as he looked down at my freshman buddy. Shoot, what was his name?

"Son, you're not on my list. What's your name again?" asked Mr. Larson.

"Alan. Alan Malloy. I was late for first, so they said to come here during noon. You can ask the office..." Alan stammered. At least I knew his name now.

"I'm sure it's just an oversight on their part. Eat your lunch and be quiet, Malloy," said Mr. Larson.

I sat down and opened my lunch sack. This was my first trip to noon detention, but I had heard the stories about the bland sack lunch they give out to the students. Cheese sandwich (1), apple (1), carton of milk (1), baggy of carrot sticks (1). It was the same thing every day. Nothing varied from the menu if you were in noon detention.

I decided that I could wait to eat something after school. Glancing over at my new detention friend, I saw that he was contentedly eating away at his cheese sandwich. He seemed to relish the bland food. Waving my hand to get his attention, I held up my sandwich and offered it to him. With a look of delight, Alan grabbed my sandwich and slipped it into his own bag. He pulled out the apple and offered it back to me. I really didn't want the apple, but Alan was really eager to give me something in return, so I took it and put it in my sack. With a huge smile, Alan went back to his sandwich. Poor dude looked like he was actually enjoying noon detention.

The forty minute lunch period seemed to drag on forever. After about five minutes everyone had eaten all of their lunches, so there was nothing to do but wait in total silence for the bell to ring. Mr. Larson would make people do push-ups if they broke silence.

"If you keep talking, you'll do pushups until *I* puke," was Mr. Larson's favorite line. We believed him, too.

And heaven help the person who fell asleep during detention. If you received a tardy for fifth period (right after lunch), then the next day you would get another noon detention. Mr. Larson would let the sleeper's slumber through the first five minutes of fifth so that they would be back with him the next day. It was a vicious cycle, of which Mr. Larson enjoyed immensely.

It was a great relief to hear the bell ring. I was glad that I had escaped a confrontation with Becky, but noon detention had really taken it out of me. Normally I feel pretty good after lunch, awake and ready to finish the day, but after detention, I felt lethargic and sleepy. On top of that, I didn't sleep real good last night for obvious reasons.

And to make matters worse, the fifth period was Social Studies. Ms. Rogers was having us watch a documentary on the Civil War. Normally war and carnage were interesting, but since there were only still photos during the time of the Civil War, the video seemed to move real slow.

I had barely sat down in my seat when Becky walked in. She shot a smug look at me. What was that all about? She couldn't be in this class because it was a junior level Social Studies class...

Ms. Rogers took the note that Becky handed her, read it through then announced, "Good news, class. Becky has been assigned as a teachers aide for this period. I'm sure I can find things to keep you busy enough, Becky."

Paul glanced at me. "Whoa. She's good! You sure about breaking up? You seem outclassed."

I slunk further down in my seat and pulled out my notebook. I would diligently take notes so that I wouldn't make eye contact with Becky. At least, that was the plan, but I was so tired.

I fought falling asleep for half of the class period. I tried everything. I shook my head, pinched myself, bit my lip, but nothing was keeping me from nodding off. Finally, I thought I would just close my eyes for a minute. Naturally I fell completely asleep. Dreaming, I felt myself straining, and pushing. My body felt unnatural and foreign again. Straining some more, I pushed one last time...

Laughter woke me from my slumber. Everyone was looking at me and laughing. Hard.

"D-dude! You just farted!" Brent told me gleefully holding his nose, his voice sounding funny because of his pinched nose. "Loudest one I ever heard! It echoed!"

"Gross!" said one of the girls behind me. "It's wafting back here. Ewww!"

A whole chorus of "Ewww's" emanated from the rest of the girls in the classroom.

"Sick!" said Paul. He was doubled over from laughing so hard. "Did they change the menu to beans in detention?"

What in the world was going on with me? This was seriously the most humiliating thing that had ever happened to me in school. I could feel myself going red in the face. Out of curiosity, I looked over at Becky. She was sitting a couple rows up and to the left. Everyone else had turned to stare at me, but she sat facing forward. Her head down, shoulders shaking slightly. She, too, was laughing with the rest of the class!

Maybe you'll stop being an ass to Becky now, came a thought. Even my random thoughts were starting to weird me out. It was time to talk with a shrink.

....

To say that I was scared to go to sleep that night is an understatement. This had been one strange day, and I had the feeling that weird things had only begun for me.

Maybe I was sleeping too lightly. I figured that if I stayed awake until I could fall fast asleep, maybe this foolishness would stop. I decided to do some of the mind-numbing homework late into the night, falling asleep when I was absolutely too tired to continue.

Not surprisingly, I decided to do my English assignment last. We were to finish a portion of "The Taming of the Shrew" and have it ready for the next day's discussion. It was around midnight when I picked up the play. My eyes were already heavy, and I knew that reading a couple of pages of the play would just about do me in.

I sat in my bed and read without really comprehending what was going on. My eyes were just scanning the words. Without realizing it, I fell asleep sitting up in bed with my back leaning on the headboard, the play in my lap. A notebook and pen lay on the bed, too, should I want to jot down any bright ideas. Highly unlikely.

Thankfully, I didn't dream that night. I was so exhausted that I slept through the entire night without any traumatic nightmares. Maybe this weird chapter in my life was thankfully over.

When I awoke in the morning, I felt pretty good. My book, notebook, and pen were on the ground where they must have rolled off when I finally drifted off to sleep. I picked them up and placed them in my backpack.

Grandma was awake and had prepared a little bit of breakfast. Do you know someone so well that you can tell that they are trying not to smile? Well, Grandma Torrey usually was smiling, but she looked like she was trying hard not to laugh. She couldn't have found out... No, that was impossible.

I took a plate of scrambled eggs and toast and began to eat. Grandma was big into vitamins and supplements, so I wasn't surprised when she placed several pills before me. They were the usual pills, except for one new one.

"What's this pill for?" I asked holding it up for her inspection.

"Beano," she said, "for excessive gas." Then she let loose with the laugh that had been bottled up.

"I...I'm sorry Marcus," she said, having trouble talking because she was trying to talk through her laughter. "Brent called last night and told me the whole story. I'm afraid it was a set-up." She sat down in a chair and abandoned herself to laughter. I hadn't seen her crack a smile in several weeks, now she could hardly breathe because of her laughter. My ego was taking an even bigger shot because now even my grandma was laughing at me!

Then there was school. The school allowed five tardies before the students were given a day of in-school suspension, so I had four more to use sparingly. I decided to burn one today to distance myself from Becky and her flock.

I normally left the house at 7:45 AM to get to school, but today I lingered. My watch, which was set to the second to school time, read 7:52 AM when I left the house. To make sure I was late, I stopped by Big Ernie's One Stop and bought a Snickers candy bar. When I arrived at school, it was 8:01 AM. Too bad I only had three tardies left. I could get used to this running like a coward thing.

Almost lightheartedly I walked up to the door, until I saw her. Sitting just inside of the door was Becky. She had been waiting for me. She looked at me with raised eyebrows as if to say, "I know your stupid little game, and I will play it, and beat you at it." Then she got up, turned her back on me and walked into her own classroom, just as tardy as I was.

You do realize that she is smarter than you, came a thought into my head. How I would love to shut off the random thoughts coming to my mind lately. They were hugely annoying.

I, of course, wasn't as prepared as I should have been for Mr. Cornwall's fourth period class. The assignment was to read through several pages of dialog between two characters of the play. Katharina, the wealthy firebrand, and Petruchio her suitor. When we were done reading, we were to come up with movements for the characters as if they were on stage. I wondered where Mr. Cornwall came up with such ridiculous ideas.

Teachers must have ESP when it comes to knowing who had the assignment sufficiently prepared or not. There were several people sitting in front of me and around me, but Mr. Cornwall scanned the faces in class and finally rested on me. "Marcus, my friend, the characters Petruchio and Katharina need animation to go along with their words. Please enlighten us as to how you would like to see them on stage."

Several very bad words raced through my mind as I vainly tried to come up with something. Acting like I had taken copious notes on the play, I opened my notebook and pretended to look at a page filled with notes. Except that I knew that it was blank. But it wasn't blank. On the page were the words, "Run away and pursue," in handwriting that wasn't mine. I swallowed hard and stared at the words that had not been there last night when I had fallen asleep.

"Marcus, can we assume that you didn't get the assignment completed?" asked Mr. Cornwall.

"Run away and pursue," I said.

Mr. Cornwall made a surprised face. "Say that again?"

"The characters should, uh, run away and pursue each other, you know, when...when, you know, they're talking to each other," I said, not knowing what I was saying, but it was all I had.

"Excellent instructions! That was well thought through! Well done Marcus!" exclaimed Mr. Cornwall.

Brent and Paul were both looking at me as if I were an alien.

"Since when are you a Shakespeare expert?" whispered Paul.

I shrugged my shoulders as if it were nothing. I was still shocked at the words written in my notebook. I didn't even have close to an explanation as to how they appeared. It was so weird.

To my horror, Mr. Cornwall wasn't through with me.

"Marcus, we need to experiment and see if your blocking works. Blocking is the name actor's use for their character's movements. That might be on a test, friends." He said as a side note with a lifted eyebrow. We all dutifully wrote down "blocking" with a vague definition of our own.

"So, Marcus, you'll play Katharina." Mr. Cornwall looked around the class to see if anyone caught his joke. Paul let out a courtesy laugh to earn points with Mr. Cornwall. "Just joking. You'll of course play Petruchio. Now, we'll need a beautiful Katharina to play across from the handsome Petruchio."

"Noooooo!" I thought so hard that it was almost audible. "Don't say it! Please don't say...."

"Rebecca, if you please." The pencil I had been holding snapped in my hand. I contemplated all sorts of bad things that could be put into Mr. Cornwall's coffee cup in return for this little adventure.

With a look of smugness, Becky came to the front of the classroom to stand next to me. Becky's temperament had changed. She was no longer weepy and sad. She was now a tiger with teeth and claws, and I was a wounded jungle yak running for my life.

"The ball's in your court, big man," the look on her face said.

"Now then," said Mr. Cornwall, "we are going to have you two act out these next lines. Experiment who will be escaping and who will be pursuing."

I had no question as to who would be escaping.

"Please begin," said Mr. Cornwall.

Petruchio/Me: *Come, come, you wasp; i' faith, you are too angry.*

("You got that right" I thought.)

Katharina/Becky: *If I be waspish, best beware my sting.*

I WAS trying to beware the sting! Stupid Mr. Cornwall.

Becky advanced towards me as she said the words, her eyes drilling holes through my skull.

"Good, good, Becky!" said Mr. Cornwall. "Very believable!"

Petruchio/Me: *My remedy is then, to pluck it out.*

Fearing the anger in Becky's eyes, I started backing toward the wall.

"Excellent, Marcus! You really look like you're scared!" Mr. Cornwall inserted. If only he knew.

Katharina/Becky: *Ay, if the fool could find where it lies,*

Becky emphasized the word "fool" to everyone's amusement. I took another step backwards just from the venom in Becky's voice.

Petruchio/Me: *Who knows not where a wasp does wear his sting? In his*   *tail.*

I took another step back.

Becky took a step forward.

Katharina/Becky: *In his tongue.*

Taking another step backwards, I found myself up against the cold unyielding wall.

Petruchio/Me: *Whose tongue?*

I asked meekly.

Katharina/Becky: *Yours, if you talk of tails: and so farewell.*

Becky turned her back and walked back towards the center of the room.

"Keep going. You two are doing great! This is very believable! Outstanding acting, if I do say so myself," said Mr. Cornwall.

Who was acting?

I took a few tentative steps towards Katharina/Becky.

Petruchio/Me: *What, with my tongue in your tail?*

The class erupted with laughter. Becky spun around towards me with a glare.

I wanted to yell, "It's Shakespeare who wrote the words!

I'm only reading them!"

"Finish the line please, Marcus." said Mr. Cornwall.

Petruchio/Me: _nay, come again, Good Kate; I am a gentleman._

Becky started to advance towards me slowly, one step at a time. I bravely stepped backwards until my back was one more against the wall.

Katharina/Becky: _That...I'll try._

I realized too late what was coming next. With a loud smack, Becky slapped me across the face!

Pandemonium broke out in the classroom as I stood there stunned by the slap. Brent had fallen out of his chair and he was clutching his ribs laughing harder than I had ever seen him laugh. Paul had tears rolling down his face. "She did it, she really did it! Did you see that?" he kept saying over and over.

Becky turned to Mr. Cornwall and said innocently, "It says that Katharina strikes Petruchio. I was just going for realism."

"No, no! That was amazing. It was...so in the moment! It was truly wonderful," gushed Mr. Cornwall. He looked so happy I wouldn't have been surprised if he wet himself. I had just been full-on slapped in the face, and the teacher not only allowed it, but couldn't find enough words to express how great it was!

I watched Becky as she walked back to her seat, her hips swaying. She gave a wink to her girlfriends and sat down in triumph, while I stood at the front of the class, a big doofus with a stinging face.

CHAPTER EIGHT

BULLIES

When I got home in the evening, I received a call from Special Agent Robbins.

"I'll be honest with you. We've hit a dead end. If you don't have any additional information to give us, then we don't have anything else to follow up on," Agent Robbins said. "Are you sure there isn't anything else you can give me?"

"There is nothing else that I can give you," I said. I wanted to say that they were probably eaten by a fire-breathing dragon, but thought that wouldn't be a great idea.

The nightly news was tapering off on their coverage of Selena's death. Early on, the FBI agent told us to change our phone number to an unlisted number so that we wouldn't be inundated with phone calls. For the most part, it had worked well. Several reporters had come knocking on our door, but grandma always politely turned them away. During the first couple days after the murder, the television stations continually posted sketches of the two men and the husband and wife. Although the FBI had followed up on all of the leads, apparently none of them were panning out. The killers had disappeared.

We received numerous invitations for interviews, but I was not interested in rehashing Selena's death again. I wanted to be left alone by everyone.

I went to bed that night with a little trepidation. Could I have subconsciously written those words in my notebook? The handwriting wasn't mine, but I had hit myself with my left hand the other night. What if I had written the message with my left hand? Wouldn't that make my handwriting more different than normal?

Although I was freaked out by the prospect, I wanted to know what was going on. I laid a notebook and pen within easy reach and concentrated on going to sleep. Maybe I would write something that would give me a clue as to what was going on. If I couldn't find out why I was having such odd things happen to me, I had no doubt that I was heading for the looney bin.

I tossed and turned, but couldn't drift off to sleep. Truth be known, I was afraid of these weird events of late. Something was wrong with me, and I didn't know what. Worse still, these strange events were escalating. Night time was also the time when I missed Selena the most. I thought about her constantly. It was also the time when I blamed myself for not being able to protect her.

I was only able to sleep a couple minutes at a time that night. Every time I nodded off, I would awake with a start. Part of me wanted to find out what was going on with me, the other part terrified at the answer. The terrified part won out and I kept awake the entire night.

When my alarm clock eventually went off, I hadn't slept more than an hour total. I was exhausted, but couldn't let myself fall into a fitful slumber, which is strange for me. Selena often teased me that I could be in the middle of a sentence and drift off. I have never had problems sleeping.

I was already exhausted when I arrived at school. Walking through the school halls, I got my share of ribbing from my friends. Even the teachers who walked past me couldn't conceal their smiles. Everyone had heard of what happened, and it didn't appear that anyone was siding with me. Had everyone forgotten that I had just lost a sister? It didn't seem fair.

Opening my locker, I found another note had been slipped in through the vent slots. I didn't have to even guess who the note was from.

"Marcus,

I know that losing Selena is the worst thing in the world for you, but her death doesn't give you the right to treat me poorly. It bothers me less that you don't want to go out with me than it does that you won't talk to me. But whatever. When you grow up and think you can handle talking to me, I'll be ready. Until then, I'm really sorry about

Selena. I hope you can work through all of this. Contrary to what you believe, I'm still

your friend. I hope your face doesn't still hurt, but you KNOW you DESERVED it.

Becky."

Deep down I knew that Becky was right. I did deserve getting slapped.

I kept to myself most of the morning, which was becoming my usual thing. Even Brent and Paul gave me space.

At noon I found myself walking past the auditorium. Mr. Larson and Alan were outside the doors talking.

"I don't have you on my list, Alan. You didn't need to come to detention," Mr. Larson said.

"Are you sure? I was late to fifth period yesterday, so I should be on the list," Alan said. "Nope, you're not on the list," replied Mr. Larson.

Mr. Larson closed the door leaving Alan standing there. Alan actually seemed disappointed that he wasn't in detention. Not seeing me, he started toward the doors that lead outside. On an impulse, I followed Alan out the door to see where he would go next. Since I was avoiding everyone, I had little else to do. Stepping outside of the door, I moved behind a large bush to witness what Alan was up to.

A group of kids were coming from the opposite direction towards Alan. Instinctively, Alan stepped off the sidewalk to give the group some room. The largest boy in the group saw Alan and yelled, "Hey Nerd-o-licious! Did I give you permission to walk on my sidewalk?" I guess I wasn't the only one to consider Alan a nerd.

"Knock it off, Eldon. I don't want to be bothered," said

Alan. The group of kids surrounded Alan and I couldn't help but notice how small he was compared to the other kids. This wasn't going to be pretty. Eldon was a senior and had gone to state several years for wrestling. He wrestled as a heavyweight. I doubt if Alan could have weighed more than one hundred and twenty pounds, with his clothes on and soaking wet. Eldon was also a bully who pushed around just about anyone he wanted. Even I had been bullied by Eldon, although that had been two years ago before I had a growth streak. Even the teachers were leery around Eldon. For whatever reason, Eldon didn't play football, although he would have been great. Maybe football wasn't violent enough for him.

"What have I told you about walking on my sidewalk?" Eldon asked, towering over Alan.

The smart thing for Alan to do was to beg for mercy and walk away. Slink into the crowd and disappear, but Alan must have been fed up with being bullied.

"It's not your sidewalk. For your information, this school was paid for with tax-payer money. I have just as much right as you do to walk on it, Eldon!" Alan said. Although I admired his bravery for standing up to Eldon, I knew that carnage was about to follow. Nobody disrespected Eldon in front of his peers and got away with it.

Eldon grabbed Alan and spun him around then grabbed him in a bear hug. Alan tried to yell, but Eldon was squeezing so hard that Alan couldn't breathe. Lifting Alan up off his feet, I realized that Eldon was going to slam him to the ground.

A forceful thought entered my mind. *Help him!*

Without thinking through the consequences, I stepped from behind the bush and yelled, "Put him down Eldon!"

With Alan still in his arms, Eldon spun around to face me. I could see he was shocked to have someone confront him. Shock quickly turned to rage.

"Stay out of this, Marcus. I'll kick your butt, even if you were just shot," Eldon shouted.

"Put him down! He didn't do anything to you. Besides,

you outweigh him by one hundred and fifty pounds," I said knowing that I was about to get it. Even if I could take Eldon, which was doubtful, his friends were all juniors and seniors and would jump in on a moment's notice.

Dropping Alan to the ground like a sack of potatoes, Eldon stepped over him and stood with his face inches away from mine. I could smell the tacos on his breath from lunch.

"I bet we weigh about the same, punk." Little droplets of spit splattered my face on the word punk. "What do you say, pretty boy? You wanna go?" Eldon said with a sneer. Eldon's friends fanned out behind him.

"Just give it a rest, huh? There's no need to get worked up about this. Besides, nobody wants detention over this," I said.

Eldon appeared to think about what I had said. "You're right. No need to get worked up about this." Turning his back to me, he seemed to be heading back to his friends. I started towards Alan to see if he was O.K. Without a word, Eldon spun around and tackled me from the side. I found myself lying on my back, with Eldon sitting with his whole weight on my chest. With his knees, Eldon painfully pinned down both of my arms. I couldn't breathe and I couldn't defend myself. Smiling, Eldon began to pummel my unprotected face over and over. Eldon's weight was positioned right on my wounded ribs, and the agony was unbearable. After a couple of blows, I could feel my lips split, and blood from my nose started running down the back of my throat making me gag.

Eldon brought a huge fist up to strike me again, and I closed my eyes preparing for the impact. I was surprised when it didn't come. Instead Eldon let out a bull roar. "Owwww! Let go of me! I'm gonna kill you, you little runt!"

Opening my eyes, I saw that Alan had jumped on Eldon's back and he had grabbed him by his ears and was pulling with all his might. Eldon's weight shifted and my right arm came free. With all my strength, I slugged Eldon in the stomach, knocking the wind from him. Turning my body, I was able to throw Eldon off my chest and scramble away. I got up painfully and looked down at Eldon who was on the ground gulping for breath. Alan was still on his back, but he had released Eldon's ears and was trying to get away. As quick as a cat, Eldon's left hand shot out backwards and caught Alan right on the nose. With a sickening crunch, blood started to pour from Alan's nose. Positioning myself next to Alan, I warily watched as Eldon's friends began to advance towards us. Although I was teammates with several of the boys, they were Eldon's friends and would back his play, teammates or not.

Taking up an athletic stance, I vowed to myself to take out at least one person before I was brought down by the pack. Alan bravely stood beside me, looking scared, but not backing away. The kid had guts.

"Hey! Knock it off!" came a shout.

Turning, I saw Mr. Turner, the school principal. Beside him were several teachers. They quickly interceded, and we were ushered inside the school and found ourselves sitting in two separate rooms. Alan and I sharing one room, Eldon and three of his gang in another. Both Alan and I were given a towel and a bag of ice. Both our towels were blood soaked. Alan gingerly had the ice resting on his nose, which had thankfully stopped bleeding. Although my face hurt, I chose to place the ice on my aching ribs.

"Thanks," Alan said simply.

"No prob," I replied shifting the ice bag to another sore spot. "Why did you mouth back to Eldon? You knew what was going to happen."

Alan took the bag away from his nose and looked at me. "I'm tired of running and hiding. I'm sick and tired of being bullied just because I'm small. Last week they dumped me upside down in one of the garbage cans, yesterday they stuffed me in my own locker. Nobody found me until second period. Something just snapped, and I decided to stand up to Eldon. I've actually been going to noon detention to get away from those guys."

I nodded my head. At least the mystery of Alan being in detention had been answered.

"You know that this isn't the end of this, don't you? Eldon won't live this down for a while," I said.

"Yeah, well you better watch your back too," Alan suggested. "You slugged him in the gut pretty good."

We were quiet for a while, contemplating the next couple of days with Eldon lurking about waiting for payback time.

"I thought he was going to knock my teeth out when you jumped on his back. I wonder how Eldon's ears feel?" I looked over at Alan and we both broke out laughing.

"Thanks," I said after a moment. "You saved me from another trip to the hospital."

Alan shrugged his shoulders. "Nobody has ever stood up for me before. Besides, like you said, it ain't over yet."

Mr. Turner came in, shutting the door behind him. He sat down across from us with a concerned look on his face.

"Are either of you two hurt badly?" he asked.

"I think Eldon broke my nose," said Alan. His nose had swollen two times larger than normal.

I gingerly felt my face. My nose was also swollen, but not as bad as Alan's. "I should be fine," I replied.

"We'll get the school nurse to look at your nose in a bit," said Mr. Turner. "Why don't you tell me what happened?"

With both of us adding details, we told Mr. Turner the events of the fight. Mr. Turner said nothing, but took notes of what we said. When we finished, Mr. Turner took off his glasses and rubbed the bridge of his nose. He seemed to be in a dilemma. Over what, I'm not sure because it was an open and shut case of bullying.

"I sure wish that you two had brought this to me instead of taking action into your own hands," Mr. Turner said.

"We just told you that Eldon started it," I said. "I thought that it was over when Eldon tackled me and punched my face in."

"Eldon and his friends say that you provoked them," said Mr. Turner.

"How?" asked Alan. "Eldon was pushing me around when Marcus tried to stop him. Eldon got mad and began to beat Marcus up." Alan's analysis stung a little, but in all fairness, I wasn't going to win that particular fight.

"Well, school rules bind my hands. You'll both serve one week of in-school detention. If this happens again, you'll serve a week of full suspension at home. Another occurrence and you will be expelled. Do you understand?" Mr. Turner asked.

"That's not fair!" cried Alan. "We were only defending ourselves! You should be giving this lecture to Eldon and his goons, not us!" I felt the same way. It was unfair that we were getting in trouble for fighting back. What were we supposed to do? Allow them to pummel us?

"Eldon and his friends will be punished accordingly for their actions in the matter. You just worry about yourselves and not Eldon," replied Mr. Turner.

In the back of my mind, I knew what this was all about. Eldon's parents were pillars of the community. They had donated thousands of dollars over the years to the school. It would look bad if Eldon was entirely in the wrong. By assigning blame all around, Eldon wouldn't be singled out. At least that is what I thought.

"You'll start your detention on Monday." Mr. Turner said. And with that Mr. Turner walked out leaving us alone in the office.

"Well, this was a lovely day," I said mostly to myself.

"Yeah, you'd think that he would give you a break, you know, with all that's happened to you recently," Alan said.

And to top it off, my fight with the school bully wasn't the biggest event of the day.

....

Grandma Torrey had gotten a call from Mr. Turner, so

she was pretty mad when I got home. She soon cooled off when I explained that I had been defending Alan.

"Your principal didn't mention that part of the story," she said.

"It was Eldon Hendrickson. He doesn't seem to get into much trouble, even though he is the biggest bully in the school."

Grandma thought for a minute. "You know I don't condone fighting, but it sounds like little Alan needed you today. You did the right thing. You've probably made an enemy with Eldon, though. I doubt that this is over." Grandma was no dummy. "Your grandfather always said to make your first punch count." With that, Grandma gave me a wink and left me to do my homework.

One thing that I knew for sure, the world could crumble at my feet, and Grandma would still be there for me. I felt a warm surge of affection for Grandma Torrey. It was the first time since Selena's death that I had even a vague moment of joy.

I was so caught up in the events of the day, that I didn't bother to think about the strange nightly occurrences. I finished my homework and then spent a couple of hours with Grandma watching T.V. Although I didn't particularly like her choice of programming, I decided that I wanted to spend some time with this great lady who had sacrificed so much for Selena and me. Grandma had been so close with Selena. Being caught up in my own little life dramas, I probably neglected to notice how lonely Grandma was without Grandpa Torrey and now Selena, not to mention my mom and dad. She had lost almost everyone in her life and I felt bad that I hadn't spent more time with her. I vowed to do better with that.

Although my face was bruised and my ribs hurt from being freshly banged around, I felt better than I had in several weeks. Something about that fight, even though I undoubtedly had lost, had released some of my demons. I was pretty wiped out after the day's events so around 9:00 P.M. I went to bed. I was asleep before my head even hit the pillow.

Almost immediately, I began to dream one of those wild dreams.

I dreamed that I got out of bed, and began to stagger across the room looking for something. Finally, I found my backpack and fumbled around and found a pen and some writing paper. Sitting on the edge of my bed, I began to write something on the pad, but I was having trouble. I soon realized that I was using my left hand to write. I was too absorbed in watching myself write that I didn't pay attention to what I was writing. I watched my hand lift the pen from the page and set it down on the dresser. Looking down, I read what I had written.

"Marcus, it's Selena. Try to contact me with your mind."

Instantly I was awake from this dream, but it had been no dream. I *was* sitting on the edge of my bed with the note in my lap just as I had seen. I realized that I was hyperventilating. I got a little fuzzy around the edges, but was able to control my breathing after a moment or two. I had broken out in a sweat that soaked my pajamas.

With hands shaking, I reread the sentence that was written with my hand, but not in my handwriting. What did this mean? Was I cracking up, or was there something to this?

Concentrating with all the intensity that I could muster, I tried to send my thoughts to a sister I knew was dead.

"IS THIS REAL?" I sent with my mind.

Nothing. I so desperately wanted this to be real, that I knew that I would be devastated if I found out it was all in my imagination. I tried again.

"PLEASE SPEAK TO ME!" I said.

I felt a tiny stirring at the edge of my consciousness.

"SELENA, IS THAT YOU?" If I focused any harder, I was sure that I would get a bloody nose. Again and again I tried to contact Selena. I was sure that I could feel something, but for whatever reason I couldn't make contact with her.

Needless to say, I spent a very focused night trying to speak to Selena. When dawn rolled around, I was totally fried.

I could almost swear that I could feel Selena's presence, but it was somehow, well, buried I guess is the word I would use. Thank goodness it was Friday. I was going to be useless at school.

My morning routine was pretty sluggish. Not even the shower woke me up completely. I had concentrated the entire night through, and I felt like I had been awake for several days.   Arriving at school, things actually took a turn for the worse. Eldon and his gang were sitting in Eldon's Jeep next to where I customarily parked. The canopy was off and loud rap music was booming from the speakers. I wasn't about to give them the satisfaction of looking scared and parking in another location.

As casually as I could, I pulled into the space and got out of my car. Looking over at Eldon and his gang, I nodded in their direction and started toward the school doors.

"Hey Harmon!" Eldon swung down from his seat. The Jeep had a lift kit and huge tires, so he literally had to swing down to exit his Jeep. Eldon leaned casually against the bumper, arms folded over his chest. Technically, we weren't supposed to talk to each other, but Eldon was never one to hold to any rules.

"You got lucky yesterday. Just to give you warning, I'm coming after you. I'll find you alone sometime and even things up." Eldon wasn't boasting or talking big. He was stating this as a matter of fact. Just a conversation between two people.

Have you even known anyone who thrived on cruelty? You look into their eyes and see that they enjoy inflicting pain. They don't respect anything but violence. As much as I disliked fighting, I knew that I would not escape another round or two with Eldon. He had been thwarted and he didn't like it one bit.

"You tell your little pal Alan that he is dead meat. I'll be looking for him too. If you want to make my day, why don't you try to protect him again? That should be worth some laughs." Snickers issued from the Jeep.

I felt cold dread wash over me as I contemplated Alan

being alone with these goons.

"Alan can't defend himself, and you know it," I said. "It was me that stopped you from picking on Alan. Leave the kid alone. You can have a shot at me anytime you want. Only a coward would pick on a kid like Alan." Of course, I knew that I would lose any fight with Eldon. As large and as strong as I am, Eldon was something of a freak. He was strong, quick, and mean. I just hoped Eldon would take the bait and come after me and forget Alan. He could easily cripple Alan, or worse.

Eldon didn't rise to my baiting. "Whatever, Harmon. I don't like that kid, and I don't care how small he is. He's going to learn a lesson. Although, I'm not going to enjoy hurting the kid as much as I will enjoy hurting you. I'm thinking of breaking your kneecap or something. A memento to last a while." Eldon gave me a wink and climbed back up into the seat of his Jeep. "See you around Sweetie Pie."

I immediately went inside and searched for Alan. He was sitting in the library, and I could tell by the way that he watched the door, that he was scared.

His face lit up briefly when he saw me. "Hey, man! How you feeling?"

"I'm fine. Ribs a little sore." I sat down across from him. "We have a problem. Eldon is hunting us."

"Yeah, I figured as much." Alan's eyes welled a little. He turned away ashamed of his show of fear. "I saw him outside and I figured he was waiting for you. What are we going to do?"

"I guess we can go to Mr. Turner and tell him," I said, my voice unconvincing.

Alan snorted. "Yeah, if you believe telling Mr. Turner will help, then I got a bridge I want to sell you. Cheap." He wiped his eyes on his sleeve and looked down at his shoes.

I chuckled. "I hear you there, man." I leaned forward. "Alan, we're in this together, OK? Where you go, I go."

Alan looked up into my face. "That won't keep Eldon away. He's just not right in the head somehow." I could visibly see Alan shiver as he thought about Eldon.

"Yeah, I know, but if we're going to go through it, let's go through it together," I said with a smile.

"Thanks Marcus." Again, tears welled up in Alan's eyes, but this time it was in gratitude. "That guy is just such a freak of nature."

I laughed. "Hey, the bell is about to ring. Let me walk you to your first class."

Alan looked slyly at me. "Does that mean we're going steady?" It broke the spell. We both broke out laughing and earned a stern look from Mrs. Welker, the librarian. Stifling our laughter, we grabbed our bags and hurried out into the hall.

When we got to Alan's classroom, I punched him in the arm. "See ya later, Sweetheart."

"I'll be counting the minutes, Pookie." replied Alan.

I looked up to see that Becky was standing with a couple of her girlfriends. They had witnessed the entire exchange.

"Oh, now it's all beginning to make sense," said one of Becky's friends. "He wants to bat for the other team. It had nothing to do with you, girlfriend!"

....

Alan and I escaped facing down Eldon the following week. Mr. Turner made sure that we served our weeks' detention apart from Eldon. Eldon, of course, was given more leeway and served his detention in the library. He was given a table to himself where he was supposed to do class work and read quietly under the supervision of the librarian. Brent and Paul informed me that he spent most of his detention playing on his personal computer and texting his friends. Brent thought that he must have hacked his way into the school Wi-Fi because they saw him surfing the web instead of working.

Alan and I had it considerably worse. Mrs. Hackett was in charge of all in-school suspensions. Mrs. Hackett had been an English teacher and was semi-retired. If we weren't doing class work or reading, Mrs. Hackett would have us read from textbooks that she had on hand then write a report on what we had read. To say that it was boring is an understatement. Alan and I were separated across the room, and we only got a chance to talk before or after school. Mrs. Hackett didn't even allow talking during our fifteen minute lunch break. Schoolwork, reading, and textbook work. Hour after hour, day after day.

I vowed I would never get suspended again. Facing Eldon was more appealing than suspension.

We had almost forgotten about Eldon as we left detention that Friday afternoon. I had taken to driving Alan home after school. Although Alan was a freshman, Paul and Brent accepted him being around. They knew that Alan didn't have a chance against Eldon and his gang and they began to look after him, too.

We were standing at Brent's locker. The coaches' polls had just come out, and Brent and Paul were excited that the team was ranked number two in the state.

"Dude," Brent said, "We'd be number one if you were playing. The other teams just know that we are weaker in the middle without you. It will be good for you to do something to get your mind off of stuff."

"Yeah, I know. Maybe when my ribs feel better." I still didn't feel like playing, but maybe Brent had a point about taking my mind off of stuff.

"That's my boy!" piped Paul. "At least you're thinking about it."

Grabbing our bags, we headed out the door. Alan followed me to my car. I opened the trunk and we put our stuff in and climbed in the seats.

Paul and Brent hustled off for a pregame meal before they headed for the football field.

"Why don't you come over to my place to get something to eat?" I asked Alan as we drove off. Alan's family lived a little ways out of town, and it would be easier to eat at my house, then we could both go watch the game. Technically, Alan could have dressed down for the game since he played on the JV squad, but since he was in detention, he wasn't allowed to practice. Although I wasn't too excited about it, I promised him that I would go to the game with him. I was still worried that Eldon would catch him alone.

"Sounds good. Can I use your cell phone to call my mom?" he asked.

"Sure." Reaching in my pocket, I realized that I had left my phone in my locker.

"Dang," I said. "We need to go back to school. Forgot my phone."

"Idiot!" Alan replied with a chuckle.

I smacked him on the back of his head.

"You know, you can give a guy brain damage if you do that too often," Alan complained as he rubbed the back of his head.

"You gotta have a brain first," was my compassionate reply.

Pulling back into the parking lot, I spotted Brent leaning against his car. He was preoccupied and didn't see us because he had a girl in his arms. Not just any girl. It was Becky. Pulling alongside Brent's car, Brent lowered his face and kissed her. Hearing the sound of the car, he looked up and spotted me and Alan. Comically, Brent pushed Becky away even though she didn't realize what was going on and was still trying to kiss Brent back. The look of shock on her face would have been amusing at any other time, but I wasn't amused.

"Hey Marcus," Brent said. In doing so, alerting Becky to the situation. She spun to see us in the car. The shock was only momentary. Upon seeing me, she linked her arm to Brent's arm. Tight. A smug look replaced her shocked look as she saw us.

"Hey guys!" she said with a smirk.

"Marcus, man, I don't want this to be a problem, OK?" Brent said.

Without a word, I exited the car and got my phone from my locker. When I came back, Brent and Becky had left.

"Hey I'm sorry, dude." said Alan. "Nobody should have that happen to them."

"It's not like we're together," I said sullenly.

Alan remained silent on the way home. After eating, we watched Sports Center and played some Madden Football.

"Marcus, you don't need to go with me tonight if you don't want to. There will be enough people around that I'm sure I'll be fine."

I let out a sigh. "There's no reason that I should be angry. I cut it off with her."

Alan had a thoughtful expression on his face. "Well, in my vast experience with womenfolk...who am I kidding. I got nothing."

Trust Alan to bring me out of my funk. I laughed and tossed my controller at him, disrupting his chance at a touchdown.

"Jerk!" he shouted.

"You two have sure been spending a lot of time together lately," Grandma said with a grateful look at Alan.

"Oh, hi, Mrs. Torrey," Alan said.

"Hi Grandma. Alan and I are going to the game tonight. Did you want to go?" I knew Grandma wouldn't want to go unless I was playing, but I was making a point to involve Grandma as much as possible.

"I think I'm going to see my sister in Seattle this weekend. I'm going to get a few things ready tonight so I can leave tomorrow." She tussled my hair and walked off to her bedroom.

"Your grandma is pretty cool," Alan said. He tossed my controller back to me. "Now stop stalling and try to stop my drive down the field you giant freak of nature."

"Bring it on munchkin!" was my reply.

CHAPTER NINE

ATTACK

The football game was going to be a challenge for our team. We were playing Dayton, and they had a huge football history in the state of Oregon. They didn't have a large number of standout players this year, but they were super-well coached and they never gave up. It would be a real feather in our cap if we won tonight.

Alan and I chose to sit in the student section right below the band. I felt a tug in the pit of my stomach as I looked at the musicians. Selena had played in the band, and I missed seeing her there. I was still trying to contact her with my mind, but I was still coming up short. There just seemed to be some kind of block there. I snorted out loud. That was assuming that Selena was really there and I wasn't some kind of loony dweeb.

Becky was there, of course. Among other things, Becky was a varsity cheerleader. I could tell that she was letting everyone know that she was now going out with my best friend. As the team was warming up, she was surrounded by her friends and they would occasionally point and giggle in Brent's direction. Once, Brent made eye contact with Becky and gave her a little wave. Fits of giggling issued from the direction of Becky and her friends. I was not even an after-thought of Becky and her herd now.

The game was exciting. Even though we had better players, Dayton was executing better as a team. The score was tied as the players left the field at halftime. Paul was trying his best to cover one of Dayton's stud receivers, but he had twisted his ankle during the first quarter. The guy he was covering had scored both touchdowns, and I knew that Paul would be fuming in the locker room.

I decided that I needed to go to the "little boy's room", and Alan wanted a bag of popcorn. We left the stands to go to the concession area. Alan quickly got in line as I headed for the restrooms. Stepping up to the urinal, I heard the doors open behind me. Whoever it was must get stage fright taking a leak in front of other people because he left without coming in.

Moments passed and I heard a commotion outside. The door opened, and I heard Alan yell out, "Marcus, watch...."

I was in the process of zipping up when I turned around and came face to face with Eldon and his pal, Bill Smalls. Smalls didn't describe Bill too well. He was a hulking brute, but slow and dimwitted. Bill had his arms around Alan who was trying to get away. Bill had stopped Alan from crying out by squeezing him so hard that he couldn't breathe. I could see that he enjoyed inflicting pain as much as Eldon did.

"Let him go, Bill!" I said. I stepped toward Bill, intent on helping Alan. I was stopped by Eldon who sucker punched me in the gut, knocking every ounce of air out of my lungs. I collapsed to the floor gulping air like a beached fish.

"Well girls," Eldon said with a smile. "We're all alone and nobody else is around. I have a question for you, Harmon. Does it hurt when I do this?" Too late I tried to dodge a kick to my rib cage. With a sickening thump, I felt my ribs scream out in pain.

I collapsed onto my side. Tears streamed down my face as I tried to gasp for breath.

"I'll take your crybaby tears as a yes," said Eldon.

Eldon spun quickly around and delivered a punch to Alan's unprotected stomach. With a grunt of pain, Alan sagged in Bill's tight grip. Bill laughed at Alan's distress and dropped him to the ground, like a sack of potatoes. Alan's face was purple and he, too, struggled to breathe.

"Well ladies, this has been fun." Eldon opened the door and let Bill go through. "Just so you know, this wasn't the beating I promised. This was just for kicks and giggles. We'll continue this another time." Eldon and Bill could be heard laughing as they walked away.

After a moment, I was able to sit up and catch my breath. Alan was writhing on the floor in pain, his breath knocked clean from him. After a moment, he sat up, his face less purple at least.

"Sorry, Marcus. I saw them too late," he said. His words came out as gasps.

"It's not your fault," I said. Although my ribs were already damaged, I could tell that they weren't further broken or cracked. I was becoming an expert on sore ribs. I'm sure the new bruises would be spectacular, however. Eldon sure knew how to hurt a guy.

"Should we report this?" I asked Alan.

"Don't be stupid," he said rubbing where he had been punched.

"Right," I said.

The second half of the game went all Dayton's way. Paul played his heart out on a sprained ankle, but it wasn't enough to shut down Dayton's stud receiver. A healthy Paul could have done it, a hurt Paul couldn't. The problem was that our team wasn't deep enough on the depth chart for someone else to play Paul's position. A hurt Paul was still better than the alternative. I knew from experience that no one would want to be around Paul this next week.

After dropping Alan off at his home, I returned to an empty house. Grandma had left a note saying that she had found a good price on airfare and that she decided to fly out that evening. I was grateful because there wouldn't be any questions about me wincing from newly damaged ribs.

I had taken to leaving a notepad and pen in easy reach of the bed in case Selena tried to contact me again. There hadn't been any strange dreams for a week, and I was beginning to wonder if it was all coming to an end. I tried again to contact Selena, but to no avail.

After taking a pain pill for my ribs, I laid down for some shut-eye. The events of the day had taken a lot out of me and I was asleep before my head hit the pillow.

I was able to sleep pretty soundly throughout the night. I woke up without having any strange dreams. For that reason, I almost didn't bother to check the notepad. When I did, I found a note scribbled on the pad.

I'm still here. Keep trying. S.

Sitting on the bed, I tried to concentrate as hard as I knew how. I could feel a stirring of Selena's presence, but I just couldn't seem to push through and communicate with her. Looking at the handwriting on the pad, it seemed to me that the writing looked forced, as though it were very difficult to write those few words. A thought dawned on me. Maybe when I was asleep, Selena was able to control my body to do those things that I had dreamed. If that was true, maybe it was difficult because she was used to her own body. Body movements and motor skills would suffer. Of course she would be clumsy and uncoordinated. The more I thought through it, the more I found this made sense. I somehow needed to make things more convenient for her to communicate with me.

Maybe writing was too difficult for Selena to accomplish using my body. I wondered if speaking would be as difficult. Getting up off the bed I walked into Selena's room. Grandma hadn't changed anything in her room, and I had only entered her room once or twice since her death. The memories were just too strong.

I found what I was looking for on Selena's dresser. It was her phone – the one that she had recorded me with. Picking up the phone, I put the earbuds into my ears. I pushed the "play" button.

"Stop doing that! Heeeeee, oooh, oooh! Eeeeee! No, no, no! OK, ok! Dishes for the week! Just please let go!" I shook my head. I had one of our last conversations right in the palm of my hand. It was surreal.

Returning to my room, I placed the phone next to

my bed. Hopefully, Selena would be able to record her/my voice and communicate better with me should I have another "dream".

While I was getting some cereal in the kitchen, I heard a knock. When I turned around, Brent was peeking his head through the doorway.

"Hey man, I thought we should talk," he said. I noticed that he stayed partially outside.

"Sure," I said nonchalantly. "What's up?"

"Don't give me that, Marcus. You know what's up. Are we gonna talk about it?" He still remained behind the door. I was stronger, but he was faster. I think he was ready to bolt and run should I show any violent tendencies.

"What's to talk about? Obviously, you and Becky are together. I broke it off with her. It's a free country, the last time I looked. Do what you want." I couldn't hide the sarcasm in my voice.

"Are you gonna let me in, or are you gonna pummel me to a pulp?" he asked, still in his defensive position outside.

I let out a sigh. "Since Eldon smacked me in the ribs again, I guess I'll spare your life."

"Eldon got you again? How did that happen?" he asked. Sincere concern showed in his eyes.

I related the story of Alan and me in the restroom.

"Man, that dude is just wrong in the head," was his reply after I told the story. "Marcus, I'm sorry man. You've really had a rough couple of weeks, and now I'm hurting you too." Brent looked down at the floor. "I'll...I'll break it off. I don't want to hurt you any more than you have been..."

We both sat down in front of the TV. I absently began to rub my ribs.

"Forget it, man, forget it. I don't even know why I'm upset. I broke it off, right? I mean, I actually felt relief when I broke it off. It's not like I even want to get back with Becky. It's...it's kinda weird. I don't know," I said.

"Do you want me to break it off? I mean, I will if you

can't handle it..." I could tell that Brent was being sincere. He really was a good friend.

"No. You seem to really like her, and she really digs you. You two kids have fun. I'll be fine." I actually meant it. I was beginning to see how foolish it was to be jealous of a situation that I had caused.

"She's going to be hanging around with me, and you're going to be around. It's not going to be all weird and stuff is it?" Brent asked with a raised eyebrow.

"Oh, yeah. It's gonna be weird all right." I laughed at Brent's downcast expression, "But we'll get through it. We're almost adults anyway. We might as well act like it."

Brent couldn't hide his relief. He must really like Becky. Actually, this was the first time Brent really had a steady girlfriend. I silently wished him luck.

"That's great! Really man, great!" Brent gushed. "Hey, uh...Becky wanted to talk with you too. Can she come in?"

"Becky is here?" I asked incredulously.

"Well, yeah. She wanted to sit in the car until you calmed down."

"And you were worried that it would be awkward?" I asked.

Brent jogged out to the car and in a couple of moments both of them were sitting side by side in the love seat. I couldn't help but remember that Becky and I used to sit in that very chair not too long ago.

"Marcus, I don't want this to be weird," Becky said,

"It's unanimous, then," I said. "We all don't want this to be weird."

"I mean, you did break up with me, right? You didn't expect me to sit around and wait for you, right?" Becky asked.

"I'm fine with you and Brent. You guys just took me by surprise. It just seemed to happen so fast," I said.

"It's just that, you know, with everything happening over the last couple of weeks...well, I don't want to be the cause of more sadness for you." I could see that Becky was also being sincere, and trying to be a good friend and not intentionally hurt me.

"It's cool. Seriously. It stung a little, but it's better this way. Really. I'm happy for you both. And don't worry about me. Things are getting better."

"Well, we're here for you Marcus, regardless of the past," said Becky.

"Yeah, buddy, we're here for you. Even if it means that we got to take on Eldon and his gang. Which reminds me, I need to put the baseball bat in my car." I don't think that he meant that as a joke.

Brent stood and helped Becky to her feet. "We're going into Gresham to take in a movie. You don't...you know, want to tag alo..."

"I will hit you in the face, hard, a lot of times if you finish that sentence," I said with a doleful glare. "You two kids run along. I've got better things to do than hang out with my ex-girlfriend and her new boy-toy."

"I always was the pretty one of our group," replied Brent with a huge smile.

"Yeah, yeah. Now get outta here before I call the cops," I said as I ushered them out the door.

....

That weekend was pretty slow. I actually had some catching up to do with homework because Mrs. Hackett didn't allow us to use computers while in suspension. That meant that I needed to spend some time with some writing assignments that were due this next week.   Throughout the weekend, I would occasionally try to contact Selena. Even though I faithfully made sure that the pad, pen, and phone were in place before I went to sleep, nothing had come from it. Something was missing and I was frustrated that I couldn't solve the problem. I know it sounds weird, but I really believed that Selena was there. I could feel little sparks, like she was trying to communicate with me too. Little glimpses of her presence would come and go. I guess that she was a ghost or something. Not sure how ghosts communicated. Maybe I needed to get some chains for her to rattle.

Sunday night rolled around and I was lounging on the couch watching TV. Grandma had just called to check on me and inform me that she decided to stay with her sister for the remainder of the week. She was concerned that I was all alone, but I assured her that I was fine. I knew that she needed to spend some time with her sister more than she needed to be watching after me.

The phone rang and I jumped up to get it.

"Hello," I said.

"Hey, man, this is Alan. Mom wanted me to ask if you wanted to have dinner with us."

"Uh, sure. Grandma decided to stay another week, so I'll be cooking for myself," I said with regret. My cooking wasn't even close to Grandma's.

"Yeah, we heard. Your grandma just called us to see if we could watch out for you this week. You know, babysit you." Alan laughed at his humor. I made a mental note to smack him in the back of the head when he wasn't expecting it.

"Whatever, punk. OK, I'll be over in a little while." I hung up the phone and decided to shower and change clothes before going over to Alan's.

Dinner at the Malloy's was fun. Alan was the oldest of three kids, a five year old sister named Allie, and a one year old brother named Tim. Alan pretended that they were hugely annoying, but I could tell that he loved them. Alan's mom stayed at home to watch the kids; Alan's dad owned a carpet cleaning business.

"I hope you like barbecued beef ribs," said Mrs. Malloy.

My mouth watered. "Oh, yeah," I said, nodding my head. "I love ribs!"

Dinner was more lively than I was used to. Even when Selena was alive, dinner with Grandma was a quiet time to eat and talk about the day's activities. I was accustomed to nice quiet dinners.

Not so at the Malloy's. With six of us at the dinner table, it was constant commotion. Allie apparently had taken a shine to me because she wouldn't let anyone else but me help her eat. I dished up her plate and cut the rib meat into bite sized chunks for her. Timmy contributed with excited shrieks about his food, some of which actually got into his mouth. Most of the food went onto the floor where the dog had strategically placed himself.

When I wasn't helping Allie, someone would veritably ask for something to be passed. Since I was sitting at the middle of the table, I would have to stop eating to pass whatever was wanted along to the next person. It seemed that every time I raised my fork, someone asked for something. I had raised my fork to my mouth five times in a row without being able to take a bite when I discovered that the basket of bread that I was passing was empty. I turned to Mrs. Malloy to tell her that the basket was empty when I caught sight of Alan who was having some sort of conniption.

Alan's face had turned completely red from holding in his laughter. He was successful about holding the laughter in, but his whole body was bouncing violently from internal laughter. Alan's parents seemed to have the same affliction. That's when it dawned on me that I was the center of a joke.

"Haaaaaa, ha, ha, haaaaa!" bellowed Alan with a mighty laugh. "You....you...should have seen yourself! You must...ha.. have passed that empty bread basket thr...three or..or four times before you figured it out. Oh, my sides hurt." Alan abandoned himself to laughter, occasionally slapping the table. Alan's parents also let loose, and even the two young ones joined in the laughter.

I couldn't help but join in with this happy family. No malice was intended. In fact, I felt strangely honored that they would treat me as one of the family, even though I had met Alan's family for the first time that night.

"You do know that this means that turnabout is fair

play," I said to the laughing family.

"Marcus, you are SO out of your league if you think you can compete with my mom," said Alan with a grin.

"Alan's right, Marcus," said Mr. Malloy. "The best word of advice I can give you is to hang your head in shame and admit your defeat like a man. Now that I think of it, that's good marriage advice too."

Mrs. Malloy playfully smacked Mr. Malloy in the head with an oven mitt.

"You didn't include begging for forgiveness, just for being a man," added Mrs. Malloy.

"I thought that was implied," said Mr. Malloy as he was reaching for the FULL basket of bread sitting beside him.

After dinner was over, I offered to do the dishes. "It's the least I can do for saving me from mac and cheese."

"Well, I guess we'll just have to have you over more often," said Mrs. Malloy with a smile.

Mrs. Malloy asked Alan to help me, but he conveniently had to go to the bathroom. Mrs. Malloy came into the kitchen after he had left.

"Marcus, can I talk with you for a minute?" she asked.

"Sure thing," I said as I rinsed out a salad bowl.

I could tell that she didn't know where to start. "I'd like to thank you for sticking up for Alan against that Hendricksen bully. He doesn't have many friends, so..." her eyes welled with tears.

"Hey, Alan is a good kid. No one should have to put up with bullying from that jerk," I said.

"Is the bullying over?" she asked hopefully.

I didn't want her to worry, but telling the truth seemed like the right thing to do.

"I wish I could tell you otherwise, but Eldon isn't the type to give up bullying. He actually thrives on it," I said with sincerity.

Mrs. Malloy nodded. "We kind of figured that it was that way. Alan doesn't say much, but we noticed that he's been jumpy lately." Her eyes welled with tears again. "Thanks for being his friend. You have no idea how much he looks up to you. He talks about you all the time. You're like the big brother that he has never had."

"He's a good kid," I said again. "Me and my buddies will keep a watch on him. Don't worry, he'll be alright." I wished that I could believe that completely.

"We talked with Mr. Turner, and he said that Alan provoked the Hendricksen boy into fighting. Can you believe that? Alan against that boy who is like a full-grown man! What a load of crap!" Mrs. Malloy said angrily.

I agreed.

"Well," she said with a smile. "Thanks again for being Alan's friend."

The bonus part of the evening was that I was allowed to take home a brimming plate full of ribs. I would eat well for a day or two.

When I got home, I went straight to the kitchen to put the ribs in the fridge. On second thought, I grabbed a rib to eat on the way to my bedroom. My bedroom was upstairs and there were seventeen steps. A guy could starve to death without proper provisions for a trip of that distance.

At the top of the stairs, I noticed that Selena's bedroom door was opened a crack. By unspoken agreement, Grandma and I had made sure that the door was closed. I guess not enough time had passed for either of us. I was certain that I had closed the door after I had found the phone. Maybe I hadn't pulled it tight.

Peeking in the room, well, it just didn't look right. The mattress of the bed seemed a little askew for some reason. I entered the room and looked around some more. Minute details just seemed a little wrong.

I closed the door behind me and went to my room. Immediately I knew that someone had been there. Again, it was little details. Like whoever that had been in the house didn't want anyone to know that they had been there. The dead giveaway was my guitar case. I really didn't take my guitar anywhere, so I was just in the habit of latching only the middle clasp on the case. Whoever opened the guitar case must have forgotten how it was latched before closing it again. Two clasps were latched

Who was going through our house, and what were they looking for? Immediately, I thought of Selena's killers for no other reason then that nothing appeared to be taken. Somebody was looking for something. It didn't seem to be a robbery.

Going from room to room, I found the same sort of evidence. Nothing overtly out of place, just a general feeling that some minor things weren't the same.

Without knowing why, I felt for Selena's crystal that I was wearing on a chain beneath my shirt. I continued to wear it everywhere, except in the shower. Could the crystal be what was being searched for? Selena's killers had mentioned it, but had seemed to dismiss it as being unimportant or no longer necessary. That somehow the crystal wouldn't be useful after a couple of hours, whatever that meant. Well, it had been more than a couple of hours since Selena's death. What use would the crystal have for them now?

I decided to call our local police. Maybe they could find something that I missed, or maybe there were similar break-ins that they knew about.

It took about twenty minutes for the patrol car to pull into my driveway. In the driver's seat sat Jimmy Walton. I could tell it was Jimmy just from the sheer girth. Jimmy must've weighed a good three hundred and fifty pounds wearing only socks, but don't let his weight fool you. Jimmy could flat-out move when he wanted to. He was not good for long-distance, but there were more than a couple guys sitting in jail who underestimated Jimmy's speed for the first thirty yards of a foot race. The strategy was to keep out of Jimmy's reach for the first hundred yards. After that Jimmy would tire and end the chase.

"What's up Marcus?" Asked Jimmy as he climbed out of

the car.

"Hey Jimmy," I said, "I think somebody's been in the house."

"Is anything missing?" He asked.

"Nothing's really missing, there's just some little things about the house that just aren't right," I said.

I took him to the house pointing out various things I found. I kind of expected Jimmy to discount my feeling that somebody had been through the house, but to my surprise Jimmy seemed to believe me.

"It's probably just some teenage kids doing something for thrills," he said. "I wouldn't put much stock in, but if you find something missing, give me a call. Not much we can do now when nothing is missing."

I thanked him for coming over. At least he believed me, but I didn't buy into it being a random act by teenage kids. It was just the feeling I got.

With Grandma being gone, I thought it might be fun to have Alan over to play video games and watch television. After clearing it with his parents, I drove back out to their house to pick Alan up.

"Marcus is afraid of the dark, so he just wants me around for protection," he explained to his parents as we were walking out the door. Not wanting to upset his parents, I waited until we were in the car before I smacked him upside his head.

On the way home I explained to Alan about the break-in.

"Dude, that's kind of freaky," he said. "You don't suppose it was Eldon or any of his gang, do you?"

I hadn't really considered that. As I thought about it, it just didn't seem right. I couldn't shake the feeling that it had something to do with Selena, as odd as that seems.

When we got to the house, Alan insisted on walking around to see firsthand what I was talking about. I pointed out all the things I discovered.

"Did you check around the house and all?" Alan asked.

"What do you mean?" I asked.

"Well, it just stands to reason that someone would check around the house before they tried to break in. Maybe there's a clue as to who broke in on the outside of the house."

I was to discover that it paid to be friends with someone who watched crime shows all the time. Around the back of the house was a large rhododendron bush that was Grandma's pride and joy. It stood over six feet tall and was the perfect concealment for someone who wanted to see the house without being discovered.

As we went to the backside of the rhododendron, we discovered footprints and a bunch of cigarette butts. Someone had spent a considerable time behind the bush watching the house. The hairs on the back of my neck began to stand up. Here was proof of what I was feeling. Someone had indeed been watching the house, and that same someone had entered the house and looked around while no one was there.

A sense of dread began to permeate my consciousness. I couldn't put my finger on it, but I began to believe that this wasn't the end of it.

We went into the house and made sure to lock the doors after we went inside.

"You don't have to stick around if you don't want to," I said.

"I'm not too worried," said Alan. "It's obvious that someone saw an opportunity and went into the house, but got scared off. I doubt anybody is dumb enough to come back."

Although Alan was diminutive in size, it was reassuring to have him around. Trying to put my feelings aside, we played several hours of Xbox before turning in for bed.

Whenever Alan had stayed at my house for the night, we would drag the inflatable bed from the garage that we used when we went camping and set it up in my room. Alan hated the inflatable bed because he thought it had a leak in it. We would fill it up to capacity then pile sleeping bags and pillows on top.

"I just don't get it," he said as he walked around the bed for the fourth time. "I just can't find the leak anywhere. Seems just fine now."

What Alan didn't know was that while he was asleep, I would often slip out of bed and let a stream of air out. It was a trick that I learned from Selena. Alan flopped down on the bed. He rolled to one corner, then tilted his head to listen for any telltale hiss. Satisfied that the hole wasn't there, he did the same to all four corners with the same result.

"Dude, I just don't get it. With how much this bed deflates during the night, we should be able to find the hole. It's got to be pretty big," he said, shaking.

I stifled a giggle. The anticipation of flattening Alan's bed was almost too much. I set the alarm on my phone to "vibrate" and placed it under my pillow. Every couple hours, the phone was set to go off so that I could get up and let more air out of Alan's bed. The goal tonight was almost total deflation.

Despite knowing that someone had entered the house while I was gone, I succumbed to sleep.

....

"Run!" came the urgent message.

I bolted straight up out of sleep. One look at the glowing digital numbers on my alarm clock told me that it was 4:27 AM.

"Wha...what did you say?" I asked Alan. There was no reply except for a quiet snore that issued from the pile blankets.

"Run!" to my astonishment I recognized the voice. It was Selena.

"Selena?" I asked.

"Marcus, run! Run for your life!" screamed Selena in my head. Like a bolt of lightning, I recognized that Selena was communicating with me telepathically, just like before she

was killed.

Mustering all my focus I asked, "What's going on?"

A very weak message from Selena came. *"Take... Alan... and run!"*

I could feel Selena's presence fading away and immediately, I felt an impending sense of peril. I knew that we were in danger and we had to move quickly. I jumped to the window and looked out. At first, I saw nothing, then a figure came around the house and looked up towards the window. I was sure he could not see me because I was looking through a slit through the blinds. Gathering himself, he took a mighty leap and jumped straight from the ground to the roof! He was now above us. My initial thought of running out the back door came to a screeching halt. The guy on the roof was positioned in such a way that he could easily monitor both doors, and with relative ease catch us if we decided to run.

I slid over to Alan's bed and gave him a shake.

"Alan, Alan! Wake up!" I whispered urgently.

"Just a couple more minutes, okay mom?" came his sleepy reply.

Knowing that we didn't have time for Alan to wake up completely, I physically grabbed him and threw him over my shoulder, sleeping bag and all.

He began to struggle, thinking that I was playing some kind of trick on him. My only hope now was to hide from the intruders. Knowing the speed and strength of the man on the roof tempered my first instinct to make a run for it.

Grandma's house was built sometime in the 1970s. It had one peculiar feature. The owner had dug out a small underground cellar that attached the house. Grandpa had blocked the cellar off by placing a tall bookshelf in front of the door. If you didn't know the cellar was there, you'd never expect it to be behind the bookshelf. It was Selena's favorite hiding space. For years we had played hide and seek and she had beaten me every time. No matter how hard I tried, I could never find her.

Once when we were camping, she let me in on her secret. When we got home from the camping trip, she took me down to the basement and showed me how to pull the bookcase out of the way and expose the door to the seller. She also showed me a little makeshift handle that she had placed on the back of the bookshelf so that she could pull the bookshelf closed behind her.

With Alan still over my shoulder, I raced downstairs to the background. A crash sounded from the front of the house that signaled the door had been broken down and someone was in the house. More than one someone, because I heard several voices.

Alan must've sensed something was wrong because he stopped struggling and making noise. I set him down and pulled the bookcase out from the wall. Opening the door to the seller, I pushed Alan through, and then pulled the bookcase back into place. I closed the cellar door most of the way, but left it open a crack so that we could hear what was going on in the house. I couldn't hear much because the bookcase blocked most of the sound.

I felt Alan sidle up to me. It was pitch dark, except for the small stream of light that came from the crack in the door. Alan had the sense to remain quiet as we both listened. We listened for what seemed like hours, but was in reality probably only a couple minutes. No sounds came from the house, but we were in the backroom behind a door, so we couldn't have heard much anyway.

It was frustrating not being able to hear what was going on in the house. I reached out to push the bookcase out a fraction.

"No!" came Selena's voice.

Almost on cue we were able to hear two people come into the room. They were talking, but I wasn't able to understand what they were saying. It was a different language. We could hear them opening drawers and cupboards, obviously searching the house.

A third voice entered the room. Again, we could not understand what anyone said, but it was obvious that the third person was in command and was very agitated. An argument broke out between the three people and then came the sound of something being thrown up against the bookcase.

Both Alan and I jumped at the sound. I could hear Alan's breathing become more rapid and raspy. I couldn't blame him. My heart was beating a mile a minute.

We both listened as the three men exited the room, still arguing. By common consent, both of us sat down on the cold concrete and let out a breath of air. Alan still had a sleeping bag, and he draped half of it over my shoulders.

"How long do you think we should stay in here?" whispered Alan.

"I don't know," was my honest reply.

We sat there for hours dozing on and off. Occasionally one of us would go to the door and try to listen. There was no sound coming from the house, but we didn't trust our ability to hear whether the intruders had left the house or not.

All the while we were sitting there, I tried to make contact with Selena. Occasionally I felt a flicker of her presence, but then nothing.

Hour after hour passed before I got another message from Selena.

"Go!" she said.

I got up and gently pulled the door open.

"Dude, what are you doing?" Alan whispered.

"I think it's safe now," I said.

"How do you know?" he asked.

I shrugged my shoulders and gently pushed the bookcase out of the way. Walking as quiet as we could, we exited the room. Stopping in the hallway, we paused to listen. Hearing nothing, we headed upstairs. I needed to grab my car keys, then my plan was to head to the police office to explain about the break-in.

We quickly changed out of our pajamas and into our

street clothes. When we were dressed, we headed downstairs. The front door had indeed been broken. It hung crookedly with one of the hinges completely torn free.

My first thought was to get to the car. I moved the broken door aside, then sprinted to the vehicle. Alan was right behind me. It took us only a moment to realize that the car was unusable. Four slashed tires. We were on foot.

"Call the cops," said Alan.

That seemed like a good idea. I reached into my pants pocket to retrieve my phone, but I had left it under my pillow.

The dilemma now was whether to return and retrieve the phone or set off on foot. Neither option was good.

It dawned on me that there was another option. Grandpa's 1958 dodge power wagon was sitting in his old shop. The dodge hadn't been started in over a year. It was our go-to vehicle when we went camping. It wasn't fast, but it was rugged and you could practically climb a tree with it.

"Come on," I yelled to Alan as I sprinted for the shop. He easily caught up with me. Alan wasn't very big, but he was a speedster.

"What are we doing?" Alan asked.

"Plan two," I said.

We slipped inside the shop just as two headlights appeared coming down the road. Instantly I knew that these were the same people that were after us.

I opened the driver's door and Alan jumped in and scooted across the bench seat to the passenger side. I jumped into the driver seat and pulled down the visor. The dodge keys dropped into my lap.

"*Hurry!*" said Selena.

We could hear the car pull into the driveway. It was now or never. Jamming the keys into the ignition, I pumped furiously on the gas pedal. The old truck needed some loving care when it came to starting it, but it was the vehicle that I had learned to drive when I was a kid getting firewood with my grandpa. It was a testament to the loving care my grandpa gave the dodge that it turned over and started on the first try.

We heard a shout and it didn't take a genius to realize that we had been heard. The dodge wasn't a stealthy vehicle by any stretch of the imagination.

I punched the button on the automatic garage door remote and it began to open. We could see two pairs of feet as the door began to raise. They were waiting for us. Slipping the dodge into gear, I dropped the clutch and punched the gas. The two pairs of feet disappeared, and then we crashed through the door.

The dodge had a very high suspension and ground clearance. Although the car was blocking our path to the street, I simply plowed through the fence, scooted across the lawn, jumped the curb, and headed on down the road. The dodge was built like a tank.

"Head for the police station!" yelled Alan.

That was as good an idea as any, so we raced off in that direction. When I say raced, I mean that we might've broken forty miles an hour, maybe. The Dodge might be built like a tank, but it wasn't going to win any speed records.

Alan kept a close watch through the back window. After a couple blocks, he announced, "Here they come!"

Up ahead I saw the headlight of a car coming our way. Immediately I knew that the car was part of the team that was out to get us. It stood to reason that they were all in contact with each other. It wouldn't take much to call and inform everyone what type of vehicle we were driving.

My fears were confirmed when the car veered into my lane and started heading right for us. I could see the passenger leaning out his window. I've seen many, many, action shows in my time and that could only mean one thing.

I knew I couldn't outrun the people in the dodge, but that didn't mean that we were helpless.

I gunned the accelerator and shifted into a higher gear. An orange blossom of gunfire flared from the oncoming vehicle and the passenger side window fractured.

"Are you all right?" I yelled.

"Yes!" Alan yelled back.

"Hold on!" I yelled.

Cranking the steering wheel to the left, I swerved across the oncoming lane of traffic, over the curb, and into the grass of the city park. Cutting across the park, I hopped the sidewalk and the curb and pulled onto the street on the far side of the park.

Neither car pursued me across the park, but that didn't matter too much because the lumbering pace of the truck was no match for the cars. Within moments they were back on my tail.

Remembering the gunfire from the oncoming car, I made erratic swerves to make it hard for someone shooting at us to draw a bead with a gun.

As we pulled onto the street where the police station was located, we saw another car coming towards us. Again I knew without a doubt that the occupants of the car were part of the same group of people who were out to get us. They had obviously guessed where we would run to, and they were here to block our path.

"Right!" said Selena.

Taking a right would take us out of town. To me that sounded like a foolish idea because a kid on a bicycle could catch us in the truck. I hesitated.

"Right turn now, Marcus!" yelled Selena.

Cranking the wheel to the right, we screeched around the corner and headed out of town. As expected, both cars were right on our bumper.

I continued to swerve erratically, but to my surprise there was no more gunfire.

"Where are we going?" asked a wide-eyed Marcus. He looked scared. I caught my reflection in the rearview mirror. I looked scared, too.

"Uh... I'm not sure. Maybe we can lose them." How could I tell him that I was hearing the voice of my dead sister giving us directions?

Just as we crested a hill, Selena spoke to me again.

"Left....dirt road...follow..." she instructed.

Sure enough, there was a dirt road on the left. It was primitive to say the least. Instead of a flat gravel road, we followed the ruts of two tire tracks. The ground was brutally rugged with large holes, mud, and large rocks and branches. It occurred to me how brilliant Selena's plan was. The truck was made for this kind of road, wherein the sedans were better suited for highway travel.

We could clip along at a good thirty miles an hour. The sedans had to creep along to keep from bottoming out or getting stuck in the mud.

Just when I thought that we were going to make it, the road came to an end.

"Run!" yelled Selena.

Now, this did not make sense at all. Selena knew that the occupants of the car could easily catch us on foot, so why did she lead us to this dirt road that dead ended?

"Run now!" screamed Selena in my head.

"Come on!" I yelled at Alan.

To Alan's credit, he didn't dilly dally. As soon as the truck came to a halt, he jumped out of the passenger side door.

"Straight ahead!" said Selena. *"Fast!"*

The morning sky was beginning to brighten in the east. Night was becoming day. We sprinted down a path that opened up into a meadow. On the far side of the meadow were some large boulders. We sprinted to the boulders and came to a screeching halt. Several men had stepped out from behind one of the larger boulders. We were trapped! Selena had led us into a trap.

I stooped down and picked up a large rock. I wasn't going out without a fight. Alan followed suit and picked up a large branch.

I was about to chuck my rock at the nearest man when the hot brunette also stepped out from behind the rock.

"Hey there, Tiger," she said. "I guess I was wrong. They came after you."

Both Alan and I were breathing hard from our Sprint.

"What...what's... going on?" I asked.

"Vesuvius and Selena sent us," was her reply.

"Selena... Selena's alive?" I asked.

"No. I don't have time to explain now," said the brunette as she nodded back towards the way we had just come. Four of our pursuers were now in the meadow. They had got to the meadow inhumanly fast, but once they saw that we weren't alone, they slowed to a walk and spread out and advanced slowly towards us.

The leader of our group called out in a language I didn't understand. The reply was also in an unknown language.

The brunette appeared at my elbow.

"We're hoping to resolve this peacefully, but if it doesn't, you need to do exactly as I say," she said.

I looked over at Alan. He was as pale as a ghost. I can't imagine what he was thinking. My mind was reeling also. Somehow I was communicating with my dead sister. We were being pursued by Selena's killers. On top of that, the brunette had told us that Selena had sent them. I didn't know what to make of any of this.

The two leaders were shouting to each other from about fifty yards apart. It was frustrating not knowing what either one was saying.

"What are they saying?" I asked the brunette.

"We surprised them," she said. "They're trying to negoti-ate handing you over to them, but don't worry, we would never do that. Normally these men would have attacked, but we have the numbers on our side."

I glanced over at Alan again. Instead of watching the ac-tion, I could see that he was watching the forest line around us.

"Marcus, I think there's more of them," he said.

"What do you mean?" I asked.

"I think there were four people in the car at your

grandma's house, so that means whoever was driving the second car isn't accounted for," he said as he scanned the trees nervously.

"Is this true?" asked the brunette.

"Yes," I replied. "Two cars chased us, so there must be at least one more person out there."

And then they attacked. Alan had been watching the tree line, so when the enemy appeared, he shouted a warning.

"Here they come!" he shouted.

I had seen the enemy move before. It was no less shocking to see how fast they came at us. Each stride covered a remarkable distance, and the leaps that some of them made can only be described as inhuman. I felt the chill of fear shoot up my spine.

"How...." asked Alan.

Instantly, the brunette and several others rushed to meet the oncoming attack. Turning, I watched as the two leaders lunged at each other, and a small battle erupted in the middle of the meadow.

As scared as I was, I was also enthralled with the athleticism that was on display. I could hardly take my eyes off the two leaders as they jumped, lunged, and struck vicious blows at each other.

Alan came up beside me.

"How are they doing this?" he asked. His eyes darted around as he took in the fight.

"I don't know, dude," I replied. "I wish I knew myself."

I was so enthralled with the fighting that it came as quite a surprise when I was hit with a blow that knocked me to the ground. I got up quickly thinking someone had attacked me, but there was no one within fifty yards of Alan I.

It was then that I saw what struck me. Along with the fantastic displays of athleticism, something else equally unusual was going on. Interspersed between the fighting, suddenly a rock or a branch would seemingly fling itself at one of the combatants. I watched in amazement as one of the enemies froze in his tracks, focused on a rock and flung it through the air using only his mind. The intended target saw the rock coming, and with the same focused energy, deflected the rock aside using only his mind. Either I was hit with a stray rock or someone intentionally launched it at me.

I looked around the battle scene. There were more of us than there were of them. One of the enemies caught my attention. He was looking intently at Alan.

"Alan, duck!" I yelled. Just as Alan hit the ground, a fireball swept over him. The fireball brushed his sleeve and it caught fire. Alan began to furiously beat the flames on his sleeve to put out the fire. Wide-eyed, Alan lifted his arm to show me the smoldering sleeve.

Shifting focus, the flame thrower locked in on me. I jumped behind a large boulder just as the fireball struck the front of the rock. The heat from the flame was intense.

How were they doing this? To say that I felt weak and hopeless was an understatement. Past experience from fighting the older couple, I knew that I wasn't strong or fast enough to defend myself. I was completely at the mercy of my new friends, whoever they were.

Things didn't appear to be going well for my friends. The surprise attack wasn't as successful as the enemy had wanted due to Alan's alertness, but the battle began to come closer and closer to me and Alan, and there didn't seem to be much that my friends could do to stop it.

I noticed that the brunette was limping, and several of our new friends were singed and smoking pretty good from the guy chucking the fireballs.

One man appeared before me. His scarred face was grinning evilly at me. With that unearthly quickness, he attacked. I dodged, or I tried to dodge and tripped over a branch and went down. Instantly he was on me with one hand raised. It held a machete.

As he brought his hand down to kill me, something very powerful knocked him off of me. The man's scream was cut off abruptly, and I looked up just in time to see the man, now limp and lifeless, in the dragon's jaws. With one last violent shake, the dragon released the clearly dead man and turned to face the remaining attackers.

What once was bravado and strength turned to fear on the faces of our attackers. Even more interesting was the reaction of our friends. They seemed as surprised as the attackers. I guess I just assumed that the dragon was with them.

It ended as quick as it started. When the attackers realized that there was a dragon in the fray, they disappeared quicker than they had appeared.

I looked over at Alan. He was physically shaking from the experience. He was glancing from one person to another, trying to process what he had just seen. Not to say that I wasn't shaken, I had seen this before, but nothing can prepare you for something like this.

"How are you doing, Tiger?" asked the brunette.

"Just swell," I said with some sarcasm and anger. "People that I don't even know are trying to kill me, and not just any kind of people, people with superpowers that defy any logical explanation on my part. Furthermore, you claim that my dead sister, Selena, has sent you to defend us. Have I left anything out? Oh, yeah. A freaking dragon! A DRAGON! Oh yeah, I just found out that my entire life has been a lie. Yup, I'm doing just swell."

I was glaring at the brunette as I vented.

The brunette looked down at the ground and half-heartedly kicked at a pine cone. Her face looked indescribably sad. For what reason, I had no idea.

"Marcus, please don't blame Selena for all of this. She was only trying to protect you, and protect, well, things that you have no idea about," she said.

The others slowly trickled in. I noticed that they had not let down their guard. Several of them were circling the perimeter, and every one of them continued to scan the trees looking for potential danger. The dragon was circling overhead, and it was a terrible sight to see.

Alan finally found his voice, "Who are you guys?" he asked.

"Friends," said a voice behind us.

Turning, we found the leader of the group striding up to us. He had a nasty cut over his right eye. His jacket and pants showed signs of singe marks.

"So, is anyone going to tell us what's going on?" I asked.

"I guess this is all shock to you, Marcus," he said. He turned and looked at Alan. "You'll be Alan, I suppose?"

Shock must have shown on both of our faces. "Vesuvius told us about you, Alan. He's been watching you two. He said that you have been a loyal friend to Marcus."

For whatever reason, everyone talking about Selena and Vesuvius angered me. "Now you listen to me," I yelled. "Stop talking about Selena as if you know her!"

I had stepped up to the man and had jabbed my finger into his chest. I was several inches taller than him, and I probably outweighed him by a good twenty five or thirty pounds. In most cases, this would have intimidated just about anyone, but he just looked at me calmly. He wasn't intimidated by me even in the very least bit.

"I know this must be confusing and shocking to you, Marcus, but you need to trust...." he began.

"I don't know who you are, or even where you come from for that matter!" I yelled. "Thank you for helping us out back there, but don't ask me to trust you."

Alan was quietly taking everything in.

"So the real question," said Alan softly, "is how you're communicating with Selena? Do you mean to tell us that she is alive?"

I knew that I had been in contact with my dead sister, but it appeared that these people thought she might be able to communicate, too. To say I was curious about this was an understatement.

The brunette was eyeing me closely.

"I think Marcus can tell you about that, Alan," she said.

I wasn't sure about spilling the beans about hearing Selena's voice in my head.

"What are you talking about?" I asked as casually as I could.

"I don't suppose that you are wearing Selena's crystal by chance, are you?" she asked.

"What does that have to do with anything?" I always wondered why Selena was so adamant about me having the crystal. To me it was hugely sentimental because it belonged to both my mom and Selena, but now, a relative stranger was asking me about the crystal. How would she have known about the crystal?

"Selena's crystal," said the brunette pointing towards my chest. "Why do you suppose that Selena insisted that you find the crystal after she had died?"

"I just figured that the crystal was just sentimental. It originally belonged to our mom and it was passed to Selena after our parents death," I said.

The brunette reached under her collar and pulled out a necklace with a crystal on it. The crystal was very much like Selena's crystal, with the exception that the crystal I was wearing was clear wherein the brunette's crystal was dark blue.

The leader of the group stepped forward.

"Marcus, it's going to take a great deal of time to explain everything. To be quite honest, the attack on you and Alan came as a bit of a surprise to us. If Vesuvius hadn't contacted us, we wouldn't have been here to protect you," he said.

The brunette looked thoughtful.

"May I see your crystal?" She asked.

Somehow, the crystal was very important to why this was all happening. I hesitated.

"It's okay," said Selena.

I removed the chain from around my neck and held it out to the brunette who took it out of my hand.

Focusing intently on the crystal, the brunette spoke

three words, except it was not verbal. I heard her the same way I heard Selena.

"*Illuminoro, va Seleni,*" she said.

Instantly, Selena's crystal began to glow. To begin with, it glowed bright white light, but as we watched it, it turned a deep blood red color.

A gasp of surprise came from some of the men who were standing around. Even the leader of the group and the brunette were startled.

The brunette quickly handed the crystal back to me.

"We need to take them to the council," she said to the leader "they meet tonight, and tonight is also the choosing."

He nodded, looking thoughtfully at me.

"The choosing presents a problem. This, of course, changes everything," he said.

The dragon landed with a whoosh. Instinctively, I held the crystal eye-level with the beast. Again, the unusual ritual of taking the crystal gently in its lips, then blowing fire until we heard the curious popping sound.

I had failed to notice that everyone but me had taken a healthy couple steps back from the dragon.

The brunette eyed the dragon.

"Changes everything," echoed the leader's words.

CHAPTER TEN

THE HEAVY PLANET

"I don't know what's going on," I said, "but I'm not going anywhere until I get some answers."

"We don't have time..." began the leader.

I was in no mood to be ignored. Again, I stepped up chest to chest with the leader. Again, there wasn't even a hint of fear in his eyes.

"Then make time."

"It's okay, Marcus," said Selena. *"Where we need to go will take some time, and I can explain as we go. I have Vesuvius to recharge the crystal if I get low on energy."* Selena chuckled. *"Your world is about to be rocked, Bro. Hope you're in good shape."*

Apparently where we were going was going to be some rough hiking. Alan was wearing his normal nerd attire with a flannel shirt, jeans, and hiking boots. I was dressed in cargo shorts and sandals. The brunette eyed me with disapproval.

"He won't make it dressed like that, if he can make it at all."

What did that mean?

"Let's split into two groups," said Selena. *"Marcus, Alan, Abigail, and I will go home and get Marcus ready to travel, you can go ahead and warn the council."*

"I don't like the idea of us splitting up...." the leader said.

"Leo," said Selena, *"we have Vesuvius, and we also have Abi. We'll be fine."*

I deduced that the brunette was named Abigail and the leader was Leo. At least I knew some names now.

Leo didn't like the idea, and it showed, but apparently

we were on a time crunch and he finally consented to splitting the groups. With a final glance back at us, Leo and his men disappeared into the woods with that incredible, unearthly speed.

The ride back into town was unexpectedly quiet, except for Alan.

"So, funny story," he began. "This morning I woke up and had a bowl of Cap'n Crunch, the ones with berries. We had the plain and the peanut butter Cap'n Crunch, but the ones with berries sounded good. We also have Grape Nuts, but those are just nasty. All the little spoons were dirty, so I used a big serving spoon. The birds were singing, the bees were buzzing and....*ARE YOU FREAKING KIDDING ME? A DRAGON! AND FIREBALLS! WHAT? WHAT? SERIOUSLY?*"

I looked out the window overhead, and sure enough, there was the dragon easily keeping pace with the truck.

"Hello, Alan. I'm Selena."

"Whoa! I heard that!" Alan said. He was beaming. This was turning into a big adventure for him. We didn't see eye to eye on that fact. I was getting more angry as the minutes passed by. "Hey Selena! I've heard a lot about you."

"Thank you for being such a good friend to Marcus. That means a lot to me," she said.

"No problem. Someone needs to keep the dumb jocks in line." Alan was adjusting to this new world much faster than I was. Each new discovery was met with awe and wonder. Each new discovery took me further and further away from what was in my comfort zone, and I felt my life was a total lie, and I was mad.

"Now would be a good time to tell me what's going on," I said, not without a little anger in my voice.

Selena was silent.

"Selena, I need answers now or I'm not going anywhere," I said with my mind. It just seemed a more forceful way of communicating.

"It's not that I don't want to give you answers. I just don't know where to begin," answered Selena.

"Oh, I don't know. How about: who are you? It seems like everything I have known is now a lie. How about that? Why don't you start there?"

"I don't suppose it helps to know that all this was done to protect you?"

"Nope. Doesn't help even a little bit. It makes it even worse. You didn't have faith that I could be trusted? That I wasn't strong enough to know the truth? Pick one and run with it."

"Marcus..."

"I don't want to hear from you right now!" Contradicting myself, I know, but I was angry.

Abi had been listening in silence.

"Selena is...was one of our last hopes for defeating a very great evil," she said.

The glance I gave Abi wasn't very kind. She was part of the mystery, and even though beautiful, she was beginning to wear out her welcome.

Pulling up to the house, Abi hopped out quickly. "I'm going to check the house first. Wait a minute."

After a few minutes she came trotting back. "All clear. They definitely searched for the crystal, but no one is here now." She turned to me. "You have fifteen minutes to get ready. Travel light."

Travel light? What was that supposed to mean?

I jogged into the house. Somehow I knew that Selena was anxious to get on the move, and even though I was angry, I felt time was of the essence, so I hurried.

I was processing recent events. I both wanted answers, and to be left alone. Selena was wise enough to remain silent while I changed. While I changed? You would think that would have occurred to me sooner, but no.

"Please tell me you have your eyes closed right now," I pleaded.

Selena's laughter was genuine and full of the joy that I remembered and loved about her.

"I wondered when you were going to realize that!" She then abandoned herself to laughter while I quickly zipped up my fly.

"Ewwwwww!" and then the obvious realization. "What about when I shower or when I..." The horror of the thought didn't allow me to finish the sentence.

"Go to the bathroom?" she finished.

"Noooo! Please no! Even if it's a lie, tell me that you can close your eyes."

"Do you know that you fart in your sleep?"

"Arrrgh! This just gets worse and worse! Wait! That was you in the classroom that day! The day I farted. I know it was you! And the bed-wetting thing! That was all you!" I bellowed.

Selena had abandoned herself to mirth. Her laugh was clear as a bell. Somehow telepathy allowed me to feel some of the emotion as well as hear her laughter. There was genuine joy coming from her, and I finally understood a little of the joyless situation she was in, trapped in a crystal hanging around the neck of her brother. This was the first happiness she had had since being killed.

Soon I was chuckling despite myself.

"But seriously, you can look away, right?" I asked. There might have been a little bit of anxiety in that question.

"I can look away. But tick me off and I'll be in your head when you try to pee or shower. Hope you don't suffer from stage fright," was her mirthful reply.

Selena's laughter was contagious, and I found myself laughing at the absurdity of the situation we were in.

Alan and Abi knocked, then entered.

Abi looked at me quizzically.

"This is a strange change of events, I must say. Am I to understand that you two are OK?" asked Abi.

"I still need answers, but I guess we're Ok."

I had changed into jeans, a tee shirt with a hoodie, and my hiking boots. I also grabbed a baseball cap.

"Should I bring a water bottle or something to eat?" I asked.

"You will need both of those things," answered Abi, "but one of us will need to carry your and Alan's provisions. You are going to have a very difficult time as it is."

I was a little offended. I was big and strong, and in pretty good shape.

I was about to argue, but Alan interceded.

"Dude, you need to hear Abi out. You aren't going to believe where we're going."

So, even Alan knew more than I did.

Selena handled the explanation.

"You know about parallel universes? We will be going back to the world you and I were born to. We were brought here because of some special traits our family possesses."

Alan couldn't contain himself.

"We're traveling through a wormhole! A real wormhole! Rock on!" His air guitar needed help.

"Before you get worked up, Alan, you both need to know that there is real danger." Selena warned. *"You've already experienced some of the, uh, interesting differences that the people of that world have. But there are other things. That world is larger than the earth. The gravity is substantially more. The air is also thinner. You will feel the effects immediately, and it won't be pleasant, because we have to hike several miles."*

"Which is why everyone has such great physical strength and speed! That totally makes sense now!" Alan looked like a kid on Christmas morning. "Their bodies are used to the heavy gravity, and when they come to earth it's like us going to the moon!"

Abi was also concerned. "On top of everything else, we're going into a situation that is tenuous."

"The world we come from has a great evil. Abi and I are a part of a small group of freedom fighters. We're led by a council of leaders from different tribes. They meet tonight, and outsiders are never invited. We're just assuming that the events today will warrant us crashing their party, but you never know."

"And the tribes don't necessarily like each other. We're

bound together out of necessity," Abi added.

I directed my thoughts directly at Selena.

"Selena, is this all worth it? We could always run and hide," I said.

"I hope you realize that I would never put you or Alan in danger unless I thought it was necessary. I wish there was another way, but there isn't. The good thing is that once we've delivered our report, you and Alan can probably go back to normal. You won't be useful to our enemies after that."

"Why do Alan and I need to go at all then?" I asked. *"Abi and the others know as much as we do at this point."*

"There is something that you will physically need to do. Something only you can do. You need to unlock a very special crystal with your DNA. After that, you are useless to the enemy. You can come home and forget this ever happened and live happily ever after."

Like I could ever forget something like this.

And then the question that I dreaded to ask.

"What about you, Selena? What happens to you? I don't want to lose you again. Even if you are an annoying ghost."

"This is a special kind of hell, Marcus. The crystal houses my intelligence, but I'm bound to it. Most people tied to a crystal choose to abandon it days after. They choose to die. Do you understand that? It's a necessary evil that we use to pass on important information, even after mortal death, but everybody chooses eventually to die rather than be enslaved to a crystal. Well, almost everyone. There are exceptions, and none that I know of are good."

"So you will choose to move on?" I asked.

"If I could right now, I would. This is not a natural state. It really is a hellish existence." I heard the pain in her voice.

Abi pulled us back to the immediate situation.

"We need to get moving," she said. "We have a long ways to go, and little time to do it in."

Not surprisingly, we drove back towards the area where Selena had been killed. It was the first time I had been back since that night, and I had a sick feeling in my stomach as we got closer and closer.

An obvious question popped into my head.

"Why are you able to speak with us so clearly now? Why weren't you able to do so before?" I asked.

"Vesuvius is the answer to that question. He powers the crystal with his fire. The crystal can charge itself over a long period of time...like years. The crystal can also take energy from the wearer, like you, but you have to allow it by connecting to it. That is why I wanted you to contact me. I expended a lot of energy protecting Becky against your Jack-Assery."

I shuddered as I remembered the farting and bed wetting incidents again. That just wasn't right.

"Yeah, I owe you for a couple of things," I grumped.

"You'll never go to the bathroom alone then," she said smugly.

Game, set, match. For-ev-er.

"Abi, could you give them an idea of what to expect? I need to save my energy in case I can't recharge. I will need to be able to speak directly with the council tonight."

Alan piped up.

"How do you know Selena, Abi? I'm missing something there."

That was a fantastic question. Why didn't I think of that?

Abi teared up.

"I am...was Selena's...squire, I guess is the best definition. Selena was training to be a dragon rider, and I was her attendant. I would take care of Vesuvius and make sure her armor and weapons were in good working order."

"Awesome!" was Alan's response. "Selena was a dragon rider!"

"It was also my job to protect her..." Abi began.

"Abi! We've been over this before. There was nothing, and I mean NOTHING that you could have done to save me, and you know it. I don't blame you, and you shouldn't blame yourself!" Selena said.

I know that my guilt was there daily, so I doubted that Abi would forgive herself anytime soon. I know I wouldn't be able to for the rest of my life.

"Both of you. I can feel your guilt too, Marcus." Then Selena added, *'Let's get into game mode guys."*

Abi cleared her throat and wiped her tears. I had a feeling that there was more to her story than met the eye. Now was not the time to hear it, though.

"We're going to be traveling through a wormhole shortly. The wormhole will be taking us to a world with some familiar things, and some things that you won't be prepared for, even with us telling you about them before."

"Like the gravity thing?" asked Alan.

"Yes, and that the air is thinner, and that there are multiple moons..."

"Awesome!" interjected Alan.

"And we're walking into an unknown situation with some arguing tribes. Tonight is not just a council meeting," Abi said.

"The Choosing, whatever that is," I said.

"Yes, the Choosing." Abi remained silent for a moment, trying to find the words to explain.

"I guess maybe I need to explain the next part," said Selena. *"The choosing is an event that takes place every five years. Dragons are an ancient animal that were nearly wiped out due to a very evil society that actively hunted them."*

"They seem so formidable. How would humans defeat dragons?" asked Alan.

Abi fielded that question.

"Infant dragons imprint the same as some birds do. If you know where the ancient breeding grounds are, and you are the first thing the dragon sees after hatching, well, you control that dragon."

Alan was fascinated. "What about the parents, the adult dragons?"

"Typically, the breeding ground is guarded by one dominant male dragon after all the eggs are laid by the female dragons. Normally, that would be enough against any other predator, but humans are uncommonly smart, and there are ways to kill even a dragon. Once that one dragon was disposed of, the rest was easy. Some dragons were spared to be used by evil men, but most infant dragons were killed," explained Abi.

"So how does this relate to the Choosing?" I asked.

"Dragons were killed because they were considered dumb animals without any intelligence, and they can be very destructive to cattle and other livestock. It was mostly economics that caused their demise. It wasn't until our ancestors discovered the crystals that we learned that the dragons were actually intelligent beings with a complex social system, capable of working with human riders. You see, there isn't a way for humans and dragons to communicate without the crystals. Dragons don't have the ability to decipher verbal language. The crystals allow us to communicate and work with each other, and they also have other properties. The fireballs and levitation are a function of certain crystals. That is why they are being sought after, and is the reason we're in the current situation."

"And somehow your crystal is unique?" asked Alan.

"I guess that's obvious."

"And the choosing?" I prompted.

"When dragon and rider imprint, they become inseparable. The dragon won't leave the human for the rest of the rider's life. This puts the dragon at a disadvantage since they are tied to their rider, good or bad. In the past, riders chose the dragon. As dragons became more and more scarce, they made a pact with our ancestors to allow dragons to choose the rider. The crystals were even more rare than the dragons themselves. Each crystal was gathered and placed in control of the dragon elders. Every five years, the elders from the human tribes choose the best candidates from their tribes to go before the elders of the dragons. The dragon elders then choose from the human candidates, which ones they deem to have the proper qualities of a rider," said Abi.

"And this was how you were selected to be a rider?" I asked Selena.

"Yes. But in a very unusual way. Before our family crossed through the wormhole, I was chosen as an infant. Mother was considered as a top rider candidate. She was holding me during the ceremony, while dad held you. It was no surprise when the dragon elder stopped before our mother. It was a little more of a shock when the crystal was presented to me, not her. We don't know why the elders chose me, but it was assumed that there was something unusual about the crystal. Some tests were run, and it was discovered to have...unusual properties. The decision to hide us came shortly after."

"What properties?" I asked.

"Another time," said Abi. "We're about there. You are going to need all your strength in a couple of minutes."

....

The hike was familiar. We headed back to the area where Selena was killed. It was the same game trail that Selena and I had been carried down.

"Think of the wormhole as a doorway. There isn't really any sensation as you pass through the door itself, but you will know without a doubt you are someplace other than earth when you reach the other side."

Abi looked at me.

"You are going to feel the effects the most, Marcus, because of your size."

We came to the clearing where I had found Selena's body.

"I was so close," Selena said with sadness.

About one hundred yards past the large rock where I had found her body was a sheer cliff that dropped sharply. I could see the tops of some pine trees below us.

"Selena actually sacrificed herself to keep this wormhole hidden. Our enemy knows of only a few. They are constantly searching for others," said Abi.

"Only a couple of minutes. So close."

Alan had been searching all around us. "Where is it? I don't see anything."

I could see that Abi had a strange smile that I couldn't place. "It's close. Real close," she said with a chuckle.

Vesuvius landed with a thud. I had forgotten all about him. You know you are having a weird day when you forget about a dragon.

"Another reason dragons are sought after by our enemy is that some have the ability to find wormholes. You wanted to know what is so important about Selena's crystal? She has one of the crystals that open wormholes. I can't believe I hadn't figured that one out. It is so obvious now."

"Crystals have different properties. When Vesuvius and I access it together, we can open certain wormholes that our enemies don't have access to. This is how I was able to cross over and train to become a rider without our enemy knowing. Dragons can find wormholes, but can't necessarily open them. The crystals, which are very rare, enable us to open and use hidden wormholes."

"Do we know how you and Marcus were discovered?" asked Alan. Great question kid.

"We've expended a lot of resources trying to figure that one out," said Abi. "We're not sure, but we think we must have a spy within one of our tribes. We're still looking, unfortunately."

"Hold the crystal up for Vesuvius," instructed Selena.

Vesuvius focused intently on the crystal and it began to glow brilliant white. Without a loud cracking sound, a vortex appeared over the side of the cliff, about half-way down, in mid air. I quickly stepped back fifteen feet.

"Are you serious?" gushed Alan. "This is so cool!"

"Nope," I said. "Not going to happen."

"Marcus, it's really nothing. You jump..."

"Nothing? What happens if I miss the wormhole? Need I remind you that we're looking *down* at treetops?" I asked.

Abi wasn't impressed with my manly display of being protective of our group.

"Marcus come here and watch me go through. It's really nothing," she said.

Despite being terrified of falling off the cliff, I was also fascinated at the prospect of watching someone else going through a wormhole.

Edging closer to the cliff, but far enough back that I wouldn't fall over, I peered over to again see the swirling vortex.

"Give me some room and move to your left so you can see how I do it," instructed Abi.

I shuffled left a few steps, which gave me a better view of the...

I felt the shove and could do nothing about it. Just in case you're wondering, a high pitched scream does not stop you from falling headlong off a cliff and into a wormhole to another world. I've done the research for you. You're welcome.

I knew the second I collided with the wormhole. Instantly my body felt incredibly heavy, and my downward falling was translated into forward motion. I felt solid ground under my feet, but the forward motion toppled me to the ground. The heaviness was oppressing. Just lifting my arms seemed to take effort.

"You'll want to roll out of the way, Marcus. The others need to come through, and you don't want Vesuvius to trample you," warned Selena.

With what seemed great effort, I rolled out of the direct path of the vortex.

Vesuvius was the next to come through, and once free of the vortex, immediately went to the air, presumably to scout for danger.

Alan came next, and his entrance was no better than mine. He went to the ground, but bounced up instantly, his eyes shining.

"Best day, EVER!" he shouted.

Abi came through sprinting. She had anticipated the forward motion and planned accordingly. She gracefully came to a stop and walked back calmly to us.

Helping me to my feet, she said, "Sorry. Had to be done, Marcus. We don't have time, and now that you know how the gravity is going to affect you, you know why time is of the essence."

The gravity was one thing, but what about the air? There was no air! My breathing was long, deep gasps.

Alan didn't seem as distressed by the gravity and lack of oxygen. He was breathing more heavily than usual, but nothing close to what I was doing. Instead, he was looking around with curiosity and excitement. His slight size, and being a long-distance runner paid off on this particular planet.

I felt light-headed.

"Abi, Marcus will need some water and one of those chocolate bars in your backpack."

Between gasps of air I ate the candy bar and downed half a bottle of water. After a couple of minutes, I felt better.

"It's going to be a struggle, Marcus, but we need to get moving now. We'll take short breaks so that you and Alan can maintain a good pace."

It was agonizingly slow going. We were stopping every five minutes for me to catch my breath. Alan seemed to be taking everything in stride. He would get tired, but recovered so much faster than I could. It annoyed me every time he pointed at something new and interesting. My focus was on the trail ahead of me and placing one foot in front of the other and trying to catch my breath, not on the bright purple birds the size of an emu flying overhead. By the way, when one of those poop mid-flight, it's way worse than getting strafed by a Seagull at the beach, and the smell... like a thousand rotting fish. It was sticky and impossible to scrape off, and it only hit me, of course.

Breaks were supposed to be every five minutes, but soon I was stopping every couple minutes, and I felt I needed longer and longer breaks to catch my breath.

"We're not going to make it," Abi said with what I

thought might be disapproval. I couldn't help myself. Where was the air?

"I don't know what else we can do," answered Selena.

"What about the dragon?" asked Abi as she scanned the sky.

"You know that's impossible. Dragon's will only allow one rider. They will kill anyone who tries to mount them that isn't their rider, friend or foe."

"Have you tried to communicate with Vesuvius?"

Selena's answer was heated.

"Of course I've tried to talk with Vesuvius! How do you think I feel about being within feet of my dragon and not being able to comfort him or talk with him?" she "yelled." It was weird hearing the anger in her voice but also feeling the emotion.

Abi seemed unfazed at Selena's outburst.

"I've been thinking about that. What if we have Marcus activate the crystal? With an active crystal, Vesuvius might be able to communicate with both of you."

Selena took a minute to think about Abi's solution.

"As far as I know, that's never been done. There are a couple of possibilities. One would be that it doesn't work. Another would be that Vesuvius would see that as a threat and kill Marcus. I'm not sure it's worth the danger."

I had been standing still, bent over at the waist, trying to get enough air in my lungs to take a few more steps. Feeling sick to my stomach, I staggered a few steps off the trail and vomited. The others looked away to give me some privacy while I vomited again. There is no way to look cool while vomiting, covered in bird poop. Becoming lightheaded, I took a knee and placed my hand on a nearby tree trunk. Instantly I felt a sharp sting on the back of my hand. I let out a surprised yelp, and pulled back my hand to find puncture wounds. My yelp caught the attention of Abi who went into instant action.

"Where is it? What bit you?" yelled Abi as she scanned the tree trunk and surrounding area.

"It's too late, Abi. I saw it. It was one of the vipers. We have

to get him to a healer now!" Selena's fear was palpable.

"If we were on your world, I could probably just carry you, but in my world that would be impossible," Abi said.

"I guess we risk it. Marcus, you need to listen to me. You will need to activate the crystal. Once you are "in," let me do the talking to Vesuvius. Don't say a thing or he will kill you. Do you understand?"

"I don't feel anything. Maybe I'll be alright...." I began.

"Dude. Look at your arm," said Alan, pointing.

Dark black streaks were starting to inch up my arm, and I began to feel the burn.

"Abi please..."

Grabbing my good hand, Abi withdrew a knife and flicked the tip of my index finger. Blood immediately started dripping from the wound.

"Take the crystal and smear some blood on it," commanded Selena. *"The DNA in your blood is the only thing that can activate the crystal."*

Abi's knife must have been razor sharp, because I was bleeding pretty bad. I soon had the entire crystal coated in my blood.

"Now, you need to focus like you're trying to communicate with me, but you're going to try to connect to the crystal. It's not alive. It's more like a computer hard drive programmed to react to various commands."

Focusing all of my attention on the crystal, I tried to connect to it. Nothing, and my arm began to tingle and burn more.

"We're running out of time," said Abi. "He can lose consciousness any moment now."

The pressure didn't help. I failed over and over and started feeling woozy.

"Marcus, try something visual, like imagine you plugging in an HDMI cable to the crystal. I don't know. Worth a try," said Alan.

Focusing again, I closed my eyes and imagined plugging

into the crystal.

I felt the crystal vibrate in my hand. Instantly, an unworldly and very horrible screech emanated from somewhere above the treetops.

More importantly, I felt the anger and fear of Vesuvius as the crystal was activated.

"I'm going to kill you for that, brother of my rider," said a very audible Vesuvius. I fleetingly wondered how he knew English.

With a sudden whoosh and a thud, Vesuvius was on the trail in front of me. I have never seen something as fierce and menacing as a dragon slowly bearing down on me.

"Explain yourself!" screamed the dragon. My whole body seemed to vibrate with his words.

It was now nose to nose with me. I was going to die with vomit breath and bird poop all over me. Somehow, I had always imagined my death differently.

The crystal vibrated again in my hand.

"Hello, Suvi, my faithful friend. We desperately need your help right now," said Selena.

Vesuvius stiffened, his eyes widening to the size of small dinner plates at the sound of Selena's voice.

"Is that really you, tiny rider?"

"It is I, old friend. We need your strength and speed, Suvi. Can you once more trust me?"

"Always, tiny rider. Always."

And with that I sank into darkness as the viper poison took over.

CHAPTER ELEVEN

CHOSEN

I woke up to Abi wiping a damp washcloth across my forehead. I had a horrible headache, and I still smelled of vomit and giant bird poop. We appeared to be in some kind of tent.

A lady held my wrist, seemingly taking my pulse. She wore a bright red crystal around her neck. Giving Abi a focused look, she grabbed a large bag and left the tent quickly.

"Welcome back to the land of the living," said Selena. *"The healer says you should be fine now. She was able to administer an antidote to the viper's poison. How do you feel?"*

"Like I could sleep for a hundred years. I'm exhausted," I replied, my words slurring.

"We don't have a hundred years. The council meets in a few moments," said Abi.

Alan burst into the tent. It irritated me that the lack of air and the abundance of gravity had such a minimal effect on him. Sure, he was breathing hard and he moved slower than usual, but his eyes were wide with excitement, and he wasn't covered in giant bird droppings.

"Marcus, we flew on the back of a dragon!" His face more animated than I have ever seen. "BEST DAY EVER!"

I must have looked horrible because he pulled up short when he saw me, or maybe it was the smell.

"Dude, how are you feeling?" he asked.

"You don't want to know," I said.

A horn of some sort sounded some distance off.

"Alan, get on the other side of Marcus. We'll need to help

him to the gathering," said Abi, as she grabbed one of arms to help me up. She made a face as I stood up next to her, the smell of bird droppings intense.

Alan started coughing.

"Kind of makes a guys' eyes water a little," he said, his face also contorted in repulsion.

The meeting place was in a large natural amphitheater. Torch light lit the area, as it was beginning to get dark. There were hundreds of people crowded into rows facing a raised platform at the front of the amphitheater. Both men and women were dressed in some kind of highly polished armor, both metal and leather.

"Let's just sit in the back out of the way. We'll speak with the council after the choosing," said Selena.

Despite how horrible I felt, I was fascinated with the prospect of seeing the choosing ceremony.

Near the raised platform was a sectioned off area with what could only be the candidates for the choosing. Most appeared very fit, in their late teens or early twenties. They were especially groomed and polished, their armor shone brightly in the torch light. Several of the young men and women who came to our rescue in the clearing were stationed within the sectioned off area. There was a feeling of excitement and anticipation throughout the crowd. I wondered absently how we were going to hear what was going on, because I couldn't see any sort of amplification system.

To say that we attracted attention is an understatement. As we were preparing to sit on one of the back benches, the people around us took notice. Soon it seemed that everyone in the audience had turned to look at us.

A very large man, clad in magnificent armor stood up from his seat. Seconds later he was striding towards us, a scowl on his face. As he neared us, his scowl turned to anger and he began to shout. His stride didn't let up as he neared us. Abi stepped forward and began to speak in a reassuring manner. As quick as lightning, the man slapped her in the face

147

and she crumpled to the ground. Anger surged through me and I stepped forward to protect Abi. With the same speed, he punched me in the face. The force of the blow drove me to the ground, and I felt blood dripping from my nose and pulverized lips.

I apparently was the object of his anger because he stood over me, his voice booming. I had no idea what he was saying, and he raised his fist to strike me again.

A scream from above us was heard, then the man was knocked to the ground with great force. Standing between us and the angry man, Vesuvius was crouched, ready to pounce.

"*Thank you, Suvi. I think that will be enough,*" said Selena.

Vesuvius came out of his crouch, but remained positioned between us and the rest of the crowd. His tail flicking back and forth, his eyes never leaving the large man slowly getting up off the ground.

A small group of men and women were making their way towards us. I couldn't help but notice that everyone stood aside for the group.

"The council members," whispered Abi in my ear. She also had a trickle of blood on her lips where she had been struck.

By now my shirt was covered in blood. And vomit. And bird poop.

The leader who had come to our aid in the clearing when we were attacked, was conversing with the group. He was seemingly trying to explain the situation. An argument appeared to be happening among the various leaders.

After several minutes of arguing, a huge but aged warrior stepped forward from the group. He was battle scarred, and I saw that he was missing his left hand. His attention was on me.

His question to me was in the same language. I looked questioningly at Abi.

"Qurum wants to know how you can command the dragon of another rider," translated Abi.

Qurum took another step forward looking intently at me.

"You are from other side?" His English had a strange accent, but was understandable.

"Earth? Yes, I'm from Earth," I said, my stomach in my throat.

"How do you command the dragon of another rider?" he asked again. His expression was menacing.

"I can answer that, Qurum," I could tell that Selena was heard by all. A great gasp went out from the congregation.

"Selena. So it is true, just as Callum suggested. My apologies for not believing," he gestured towards the leader from the meadow who bent slightly at the waist to acknowledge Qurum.

"Just because Callum and Abi are outcasts doesn't make them liars," said Selena, her voice had a reproachful sound to it. Another murmur was heard from the crowd. Some very angry looks were cast in the direction of Callum and Abi. Especially from the large man who had attacked us. If Qurum hadn't been there, I was convinced that he would have killed us.

"Nevertheless, perhaps tonight, the night of the choosing, wasn't the best choice of time to come before the council. You know that outsiders are not permitted, Selena," said Qurum.

"Marcus is not an outsider. We are of the same blood. We were born on Vocce and he was hidden on the other side, as was I."

"Bah," shouted the large man who had struck us. "Your words can't be proven, and your presence is an abomination to our customs!" Shouts of agreement echoed his words from several in the crowd.

"Marcus, hold up the crystal," Selena commanded me. I could tell, somehow, that her words were focused on me and not the whole group.

I held the crystal high over my head. The crowd once more reacted with a murmur.

"Abi, help Marcus activate the crystal."

Taking the same amazingly sharp blade, Abi pierced the skin on my forefinger and smeared some of the blood on the crystal. It began to glow.

Vesuvius, who had been standing next to us in a protective stance, swung around and gently took the crystal from my hand. Placing it on the ground, he again heated it with flames from his terrible mouth, and just like that, my dead sister stood before us.

My gasp might have been the loudest in the crowd that day.

"The name of my crystal is Larzi. The record keepers can confirm the name and properties of the crystal, and they can also confirm that it belongs to my family's bloodline," said Selena. Her voice had an air of authority about it.

"That crystal is said to be destroyed," said Qurum, his head tilted, his eyes had a quizzical expression.

"Part of the deception to hide the truth."

Vesuvius startled and peered into the sky. *"They come, tiny rider,"* he said to Selena.

"Suvi has informed me that the dragons are near," said Selena.

Instantly, all eyes were scanning the dark sky. In the distance, streaks of flame would appear briefly, then go out. They got nearer and nearer.

I couldn't take my eyes off my sister. Naturally, I stepped over to her to give my sister a hug.

"Marcus…"

And my arms passed right through my sister.

I stepped back, realizing that she was just a projection of some sort.

"…when Larzi is fully charged I can project my image. Sorry, I should have told you sooner."

"There's a lot of things you should have told me. I'm not prepared for any of this," I replied, not hiding the hurt in my voice.

"Of course you're right. Hindsight is 20/20. Things went

horribly wrong as you can see," Selena explained calmly, and then the ground shook as the dragons landed.

With a shrill scream, Vesuvius rose into the air and with a few wing strokes, landed into the center of the dragons. Instantly, he was nose to nose with a large crimson colored dragon.

"His mother," said Selena.

I thought I would be prepared to see dragons since I was sort of familiar with Vesuvius. Now I saw that he must have been a juvenile dragon at best. I would guess that Vesuvius was just larger than an adult elephant, but most of the other ten dragons were at least double his size, and two that stood even taller. They were multi-colored, ranging from red to green and blue. And they were terrifying. A hush had fallen over the crowd, and everyone returned to their place in the Amphitheater.

Qurum stepped forward and addressed the dragons and the audience. The mystery about how everyone would be able to hear the proceedings was answered, because of course he just used telepathy. Qurum was holding a large crystal that appeared red and glowing.

"The crystal allows him to speak with the dragons. Without crystals we have no basis of communication," said Selena.

"So, not everyone will hear the dragons?" I asked.

"Well, you will. You've got Larzi. When you're connected to the crystal, you can communicate with dragons. Another trait of this crystal is that it can translate languages. You will be able to understand any spoken language. It's kind of like one of those Kung Fu movies. You'll see their lips move, but hear the translation in English. It's hysterical sometimes. In time, you'll learn the language. What works best is the telepathy translation," Selena informed me.

Qurum held his crystal high, and the largest, most fearsome green dragon stepped forward and gently took the crystal in its teeth. The dragon went through the same ritual that Vesuvius had when he powered Larzi.

"That green dragon is Lowry, king of the few remaining dragons. Also, Vesuvius's father,` said Selena.

"Welcome, Lowry, we are grateful for your presence in these most dangerous of times," said Qurum.

"My son informs me that there are some unusual circumstances this evening?" inquired Lowry.

"Most unusual indeed. The return of Selena and her brother Marcus. Plus an outsider. Selena claims that her crystal, Larzi, is thought to have been destroyed," said Qurum.

"We will speak of this later. The ancient ones approach," said Lowry.

Again a whoosh, and three ancient dragons landed near the other dragons, and ancient they were. Where the other dragons were heavily muscled and toned, these new three seemed withered and somehow, brittle. Their colors were less vibrant than the younger dragons. Ancient was a good descriptive word. Their movements slower and more deliberate.

The hush among the crowd was more pronounced. Total silence was observed.

"Welcome, Ancient Ones," said Lowry, at the same time dipping his head in reverence and respect to the old dragons.

"It is well to see you again, Lowry. What of the candidates?" asked a withered dragon. Her skin was battle-scarred, which gave her an even more ferocious appearance.

"Twenty of the various clans' best young people, I'm assured," was Lowry's reply.

I glanced down at the candidates. Their ages ranged from middle teens to young adults. All were very healthy, and I could tell that they were all physically fit. I noticed, again, that they were all clad in their best armor and their tunics underneath were of the best quality. Any one of them could be called beautiful.

The old dragon glanced over at the candidates.

"Mostly useless baubles, I see," she said.

I let a snort of humor escape. Several rows of audience members turned to look at me, and I realized they couldn't hear the dragons, so they wouldn't have heard the insult.

"The choosing should be quick then," said Lowry. *"Have you decided on the number of dragons to be paired with a rider?"*

"There are less and less worthy. To be paired with a rider is a lifelong commitment for dragons, as you know. We must be diligent to pair only with the most worthy. I think no more than five dragon infants will be paired on this day," said the ancient dragon.

Lowry bowed his head again.

"As you wish. The clans will be unhappy, but we must protect our own," he said.

Turning away from the ancient dragons, Lowry once again addressed Qurum and the rest of the audience. It was strange having heard the conversation between the dragons, and knowing that all the others in the audience had not.

"Qurum, the ancients will choose five riders this day." The shock in Qurum's face was visible to all. He quickly relayed to the audience that there would only be five riders chosen this day.

The reaction from the audience was immediate. Qurum had to signal for silence to continue.

"Five? Lowry, how do we fight with only five dragons and riders? We were expecting at least ten. How do you expect us to survive with only five this cycle? We will be wiped out before another five years and another choosing." said Qurum, shock and dismay sounding in his voice at the news.

"We are fewer in numbers than we have ever been, and we must choose wisely. Five is what our elders have allotted. Hopefully, your very highest quality candidates are here. It is the best that we can do. Sorry old friend, we are also in a desperate situation. We must think of our extinction as do you," said Lowry, and added, *"You know as well as I that the betrayal decimated our ranks."*

"The betrayal?" I asked

Abi fielded the question.

"The Gonosz seemed to have an unnatural ability to find

the hatching grounds of the dragons. Many of the unhatched dragon eggs were either destroyed, or captured for many breeding seasons. It was discovered that there was a rogue dragon that betrayed their location." she said, sadness in her voice. "The betrayal wiped out a generation of young dragons."

Qurum was silent for a moment, contemplating this new development. *"Of course five dragons are better than none. Please proceed."*

A hush fell over the audience as the aged dragons walked over to view the candidates. One by one, the dragons would peer into the faces of each candidate. Sometimes the re-action was immediate. If the candidate was rejected, the three old dragons would take a step back and blow streams of red fire into the air. The rejected candidate would then leave to find a place in the amphitheater. When a candidate was accepted, they blew white flames into the air. It was a source of great joy and pride to the families and clans if one of their people was chosen.

"It is a great status symbol to be chosen as a rider," Selena told me. She had long since stopped projecting her image to save Larzi's energy. Apparently, that was particularly draining.

Alan's eyes were wide with awe and excitement. He couldn't hear or even understand what was being said, but he was flush with wonder all the same. I wish I felt the same, but truth be told, I was overwhelmed. I sat contemplating how I might fit into this new reality. Maybe it would have been better that I stayed in ignorance of this whole other life my sister led.

In the end, there were only three riders chosen. One rider was a young teenage girl from the meadow named Marrle. She had a skill with fire, as I recalled. One was a mighty young man, about twenty, who was the spitting image of the large warrior who had attacked us. Kal was his name, and he stood proud and tall when chosen by the dragons. The third seemed an unusual choice. Not much larger than Alan, but fit and well-muscled, Chayl was quiet and reserved, but I could sense that he was capable and smart. There was an air of competence about him.

"I know Chayl's family," whispered Abi. "They are all brilliant. A good choice for a rider in my opinion."

The crowd had begun to murmur. They had expected ten dragons and riders, and only three were ultimately chosen.

"I know that the dragon's must be selective, but three isn't anywhere near enough to make a difference. Surely you can find two more candidates worthy of a dragon?" asked Qurum. His face was pale. The crowd had gone from total silence during the choosing to a steady murmur. I was also hearing some of the telepathic conversations between people. Expressions of shock and anger were the norm.

"We are not without sympathy, Qurum. This is the choice of the ancient ones. Their say is final, you know this," said Lowry. *"My advice is to train them well. Remember, one dragon and rider can change the course of a battle. Please present your riders."*

Qurum motioned for the three chosen candidates to come forward. All three were amazingly dressed and groomed. They carried themselves with assurance and confidence. I could easily imagine Selena up there.

The ancient dragons approached, and stood behind the candidates.

"Chayl of clan Imor, do you accept your chosen role of rider?" asked Qurum. In his previous conversations, I could tell that the audience hadn't been privy to the conversations, but with this part of the ceremony, Qurum had somehow broadcasted so all could "hear" the ceremonial proceedings.

"Yes," was Chayl's simple telepathic answer.

"Name your attendant," commanded Qurum.

"I name Leor, also from clan Imor," replied Chayl.

Leor, who was also clad and groomed magnificently, stepped forward. The two quickly embraced then stood side by side. One of the ancient dragons stepped forward. His neck convulsed twice, then regurgitated two crystals onto the ground in front of Chayl and Leor. With a mighty blast of fire, the dragon breathed on the crystals until they glowed. The dragon finished breathing his fire and returned to his place with the other ancients. Stepping forward, Leor and Chayl picked up their crystals.

"*The crystals absorb all the heat energy from the dragons. That is why the riders can handle them directly after being charged without burning themselves,*" said Selena after I questioned her.

"*Marrle of Clan Imor, do you accept your chosen role as rider?*"

"*Yes,*" was Marrle's answer.

"*Name your attendant,*" said Qurum.

Marrle hesitated.

"*Please name your attendant,*" commanded Qurum again.

"*I name Abi who is Clanless,*" Marrle said looking in our direction. There was defiance in her voice as she made her decision known telepathically.

The response at her choice was immediate and frightening. A great vocal roar erupted from the audience.

The large warrior who had attacked us strode to the front.

"*Qurum, I, Kalam, leader of clan Reylor, formerly protest this choice! She already failed her rider once, resulting in the death of the rider, and of more importance, losing a valuable dragon. Abi should not be given another chance to fail. We demand another choice as attendant, and I don't have to remind you that she is an outcast!*" Kalam's face was livid.

A roar of agreement went out, especially from the clan Reylor.

Abi, to her credit, stood tall and unflinching. And even after our trip through the wormhole, she was stunning. She could easily have been one of the beautiful people chosen to be a rider.

Apparently the ancient dragons felt the same way. They had quietly come up behind Abi, obviously inspecting her. As one, and to the utter astonishment of the crowd, they unanimously stepped back and blew three white streams of fire into the sky, accepting Abi as a rider, not an attendant.

I expected a huge uproar from the crowd, instead the action was met with total silence. Kalam's face was red and veins stood out in his neck, he was so angry. Other clan leaders had also stood in protest.

"YES!" was the only voice I heard, and it was from Selena.

I expected an outburst, especially from Kalam, but his telepathic voice was strangely subdued. Maybe suppressed is a better word. It was evident to all that he was trying to control his anger.

"If I may speak, Qurum?" asked Kalam.

"Proceed," was the answer.

"Could you please inquire of the dragons why an outcast who has limited time, in Abi's case, a matter of years, over one of the clans' own candidates?" Was Kalam's question.

"Limited time?" I asked Selena.

"Later," was the answer.

"This is a highly unusual request, Kalam. We have always trusted the will of the dragons in this matter," said Qurum.

"This is a highly unusual selection. I believe my question is warranted." Nods from many in the audience suggested that most wanted an explanation.

Qurum turned to Lowry.

"I don't need a translation crystal to see that Kalam doesn't like the choice of our ancients. Please relay to Kalam that it is the choice of the dragons who is worthy to be a rider. We can select anyone, but have allowed the clans to be a part of the choosing by selecting their best, but ultimately, it is our choice. Inform Kalam that the choice stands!" said Lowry.

"Your protest has been heard, Kalam. As per the Ancients and dragons, Abi as rider is a choice that stands. *Approach Abi,*" commanded Qurum.

Again a murmur went out, but was muted. It was apparent that the word of the Ancients was final.

Abi, with her head held high, strode to the front looking forward, ignoring the looks of hatred from most of the audience.

"Marrle did that on purpose! She knew the ancients would be impressed with Abi! I surely underestimated Marrle. Never would have thought she had it in her!" said an elated Selena.

As if to confirm Selena's words, as Abi stepped into the lineup of riders, Marrle embraced Abi, and they both stood side by side beaming.

"Marrle, as your choice of attendant has been promoted to that of rider, please select another attendant," said Qurum.

"I choose Jazmyne, from clan Imor," said Marrle.

A roar of approval erupted from clan Imor, as a strawberry blond woman stepped forward.

"Are there no ugly women on this planet?" I asked Selena.

"Calm yourself, Captain Barf-Shirt," was my loving sisters' reply.

Again, the same dragon stepped forward to present the crystals. Once again crystals were given to both rider and attendant.

"Abi, who is clan-less, do you accept your chosen role as rider?" was the question.

"Yes," said Abi, standing tall, and seemingly unfazed by the obvious fervor of her being selected had caused.

"Name your attendant," Qurum commanded.

"I select Sabrynna from clam Wyr," said Abi.

The girl that had been with Abi the day that Selena was killed stepped forward. Striding proudly to the front, Sabrynna stood tall and brave next to Abi. Her face was defiant and fierce. That would be a pair that I wouldn't want to mess with.

Kal stepped forward without being asked.

"Kal of clan Reylor, do you accept your chosen role as rider?" asked Qurum.

"Of course," Kal said with a smirk.

"Name your attendant."

"Kylor of clan Reylor will attend me," said Kal.

A large, but awkward young man stepped forward. Even though he tried to hide it, he appeared unhappy with his new position.

"Kal's younger brother. Kalam is very hard on Kylor. Strictly a political move to bolster the image of the family. Kylor is no warrior," said Selena.

The ancient dragon stepped forward and presented the crystals to Kal and Kylor. As Kylor picked up his crystal, he accidentally tripped and bobbled the crystal which skipped off under the front row of benches. Retrieving the crystal, he stepped back in line, red-faced. Kal's face was also red, but not from embarrassment. I hated the thought of Kylor being alone with Kal after the ceremony.

"I present to you our newest Riders. Riders and attendants, please accompany the Ancient Ones for final rituals," said Qurum.

As one, the audience stood. The ancient dragons slowly made their way down the center of the amphitheater. The remainder of the dragons fell in line, including Vesuvius. Finally, the newly chosen riders and attendants brought up the rear. As they neared the back, I again marveled at the size and strength of the dragons.

The lead dragon was the ancient female dragon. Her pace was slow and deliberate. As she neared where we were, her head suddenly snapped up and she appeared to sniff the air. She scanned the nearby audience looking intently into their faces. More than one person stepped back from the ferocious scrutiny of the dragon. Looking around, I tried to locate what the dragon was searching for.

Surly it had to be the strong looking young woman several rows down. She was tall and athletically built. Her armor practically glowed, it was so polished. I bet the dragon's realized that there was another potential rider they had missed.

As the dragon passed behind us, I felt the hot breath on the back of my neck as the dragon sniffed me. I jumped in surprise as I realized she was within inches of me, her nostrils searching me up and down. Her eyes opened wide as she bent to sniff me again.

With some effort, she turned and headed back towards the front of the audience. Confused dragons, along with new riders and attendants dutifully followed. When again in place, the ancient dragon conferred with both Qurum and Lowry. Both repeatedly turned to look in our direction, incredulous looks on both faces. This time, I wasn't able to hear what was being discussed.

"*Wow. Oh, wow,*" Selena said.

"*What? What's going on?*" I asked.

"*Uh, your world just got one hundred times more interesting, I think,*" she said cryptically.

Qurum turned towards the audience, looking in our direction one last time, this time visibly shaking his head this time.

A young woman appeared at my side.

"Please come with me," she said.

"*Selena, what's happening here?*" I asked.

"*Follow her. Don't trip and fall. You already look like death warmed over,*" she said.

I followed the young woman who led me over to the other candidates. Just the effort of walking to the front caused me to wheeze uncontrollably. I had to bend over and catch my breath to the amusement of most of the audience. The candidates looked as confused as I felt. I stood next to Abi, and became acutely aware of my appearance as I stood in front of the audience. I was bloody, had vomit breath, was covered in bird poop, and was standing next to some of the most beautiful people I had ever seen in my entire life. It still hadn't set in, what was going to transpire.

Qurum gestured for me to step forward. The three ancient dragons stepped forward before me, and in unison blew white flame into the air. Everyone, including me, was silent with shock.

"*Marcus, sole member of the tribe Musi, do you accept your chosen role as rider?*" asked Qurum.

Instantly, the large warrior leaped to his feat, this time a sword was drawn. His eyes never left my face as he charged at me.

Ten feet from me, he raised his sword as though to strike. I was in no shape to defend myself.

Vesuvius landed with a fearsome shriek that stopped Kalam in his tracks. With incredible quickness and dexterity, Vesuvius lashed out with his tail, snapping the sword in half. Vesuvius raised his tail again, appearing to get ready to strike Kalam.

"STOP!" was the command from the ancient female dragon.

Vesuvius's tail instantly dropped, but his stance remained defensive. There was both fear and hatred in Kalam's face.

The ancient dragon stepped forward.

"Qurum, if you will please allow Kalam to use your crystal, I wish to communicate directly to Kalam," ordered the dragon.

Qurum didn't look happy relinquishing his crystal to Kalam.

"I assume that you disagree with our choice of rider?" asked the ancient one, her voice low and ominous-sounding.

Clearly, Kalam vehemently disagreed with her choice.

"There are many candidates more worthy than this stinking outsider, regardless of his tribe and family. First Abi, and now an outsider? I don't care if he is the last from the Musi tribe, he is not worthy," said Kalam. His eyes never left me. Hatred and disgust written all over his face.

"Selena was chosen and proved herself," replied the ancient dragon.

"Selena was trained from birth. She was one of us. This whelp can't even handle our atmosphere, and he stinks of vomit, and fear!" said a red-faced Kalam. Spittle shot from his lips in my direction, landing at my feet.

"The choice of the ancients has never been questioned," said the dragon.

"The choice is wrong!" Nods from many of the audience confirmed that most thought the same. Kalam's eyes seemed to drill holes right through me.

"Perhaps we were wrong about the worthiness of... one of the riders," said the dragon. She turned and looked at Kal, her meaning apparent.

Kalam appeared to be caught short. To continue to complain about the decision of the ancients could cause Kal to lose his place as a rider. Kalam's family and clan could lose face, should that happen.

His facial demeanor changed to calm and reasonable, but his eyes couldn't hide the truth. He hated me. A burning, hot hatred.

"Perhaps I was too quick to action. Forgive me, Ancient One," he said, retiring to his place among his clan after restoring the crystal back to Qurum.

"Marcus, sole member of the tribe Musi, do you accept your chosen role as rider?" asked Qurum again.

"Uh, what?" I answered audibly. My voice only loud enough for the first row or two to hear.

"Answer telepathically," prompted Selena.

"Yes?" I said to Qurum telepathically.

"Please answer to the entire audience. All must hear you accept," replied Qurum.

"You've never done this before, Marcus. You know how to address individuals, not groups. Focus on everyone in the audience and answer," Selena said.

Concentrating on the audience I focused my attention and answered "yes."

"Nope. That wasn't it."

I tried again. No use. The blank stares from the audience confirmed that I had failed again.

"Focus on the last row of people," whispered Abi who now stood at my side. "Close your eyes and focus on talking to the last row of people. That's the amount of concentration you will need to broadcast to all."

Closing my eyes, I could picture how far away the last row was. It seemed a mile away.

Focusing all my attention, I tried to send my message all the way to the back of the amphitheater. It took all of my concentration, and it worked. A roar again arose from the audience at my acceptance to be a rider, and not a good roar of approval.

For some reason, the next question caught me by surprise.

"Name your attendant,"

"Uhh… Alan, I guess," I said. I didn't know anyone else. Another outburst from the audience. At least they heard me this time.

Kalam had jumped to his feet, but this time didn't say anything. He didn't need to. A very confused Alan was brought to the front by the same girl who had fetched me. Alan, of course, didn't have a crystal to interpret for him, so he had no idea what was going on.

Alan stood beside me, a questioning look on his face.

"Please join the ranks of rider and attendant," said Qurum, gesturing to the four newly chosen warriors. And just like that, we became the fifth team. Qurum shook his head in disbelief looking at the two of us.

As we lined up with the other riders, it dawned on Alan what had happened.

"You got to be *freaking* kidding me!" he whispered out of the side of his mouth. He couldn't conceal the huge smile on his face. It was better than Christmas, his birthday, and Halloween all in one.

As we found our places, I caught our reflection in the shining armor of Qurum. It was worse than I had thought. I had been splattered from head to toe by the bird, with my hair and shirt getting a fair share of the droppings. The vomit on my shirt was also obvious, and my eyes were bloodshot. I'm pretty sure that I was the lamest rider choice of all time.

To stand next to these beautiful specimens of what riders should look like, I've never felt so inadequate or foolish in my life. From the stares from the audience, my self analysis was fairly accurate.

The dragon stepped forward to present us with our crystals. Another gasp went out from the crowd. I looked up to see that it was a female dragon that was to present them.

Even Selena seemed surprised.

"This has never happened. The female ancient has never presented the crystals. The records go back several hundreds of years," she said with awe in her voice.

Stopping in front of me, she looked expectantly at me. Naturally, I stood there looking like an idiot, not knowing what was wanted of me.

"Present your crystal, young one," she finally prompted.

"This is Selena's crystal, not mine," I said.

"Crystals can be used within family units. Please present Larzi," she said.

Holding Larzi high, the ancient dragon took the crystal and placed it on the ground, then proceeded to regurgitate two other crystals. Again there was a reaction from the audience.

"Never has anyone received more than a single crystal," said Selena's voice in my head. *"This is unusual indeed."*

Bright blue flames shot from the ancient dragon's nostrils. The heat was intense.

Stepping back, she looked at us expectantly.

"I think you're supposed to go first, Marcus," said Alan.

Reaching down, I grabbed Larzi then looked at the ancient dragon. The dragon nodded her head, and I picked up the other also.

Alan appeared at my side and quickly scooped up the remaining crystal. He stared at it in total awe and wonder.

"If you please, Qurum," said the dragon.

Alan looked startled as the dragon spoke.

Leaning close to me, he whispered, "I *totally* heard that!"

I had forgotten that only those with special crystals could communicate with the dragons.

CHAPTER TWELVE

HOMEWARD BOUND

The dragons, along with the new riders and attendants lined up to exit the amphitheater once again. The major difference was that Alan and I were now a part of the processional. I followed directly behind Kylor. Alan and I brought up the rear, which seemed fitting. There were mighty dragons and newly appointed riders and attendants, but Alan and I were by far the most scrutinized. There were curious looks, but many were looks of revulsion or even hatred.

After we had cleared the amphitheater, I was once again huffing and puffing. I dropped to one knee, trying to breathe. I was getting tunnel vision and feeling nauseous again.

A strong hand grasped my shoulder.

"It must be hard coming to our world," said Kylor. *"Here, let me help you up. Just lean on me and I'll help you walk."*

Kal turned to see his brother helping me. His disgust was not disguised, and he appeared to begin to say something, but thought better of it and turned away to continue to follow the dragons.

"You'll have to forgive Kal. He is more like our father. I guess I'm more like my mother. She died some years ago," said Kylor.

I was too busy concentrating on breathing to answer, even telepathically.

Our little parade took about half an hour, and concluded in a large meadow. Thankfully, there were benches for us two-legged creatures.

I sat on one of the benches, wheezing. I was surprised

that my intake of air didn't strip the surrounding foliage of their leaves. My legs felt rubbery, despite Kylor practically carrying me the entire way.

I sat next to Abi who sympathetically rubbed my back.

Alan, of course, recovered much quicker than I. Kinda hated him right now.

The meadow seemed unusually bright. Looking into the sky, I saw that two moons lit up the night. Even as tired as I was, I marveled at the beauty.

"There are actually three visible moons," said Selena. *"You have no idea how badly three moons affect tides on this world's lakes and oceans. The third one has a higher orbit than these two. It won't be seen tonight."*

Lowry stepped forward directly in front of us. I hadn't seen Qurum follow us, but he too, stepped forward.

"Qurum, please begin the ceremony," said Lowry.

"Riders, please rise. As newly chosen riders, you will need to use the power of the crystals to communicate with dragons. Connect your minds to the crystal now, please." Qurum said.

The other riders concentrated on their respective crystals. In unison I saw a sense of awe as they connected.

I had already connected with Larzi, so I just stood there.

"Marcus, you have a remaining crystal," said Qurum.

Focusing on the other crystal, I thought back to when I had first connected with Larzi. It came easier this time. In an instant, I was connected with both crystals. I felt a surge of energy pulse inside me, that was gone almost instantly. But for that instance, I felt strong.

"Riders, you should be able to hear and understand me," said Lowry. *"As your first test, reply 'Aye' if you hear and understand."*

A chorus of "ayes" rang out from all five riders. Of course Captain Barf-Shirt said it verbally. I could almost hear Selena's eyes roll.

"Aye," I said telepathically after all eyes turned to me.

"Good. Please be seated. Qurum, please instruct the attend-

ants of the properties of their crystals."

"*Attendants, please rise and come forward,*" said Qurum. All five attendants went forward. Alan seemed tiny standing next to Kylor. Truth be told, most anyone would look tiny next to Kylor. He was well over six feet tall. Kal only slightly shorter.

"*You also have crystals. They are given to you to assist your rider and dragon. Often, they are paired with the rider's crystal to maximize strengths. During your choosing, the ancients looked for your various strengths and weaknesses. As you know, you will be put through a series of tests prior to becoming a rider and attendant.*"

"*Tests?*" I asked Selena. "*You know I'm not good at tests.*"

"*I will be here to help you for the mental stuff. The physical stuff is all up to you,*" she answered.

"*Before you are paired with a dragon, the most important thing that you will do is find out the properties that your crystals hold. Their strengths and weaknesses. These are gifts from the dragons, and while some crystals are known to us,*" Said Qurum, nodding in my direction, "*most are new crystals that need to be explored and tested. As most of you know, crystals allow us to speak with the dragons, but they also hold other properties that can be useful. As your first challenge to becoming a rider, you must return to your homes for sixty days. During that time, you will become familiar with your crystal. When you return, the dragons will put you through a series of trials to prove that you have mastered their use. Only the dragons themselves know the full properties of each crystal. You'll want to be fully prepared. These trials are not easy. They are to prove that you are suitable to be paired with a dragon for the remainder of your lives.*"

Lowry stepped forward.

"*Congratulations riders. You'll want to protect your crystals with your life. Loss or destruction will disqualify you for Rider Training. We will return to this meeting place in sixty days. Riders and attendants are dismissed. Selena, Marcus, and Alan, you'll stay please,*" said Lowry.

The others quickly disappeared into the night. Selena

had reappeared, and I noticed that Vesuvius had quietly come up behind us. Amazing how light on his feet he could be.

"You present a very difficult problem for us, Marcus," said Lowry towering over me.

"I'm sorry. I didn't know this was going to happen," I said.

A low rumble issued from deep inside Lowry. The properties of my crystal let me know that it was laughter, but it sounded terrifying regardless.

"No, I suspect that you didn't know this would happen. The ancients have their own reasons, and by and large their reasoning is dead on, but I confess that I question their wisdom on this one, no offense to you," said the dragon.

"No offense taken," I said with sincerity. I, too, questioned their wisdom on this one.

Qurum came and sat down beside me and Alan. On closer inspection, he looked older and more tired up close.

"We have a problem to solve. Just what do we do with you? You are not strong enough to effectively train here, but you're unprotected in your world. We can't afford to send you the protection you need, and it won't be long before our enemy knows that you've been selected as a rider. You'll be a prime target, especially with three crystals between you and Alan as a prize," he said.

"Qurum," said Selena. *"I have a suggestion. The known worm-hole of the enemy closes in a matter of hours. It will take another half year before it opens again. I'm sure they left trusted soldiers on the other side, but not many. If we were to return, taking Vesuvius, along with Abi and Sabrynna, we should be strong enough to scare off any attack. Marcus and Alan could continue their training and also get into better shape to handle the rigors here."*

"I don't relish the idea of you being on the other side alone," said Lowry, *"but if Vesuvius agrees, that should be more than enough protection."*

"Of course I will go with Selena," said Vesuvius. *"After all, she is still my rider, father."*

I realized that it was going to be necessary to know how

everyone was related on this world. It might be a matter of life and death.

"It is settled then. Sixty days will go by fast, young ones. Mighty fast, indeed. Farewell!" and with a mighty flapping of wings Lowry disappeared into the night.

....

The trip back through the wormhole had gone a lot smoother because Vesuvius agreed to carry me and Selena. The conversation between Vesuvius and Selena almost broke my heart, they were so close. There was tangible love between the two.

Alan was proving himself as a real trooper. He was able to trudge the entire distance, stopping often for sure, but still managing to make it the entire way.

From Vesuvius' back, I was able to take in all the things I had missed due to me trying to breath and walk at the same time, on the way to the meeting. The daylight had broken, and we were able to see a great deal of the forest. Many of the plants and trees were the same, but there were also some real surprises, too.

The animals were diverse. Rodents, birds, and insects were abundant. Once, Vesuvius startled and took to the air before I knew what was going on.

"Grip with your knees," was Selena's instructions.

We circled above the group below, before spotting what Vesuvius had smelled. It appeared to be a huge hippo. It was wallowing in the river, but when we flew over it, it blew warning flames out of its nose at us.

"They are even more dangerous to humans here than they are on earth. Those flames can shoot fifty feet or more," said Selena.

Flying on Vesuvius's back was terrifying. Each movement felt as if it would dislodge me. I gripped as tight as I could with my knees, but it didn't seem enough.

"Will I have a bridle or something to hold on to when I get my dragon?" I asked Selena.

"No. You'll be holding a weapon and shield. Both hands will be full. Part of your training is getting to know the dragon movements. Once you're in sync with your dragon, you become a single fighting force."

"If you say so," I said dubiously.

Arriving at the wormhole, Selena prepped us for crossing.

"Remember, we fell through the first time. When we cross this time, we'll need to climb up. As you pass through, there will be some handholds on your right for you to grab. They are recessed into the rock, so they can't be seen from above. Abi, maybe you should go first to show the way."

Holding the crystal up, Vesuvius used it to open the wormhole again. With a loud popping sound, the swirling vortex appeared.

Without hesitation, Abi passed through the vortex.

"Marcus will go next, followed by Alan. Sabrynna, if you will make sure these two get through first, then come through last."

"Vesuvius can fend for himself," said Selena.

Walking through the vortex was as strange as before. After being weighed down by oppressive gravity and limited oxygen, I felt as light as a feather crossing back to earth. I stepped through and found myself looking up at the sheer cliff. Abi was several feet higher than me, her hands and feet in the hand-holds. It was a strange sensation because I was essentially standing perpendicular to the wall because of the location of the wormhole.

"Stop! You're going to need instructions before you come too far. This is going to be a strange sensation." Warned Abi. "As you exit the wormhole, you're going to be subject to this world's gravity again. You're going to want to step with your right foot and place it in this foothold," pointing at a foothold to my right. "Then lean forward and grab a hand hold."

Doing as Abi said, it was indeed a strange sensation. As I stepped with my right foot, I could feel the gravity of earth pulling me down. Leaning forward, I grabbed a hand hold and pulled myself clear of the wormhole. It felt as though gravity shifted, which I guess it did. I was now on the sheer cliff. I followed Abi up the cliff and turned around to see Alan. He cleared the wormhole without any instruction. He was a natural at all this other-worldly stuff. He was followed by Sabrynna, and then with a whoosh, Vesuvius flew through the vortex and into the sky.

The ride back to Grandma's house was strangely quiet. It had been such an eventful two days that it was impossible to take in. Even Alan was quiet, although the smile never left his face. I was exhausted. Furthermore, sitting in close quarters with everyone, especially two very attractive women, exposed just how awful I smelled.

"Still kind of makes your eyes water," said Alan, his face hidden behind his shirt that he had pulled up.

It seemed like a lifetime since we were attacked and had to flee in Grandpa's truck.

"*I scouted the house and area around, tiny rider,*" said Vesuvius. "*All is clear.*"

I looked up to see if I could spot Vesuvius.

"*You won't see him. He can camouflage himself in the sky when he wants to. One of the reason's dragons are such a formidable fighting animal,*" said Selena.

"I guess I better check in with the parents and let them know I'm alright," said Alan. "If my mom knew..." he shuddered visibly. He grabbed his phone to find a private place.

"*Abi and Sabrynna can stay in my room. We'll need to find another solution before Grandma gets back, and then we'll need to start training.*"

....

Morning came quickly, and I was more than tired. The weekend events didn't seem real, but the presence of Abi and Sabryyna confirmed that we did in fact cross to another world. Then there was the pile of foul-smelling clothes I had left in a pile, too tired to throw them in the hamper. Alan, of course, seemed unfazed. He had gotten permission to stay one more night.

"Mom says you're a good influence on me, and you won't do anything stupid," said Alan with a wide smile on his face.

I was undressing to shower when, *"We should start your training right after school,"* said Selena.

"Arrrghhh!" I shouted as I quickly covered up with my towel.

"Oh, grow up, Marcus!" said Selena. *"You're going to have to get used to me being here! I don't enjoy this any more than you do, I just thought some mundane conversation would make this less uncomfortable."*

"Well, you thought wrong," I said. "Please give me some privacy? You said you could lock yourself away or something?"

An exasperated sigh. *"It would make a lot more sense for you just to grow up, but whatever. I'll check back with you in fifteen minutes. Seriously!"*

And I actually felt Selena's presence leave.

Fastest shower of my life.

The other three were already downstairs eating some breakfast that Abi had cooked. I realized how famished I was when she placed a plate of eggs, sausage and bacon in front of me.

"Shouldn't one breathe while one eats?" Sabryyna asked Abi with a smirk as she watched me inhale my food.

I learned with some surprise that Abi and Sabryyna were going to register to attend school. They had all the proper documentation arranged. I was also surprised to learn that three others had crossed to act as security for us. Two women and one man. The man and one of the women would pose as parents to Abi and Sabrynna. They would remain mostly on patrol around Grandma's house.

"Sabryyna and Abi will serve as additional close security," said Selena."*You will be introduced to the others after school.*"

"Won't it be difficult for Abi and Sabryyna to attend

school on a different planet?" I asked.

"Both of us have been trained to operate on this side of the wormhole. That was my sole training, in fact. I was raised from birth to function here," said Abi. "Don't worry about us. We will be fine."

As you can imagine, school was pretty weird after such an eventful weekend. Of course there was no time to finish homework, and I knew for sure there was going to be a pop quiz in English. Even though I had made peace with Becky, I was still fuming over being put on the spot by Mr. Cornwall.

The plan was for Alan and me to go to school as usual. Abi and Sabryyna would check into school with their "parents," later that morning.

Alan and I must have been off of our game because of the weird weekend. We totally forgot about avoiding Eldon and his entourage. Before, we had been slipping into the band room entrance to avoid Eldon, but today we went right through the main entrance of the school.

I felt someone come up behind me. Too late, I tried to spin and defend myself, but I was quickly wrapped in a bear hug, my arms pinned to my sides.

Eldon appeared in front of me, and without warning, slugged me in the gut, knocking all the air out of my lungs. I was released from the bear hug and sunk to the ground, gasping for breath. I looked up to see Alan, suspended in the air in an Atomic Wedgie. His face contorted in pain. After several seconds, he was dropped unceremoniously to the ground.

"Morning ladies," Eldon said as he walked off, accompanied by snickers from his admirers.

"I really, really hate that guy!" said Alan, as he gingerly undid the aftereffects of being suspended in the air by his underwear.

As I caught my breath, I stood to find myself staring at Abi and Sabryyna sitting in the waiting room next to the entrance. They had seen the entire ordeal. My humiliation was now complete.

"We're going to need to take care of that situation," said Selena.

"Maybe Suvi needs a snack?" asked Alan hopefully.

The rest of the school day went without further issues. Alan and I successfully avoided Eldon by camping out in the library when we weren't in class. It was the only place Eldon wouldn't be caught dead in.

"His lips probably move when he reads," Alan said, his face in a scowl. "Sounding out those long two-syllable words can be difficult for neanderthals."

Abi and Sabryyna had joined us. They had successfully registered for school and were causing all kinds of a stir among the male population. Have I mentioned that everyone from that world was gorgeous? It confused the school population that these two supermodels would hang out with Alan and I.

"Part of your training will be to find out the properties of your crystals. The ancient dragons were capable of infusing special capabilities into each individual crystal. It is up to the rider and their dragon, along with their attendants to discover what those capabilities are, and how to use them to their advantage," Selena said. *"I must warn you that this isn't always straightforward or easy. In fact, Suvi and I constantly found little bits of capabilities that we initially didn't know about. It's a continual learning process. That will be the first thing that we start with today after school. You'll have better success finding the capabilities after you are paired with a dragon, but it doesn't hurt to start as soon as you can. That, along with our conditioning program."*

There was little doubt as to who needed the conditioning. Abi and Sabryyna were fit as Olympic athletes, and Alan hadn't passed out or vomited all over his shirt, so that left me.

The lunch bell rang, and I reluctantly got up to go to Mr. Cornwall's class and face the dreaded pop quiz. Thankfully, we had ended our section on Shakespeare, and now we were reading, "To Kill a Mockingbird," and of course, I hadn't read any of the assignment. Abi walked with me to class. Abi was the younger of her and Sabryyna, so Abi's cover was that of an eleventh grader, like me, and Sabryyna that of a senior.

Alan had taken it upon himself to show Sabryyna her next classroom because "it was on the way." He must have had to sprint to his classroom which was on the other side of campus after he dropped Sabryyna off. Had to admire the kid for trying.

"My feelings are hurt, Marcus," said a voice behind us. We had just rounded the corner to enter Mr. Cornwall's class. I didn't have to turn around to know it was Eldon.

Great. I was about to be humiliated in front of the beautiful Abi, once again.

"It's almost like you've been avoiding me, son," Eldon said. He was talking to me, but was eyeing Abi up and down. "But I can see why you were distracted, so you're forgiven."

"We're just trying to get to class, Eldon," I said. "We don't want any trouble."

"We?" Eldon asked, again focusing on Abi. "Let me give you some advice, pretty lady. Marcus here isn't the man you're looking for. I would be happy to escort you around school. It would give you instant credibility to be seen with me. You don't want to be tainted by being seen with the king of the nerds."

"If I had a body..." said Selena.

Abi slipped her hand into mine and laid her head on my shoulder.

"That's OK, Elron." A couple of snickers were quickly stifled at the deliberate wrong name. "I'm attracted to strong men that don't need a gang around them to pick on others. Marcus would kick your butt if you weren't surrounded by your thugs."

It was almost worth the violent and painful death I was going to receive from "Elron" to hold Abi's hand. The smell of her hair was intoxicating. I inhaled deeply, realizing that it was my last chance before being curb-stomped.

Eldon smiled with his mouth, but his eyes were burning with hatred. Not just for me, either. He now hated Abi.

"Well, when you change your mind, and believe me, you will change your mind, be sure to shower and disinfect yourself of his taint. I might forgive you, but only because you are gorgeous. I don't give second chances to ugly girls," Eldon said with a smirk as he turned and walked off.

"You know he's going to kill me, right?" I asked Abi.

"I've got him right where I want him," said Abi as she let go of my hand.

"You are going to fight him?" I asked.

"No," she said, "you are."

CHAPTER THIRTEEN

TRAINING

I recognized the three adults from Qurum's clan. Abi and Sabryyna's "parents" were two middle-aged adults named Wynn and Maria. The other woman, Lydia, was younger and was the real sister of Maria. She would pose as the eldest sister already graduated. They were athletically built and spoke with no accent. Wynn and Maria were also the "parents" of Abi and Sabryyna when I first met them the day Selena died, so this was a group that had worked together often, I gathered.

"It's good to see you again, Marcus," said Wynn. "Congratulations on being chosen to be a rider. It is a greater honor than you can possibly know. If you're anything like your sister, you will be a great dragon rider."

"We have limited time, so we best get started," said Selena. We were in a secluded clearing in the forest, several miles out of town. *"Each day we will need to maximize your training. Wynn, Maria and I will be your trainers. Lydia will serve as a combat training partner and will also see to your physical conditioning."*

"It is critical to focus on two training issues," said Maria. "First and foremost is discovering the properties your individual crystals hold, and secondly," looking directly at me, "your conditioning."

Sure, pick on the chubby guy. I already dreaded the conditioning.

"I suggest you find a quiet spot and try connecting with your crystal as your first assignment. Alan, we will need to instruct you on how to use telepathy to connect to your crystal."

"Uh, I already did the connection thingy," said Alan. His face showed concern. "Nobody told me I wasn't supposed to, so I've been trying and trying, and I finally got in. The name of my crystal is Medic."

Everybody in the group was looking at Alan, shocked looks on their faces, mine included.

"Did I do something wrong?" he stammered. "I was just trying to get started... you're not going to kick me out, right? Oh, please don't kick me out! I mean, I was just..."

A loud laugh from Wynn broke off Alan's sentence.

"And here we were, worried that a native earth human might not be able to access his crystal. That was one of our largest hurdles," said Wynn with another laugh. "No, Alan, we're not going to kick you out. We're actually impressed with your effort."

Alan was positively glowing with the praise. Not going to lie. I was kinda jealous.

"Were you able to find any skills?" asked Selena.

"Yes," said Alan. "I found what appears to be healing skills. I don't know how to use them, but I believe the crystal to have healing properties."

"An excellent gift," said Maria. "Healers are few and far between. It takes skill and intelligence to be a healer."

"It was my experience that there are other skills that you will need to discover, but the healing skill is a major gift," said Selena.

Doing as Wynn suggested, we found quiet spots around the clearing. Lydia jogged off to make sure that we were not being observed.

"You have an especially interesting challenge. Two crystals. That's never happened before," said Selena. *"Fortunately, I can help you with most of the properties that Larzi has. There seems to be a few more properties, but Suvi and I never were able to get a fix on them. Maybe you'll be able to access those. Let's try connecting with Larzi."*

Concentrating, I focused my efforts on Larzi. Having

connected before, I was able to connect fairly quickly.

"I don't know what I'm looking for," I said to Selena. "I just feel the connection, but nothing else."

"That's normal for the first couple of times. Think of the crystal like a hard drive on a computer. Information is stored in different areas of your hard drive. You'll want to explore every area you can. It seems weird now, but you'll understand after you find how to navigate the crystals. Don't get discouraged. It takes time. The cool thing is that we have a short cut. I can show you around Larzi, since I live here."

And with that, Selena appeared in front of me.

"It helps to have a visual," said Selena, *"Take out Larzi."*

I took Larzi from around my neck and held the crystal in my palm.

"Larzi has a couple of capabilities that I can show you. First, let's focus on the upper left corner of the crystal. You'll need to really focus your entire attention on that area to activate it."

"What am I looking for?" I asked, "I still don't feel anything different."

"You'll know when you experience it."

Concentrating as best I could, I focused all my attention on the crystal. At first I felt nothing, but my attention kept being attracted to a place higher up on the crystal than I had been focusing. Little by little, I followed my instincts until...

"You've got to be kidding me!" I exclaimed as a rock levitated in the air, then dropped as I lost focus.

Selena's face was like that of a proud parent.

"Cool, huh?" she asked. *"Levitation is a fairly common gift. Comes in handy for a lot of things."*

"How big of things can I lift? Are there limitations?" I asked.

"See that log over there? Try lifting it."

Focusing in on the log, I tried to lift it. Immediately I felt drained. Not physically, but mentally drained. It was a weird feeling, to feel that kind of exhaustion.

"That's an important lesson, right there. You have limita-

tions. It's just like weight lifting. As you work out more and more, you will be able to do more and more, but we all have limitations. When you get your dragon, your abilities will be compounded. They bring a lot of power both mentally and physically to the game, but you will both have limitations. It's important to know them, especially while in the heat of battle."

I could feel my strength return a little, so I tried levitating a small stick. It was immediately blasted out of the air by what appeared to be a bolt of fire.

I spun around to see a smiling Alan.

"Best day ever!" he yelled, and disappeared to wherever he had come from.

"Let's try your other crystal. I can show you around Larzi, but you will need to explore your new crystal by yourself."

I returned Larzi back around my neck and took out the other crystal. Using the same focused attention, I tried connecting with the crystal. Nothing.

I shook my head and tried again. I just needed to focus my attention. Still nothing. It was as though what I held in my hand was just a regular crystal found on the ground. It felt dead. No spark of anything.

"You don't suppose the dragons gave me a defective crystal?" I asked, concerned.

"No. Like I said, it takes time. You'll need to find the unique way to access the crystal. Each one is different," Selena informed me.

The conditioning was brutal. Lydia had me gasping for breath seconds after we had thoroughly stretched. She had us running the entire hour of conditioning. Abi and Sabryyna took the running in stride and hardly broke a sweat. Alan was breathing hard, but recovered quickly. No amount of running could wipe the smile off his face.

I, on the other hand, was stripping leaves from trees with every intake of breath. Every time I was able to catch my breath, we immediately started sprinting again. My legs were shaking, and I began to feel sick to my stomach. Great. The return of Captain Barf-Shirt.

Lydia seemed to be legitimately sad to see the sun dip behind the mountain, thus ending our torture session.

"That's a good first day," said Wynn. "We'll pick this up again tomorrow." The three of them disappeared as they ran off towards where our vehicles were parked. I marveled again at how unhumanly they moved.

I couldn't help but notice that my clothes were soaked through with sweat. Abi and Sabryyna both lightly mopped their brows, but otherwise, I couldn't tell that they had been running for the best part of an hour.

Alan had a ring of sweat around his collar and armpits.

I had to wring out sweat from my shirt before I could get into the car, and then the cramps came.

"You'll want to stay more hydrated tomorrow," said Sabryyna as I massaged my leg, trying to work out the painful knot.

With the cramps and how bad my legs were shaking, I needed someone else to drive us all home. I had drove us up, but Lydia's death march had incapacitated me. I sighed, realizing I would never look good in front of Abi. My manliness was taking a lot of hits lately.

"So, your grand scheme is that I'm going to fight Eldon? You know that he's fairly easily beaten both me and Alan up several times, right?" I asked Abi as we were driving home.

"That wind bag?" she asked, with a snort. "You and Alan will both be able to handle ten Eldon's with a little training." Sounded good to me, but I was dubious to say the least.

The next couple of weeks went by quickly. Alan, of course, was the star student. He had found a total of eleven different skills within his crystal. Not only could he shoot bolts of fire, but he could levitate items, and instantly heal all sorts of cuts and wounds by utilizing the crystal energy. He could also translate languages, and most importantly, the crystal held a vast store of knowledge regarding the healing and nutritional properties of plants and minerals on both earth and

Vocce, which we learned was the name of the planet through the wormhole.

I, on the other hand, had only been able to access three skills using Larzi, even though Selena swore there were other skills that I just wasn't able to access. So far I was able to levitate small items, start small campfires with a spark, and find drinkable sources of water. I still couldn't connect to my other crystal.

"I feel great power emanating from it," said Vesuvius. Selena had asked him to examine the crystal for fear that it was indeed just a chunk of rock.The crystal was powerful and authentic, I just couldn't do anything to connect to it. This did nothing to bolster my confidence.

Abi and Sabryyna both found some pretty cool warrior skills. Sabryyna was a skilled archer already, but discovered that she could access limited night vision. Soon she was making incredible shots.

"I'm only limited to the strength and range of my bow," she said after hitting a target at one hundred yards. Throughout the day, she would curse at the limited range of her compound bow. Her and Vesuvius even made a game testing her skill.

"It's one thing to hit a stationary target," said Sabryyna during weapons training. "It's quite another to hit a target that is moving."

Since Vesuvius's skin was so thick, regular arrows had no effect on him, especially at a long range when the energy from the arrow was mostly spent. He would dive through the heavily forested trees, and Sabryyna would try to shoot him. She soon became so accurate that they had to change the rules. She now had to hit a drawn target on Vesuvius, or it would be considered a miss. My effective range on a stationary target was about thirty yards. I had a better chance of hitting a moving target by throwing the bow at it.

Abi's skills were discovered in heavy weapons training with Wynn. As Alan and I learned, the inhabitants of Vocce were mostly behind on technology compared to that of Earth. Our worlds had developed in different directions. On Vocce, hand-to-hand fighting was still the norm. Swords, spears, bows, arrows, and armor were still the items of war.

While sparring with Wynn with long swords, Abi suddenly sprang into a series of thrusts and parries that caught the expert, Wynn, totally by surprise. She easily disarmed the startled warrior time and time again. Once, while practicing killing thrusts and blows on a dummy soldier filled with straw, she was able to strike with such force as to shatter the supports behind the dummy.

"I can magnify the blows," she said as we gathered around to see the destruction. "It took such little effort."

"I think I have something similar," said Alan "but it is when I punch or strike something. I just can't focus on it, and it happens only occasionally. What are you doing to magnify your blows?"

"You have to focus your attention on the instant of impact," said Abi. "It's a timing thing."

Alan turned and struck an old punching bag that we had brought up to practice hand-to-hand combat on.

"Ow!" he yelped, shaking his hand in pain. "That definitely wasn't it."

"Picture your fist going through the bag," Abi said. "Your point of impact isn't the face of the dummy, it's the back of the skull, if that makes sense."

Cocking his fist back, he tried again. This time the results were shocking. The one hundred and fifty pound punching bag flew through the air and landed in a heap ten feet away, some of the stuffing clearly visible through the split from the impact that his fist had caused.

"I was picturing Eldon's ugly mug," said Alan with an evil smile.

We had been able to avoid Eldon these last couple of weeks. Having Abi and Sabryyna around was a good deterrent. After his showdown with Abi, Eldon didn't seem anxious to lose any more face. I could tell it baffled him that they weren't in any way intimidated by him. Also, they were women, and he couldn't physically assault them like he could another male.

"One of the abilities that you should be able to access is that same focus of force that Abi and Alan are able to do," said Selena as I drove to school. *"That would be a real surprise to that baboon."*

....

Alan had been spending an excessive amount of time at our house, and Grandma would be returning the coming weekend, so this week he was spending some time with his family.

Abi and Sabryyna had moved in with their "family" to a rented house. Before everyone left, we had a big house cleaning so Grandma wouldn't come back to a big mess. It had only been a couple of weeks that Grandma Torrey had been gone, but it seemed a lifetime. Now that I know that she knew about Selena all along, I was a little resentful that I had been lied to. Looking back, it all started to make sense. Selena had to have a cover story for all the time she spent on Vocce. Of course grandma knew.

"Don't hold that against her," chided Selena. *"She was doing what mom and dad asked her to do, and it seemed the best thing to do at the time."*

Wynn was concerned about our safety, so it was decided that Abi and Sabryyna would be "sick" for a day or two. In reality, they were scouring the surrounding area for any sign that we were being watched. Vesuvius had been flying regular reconnaissance missions, but Wynn had wanted to take a more thorough look around, just for safety, and Eldon and his crew must have noticed their absence.

"Watch out!" Selena shouted as I was walking down senior hall at school, heading for my first period class.

Too late, I found myself flat on my face, both my ankles tightly bound in loop from a lasso, the kind they use for roping steers. It always amazed me at the skill and timing it took to rope two feet at the same time.

"Where's your babysitter?" asked Eldon as I sat up. I tried to quickly reach down and get the rope off, but the goon who had lassoed me kept the rope taught, effectively making my efforts futile. His nickname was Cowboy, and he was stocky and tough from working on his family ranch.

"What's she see in you anyway?" asked Eldon with a sneer. "I mean, what's attractive about you? All this time I just assumed that you were gay."

I was struggling with trying to get up, but the rope around my ankles was tight. Cowboy competed on the high school rodeo team, and knew how to keep tension on the rope making it impossible to escape. Eldon was circling behind me, inflicting some sort of pain.

A surprised "yelp" stopped Eldon in his tracks, and the rope went slack and I was able to slip my feet out and scramble up.

Cowboy had dropped the rope and was slapping madly at his backside, unmistakable singe marks on the back of his pants. He was looking wildly at the crowd that had gathered, undoubtedly looking for the person that had torched him. Naturally, his eyes lingered on Alan who had appeared in the crowd, but Alan had been nowhere close to him when he got burned. The grin on Alan's face was suspicious, but it was impossible for him to be the culprit from his location in the crowd.

In confusion, Cowboy gathered up his rope. Eldon, mad about losing his chance to inflict pain, crossed to Cowboy.

"What was that all about?" he asked angrily.

"Somebody burned me," Cowboy said, glancing at the laughing Alan. "Don't know who. Nobody came close enough."

The five-minute bell rang and the crowd began to disperse.

"You'll want to be careful about stuff like that in the future, Alan. The last thing you want to do is bring attention to yourself like that, but nice job!" There was pride in Selena's voice.

"Just learned how to do that yesterday. Instead of a fire bolt, I can make a fireball appear anywhere I wish. No one can see where the fire ball originates from." His smile was wide. "Toasted buns, baby!"

The rest of the day went by without incident. We found out later that Cowboy had been admitted to the hospital for second degree burns. Even though there was no evidence that Alan or I were responsible for the burns, it was inevitable that Eldon and his pals would attribute it to us somehow. Retribution was surely on its way.

Later, we met up with our training group. Wynn reported that they hadn't found anything unusual, but wanted us to still be careful.

Everybody looked forward to our training sessions. Everybody except for me, that is. For the other three, training was all about finding new and cool skills and how to best utilize them. I was struggling to make the three skills I knew useful, and I still couldn't link with the second crystal. It felt dead to me, despite Vesuvius insisting that it was powerful.

And then there was the conditioning. When we were sent out on a long-distance run, the girls easily finished forty five minutes to an hour faster than me. Even Alan was able to finish at least twenty minutes faster. Then there were the wind-sprints. Lydia would say, "Running is a skill that warriors need, either to catch the enemy...or to run away when necessary." Kinda was starting to hate Lydia.

"It's time that we talk about our enemy, who are called the Gonosz," announced Selena after Lydia's sadistic conditioning. Wynn, Lydia and Maria all had left, leaving only the riders and attendants, and Selena, of course.

"This is the reason that we are doing all this training. Abi, I think you are the best suited to explaining this."

Abi looked uncomfortable as she stood up and sat directly across from us. She addressed Alan and I, Sabryyna already knew the story.

"I'm going to speak with you with telepathy. I can describe

our enemy better, but more importantly, one of the hidden secrets of the crystals is that we can share visual memories among the dragons, attendants, and riders. We keep this a secret from all, even our own clans. It is a way in which we share vital information."

A scene appeared in my head. From Alan's gasp, he too, saw what I was seeing. What we were seeing was a village on Vocce. It was a village unlike that of which we have here on Earth. Positioned in the deep forest, instead of cutting down the majestic trees, the homes were built among them. A few of the structures were built on the ground, but the majority were built high off the ground. Beautiful wooden walkways connected the structures. All the building material was organic.

Gardens were also suspended among the trees. Fruits and vegetables growing in great abundance and variety, and the homes...how to describe the homes? The sleeping quarters were the only rooms that were fully enclosed. Everything else was open-air rooms.

We saw rooms that were obviously built for food preparation, and also large living rooms with some of the most comfortable-looking furniture I've ever seen. Carved wooden art adorned most rooms. Beautiful beasts of all kinds, but the most beautiful animals were carvings of the dragons. They were incredibly detailed, and painted with skill, artistry, and such subtlety. Nothing garish or overly gaudy. Colorful crystals also adorned the homes, arranged in mosaics and suspended to hang and give color to each room.

The inhabitants were, of course, beautiful like Abi and Sabryyna.

There was a large area suspended in the trees that had seating for hundreds of people. At the front was an unmistakable stage. Shops were also found among the trees. They could be distinguished from living quarters because they were the only structures to feature any signage, but even the signs were works of art.

It looked like paradise. People were going about their

lives in what appeared to be a peaceful and happy existence.

The scene shifted. The village was attacked. They fought back mainly by defensive measures. Walkways were pulled up that connected the tree dwellings and the ground, depriving the attackers access. It looked as though the defensive measures were going to work.

The villagers were raining down arrows upon the attackers with high accuracy. The attack was being repelled with great success.

In an instance that changed. With a great scream, a huge dragon dropped into the treetop village, and with great bursts of flame began to destroy the structures, along with the inhabitants. The arrows were ineffective against the huge dragon.

On the back of the dragon was a highly armored rider, but not just any rider.

The rider was Abi.

The villagers were quickly defeated by the huge dragon. Those that had survived were rounded up and put in chains. Men, women and children were marched a very long distance. Great enough distance that the vegetation turned from jungle to grasslands. They were taken to a large city made from adobe or mud bricks. No beautiful artwork, no more open living quarters, just drab clay-colored dwelling.

The villagers were lined up at a very large tent. Inside the tent was equipment that looked to be surgical in nature.

"Although the inhabitants of Vocce are behind in many of the technologies of Earth, our medical abilities are, in some respects, ahead of those here," said Abi.

Each of the villagers were lined up and taken into the tent. One by one they were placed on a bed, face down, the backs of their necks exposed.

A tiny slit was made at the back of the neck where the neck and the base of the skull met, exposing the vertebrae. A small chip of some type was fused to the topmost vertebrae. The skin was then stitched back together.

"The chip is a small but powerful explosive. It also can inflict a strong electronic impulse that renders the wearer temporarily paralyzed. It is horribly painful," said Abi. *"If you disobey the Gonosz, the least you can expect to get is a very painful shock. The worst is when the explosive gets triggered. Death is instantaneous and gruesome. The sight of someone being killed in this manner is a great deterrent to everyone. It is one way in which the Gonosz control the population."*

The next scene showed the villagers forced to labor for the Gonosz. Gone were the laughing, singing, beautiful people we saw in the trees, now replaced by sad dreary slaves. The strongest males and females were also selected as warriors. Their knowledge of other tribes enabled the Gonosz to enslave even more of the population. Either do the bidding of the Gonosz or suffer pain or death.

"You can imagine how they use family members as hostages," Selena chimed in. *"If you have a spouse or children, the Gonosz would threaten to kill your family members if you disobey. People brave enough to risk hurting themselves will not risk hurting a loved one."*

The enslaved warriors were sent out to capture the other villages, many of which were close friends or relatives of the enslaved people, and leading those warriors was Abi riding the huge dragon.

The scenes disappeared from our minds.

My face must have displayed the shock of seeing Abi riding the giant dragon, fighting for the enemy. Her eyes locked onto mine. Neither one of us would look away. I felt betrayed, confused, and sickened. She looked haunted and sad.

"Now you know why the clans hate me," she said, her voice cracking with emotion, "and now I suppose you hate me, too."

"Why...." I began.

Turning, she lifted her hair to display a scar where the others had received the explosive chip.

In our minds flashed a scene from the forest village. It

was of a family, a mother, father and three young children.

"Abigail, watch your brother and sister while your mother and I are out gathering honey. I followed a bee the other day, and it led me to a large hollow tree. There must be fifty buckets of honey for us to gather! You would enjoy some honey on your bread, wouldn't you?"

The oldest child, who was brunette, jumped up, clapping with joy.

"Oh, papa! We haven't had honey in months!" she said.

"Then watch Delma and Jown. We'll be gone for most of the day, but be back before dark," said the mother.

The parents left, and the three children spent most of the day playing in the forest around the tree village.

"It's getting dark," said Abigail to Delma and Jown. "Let's return home and see how much honey mama and papa have gathered."

Laughing and skipping, the three returned to their home.

"If you two will set the table, I will slice some bread so that we can have it with our meal when mama and papa get home. Won't the honey be delicious on this fresh-baked bread?"

But the parents didn't return that night.

"They probably had so much honey that it will take more than one day to bring it all home," said Abigail. She was putting on a brave face for Delma and Jown, but the concern could be seen on her face. Nevertheless, she tucked her younger siblings into bed then went to bed herself.

The next morning, she woke up early and checked her parents bedroom.

"Mama? Papa?" but the bedroom was empty.

The concern was now very noticeable on Abigail's face, but not wanting to frighten her brother and sister, she warmed the stew from last night's meal, along with the remaining bread.

That entire day, the three siblings stayed at home

watching from their open-aired living quarters, for signs of their parents and the honey, but the parents didn't show. They didn't show the next day either. By now, the children knew that something was wrong. Their parents would never leave them alone for that long without getting in touch with them.

On the morning of the third day, Abigail got her siblings dressed and walked through the tree pathways. They found their way to one of the structures with the beautiful signs in front. The wooden sign was hand-carved and featured various herbs, flowers, and other foliage. Also on the ornate sign was a mortar and pestle.

"How are my favorite nieces and nephew," boomed the large man behind the counter. He was the spitting image of their father, if their father was ten years older and fifty pounds heavier.

Immediately, the large man could see that something was amiss with the children. His face showed his alarm.

"What's wrong? Where are your parents?" asked the man.

"Uncle Bren," said Abigail, her eyes brimming with tears, "Mama and Papa went to gather honey in the woods and haven't returned."

"Well, I wouldn't be scared. They'll be back I'm sure. It's not yet afternoon. I'm sure they will be back before dark."

"They have already been gone three days, Uncle Bren," wailed Delma, wringing her hands in anguish.

"Three days...." and Uncle Bren went into action. He quickly removed his apron and tossed it onto a chair.

"Come children. Let's go see aunt Lyn. She will have some supper for you, and I will go look for your parents. Don't fuss. I'm sure your parents are fine. Must have been lots of honey."

The children and their uncle made their way among the trees to another large dwelling. Bren quickly told his wife why the children were there. She too sprung into action. Packing a meal into a bundle, she also found what appeared to be a medical bag of some sort. Bandages and various herbs and powders were in the bag.

Uncle Bren had changed and had a large pack. He quickly loaded the items that aunt Lyn had gathered.

"I'm going to alert our trackers. They have the best chance of finding Wil and Loleh," he said. Turning to Abi, he asked "Do you know where they went?"

"No," said Abi, shaking her head. "Papa said he followed a bee that led him to a large hollow tree that had lots of honey."

Bren hoisted the pack onto his back and was soon jogging along the walkway to gather searchers.

"Don't worry, children. Uncle Bren will get our trackers, and we shall soon see your mama and papa safe and sound. Come, let's have some fish chowder," she said.

It was decided that the children would stay with Lyn for the night. The children, exhausted from worry, quickly fell asleep now that adults were involved to help find their parents.

The next morning, the children were awakened to see the village was abuzz with action. Fortifications were being erected among the structures. Armed men and women were scurrying around from place to place, lifting the walkways away from the ground to deny an enemy access.

Bren was in the living quarters talking with Lyn.

"Our trackers found their trail, and we followed it for several hours. We found where they were scared by something and they started running. They headed for a heavily forested area, but that was a trap. They were snared and taken by a band of about ten men. We followed the tracks and came upon their camp. It was the Gonosz. The Gonosz have Wil and Loleh. It is only a matter of time before they know of us and will be coming."

Quickly, Bren and Lyn gathered articles and placed them into packs. Gathering their packs, they took the children to their home and quickly found changes of clothing and bedding for the children. Smaller packs were assembled for the children to carry.

"Come children. We must hurry!" said Bren as he led them to a platform that lowered them to the ground.

"We will need to go very fast, children. Let's tighten your packs so we can move quickly without losing items," said Lyn.

"Oh, that won't be necessary," said a very deep voice. Stepping out from behind a tree was a heavily-muscled man. He wore armor unlike any other. He was joined with several hundred other warriors. Two very familiar people were among the warriors, hands tied behind their backs with rope. Their faces showed the bruises and cuts from being beaten. The warriors had waited for the villagers to descend from the tree fortress and were now surrounded by the warriors. The few that fought were quickly killed or disarmed. Soon, the warriors were pillaging the village for anything of value. When the valuables were gathered, the village was set afire.

"That's unusual armor," I said. *"What kind of armor is that?"*

"Dragon skin armor," said Selena to our minds.

"More specifically, my sister's skin," said Vesuvius who had somehow crept into the meadow without us seeing him.

"And the man?" I asked.

"Gyilkos," said Abi. *"In the ancient language it means murderer, a title that he relishes."*

CHAPTER FOURTEEN

RANDOLPH

Grandma Torrey was home when we got there. I had texted her about knowing about my parents and Selena. It seemed like years since she left to see her sister, but in reality it had only been just over three weeks. A lot of weird stuff had happened since she left.

Grandma's reply had been simply, "I guess we have a few things to talk about when I get home."

She was sitting quietly in her living room when we arrived. I sat down without saying anything and we remained silent, the only noise was the grandfather clock tik-tokking in the corner. I don't know how long we sat in silence, but the grandfather clock finally chimed eight o'clock.

Grandma's eyes were wet when she looked up. That pretty much cleared any of the hostile thoughts I had. She had only done what she thought was best. I knew that intellectually, but it still stung.

"We were only doing what we thought was best for you and Selena," she finally said.

I got up and sat down next to her. Remarkably, Selena didn't get involved. She let me sort this with Grandma on my own terms, for which I was grateful.

Grabbing Grandma's hand, we sat quietly for a few more minutes.

"I know that you and Grandpa did your best. It's just a lot to process all at once, you know?" I said quietly. "It's like everyone was in the club, and I didn't even know there was a club."

"I know, Marcus, I know. We made a lot of mistakes along the way," she said with a sigh. "But in our defense, it was all new to us too. When your parents were married, your mother said that she had immigrated from Bulgaria. She confided in your father before they were married, and from what I understand, he went back with her several times."

We sat quietly for a few minutes longer.

"Can you forgive an old woman for the mistakes she's made?" asked Grandma.

Of course this took the wind out of my sails. Of course I was going to forgive Grandma Torrey.

"Love you, Grandma," I said.

"I love you, too Marcus," she said with a happy sigh.

"And I have a surprise for you. It's a pretty big one," I said with a smile.

"Selena isn't dead and resides in your crystal?" she said with a sly smile.

"What...how...." my mouth must have been hanging open, because she quoted one of my favorite "Mary Poppins," lines.

"Close your mouth, Michael. We are not a cod fish."

"That is what happened with your mother. She was with us for a short while. I guessed that's what happened to Selena, too." She looked hopefully at me.

"Can I talk with her?" she asked.

"I will have to translate..." I began.

"Actually, you won't," said Selena. *"She learned how to use mom's crystal. Well, this crystal actually. Mom needed to give Grandma instructions about us. Grandma picked it up faster than Alan."*

Taking the crystal from around my neck, I placed it in Grandma's hand. I no longer could hear Selena with the crystal not touching me.

I left Grandma and Selena alone and trotted upstairs. My guitar sat alone in the corner. I hadn't picked it up in weeks. The calluses on my fingers were getting soft from not playing.

Picking up the guitar, I played a chord just to see how tuned it was. After a minor quick twist to tighten the B string, I started strumming the Ovation guitar. After a few minutes, my mind and body began to relax. My mind drifted back over the events of the last several months. It just didn't seem real. In a way, the training seemed ridiculous because there was no way I was ready to fight, especially the warriors I had seen on Vocce. I would last ten seconds with even the weakest warrior.

I explored a series of chords. Bb, Eb7, Fm7, and Abmaj7. It was an odd progression, but I played it over and over. I would grow tired of the progression and try something else, but would continually find my fingers returning to Bb, Eb7, Fm7, and Abmaj7. I didn't know what drove me to play those chords, but it seemed familiar.

Something seemed not right about the notes, but I couldn't figure out what, since this was a new chord progression resulting from fooling around. I started experimenting with the chords, at first dropping the 7ths off. Closer, but not right. Minutes went by with me trying to isolate something, but I didn't know what I was trying to isolate. It just didn't seem right. Too many notes, maybe?

A thought came that I was hearing a melody within the progression. Playing the chords again, Bb, Eb7, Fm7, and Abmaj7 the melody started to form. It was simple, and decidedly odd, yet seemingly profound. Bb, Eb, Ab, and G.

I felt strangely compelled to play them again, and then a third time.

On the third time, I felt my second crystal stir. Focusing on the crystal with all my might, I continued to play the notes.

I seemed so close to a connection, but was still missing something. Again, I didn't know what I was missing, but it just felt incomplete.

After a few frustrating minutes, the stirring faded, and I was left playing Bb, Eb, Ab, and G, without any reaction from the crystal.

I felt a sharp pain on my middle finger on my left hand. I

had been pressing so hard on the strings, trying to get the melody right, that I had torn off the callus on that finger.

Grandma came into my room. She had been crying.

"Thank you, Marcus. That was a real treat, speaking with Selena," she said.

"Anytime, Grandma," I said.

Handing the crystal back, she sat down next to me.

"We need to talk," she said.

"Sure," I said.

"You know that Selena won't be able to stay around forever, no matter how much any of us wants her to, right?" she asked.

"Yes, I know. I try not to think about it," I said.

"*We're going to need to sit down and figure some things out,*" said Selena. "*When mom resided with the crystal, she thought she could stay indefinitely, but that's not how it works.*"

"Yes," Grandma chimed in, "when it came time for her to leave, it happened very quickly. She couldn't bear to stay with the crystal, even though it meant leaving both of you. I suspect that Selena is starting to feel the constraints."

I really didn't like hearing this. It sorta just seemed like this would happen way in the future some time, but apparently, it was closer than I had realized.

"*The time isn't now, but soon, and I can also linger longer if I go into a sort of hibernation. As long as the crystal is charged with energy, I can hibernate for an extended period of time to lengthen my stay,*" said Selena. "*But we can talk about that after the training and dragon pairing. I feel like I have at least that much stamina to linger.*"

....

I decided not to tell anyone about how the crystal seemed to stir when I played my melody. I had tried it several times since, and it seemed as dead as before.

Vesuvius had landed and strolled over to us. It was

strange to think that this was normal. It wasn't too long ago that I didn't know that dragons existed. It was still even stranger to think that I would be paired with my own dragon. It didn't seem real.

Vesuvius instructed us to hold our palms open, and with a flick of one of his claws, drew some blood for us to apply to the crystals.

I had connected to Larzi since I had no ability to connect to my other crystal. Despite what Vesuvius assured me, I figured that the crystal was dead.

Alan applied his blood to Larzi and focused all of his attention to the crystal. Almost immediately, I felt his presence within the crystal, along with Selena, of course.

"Whoa!" he exclaimed. *"I'm totally in! Nice!"*

"Since you are the crystal holder Marcus, you are able to allow anyone you want to connect with the crystal. You can also block anyone. This is important, because one of the tactics in a battle is for someone to try to take over your crystal. You will need to establish how to recognize Alan when he connects. The easiest way to begin is with a password. No one should know the passwords except you and Alan, and never spoken verbally. Not even Abi and Sabryyna should know. I can't help but know for obvious reasons," said Selena.

"Let's make it totally random," said Alan. *"What's your favorite animal?"*

"Orangutan," I said.

"Think of a random question for me," said Alan.

"What's your favorite food?" I asked.

"Chocolate," said Alan and Selena at the same time.

"So our password is 'Chocolate Orangutan' . That should be random enough," said Alan.

"Try blocking Alan now," instructed Selena. *"Focus on his presence and force him out."*

I narrowed down on Alan's presence, and with a couple of tries was successful at blocking him.

A thought came to me.

"Can I block you? Not that I would, but just curious," I asked.

"You are the crystal holder, so the answer is 'yes'."

Surprisingly, I was able to connect fairly easily to Alan's crystal. It just seemed to be alive and easy to connect to. No surprise, Alan was able to block me on his first try. Abi and Sabryyna were also successful at connecting to each others' crystal. Of course, Abi had experience with this from being Selena's attendant.

"We need to talk about the dragon pairing. We will need to travel through the wormhole on Saturday. The pairing takes two days, so we will need to come up with a reason to miss school on both Monday and Tuesday," said Selena. *"Alan, that mostly means you since Abi, Sabryyna, and Marcus can get excused easier than you. Any ideas?"*

We hatched a plan to have Grandma invite Alan to go with us to Eugene to visit the University of Oregon. That would make it legitimate for us to miss school, since we needed to make the visit on a weekday. We would say that we wanted to leave early so we could spend a day at the Oregon Coast.

When we got home, we pitched the idea to Grandma.

"So, this really is happening?" she asked quietly. "I'm frightened for both you and Alan. Selena was a renowned rider, and we know how that turned out."

Grandma turned to me.

"How do you feel about fighting, Marcus? Do you even know what you're training and fighting for?"

That question stumped me. Up to this point, it all seemed unreal. I mean, even though I went through the wormhole to Vocce, in the back of my mind, it just felt like it would never actually happen. I was silent for a long time.

"Ms. Torrey," said Alan in a voice that was unusually subdued for him, "Abi was able to show us some of her memories. Entire villages were wiped out by the Gonosz. I know that Selena, Abi, and Sabryyna haven't said anything, but I feel like they think that the Vocce are planning on coming here to Earth."

Abi spoke up. "You are correct in that it is a fear of ours. Earth is technically advanced in many ways, but the Gonosz have ways of war that would be very difficult for the military to adapt to."

"But why, children?" asked Grandma. "Why are you chosen as dragon riders over adults?"

"Dragons only pair with one rider in their lifetimes, however dragons have a much longer lifespan than humans, by hundreds of years. That makes it imperative that the riders that are selected are chosen young so that they can maximize the pairing with the dragon," answered Abi.

"I just can't bear the thought of losing Marcus and Alan, too," said Grandma.

I have to admit that I wasn't sure about my participation in this battle. For starters, I couldn't possibly physically fight one of the Gonosz. Having fought (and lost) to several of them, I knew I couldn't last more than a few minutes, and I didn't even want to contemplate how Alan would fare.

"Are we required to go through with all of this? I asked. All eyes, including Alan's, turned to me.

"No," said Abi. "But you better make up your mind. If you pair with a dragon, then back out... Well, I don't need to tell you how devastating that would be for our fighters, especially because there are fewer and fewer dragons made available to us."

The room had a different feel all of a sudden. There was no doubt as to the commitment of Abi and Sabryyna. Even Alan seemed to be all in. I was the only one, aside from Grandma of course, that was unsure.

"What did you think this was all about?" asked Sabryyna fiercely. "What did you think all this training was for? Some kind of game?"

"I don't know what I thought," I said. "Everything just happened so quickly that I just kinda went along with it. Some aspects were fun and exciting, I guess. I just never thought it was for real. I know that sounds strange."

Sabryyna's eyes were drilling holes through me. Alan looked confused. He had made up his mind that he was fully committed. Abi was staring at me thoughtfully.

"We have a couple of days to make a decision," said Selena. *"Let's get some rest and we'll figure out our course of action in the morning."*

The drive to Alan's house was quiet for many moments.

"I didn't know that you had questions, Marcus. I wish you would have told me," said Alan. "If I am to be your attendant, I should know what you're thinking."

"It's just been creeping up on me," I answered. "Now that we're going to get an actual dragon and be expected to go into battle..."

"I just think this is something worth fighting for," said Alan quietly. "It's like Eldon. Whole nations and civilizations can be bullies, too. That's how I see it."

"I know, but what is the reality that we can make a difference?" I asked. "Abi's memories are scary. How do we fight against entire armies?"

"The dragons," Selena said. *"The dragons make a difference. But you will need to go through the training to find out just how effective they are as fighting weapons."*

We pulled up to Alan's home. Immediately, we could tell that something was not right. Emergency vehicles were crowded into the driveway. Flames and smoke were issuing from the house. Even a quick view of the carnage told us that the house couldn't be saved. The car hadn't even come to a full stop before Alan had opened the door and jumped out.

"Is anyone hurt?" he asked on the run. "Please tell me no one is hurt!"

An ambulance was sitting off a little ways from the house. Alan's father jumped out of the back as Alan ran up to him.

"Please, dad! Is everyone alright?" he asked in panic.

"Your mom was burned trying to save Allie and Tim. She should be alright, but she suffered some serious burns." Alan's dad paused. "Allie got burned pretty bad. The fire started near her room. They are taking Allie and mom to the emergency room. I'm going in the ambulance with them. Tim is alright, no injuries. Can you take care of Tim and follow us to the hospital?" Mr. Malloy asked with tears in his eyes.

Alan could only nod his head as a sob escaped his throat. He rushed to hug his dad.

"Don't worry, Mr. Malloy. We'll take care of everything. Just take care of Mrs. Malloy and Allie. We'll grab Tim and bring them after awhile," I said. I had a lump in my throat because the Malloy's seemed like my own family.

"*I can sense that* Vesuvius *is around. He wants to talk with us,*" said Selena.

"*Can we do that some other time? We need to take care of the Malloy's,*" I replied.

"*I think it has something to do with the Malloy's,*" said Selena.

Alan had grabbed Tim who was unhurt, and was in the process of finding the spare diaper bag in the Malloy's mini van.

"I will be right back," I said to Alan. He looked up quizzically, but then returned to the task at hand.

"*Just on the other side of those trees,*" said Selena.

As we cleared the trees, we could see a large object lying on the ground. It was Vesuvius, but a very wounded Vesuvius. Singed marks showed on his sides, and one of his legs had a nasty-looking claw mark.

"*It was the Gonosz. They brought a captured wild dragon. They were controlling him with an electric bridle. He wasn't a dragon that I recognize,*" said Vesuvius.

"*I thought the only way to pair with a dragon was with the crystals,*" I said. "*How were they communicating with the dragon?*"

"*They have some dragons that they have captured that they enslave with the electric bridles. They don't communicate with the dragon. They control through pain and fear. Not as effective as how our riders and dragons are paired, but any dragon is fearsome,"* said Selena.

"The dragon was responsible for the fire," said Vesuvius. *"I was patrolling in the air and sensed that another dragon was in the area. It attacked me before I was fully ready for a fight. I was wounded before it targeted Alan's home. This attack was planned. They knew to target Alan's home."*

We hadn't noticed that Alan had come up behind us, packing Tim. The look on Alan's face told me that he had heard what Vesuvius had said.

"I was able to fight the dragon off before it attacked again, but the home was burning before I was able to disrupt the attack. If the dragon had been able to make a final pass, the fire would have spread too rapidly for Alan's family to escape," said Vesuvius. *"I'm sorry that I wasn't able to do more, Alan."*

"It's not your fault, Suvi. Thanks for defending my family. If you hadn't been here..." Alan's voice trailed off, but his face showed his emotion.

The home ended up being a total loss. Thankfully, Mrs. Malloy and Allie were both in stable condition, with Allie suffering the worst burns. Part of her face was burned pretty badly, and she would wear the scars the rest of her life. Her face and head remained bandaged when we visited. Mrs. Malloy was treated for several days, then released. She chose to stay with Allie on a hospital cot that was brought into Allie's room each night.

Alan, Tim, and Mr. Malloy had stayed at Grandma's house while trying to figure out what to do next with their lives.

One of the sources of concern from the fire marshal was how the fire started. Apparently, there was also an explosion component with the fire. Mr. Malloy operated a small farm on the side of his carpet cleaning business, so he had some tractors and a backhoe that he stored next to the house. He also had a large above-ground gas tank to fill up his farm equipment and his work van. It was discovered that this was the cause of the fire. The above-ground gas tank had exploded, showering the house with a fireball and more raw gas that quickly also caught fire. There was no chance for the house to survive. If it hadn't been for Vesuvius, the Malloy's would have been consumed in the fire, but why did the gas tank explode?

Mr. Malloy had been cleaning the carpets of one of the restaurants in town and had just pulled up to the house after Mrs. Malloy had pulled the kids out and had called 911. At first, Mr. Malloy was suspected of starting the fire, but fortunately there was a camera located in the restaurant parking lot that showed he was indeed loading his van when the emergency call from Mrs. Malloy came in. The fire marshal was certain that the fire was started by someone, since gas tanks don't just blow up. We, of course, knew that he was correct, but couldn't offer any help. That a dragon had started the fire was pretty much the farthest end of the far-fetched spectrum.

"I saw the wild dragon target the tank," said Vesuvius. *"It purposely heated the tank with a fireball, and after it exploded, was turning to make another pass to ignite the rest of the house. It was well-planned. Would have worked if I had been a minute or two later."*

We had taken a couple of days off to take care of the Malloys, and just like that, it was time for us to cross over to Vocce for the dragon pairing. I had almost totally forgotten about the pairing. Taking care of the Malloys seemed more pressing.

"Marcus, can we talk?" asked Selena. She had been hibernating to build crystal strength.

"I still don't know what I should do, if that is what you want to know," I said telepathically.

"That's what I figured," she was silent for a moment. *"Alan plans to attend with or without you. Did you know that?"*

"There wouldn't be any reason for him to attend if I decline being a rider. What use would that serve?" I asked.

"He wants to go through warrior training regardless. Even if you decline, the crystals are yours, as is Alan's. There is power

in the crystals that could make you both effective warriors, even against the inhabitants of Vocce. Crystals are rare indeed," she said.

"Why hadn't he spoken to me about this?" I asked.

"Alan wants you to not feel pressured. His family was attacked, so he is all in because he wants to be able to defend his family should this happen again."

Selena let that set in a moment. I sat in silence thinking over the options.

"Marcus, there's something else," she said, interrupting my thought process. *"You've seen some of the Gonosz strategies. They are ruthless. Even if you decide to back out of being a rider, they will still come after you and Alan."*

"Because of the crystals," I said out loud.

"Yes, because of the crystals. And that's not all. You notice that they went after family members right off the bat, right? This is their favorite strategy. Targeting family members to get what they want, and it nearly always works. Who wants to see their family and friends tortured and killed?" she asked.

"You're trying to tell me that Grandma is in trouble, aren't you?" I asked, knowing the answer already.

"Yes," Selena said with a sigh. *"Grandma is now in trouble, regardless of what you do now. Choose to be a rider, and they come after her, choose to decline, they still come after her. Do you see what I'm getting at?"*

"Sure. That it now doesn't matter what I want. I am locked in whether I want to be or not," there was some bitterness in my reply.

"I won't sugar coat it. Yes. You are locked in. If I hadn't been killed, things would have been pretty normal for you, perhaps, but it was only a matter of time that the Gonosz would find out my true identity and target you and Grandma. Mom and dad were trying to run from that very situation, but they were also discovered and killed. If it were my decision, I would want to at least have the best chance of surviving and protecting my loved ones. A dragon makes a huge difference. That's my advice. It's up to you, of

course."

"We can run, go off grid and leave this all behind," I said.

Selena was again silent for a moment.

"What about Alan? Abi and Sabryyna? Could your con-science let you abandon them? I know you well enough, Marcus Brent Harmon. You wouldn't be able to look at yourself in a mirror for the rest of your life, if you left them to fend for themselves. Especially Alan and the Malloys. You now know that they are targets. They will be attacked again. Will you be able to live with that?"

I felt a lump form in my throat thinking about Alan's family getting hurt again. I knew deep down that they would be targeted again.

"With a dragon, you can at least do something to protect the ones that you love," she said. *"Even if that something doesn't work, it's the only way that you will be able to live with yourself, Marcus. I think you know that I'm right."*

Of course, Selena was right. I, Marcus Brent Harmon, decided that I would go to the dragon pairing, begin the training, and probably fall to my death off of the back of a dragon, gently gliding over a field of daisies and purple pansies. I had no illusions of being some kind of great warrior.

We had employed Grandma in our plan to get out of town. Grandma pretended to want to take me to Eugene to visit the University of Oregon. Alan was invited to go. Alan's parents thought that it would be good for Alan to get his mind off of the fire by doing something "normal." If they only knew. We planned on being away about four days, leaving Saturday and getting back Tuesday night.

Abi and Sabryyna were ready when we swung by their house. The rest of Abi's "family" would remain and continue to watch after the Malloys.

If the Malloys had seen us load Grandma's car, they would have been surprised to see most of our equipment looked more like a camping trip than a campus trip. That, and we headed the wrong direction if we were going to Eugene. After a few minutes, we pulled off at a rest stop where Wynn was waiting.

"We will take good care of your grandma, Marcus. Mrs. Torrey, let me take your bags," he said. They would take Grandma back to their place and she would stay with them until we got back. It would probably be boring, but Grandma saw the reasoning behind our plan and hadn't complained.

And with that, we headed back to my least favorite place in the entire world. We would have to pass by where Selena was murdered by the Gonosz on our way to the wormhole.

Pulling up to the parking area, we spotted Vesuvius who had flown ahead and was now waiting for us.

"I patrolled the area, and it seems quiet. Abi and Sabryyna might scout around quickly on the ground, but I don't sense the wild dragon," he said, then with a huge whoosh, was back into the sky circling the area again.

We started off towards the wormhole in a trot. We were dressed for the woods this time with some camping equipment. I barely felt the added load with all the conditioning we had been doing these past weeks, but I knew the real test would come when we reached Vocce. I knew the others also wondered how I would fare.

Abi and Sabryyna had acted as scouts running up ahead. One would circle back every couple of minutes to check on Alan and I, then run up ahead again. It was amazing just how strong and fit they were.

We knew that the Gonosz had located approximately where our wormhole was, but not the exact location. That it was located halfway down a large cliff helped us, of course.

Unexpectedly, both Abi and Sabryyna returned at the same time, and with a thud, Vesuvius landed, too. They looked concerned.

"They're here," said Vesuvius. *"Only three, but the dragon is with them. You'll have to fight the two while I take care of the dragon and controller."*

"How did they know the timing? asked Selena. *"The date of the pairing was known to only the riders and dragons."*

"We've suspected spies within the clans. It was only a matter of time," said Sabryyna. "We'll have to fight for it."

Vesuvius was looking at me thoughtfully. "Rider, you possess Larzi. Perhaps you can be of assistance to me against the dragon?"

"He's not even remotely ready," said Selena. "He doesn't even know his role of rider."

"This might be a good time for Marcus to learn. This is a wild dragon that is being controlled. Not nearly as dangerous as dragon and rider team," said Vesuvius.

"I guess it's as dangerous on the ground right now as in the air," Selena consented, but I could tell she feared greatly for my safety. "But maybe seeing first hand how dragon and rider work as a team might be beneficial."

"You'll want to mount and hold with your knees directly behind my wings," instructed Vesuvius. "We don't know the reactions of each other, so I will try to fly without much evasive action. Alan, this is also where you will be of use as the attendant. All three of us will access Larzi. Remember Marcus, Larzi is your main focus in battle. You will be fighting much the same as a gunner on an aircraft. You will need to watch in all directions and use the crystal to defend and attack. Alan, you are going to be the most disoriented of us three, because you will be seeing the battle through my eyes. In this way you can direct additional fire and defense using your crystal powers. Do you understand?"

"You know that I can't use Larzi's power very well, right? I'm not so sure of this," I said. I couldn't see how I was going to be of any use in this battle, unless a small spark that could barely start a campfire was urgently needed.

"I will be focused on the dragon. Your job is to keep track of everything around us, in case we're attacked from the ground, or if I somehow lose track of the wild dragon. Having additional eyes in the air is crucial. Alan, it's best that you find a good hiding place and remain in place. This is going to get disorienting very fast."

"From past experience, Alan," interjected Abi "Treat the battle as if you are playing one of your video games. You will be *seeing everything Suvi sees. If you see him targeting the dragon or the ground enemy, use some of your skills from your crystal to assist. Understand?"*

Alan's face was fierce. He was remembering the attack on his family.

"Yeah, I got this," he said.

"Sabryyna and I will lead the enemy and battle away from you, but if we warn you, you will need to disengage with Larzi and fight. We don't expect it to come to that. Sabryyna and I are experienced warriors."

And with that, Captain Barf-Shirt mounted the dragon to do battle.

I connected with Larzi. It was familiar when Alan connected, since he had been connected before, but it was an altogether surprise when Vesuvius connected. His physical presence was scary, but his mental presence within Larzi was even scarier. Not sure how to describe the feeling. He seemed to fill up the crystal and give it life. I felt a huge surge of energy flow through me. Alan must have had the same reaction because he gasped at the sensation.

"Just be my extra set of eyes, Marcus. Alan, get ready," warned Vesuvius.

A second gasp from Alan told me that he was now seeing through the eyes of Vesuvius. Alan had found a hiding place in a clump of bushes. Unless you knew where to look, he was nearly invisible.

"Here we go, Rider. Grip tight with your knees!"

We sprang into the air, and the third gasp I heard was my own as the breath left me from the sudden movement. With several strong flaps of his wings, we were hundreds of feet in the air.

"Whoa!" yelled Alan, his excitement was palpable.

"Begin scanning around and behind you, Marcus," instructed Selena.

Turning, I started scanning behind us, but by doing so, I forgot to grip with my knees and began to slide off to my right.

Instantly, Vesuvius adjusted his flight to compensate and I was upright again.

"You have to grip with your knees at all times," warned Selena. *"Suvi won't be able to help you when we're in battle."*

As if on cue, Vesuvius dove on the wild dragon who appeared below us. The feeling of riding a diving dragon? Like the bottom of the floor just dropped from out beneath you. I may or may not have let out a very unmanly scream. One of the problems with riding a dragon is that there is nothing to grab to hold on to. It's all with the knees.

Vesuvius let a great fireball escape his fiery maw. The heat was tremendous. The wild dragon swerved to escape the fireball. The dragon was larger and faster than Vesuvius, but Vesuvius was more quick and nimble. We were now close enough to the dragon to see it had a rider on its back. As I got an even closer look, I could see a large mechanical halter-like device attached to the dragon, much the same as a horse would have. The rider had two reins in which to direct the dragon. The rider was tugging viciously at the reins, and we were able to see the dragon wince in pain at each tug.

"It's terrified," said Alan. I knew that he was talking about the wild dragon. Its eyes were bulging and scared.

The rider of the wild dragon seemed to be having trouble controlling the dragon. The scared dragon was trying to run away, even though the rider was pulling inhumanly on the reins.

"I've got this," said Alan.

Before I knew what Alan had got, fireballs started firing towards the dragon. The fireballs seemed to appear directly in front of me, about chest level, then shoot off towards the dragon. But the precision was uncanny. Not one of the fireballs struck the frightened dragon, but rather all of them struck the rider who toppled off the back of the dragon limp as a rag doll.

"Yes!" was Alan's exuberant cry.

"Excellent shot, Alan. Alas, it will be all in vain, not targeting the dragon," said Vesuvius.

"*What do you mean?*" asked Alan.

Before anyone could answer, the mechanical halter exploded. The dragon was nearly vaporized from the explosion. A second or two later, we felt the aftershock, along with bits of dragon.

We turned and headed back to where Abi and Sabryyna were. We began circling in hopes of spotting them. I was busy scanning the ground when I caught movement out of my left eye. Looking up, I was surprised to spot another dragon bearing down on us. Fireballs much like Alan's were hurtling down towards us.

"*Dive,*" I yelled. Without hesitation, Vesuvius dropped out of the sky, my heart in my stomach once again.

The fireballs passed over us, followed by one of the largest dragons I had ever seen. On its back was another rider, but there was no mechanical halter attached to the dragon, and this dragon was not scared or trying to run away.

"*You've chosen the wrong side, Vesuvius.*"

"*We thought you to be dead, uncle,*" answered Vesuvius.

"*Oh no. Not dead. Wounded terribly by your father and my own sister, but not dead,*" answered the large dragon.

"*You were trying to steal the hatchlings, uncle. They had to stop you,*" Vesuvius was now flying hard in a straight direction away from the battle.

With little effort, the larger dragon caught up and trailed us.

"*Who is the rider?*" asked the dragon. "*He is not one of us, and he appears to have gotten sick on his own clothing.*"

So, yeah. That had happened.

"*He is my brother, Randolph,*" answered Selena.

"*Ah,*" said the dragon, "*another mystery solved. I wondered why Vesuvius was hosting another rider after losing his paired rider. Most unusual. I believe you and I have some unfinished business, Selena?*"

Alan had been trying his best to hit the dragon and rider with his precision fireballs, but they all appeared to be deflected effortlessly. They would head straight towards the dragon, then veer off sharply.

"*And it appears that the rider has an attendant. Very fine accuracy, but not much power. An attendant in training. Must be a new rider then. Your brother isn't the same caliber of rider as you were, Selena. Shame. I need the practice after such a long recovery,*" said Randolph.

"*Now, nephew. You have a choice. Land and hand over your rider and his crystal, or, as much as it pains me, I will have to kill you and take the crystal by force. Truthfully, I don't care either way.*"

By way of answer, Vesuvius dove straight down without warning. "*Hold on, Rider! I can't outrun Randolph. Our only hope is out-maneuvering him.*"

Fireballs began to pass by us, some so close that I could feel the searing heat and hear the sizzle.

"*Abi, Selena, Alan! What is your situation?*" asked Selena.

"*We've fought off the ground force. They escaped, but both were wounded pretty bad. Rendezvousing with Alan in about four minutes,*" was Abi's reply.

"*We're going to need to run. Randolph is here,*" said Selena.

"*We saw him. We thought he was dead,*" said Abi.

"*Apparently, just wounded. We're going to fly through the wormhole, but Suvi will need to seal it permanently. You'll need to use the alternate wormhole. You remember where it is?*" asked Selena.

"*Yes, of course. Too bad about the primary wormhole, but necessary. We'll be a day late, as you know,*" said Abi. "*Good luck.*"

"*The alternate wormhole delivers the traveler further away from the clans than the primary one,*" Selena explained as Vesuvius performed his aerial acrobatics. My shirt now looked like tie-dye, and I had left all my gear with Alan, so I would get to wear the same clothes for the next couple of days. Captain Barf-Shirt strikes again!

With a series of crazy twists and turns, Vesuvius went into a steep dive. Fireballs started passing by, each seemed closer than the other. Risking falling off Vesuvius, I turned to see Randolph line up directly behind us. For certain he would be able to hit us with one of the tremendous fireballs.

All I was able to do with the crystal was spark a fire. Using Alan's trick when I was lassoed by Eldon and his pal, I focused on the rider, or rather, I focused on the rider's backside. A surge of energy shot through my body. At first I thought I had failed, but then the rider started to slap himself vigorously, obviously trying to extinguish the flames. I had never felt that much power surge through me when I had previously produced a spark with the crystal, so I imagine that the spark had to be substantial. The distraction caused the rider to become unseated, and he began to plummet to the ground. To save the rider, Randolph had to disengage from the fight with Vesuvius.

With a few more twists and turns, Vesuvius once more dove, but this time I knew where we were. I could spot the area where Selena had been killed, and then the cliff. It was terrifying at the speed in which we dove through the wormhole. Instantly, I knew we weren't in Kansas anymore,Toto, as the weight of the intensified gravity hit me full-force.

Spinning, Vesuvius turned to face the swirling wormhole. Fire bellowed from his mouth that he directed at the wormhole. Second by second, it faded until there was no more wormhole. He continued breathing fire on the space.

"I think we're good, Suvi," said Selena.

The fire stream stopped, but Vesuvius refused to look away from where the wormhole had been, obviously fearful that Randolph would be able to find and open the portal.

"Your quick thinking saved us, Marcus," said Selena.

"A move worthy of a rider," added Vesuvius without looking away.

"Find out how Alan, Abi and Sabryyna are doing, Marcus," commanded Selena.

"What...and just how am I supposed to do that?" I asked.

"You don't listen well, do you? I told you before that being connected to some crystals, especially Larzi, allows you to commu-

nicate with whoever else is also connected, even through the wormhole," replied Selena. "But you as the guardian of the crystal must initiate the communication."

"I can try, I guess, but you know I'm not good at those kinds of things," I said, doubtfully.

"Can you feel Alan's presence within the crystal?" asked Selena.

Closing my eyes, I reached out to the crystal. Surprisingly, I was able to detect Alan's presence in the crystal.

"Yes, he's still there all right," I informed Selena.

"Direct your thoughts to his presence within the crystal," she said.

Closing my eyes again, I connected with Larzi again and found Alan's presence. Concentrating, I focused my attention on Alan.

"Uh, testing, testing, one, two, three..." I said, feeling kind of silly at the weirdness of it all.

"Dude, it's about time! We've been waiting for you," said a concerned Alan.

"How did you know I was going to contact you this way?" I asked.

"You don't listen very well do you?" That made it official. I don't listen very well. "That's one of the greatest powers of Larzi. Of course we were waiting for your communication. Are you alright? I was able to see through Vesuvius's eyes until you passed through the portal. Nice move with the spark, by the way, amigo."

"We're good. Suvi sealed the wormhole. We're getting ready to move right now," I said.

"We're on the move right now, too. We've got to hike fifteen miles before we get to the alternative wormhole, then we have another half day's travel once through. We'll get there just in time for the pairing. Ask Selena about what the return plan is. We will be late returning if we have come back the same way," said Alan.

I relayed the question to Selena.

"Oh, we'll be able to get back in plenty of time," she said cryptically. "Tell Alan that we will contact him at the top of each *hour to get updates and make sure each other is alright."*

Vesuvius had finally turned his gaze away from the vanished portal.

"Rider, I will give you a ride to save your endurance. How do you feel right now, physically?" Vesuvius asked.

"Better than last time, but it still is difficult to move around. I can tell that I will still get very tired," I answered.

"I will allow you to ride again, then. It is best that we land short of our destination and have you complete the remainder walking. It will elevate your status, which is desperately needed," he said. *"But first, one thing, Rider."*

"What's that?" I asked.

With a swipe of his tail, Vesuvius knocked me into the nearby stream.

"And don't come out until you've washed the vomit off your shirt and pants. I have an image to uphold," said Vesuvius with a laugh.

For several minutes, I soaked and scrubbed my clothing. When I finally got out of the water, Vesuvius had started a campfire. I quickly stripped to my underwear and let my shirt and pants dry on some river rocks that were next to the fire. After an hour, the clothing was dry enough for us to continue. It felt good to think that I would be able to put my best foot forward this time, and not be Captain Barf-shirt. I just needed the change of clothing from Alan to complete the metamorphosis.

Clambering on the back of Vesuvius, we once again took to the air.

"Is there anything I need to know about the pairing ceremony?" I asked Selena.

"The ceremony is secret. It is not discussed outside of the ceremony amphitheater. You will see. There are precautions that the dragons take in order to keep just anyone from pairing with a juvenile dragon," she said.

"It is a necessity," Vesuvius said, *"without it, more and more of our hatchlings would be stolen."*

The ride was smooth, and the evening was beginning

to cool off. I was nervous and worried about the pairing ceremony. It just sounded like a good opportunity to be made to look ridiculous again. I was just hoping that we would meet up with Alan and the girls so that I could retrieve a change of clothing. Even though I had bathed, a change of clothing would still have been welcome. There was significant singeing in both my pants and shirt that left gaping holes.

I began to take notice of the new world. It was really beautiful. It must have been autumn, the same as on earth, because many of the tree leaves were multi-colored. In addition to the yellows, reds, and browns of our earth trees, many of the trees on Vocce were blues, purples, whites, and ebony. It was a palette of colors from the air.

Passing by a waterfall, I noticed that the hue of the water was a deep turquoise color.

"The minerals in the water cause the coloration," said Vesuvius.

We flew steadily. Soon Vesuvius was circling over a meadow.

"Hold on again," warned Vesuvius.

We went into a steep dive. It seemed to be one of Vesuvius's signature moves, and it always made me feel queasy.

With a jolt, we landed on the edge of the meadow.

"We'll walk for the remainder. Although we are still some distance away, I will be more readily seen if we're in the air," said the dragon. *"Lean on me when you feel tired."*

Although I was much more fit than last time, I fear that I leaned on Vesuvius for ninety percent of our short hike, but I did feel accomplished that I was able to at least walk part of the distance this time.

CHAPTER FIFTEEN

VESUVIUS' LAST BATTLE

Our plan was to hike to within a short distance of the pairing ceremony and camp that night, allowing the rest of our party to catch up with us. We had talked several times over the last couple of hours, and they were making good time. Fortunately, they were able to find the alternative wormhole without issue, and were now also in Vocce. It would take them several hours to rendezvous with us.

I had a watch that had an alarm on it, and I set it to go off at the top of the hour. It seems that I had barely closed my eyes when it went off.

"Uh, testing, testing, one, two, three. You know you need unique New York. Rubber baby buggy bumpers. Come in little buddy. Talk to me," I began.

We had set our watches to exact times on one of our first conversations, and consequent communications had been right on schedule.

Alan didn't answer, but I wasn't too concerned. Everything had been going as scheduled. I gave him a couple of moments.

"Rubber Ducky, this is Porky Pig, you got your ears on?" I asked.

Nothing. I decided to wait a few more minutes, but it was disconcerting.

"Hey, Alan! Need you to talk with me buddy. What's up with you guys?" I asked. Now I was scared. Selena was hibernating, saving her crystal energy for tomorrow's big doings. Vesuvius had taken to the air to take a look around.

"*Hey, Suvi. I'm having trouble contacting Alan. He's not answering, and it's 8 minutes after the hour.*" There was real panic in my voice, now.

With a thud, Vesuvius landed.

"*Rouse Selena,*" were his instructions. I noticed that he didn't bother to reassure me. He had gone right into action.

"*Selena, rise and shout!*" I urged.

"*What is it?*" she asked, instantly aware.

"*It's almost ten minutes after the hour, and no Alan,*" I said.

She also didn't spend any energy trying to downplay the situation. Selena also went into immediate action.

"*Suvi, they might need us. Do you know the route they will be taking?*" asked Selena.

"*Yes. There are only two direct routes. One takes longer than the other. I assume they will be following the river. It is the fastest way,*" he said. He instantly crouched down in the manner he always did when he wanted me to mount.

Without a word, I sprung onto his back. Again, the same sickening rush as he sprung into the air. Since it was dark, I wasn't able to get my bearings. The nausea was more intense that way.

I had been on Vesuvius's back several times, but I don't think that I've ever flown so fast. The wind whipped my face and caused my eyes to tear up.

"*Close your eyes and connect to Larzi,*" instructed Selena. "*Just like Alan, you can see through Suvi's eyes. It will help with the nausea while flying in the dark.*"

Closing my eyes, I connected with Larzi. Concentrating on Vesuvius, I began to see blips of light. Suddenly, I was able to see exactly through Vesuvius's eyes. Even though it was dark, everything was incredibly clear. I was able to see details on the ground, even though it was night with only one of Vocce's moons above. No wonder Alan was so accurate while he was fighting. Even though we were several hundred feet in the air, I was able to spot field mice darting in and out of the vegetation below. Selena was right. It helped with the nausea, being able to see as clearly as I did.

A large river came into view.

"That's what we're looking for," said Vesuvius. *"Look for movement. They will most likely be on the run."*

"Try contacting Alan again," said Selena.

"We're here, buddy. Talk to me," I said. Nothing. Fear for Alan, Abi, and Sabryyna was very real right now. I know that we were pretty fortunate to escape Randolph, and I was sure that he wouldn't fall for some silly trick like I had pulled.

One of the frustrating things about looking through Vesuvius's eyes was that it was like watching television. I had no ability to pan around or look at what I wanted to. I was limited to whatever Vesuvius was looking at. During a daylight fight, it would be better for me to be able to scan around independently, giving us another set of eyes. In the dark like this, I couldn't see anything, so using Vesuvius's vision was the next best thing.

Alongside the river was an obvious trail. We followed the trail, sometimes slowing to circle a heavily forested area.

"Watch out!" cried Selena.

Vesuvius seemed to just drop out of the sky as a giant fireball soared over us. We could feel the tremendous heat and hear the sizzle of the fireball. The sensation of Vesuvius's evasive maneuvers were worse than any carnival ride. The bottom just seemed to fall out from under me, and it wasn't until Vesuvius leveled out just about the tree tops, that I was able to gain my seating again. I tightened my grip with my legs, anticipating that our aerobatics were just beginning.

"Quick little reptile, aren't you?" said Randolph. *"Too bad that you are on the wrong side of this war. You might have some potential. I could train you to be quite the fighter, should you do the smart thing and join me."*

"There's no way that I would join the Gonosz. They enslave both dragons and humans. I would rather die!" said Vesuvius defiantly.

"*That can be arranged, young one. A shame, but you in-sist on being stupid,*" Randolph replied, accompanied by several fireballs that barely missed us. Only Vesuvius's skilled flying kept us safe. We darted through the trees and followed the con-tours of the ground below. It made for some scary flying, his belly was brushing the tops of the treetops, we were so low.

"*One of the properties that Larzi gives the rider is night vision and magnification. We could really use another set of eyes, Marcus. I am limited to your vision limitations. If you can access the amplified vision, we could have all three sets of eyes working while in battle,*" said Selena. "*It's more difficult to connect to than just using Suvi's vision, but it can be the difference needed in this battle.*"

I didn't want to disengage from Vesuvius' sight because it really did help with the nausea, and furthermore, I had no faith in my ability to use the crystal. It just seemed out of my ability range, but it did make sense that I should at least try.

I was already connected to Larzi, so I disconnected from Vesuvius's vision. It seemed like total darkness enveloped me, but in truth I was just seeing through my normal human-limited vision. In a matter of seconds I began to feel sick to my stomach flying blind. It was so disorienting.

I tried exploring Larzi, but wasn't even sure what I was looking for.

A quick, sudden, drop almost dislodged me from Vesu-vius's back as another fireball flew past us. The brightness of the fireball completely ruined any night vision that I had, and I saw spots when I closed my eyes. Several other evasive maneu-vers was all it took for me to ruin the bath I had taken earlier. Captain Puke-Shirt to the rescue!

"*Think of what you need, which is amplified vision, and ex-plore the crystal with that need in mind,*" instructed Selena.

It started with fleeting peripheral movements. I would catch something out of the corner of my eyes, but whenever I turned to look directly at whatever had caught my attention, it would disappear.

Randolph must have come up and was flying parallel to us, because out of my side vision, I was able to see his form. His huge wings flapped powerfully. Carefully, I turned slowly to try to bring him into my forward vision. It took a huge amount of concentration, but I finally was able to bring him into focus. And what focus it was! Even though it was almost completely dark, I was able to see features as if I were still looking through Vesuvius' eyes.

"You did it, Marcus!" shouted Selena.

Randolph was having difficulty finding an opening in which to breathe a fireball at us. Vesuvius was weaving in and out of the trees and flying the contours of the earth. With my enhanced vision, I was able to see where we were going. This improved the nausea thing, but I still felt twinges as we dodged up and down, right and left.

Randolph began to crowd us. His powerful wings allowed him to keep up, Vesuvius's only advantage was to stay quick and nimble, darting here and there keeping the larger dragon at bay. Whenever Vesuvius lost Randolph with his quick maneuvering, Randolph would launch himself high in the air so that he could survey where we were. He would then dive on us, causing Vesuvius to swerve radically to avoid the attacks from above.

"This is where you are my eyes, Rider!" shouted Vesuvius. *"Watch attacks from above. Randolph is clever. He will attack from the sides and below given the chance!"*

"My sight is as good as yours now," said Selena. *"I will scan backwards, you watch forwards. Keep your eyes moving, watch your peripheral for movement."*

It was uncanny how many angles Randolph was able to try an attack from. He constantly attacked from a different direction or altitude. If Vesuvius had been less nimble in the air, we surely would have been killed a dozen times over, but he was able to dodge out of the way of the fireballs seemingly at the last second.

"Such a shame," said Randolph. *"You fly like my sister.*

You know that the Gonosz have a bounty on her? She was one of the most dangerous dragons they had ever encountered. Such as shame."

Randolph must have been trying to lull us with his tale. Randolph's huge form appeared directly in front of us. Before we could dodge, he had breathed two huge fireballs. We were taken unaware, partially because of the story, but mostly because we hadn't expected that he would be fast enough to get directly in front of us.

Dodging the first fireball put us broadside of the great dragon. Instead of another fireball, he swiped us with his massive tail. Vesuvius was swatted out of the sky like a fly. We crashed to the ground, but before we hit, Vesuvius folded his wings around me to protect both me and the crystal holding Selena. Even still, the impact was terrible, Vesuvius letting go with a bellow of pain.

I was able to scramble free of the wings of Vesuvius, and I began to scan the air for Randolph, knowing that he would now attack.

"No!" shouted Selena *"he's hurt Marcus! Suvi is hurt!"*

Turning, I could see what she meant. Vesuvius was struggling to get up, but both wings were crumpled, and his right hind quarter was bleeding profusely. The slashes were literally inches from where I was perched as his rider. Randolph had been going for a twofer but had missed me barely, largely due to Vesuvius's skill at flying.

"Suvi!" shouted Selena. *"Stay still my friend! We will defend you! Stay still! You're hurt!"*

I had sprinted to Vesuvius. He looked up at me, his eyes showing agony and sorrow.

"I would have flown beside you and your new dragon with pride, Marcus. My one regret is that I can't be your mentor," he said to me.

"Please don't talk like that, Suvi!" whispered Selena. I could feel her heart breaking for her dragon and friend. *"Hold on dear friend. We will fight."*

"You will die!" said Randolph as he landed with a large crash. With all my might, I tried to summon a fireball, but all that appeared was a small spark that fizzled out before it even reached the rider on Randolph's back.

"Pathetic. One would never guess that you were the brother of Selena. She was a warrior, you are a useless child. Your parents were right to hide you, so you couldn't bring them shame." Randolph lowered his head so that we were now face to face. It was then that I noticed that one eye had been severely injured. I could tell that it had been bleeding profusely. His good eye showed no mercy, his breath smelled of brimstone.

His eye dropped to my chest where I wore the two crystals.

"You know, these are where riders get their real powers from. As you can see, my rider is mostly for additional eyes and ears, but otherwise useless," he said.

The rider remained still, his face blank. If he was insulted by Randolph's remarks, he was remarkably good at concealing it.

Vesuvius's breath was now labored, his great chest heaving like bellows.

"Oh, Suvi!" whispered Selena *"don't leave me dear friend."*

"Selena..." whispered Vesuvius back.

"Touching," taunted Randolph. He was now towering above us. *"When you are dead, I will be sending your dear mother your severed head, nephew. Shame. You showed skill and promise."*

Raring back, Randolph prepared to strike, his neck held high, his terrible mouth opened to bite and tear us. We were helpless against such a monster.

Randolph's eye locked onto mine. I knew he would kill me first.

With a roar, Randolph slashed down with his massive head, rows of teeth exposed.

As quick as lightning, Vesuvius sprang from the ground, his own teeth exposed. Before Randolph could react, Vesuvius' teeth sank into the larger dragon's neck. It wasn't a killing blow, however. Randolph's neck was so massive that Vesuvius was only able to wrap his jaws part way around the older dragon's neck. It effectively cut off his air, but wasn't enough to kill him instantly.

The two dragons struggled furiously, and although clearly wounded and physically outmatched, Vesuvius held his hold on Randolph's neck. Randolph combated Vesuvius' stranglehold by using his huge hind claws to dig into Vesuvius's unprotected chest and stomach. Great slash marks appeared, rivers of blood ran freely down Vesuvius's chest and flanks, but still he would not let go. Little by little, Randolph faltered. Both beasts not giving up, fighting to the very end.

Soon, it became too much. Randolph crashed to the ground, his mouth wide open grotesquely, desperate for air, Vesuvius still clinging to his neck.

"Mercy!" Randolph cried, startling me. Of course he could still communicate telepathically, even with Vesuvius's death grip.

"Like the mercy you showed us, uncle?" asked Vesuvius, his great sides heaving with exertion and pain.

With a tremendous effort, Vesuvius snapped the neck of the larger dragon. Randolph's eyes went wide, then rolled back into his head, life quickly leaving him. Still, Vesuvius wouldn't relinquish his hold.

"Suvi, he's dead," sobbed Selena *"Randolph is dead my dear, dear, friend. You did that! You defeated Randolph! You can let go now. We will find a healer. You'll be fine, my dear friend!"*

An audible chuckle issued from Vesuvius.

"Tiny Rider, even the best healer in all of Vocce could do nothing for me now," he said to Selena, the love in his voice for my sister broke my heart.

"And you, Marcus. I'm sorry that I failed you. We would have been a good pair, dragon and warrior, you and me," he said, sorrow in his voice.

"Never!" I said, *"Never have you failed me, Suvi! It is me who caused this! If I could only have been more useful! I can't even*

shoot a good fireball!"

My vision spotted movement at the edge of the meadow that we were in. I sprang to my feet, ready to defend my friend from an additional attack. The sudden movement made me remember that the gravity on Vocce was not my friend. The excitement of the fight had given me a jolt of adrenaline, but that was quickly wearing off, and I felt the full-force of gravity. Stumbling, I fell headlong into some weeds. I looked up to see the outline of someone in the wooded area across the meadow.

Out stepped Abi, followed by Sabryya, who was carrying Alan. His head was bandaged. There was a red spot where the blood had soaked through, but he was conscious and aware.

"Quick, put me down next to Suvi," shouted Alan. *"I can help him."*

Sabryyna trotted over with Alan, setting him gently by the injured dragon.

"Save your strength, young healer," said Vesuvius, nuzzling Alan affectionately with his snout. *"I'm beyond the help of anyone."*

Ignoring Vesuvius, Alan began to frantically look over the dragon's wounds. When he discovered the damage that Randolph had done to his chest and stomach, Alan sat down hard, covering his face with his hands, his chest heaving with sorrow.

"Come, come, lad! Don't be sorrowed," said Vesuvius, his body visibly getting weaker and weaker.

"You saved my family, Suvi. And Marcus and Selena, who are just as much family as the ones back on earth!" sobbed Alan. *"I can never repay that!"*

"You can repay me by staying with the ones that I love, healer," Vesuvius's voice now growing weaker, too.

Alan couldn't do anything, but nod vigorously.

"Now Abi, you were my attendant. Please sing me to sleep? One last time, friend?" Vesuvius asked.

"Of course, Suvi," she said, sitting down next to the

dragon, her arm draped over his neck. I sat down and took the great dragon's head in my lap, knowing instinctively that this is what Selena wanted me to do.

I don't know what I was expecting, hearing Abi sing, but I don't have words to explain what happened.

Her voice was as melodic as I thought it would be, but she was also able to harmonize telepathically. She was, in effect, singing a duet with herself.

> *See yon the pinewoods, draw in deeply the sea,*
> *The feel of rich soil, the joy to soar free.*
> *Small sparrow in flight, the might of the bear,*
> *Dancing and singing, no more sorrows we share.*

I was awestruck at the beauty. And just when I thought nothing could be more moving, she showed us memories of Vesuvius and Selena through the years as she remembered them. I have never experienced such terrible beauty in all of my life. Lost in that world, I stroked Vesuvius's head, a deep contented rumble issuing from deep within him.

I don't know when the song ended. Abi had continued to hum the melody long after the verses ended. It seemed an eternity. It seemed a mere second ago.

Looking down, I stared into the lifeless eyes of my friend, the dragon.

CHAPTER SIXTEEN

DRAGON PAIRING

We sat in silence for a very long while. It was Alan who asked the obvious question.

"What about Randolph's rider?"

Scrambling to our feet, we took to the woods to find the warrior. After searching for over an hour, it was the consensus that he had escaped, and was making his way back to the Gonosz. He would report the death of both Randolph and Vesuvius, and perhaps be returning with reinforcements to capture us. I had taken it as easy as I could, looking for the missing rider, anticipating that I now couldn't rely on Vesuvius to give me a lift. Captain Puke-Shirt was on his own. I was now also covered in the blood and gore that were remnants of the dragon battle.

Since Abi and Sabryyna had to carry Alan after the attack, they had to ditch all but the essentials, which was food, water, sleeping bags, and tent. All the clothing was left by the trail. I guess it wasn't meant for me to have a shred of dignity in front of my peers. We didn't have the time to wash up since we now had to walk back to the pairing grounds. We would be lucky, indeed, to make it in time.

"We had just come through the wormhole," Sabryyna was explaining their attack to Selena and I as we were walking. "We didn't have time to react before Randolph was upon us. I had gone through first, followed by Alan and Abi. The rider targeted Alan, as both Abi and I fought the more dangerous Randolph. Alan caused a fireball to explode within the armor of the rider. It was his screams that caused Randolph to lose his focus. He was forced to stop Alan from further harming the rider, which he did with a blow of his tail which knocked Alan out. We both mounted an attack at the same time, Abi going after the eyes of Randolph, I after his softer underbelly. I believe that Abi may have wounded one of his eyes rather severely," she reported.

"She did get his eye. I saw it up close when he attacked us," I said. "And good she did. It gave us a chance to run and hide while his rider attended to his wounds. Fortunately, Abi was aware of several hiding places. We were able to get away and tend to Alan. They searched for several hours. I guess they figured that we had a set destination and went up ahead to intercept us, and stumbled upon you," she said.

Even though I was in much better shape than I was the last time I visited Vocce, it was still hard going. Plus, we were behind schedule, having to battle Randolph and all. It would take us the remainder of the night, plus a good couple hours in the morning. We would make it in time, but not by much. I couldn't bear the thought of showing up with vomit and dragon gore on my shirt again, but it couldn't be helped.

Our stops were frequent, but short. Just enough for me to catch my breath and take a drink, then we would be off again. I had hated the conditioning that we had done, but was grateful for it now. Even though Alan was still hurt, he was a trooper and marched with us with a fierce determination.

We were within a mile of the pairing grounds when I spotted several dragons circling the skies. They spotted us at the same time, and changed course to meet us. I recognized one of the dragons to be Lowry, Vesuvius's father. Even from the great distance, I could see the concern in his face. Great flaps of his wings brought him to us in a very short amount of time.

Landing, he silently looked us over. Our physical condition and the fact that Vesuvius wasn't with us told a story that I'm sure he feared.

"*It was Randolph,*" said Selena quietly. She hadn't said much during our trek. I knew that my sister was hurting for

Vesuvius, much the same as we hurt from the death of our parents.

"He attacked us on both Earth and here. He has a reliable wormhole, apparently," she said.

Lowry listened without a word as Selena detailed the events. Great tears dropped from the eyes of the dragon.

"You'll want to recover Vesuvius, of course," said Selena. Upon completing her instructions of where to find Vesuvius, the large dragon launched into the air without having said a word, where he met Sharry, Vesuvius' mother, who had arrived and had listened to Selena's story while circling above. The two flew off in great haste to recover their son.

"A loss of a dragon is always terrible, but the loss of Vesuvius is especially horrible for the dragons as he was the next in line to take over leadership from Lowry. Both Lowry and Sharry are getting to the age that the transfer of power is made," said Abi. "Without a direct line of succession, there could be turmoil within the dragon clans."

Our arrival was met in silence by the other riders and attendants. I'm sure that word of Vesuvius had long ago reached them. Many of the dragons that we had seen at the gathering were there. Selena informed us that the parents of the hatchlings would also be in attendance and were already at the grounds.

"When you are paired, the parents will give the new dragon its dragon name, which only the dragons will know, so it is tradition that you give the dragon the name by which all others will refer to it," said Selena.

"I sorta wondered how Vesuvius got his name," said Alan. *"It's kind of an Earth-specific name."*

Qurum stepped forward. *"Normally, Lowry would conduct these ceremonies, but I'm sure you can understand that he and Sharry will not be in attendance today. We would wait for their return, but it is evident that time is of the essence in light of the recent attacks. Orthu will preside over the pairing ceremony."*

Orthu was one of the dragons that had been in attendance at the last gathering. He was large and powerful.

"Will the riders and their attendants please assemble," he said.

I had been kind of hiding behind Abi and Sabryyna. As expected, the other riders and attendants were dressed like warriors. With Selena's advice, I had planned to wear Grandpa Torrey's Highland dress garb. We had packed away a kilt, shirt, jacket, bodice, head wear, and knee socks. I had tried it on before our trip and was pleased with how I looked. It was how a warrior should look, in my opinion. Now I was wearing hiking boots, Levis, and of course a tee-shirt that looked like a horrible tie-dye experiment gone wrong.

As we stepped in line, I saw that Kal made a point to stand next to me. His face showed his disdain for me.

"Vesuvius made a mistake protecting you," he said under his breath. "Such a waste. It would have been better had he let you get killed and another real rider chosen in your stead. You can't even manage to dress like one who is worthy of being a rider," he said with a sneer.

Abi couldn't have heard Kal, but she suddenly appeared between us, elbowing Kal out of the way.

Kal snorted with humor.

"That's right. Let the outcast fight your battles. Can't wait for rider training. Sometimes accidents happen, you know," he said chuckling.

"Let the pairing ceremony begin," said Orthu. *"You will enter the hatchery one at a time, with your respective attendants, to be paired with a dragon. Make sure that you and your attendant both access your crystals before entering. Once in, it is important to study each of the young dragons. Dragons have different abilities and characters, as do humans. Dragons will be drawn to the capabilities of your crystals. The right dragon will enhance the abilities of your crystals. The best pairing occurs when both dragon and rider choose each other. Choose wisely."*

We were instructed to line up and follow the dragons to the actual hatchery. Of course it was up a steep hill. Even though it was only a couple of hundreds of yards, I was breathing hard and sweating profusely, making my shirt even less appealing. I hadn't thought that was possible.

Topping the hill, I found that it was an extinct volcano. After climbing the hill, I found myself now dropping down into the crater. It was a naturally protected area. At the very bottom were assembled the young dragons. I could tell that they were young, only the size of a large horse. There were about thirty dragons to choose from, and they were untamed and wild-looking. Some were snarling and biting at each other. One of the largest dragons had another by the tail and was savagely shaking its head, as if to tear the tail clean off. A sharp bark from Orthu caused the large dragon to release the other dragon's tail. The terrified dragon ran to the far side of the field where it sat down and nursed its wounded tail, sadly whimpering to itself.

"The young dragons are untamed and don't have developed communication skills," said Selena to Alan and I. *"They have been flying for about six months now, and are just large enough to take on a rider. It is your job to teach them both to communicate and to become a fighting unit. Those tasks are relegated to the rider to build rapport with the dragon. It is one of the reasons that dragon, rider, and attendants are so close...."*

I could feel Selena's sorrow as she remembered her own experiences with Vesuvius. This day would be particularly difficult for her.

Chayl and his attendant, Leor, were chosen to go first. We were permitted to watch as the two wandered in among the dragons. They would stop now and again, when one of the dragons caught one of their attention.

At first, the dragons paid little attention to either Chayl or Leor, but little by little, a few of the dragons would perk up as either one passed by. One smallish red dragon in particular seemed to pay attention to Chayl. The dragon intently watched Chayl as he walked around the holding area.

As Chayl was passing by the red dragon for the third

time, he looked thoughtfully at the dragon, but turned to inspect another dragon. This time the dragon stood and made a strange mewling sound, completely focused on Chayl.

Leor had been watching the exchange.

"Chayl, I think we need to take a good look at this red female. She seems to be alerting you."

Chayl turned and looked at the dragon, their eyes locking. Slowly Chayl walked forward, his hand extended. He was holding his crystal out to the dragon. The dragon disengaged from the other dragons and crept forward, her nose in the air, testing the scent of the unfamiliar humans. When she came within arms reach of Chayl, she focused in on the crystal.

Chayl slowly placed the crystal on the ground and stepped back. After testing the scent of the crystal for a few more moments, the dragon stepped back, sizing up both Chayl and Leor. Then, filling her lungs with a large breath, she breathed fire on the crystal until it made the same popping sound as it did when Vesuvius breathed fire on Larzi. Leor quickly placed his crystal on the ground, and the dragon also breathed fire on it, accompanied by the same popping sound.

The transformation of dragon, rider, and attendant was visible. They stood staring into each others' eyes for several moments. Finally, the red dragon stepped forward and nuzzled Chayl who scratched the dragon's ears and snout. The same deep rumble of contentment that I heard with Vesuvius in his last moments, could be heard coming from the red dragon. The pairing was complete.

"*Selena, I can't even connect with my crystal. How do Alan and I choose a dragon?*" I asked.

"*It will be more difficult, but not impossible. Dragons are alerted to the crystals. It just helps for you to be connected to them. It amplifies the properties of the crystal. Take your time, watch the dragons to see if any are alert to either you or Alan.*"

I suddenly had a fear that none of the dragons would choose me or Alan. I wouldn't if I were a dragon. What did we have to offer compared to the other riders?

Chayl and Leor, now followed closely by the red dragon, were escorted to an area in which some of the dragons had congregated. From the dragons stepped two dragons, one red and another larger green one. The three dragons nuzzled each other, then looked to be in conversation with each other. When the communication was over, the red dragon bowed her head in acknowledgment and returned to where Chayl and Leor were standing.

Chayl stepped forward and addressed the crowd.

"As per tradition, I now give this dragon her warrior name. She will be known as 'Sjer-berha' meaning 'Wise One' in the ancient language."

At the sound of her warrior name, the red dragon reared up and breathed a large fireball into the air.

Panic hit me again. I had forgotten about having to name the dragon. It seemed that I was unqualified on every level to be a dragon rider.

"Alan, I totally forgot about the naming thing. Any ideas?" I asked.

"It's kind of the sole responsibility of the rider, Marcus. You choose each other then you come up with the name based on first impressions," he answered. Great help he was.

"Selena?" I plead.

"Alan's right, Marcus. It's your sole responsibility. Don't worry. Something will come to you."

Abi and Sabryyna were next. The moment they stepped into the holding area, a sleek yellow-colored dragon shot out from the other young dragons. It came to stop directly in front of Abi, and they both stared into each other's eyes, as did Chayl and his dragon.

Without so much as looking at another dragon, Abi and Sabryyna offered their crystals to the yellow dragon. It immediately breathed fire on the crystals. Abi and Sabryyna took positions on either side and walked over to the awaiting parents.

The dragon family followed the same ritual.

"I now give this dragon her warrior name," said Abi *"She will be known as 'Hera'sha'i, meaning 'Noble Queen' in the ancient language."*

Hera'sha'i also stood and blasted the air with a massive fireball at the sound of her name.

Kal and Kylor strode forward next. Kal had been studying all the dragons intently the entire time.

"Watch," said Selena, *"He will pick the largest and strongest-looking dragon. It's all about physical strength with that clan,"* and she was right. Kal marched into the holding area and sized up several of the largest dragons, totally ignoring two medium-sized dragons that had alerted to him. The three large dragons were magnificent. They exuded power and strength, but initially did not pay any attention to Kal. I had only met Kal once before, but I could tell that this irritated him.

Kylor had noticed that several of the other dragons had alerted on Kal.

"Brother, there are several dragons here that you should consid..." he began.

"Not interested. We are going to war with the Gonosz. My dragon will fit my specifications," he said.

Kal continued to walk around the three large dragons trying to make a connection with them. Finally, the largest dragon turned his head and sized up Kal. It was the spitting image of Orthu, only this dragon had a cruel look about him. The dark gray dragon was the one that had been tormenting the other dragon as we entered the holding area. Its movements were quick and powerful. It was well-muscled and looked to be an enormous specimen when fully grown.

Interestingly enough, Kal and the dragon did not stare into each other's eyes as did the others. The crystals were presented and breathed on, just like the others, then they just turned and marched off the grounds, trailed by Kylor who was followed by one of the dragons who had alerted to them when they first entered the grounds.

A sharp bark from Orthu forced the smaller dragon to

return to the other dragons, its head hung low.

Not surprisingly, they marched up to Orthu and his mate who was almost as large as Orthu, himself. No wonder the young dragon was so large. He had incredible genes, judging from his massive parents.

"I now give this dragon his warrior name," said Kal. *"I name him 'Elu'ali'aq' which means 'Enemy Slayer' in the ancient language."*

The fireball that erupted was terrifying. The blast easily shot two hundred feet in the air. I could feel the intense heat, even though we were on the far side of the grounds. Those two would be fearsome warriors. It was then that I noticed that Orthu and his mate had similar cruel-looking features as the young dragon. I hadn't noticed it before, but there was something there that triggered my "spidey senses." Alan noticed it, too.

"Those two look like they would hurt someone, just for the fun of it," he said with a visible shiver.

Marrle and Jazmyne were next. A light gray dragon was soon marching alongside the two as they crossed to the far side of the grounds.

"I hereby give this dragon her warrior name. She will be known as 'Loem'na' from henceforth," Marrle said. *"In the ancient language Loem'na means 'protector'."*

And then it was our turn.

"Don't worry," said Selena, *"you will figure it out."*

We had to pass by Kal and Elu'ali'aq on our way to the dragons.

"We've had riders not get selected before," he said to both me and Alan. *"It's the highest disgrace to be found unworthy of the respect of an adolescent dragon."*

We wandered through the dragons, and my worst fears were realized. Not only did the dragons not pay attention to us, but several of them would retreat if I started towards them. I took another pass through the dragons, then another, and yet another. I heard an audible snort of amusement from Kal, who had walked closer to get a better view.

"Try connecting to the crystal," Alan suggested.

Focusing on the crystal, I gave it all I had. Every little bit of concentration went into connecting with the crystal. Nothing.

Circling the grounds for what seemed the hundredth time, I could hear the spectators grow restless. It felt like we had been wandering around for hours.

Desperate to try anything to connect with the crystal, I sung my weird melody: Bb, Eb, Ab, and G. The crystal seemed to stir a bit. Even Alan felt it.

"Dude, try it again!" he said.

I tried over and over, but something was just not right.

"Hey, try it again – but like Abi did when she was singing to Suvi. Sing it with your mind," Alan said.

That's all well and good, but how does one do that?

"Think of the notes and hear them in your head," instructed Selena *"and try to broadcast what you hear."*

Sweat rolled down my face from the concentration. Over and over, I tried to do as Selena instructed. It was exhausting. I had sat down on a log with my head in my hands.

"Well, that proves it. I was never meant to be a rider," I said to Selena and Alan.

I hadn't noticed that Abi and Sabryyna had walked up on us. Abi knelt beside me.

"What was that melody you were singing?" she asked.

"It's a melody that seems to be the only thing that stirs the crystal," I answered.

"So you're now trying to sing to it with telepathy, right?" she asked.

I just nodded dumbly.

"Try singing with your voice and at the same time project the notes with your mind," instructed Abi.

Taking a deep breath, I again sang Bb, Eb, Ab, and G, but also projected the notes.

"Whoa!" said Alan, "I totally heard that. Like, in my head

I mean!"

And so had the dragons...and everyone else standing in the holding grounds. When I looked up, all faces were turned to me.

"*Again!*" said Selena.

A commotion was heard from the far side of the holding grounds. Crashing through the brush came the large dragon that Elu'ali'aq had been tormenting. Lowering his head, he advanced on me slowly, an unmistakable questioning look in his eyes.

"Sing it again, Marcus," said Abi.

Again, I sang out Bb, Eb, Ab, and G. I could tell that it had an effect on the dragon. We were now nose to nose, so I sang it again: Bb, Eb, Ab, and G. But this time, the dragon sang a counter descending melody of Bb, G, F, and Eb.

Staring into the dragon's eyes, I sang the melody again, with the dragon singing his counter-melody, and on the third time I finally connected with my crystal!

"Alan, sing those notes, the notes I was singing!" I instructed.

Alan took my place and stood nose to nose with the dragon. Of course Alan had no problem singing the notes with telepathy, the dragon delightedly singing the counter-melody, and on the third time through, I felt Alan's presence connecting to my crystal.

"*Dude! We're in!*" Alan exalted. "*We're totally in!*"

The dragon, caught up in the excitement, started to caper around us, like some sort of huge dog. It was then that I saw that it had one deformed leg. Its front right paw was twisted and seemed to have mostly atrophied away. I noticed the paw because while capering around, he toppled over, almost crushing me and Alan. We both had to jump back to avoid the large dragon.

The dragon immediately looked up at me, all signs of happiness gone. His face told the story. He had seen me looking at his deformed paw, which he tried to draw back and out of sight. His eyes were wide with fear. His stare was heart-breaking. Because of the connection with the crystal, I *felt* the dragon's fear. He was afraid that I would reject him because of his deformity. Alan felt it too.

Kneeling down, I stared deep into the eyes of the dragon.

"*I choose you,*" I said.

I felt Alan kneel down beside me.

"*I choose you, too,*" said Alan.

The dragon looked back and forth between me and Alan. Our words didn't seem to have made the connection, and I knew what to do.

With a smile, I laid down my crystal in front of the dragon. Seconds later Alan's crystal was sitting next to mine.

Stepping back, we watched as the dragon clumsily got to his feet. His face showed his disbelief as his stare went back and forth between me and Alan. Looking into my eyes, I saw his eyes search mine, imploringly. With a nod and a smile, I sang out my melody: Bb, Eb, Ab, and G. The dragon responded with: Bb, G, F, and Eb.

Stepping forward, he again came nose to nose with me.

"*I choose you,*" I said again.

Turning, the dragon stepped over and happily toasted our crystals with his fiery breath.

··

"*Marcus, I've rarely been more proud of you,*" said Selena.

"*Yeah, well, it's not like the other dragons were lining up, but we sorta fit. We're both awkward outsiders,*" I said.

Sabryyna had been studying the dragon.

"There's something about this dragon. Not sure what it is, but he's unusual in more than the obvious ways," she said.

Alan and I led the dragon towards the waiting parents, but to our surprise, it was Orthu who stepped forward.

"*Are you sure of your choice?*" he asked. "*This dragon has no parents here to name him. His sickly mother died months ago,*" *and his father was a wild dragon whose whereabouts are unknown."*

Again, I got the feeling that there was something sinister about Orthu, but couldn't put my finger on it. I couldn't help but feel that he was amused with our choice of dragon and that he was more than pleased that we had made that particular selection.

Kal didn't try to disguise his feelings.

"A fitting selection for you, rider," he said with a mocking bow. "You two are meant for each other. We'll see you on the training fields."

He found what he said amusing and walked off chuckling.

"As this dragon has no parentage present, he will receive his dragon name from the eldest dragon," said Orthu.

I recognized the ancient dragon who stepped forward as one of those from the gathering. His movements were slow and deliberate.

The two dragons seemed to converse nose to nose, and after a brief period of time, both stepped back from each other and the young dragon returned to Alan and I.

Stepping forward to meet me nose to nose, he looked at me expectantly. I was wracking my brain, trying to think of an appropriate name.

"How do I name a dragon?" I asked my small group. "All I can come up with is Puff, Elliot, and Smaug."

"It has to be personal. Something meaningful," said Abi.

Sweat dripped off my face as I tried to come up with something. I could hear Kal chuckling as he watched me fail at such a simple task.

The dragon moved even closer, our noses now touching. His eyes were pleading with me to give him a meaningful name.

One of our last family trips with mom and dad had been to Europe. I know where Selena got her inspiration to name Vesuvius, but since that name was already taken...

Taking a deep breath, I tried to calm my mind. I went to one of my favorite "happy places," which was the countryside of Ecuador. My freshman year in high school, our choir had earned money and were able to spend two weeks there. I especially loved the small towns outside Quito, which was the capital city of Ecuador. I was glued to the bus windows as we drove through the Andes. There was one huge mountain that we drove past that was....

"*Cotopaxi,*" I said to everyone. "*Cotopaxi is the name of this dragon. Cotopaxi is a Volcano in my world. The ancient people considered it a sacred place, and it was thought to be the source of rain. The summit was the home to the Gods. I name this dragon, Cotopaxi.*"

The dragon seemed to love his name, or so I would assume from how he gave my face the wettest, most slobbery lick ever!

"*That's an awesome name for a dragon!*" exulted Alan. "*How about it, Paxi? How do you like your warrior name?*"

Alan, too, was rewarded with a drool-filled, slobbery lick to the face.

"*Gross, you big lizard! That's disgusting!*" but he was laughing with his arms wrapped tightly around the dragon's neck.

We were gathered in a group of riders, dragons, and attendants when Lowry and Sharry landed a short distance away. Their sorrow was palpable.

"*I'm glad to see that the pairing is complete,*" said Lowry. "*Thank you, Orthu for presiding in my absence. As most of you know, there is a period of time allotted for rider, dragon, and attendant to become familiar with each other before true training is to begin. The council believes that time is of the essence, especially in light of the recent attacks. We believe that we've become too predictable in our training habits and practices. It is the will of the council that the clans separate for a period of time to make war preparations then meet again when our individual units are stronger. That leaves us with a dilemma as to what to do with Mar-*

cus and Cotopaxi. Any suggestions?" asked Lowry.

"Does it really matter?" asked Kal, with a sneer.

Abi stepped forward. *"May I suggest that Marcus returns to earth? Sabryyna and I volunteer to remain with him and Alan. That will give us all time to prepare for training. Sabryyna and I will be valuable resources to both Alan and Marcus. With Randolph's death, we feel that another dragon attack is unlikely, and we believe that the Gonosz still must not have a reliable wormhole to cross at will."*

"Dangerous," answered Orthu immediately. *"They have shown that they are incapable of protecting themselves. They should remain here, under the protection of the dragons and clans."*

"On the contrary," said Sharry, speaking for the first time. *"They managed to fight off Randolph, my brother, a fully-grown dragon with real fighting experience. They have shown themselves to be a functioning fighting unit, able to utilize each other's strengths. I see no reason to hold them here."*

"We all know that if it were not for Vesuvius, these children would all be dead. I feel for your loss, Sharry, but I cannot agree that they are anywhere near a functioning fighting unit," said Orthu.

"Then you should hear the reports of one of our spies within the Gonosz. There is a report of a certain rider with burns over most of his body. The outside of his armor seems unharmed, but the inside tells another story," she said with a sideways glance at Alan who visibly swelled with pride at being singled out.

"A lucky fireball does not make a warrior," Kal said. Apparently, the sneer was a permanent expression.

"Maybe not, but it shows that they are thinking as a fighting unit already. I say that Abi's plan be accepted, as both Abi and Marcus are clan-less. It is obvious that Marcus is not ready to train in our atmosphere..." said Sharry.

"Another reason to keep him here, to force him to get stronger..." interrupted Orthu.

"...but as you can see," continued Sharry, ignoring Or-

thu's interruption, *"he has worked hard to gain more strength. He will be able to train harder and longer in his own atmosphere. Plus we already have assets on earth who will continue with the training, and he will be able to say his goodbyes."*

Goodbyes. That brought me up short. We were talking about a real war, where real people and dragons got hurt. It was pretty obvious that I was the weak link. I wouldn't last ten minutes in a real fight.

"When do you propose that we meet again for formal training?" asked Qurum quietly.

"If I may," said Selena, *"Marcus can finish out the school year. That will give him time to prepare and gain strength. Several times a month, we can cross and get instruction, much the same as when I was trained as a rider. I can speak from experience, that it takes time to get used to the atmosphere here. If Marcus is introduced little by little, his body will adapt more readily, and be able to repair itself. Once acclimated, he will do better."*

"I am fine with that proposal," said Qurum. *"Lowry, what say the dragons? Would the training work for you?"*

"Our young dragons need training from more experienced dragons, just as their new riders. I see the wisdom in letting Marcus and Abi train on Earth, but I would feel more comfortable sending a battle-trained dragon who has once had a rider to function as a trainer, and for added protection. Lloyd will accompany the young dragons and their riders," said Lowry.

"You would risk one of our venerated council members to train the young dragons?" asked an incredulous Orthu. *"Lloyd was once a formidable dragon indeed, but age has slowed his reflexes. It should be I that trains the young dragons and their riders."*

"I believe my decision has been made. Lloyd will accompany our youngsters," said Lowry.

And with that, out stepped one of the dragons from the pairing ceremony. While he was definitely one of the older dragons, there was a youthful twinkle in his eye.

"Yes!" exulted Selena. *"Lloyd was one of my trainers. You'll*

love him, Marcus."

"I suggest that we meet to train at least twice a month," said Qurum. *"Now, if I'm not mistaken, Vesuvius closed your main wormhole. You will need to use the alternative wormhole, which closes in a few hours. You had better leave immediately, or be forced to stay on a few more days."*

I had figured that we would use the same wormhole that Abi, Sabryyna and Alan had crossed through.

"We're pretty sure that the wormhole is now compromised," responded Selena when I asked why we weren't using it. *"Although the Gonosz should not know how to access the wormhole, they now have an idea of its location. They are sure to have people watching that area day and night."*

The dragons and clan members quickly dispersed from the area after the details of when and how we would meet each month. Soon, Qurum, Lowry and Lloyd were the only ones left as we prepared to leave.

"Well, young ones," said Lloyd. *"Our first test is upon us. Dragon and rider will need to fly together for the first time in order to make it to the wormhole in time. I can also carry an additional rider to lighten the load. Alan, you will ride with me. Abi and Sabryyna will need to both ride Hera'sha'i. Marcus, you and Cotopaxi will fly solo. Ready?"*

Cotopaxi looked at me, his eyes large.

"It will be fine," I said, not feeling like it was going to be fine at all. Vesuvius had been an experienced flier. If I got sick riding Vesuvius and had nearly fallen off his back then...well you know.

"Very well," said Lloyd. *"Riders and dragons mount up and ready yourselves for flight."*

Alan scrambled to the back of Lloyd. Sabryyna climbed onto Hera'sha'i first, then scooted back to allow Abi to take her place in front.

Cotopaxi had watched the other dragons crouch down to allow the rider ease in mounting. Crouching, he looked expectantly at me. I had done this several times with Vesuvius, so no big deal.

Taking a short run, then a hop, I landed on Cotopaxi's shoulders. My momentary proud moment of successfully mounting my new dragon was short lived, as Cotopaxi toppled over, my right leg trapped painfully underneath the adolescent dragon.

Cotopaxi staggered to his feet, then glanced down at his withered front paw. He had fallen over because the paw couldn't hold both his and my weight. Again, Cotopaxi looked at me with terrified eyes, expecting me to reject him because of his disability.

"It's alright," I said, stroking his head. "We'll figure it out."

The lick of gratitude was especially wet and slobbery.

An idea seemed to hatch in Cotopaxi's head. Walking over to a large tree, he braced his shoulder against the strong trunk. His meaning was clear.

"Right on, Paxi!" said Alan.

This time, I was able to clamber onto Cotopaxi's back without toppling over. Once situated, Cotopaxi moved away from the tree. He was a little wobbly, but at least he was able to carry my weight, even as large as I was.

"The worst part is over, Paxi," I said soothingly.

I was wrong. The worst part was significantly worse, and still ahead of us.

CHAPTER SEVENTEEN

FIGHT CLUB

Our plan was that Lloyd would lead off and set the pace. Cotopaxi and I would follow, and Abi, Sabryyna, and Hera'sha'i would bring up the rear.

"We don't expect that there will be other issues with the Gronosz since Randolph has been slain, but one never knows, so you should be vigilant always," said Lloyd. With that he launched into the air with Alan clinging to his back.

Cotopaxi turned and looked at me.

"You've got this," I said. *"Just follow Lloyd's lead."*

With a determined look on his face, Cotopaxi took a running start and launched into the air. And what I mean by, "launched into the air" is that our combined weight made taking off a little challenging for the young dragon. Several saplings were sacrificed as we tried to gain altitude. We had to dodge large tree trunks before we gained enough clearance to soar over the forest. Even then, we couldn't fly high enough to keep Cotopaxi's tail from occasionally removing the top of tall tree tops. Each time I would feel a jolt and hear a large crash, but little by little, we were able to gain altitude and soon we were flying level with Lloyd and Hera'sha'i. Hera'sha'i didn't seem at all bothered by the combined weight of both Abi and Sabryyna. The three of them seemed to be enjoying their first solo flight together immensely.

Wherein Lloyd and Hera'sha'i were able to maintain

level flight, Cotopaxi's flying motion was more like a dolphin racing on the top of the water. Up and down, and up and down. You probably see where this is going.

The nausea was returning with a vengeance, with his peculiar flying motion. If only I could use Larzi to enhance my vision. It had worked before with Vesuvius, but Larzi wouldn't work with Cotopaxi. Crystals were dragon specific. Maybe...

Singing the melody, I tried to connect with my new crystal. Cotopaxi heard me and started to sing along, and in no time I was connected. Since I was a little more familiar with what it felt to use enhanced vision, maybe I could find the skill more readily.

At first, I couldn't feel a thing, but as I concentrated on the enhanced vision, I felt a sensation more and more that it was indeed a function of my new crystal.

Focusing on the enhanced vision, I also concentrated on Cotopaxi. All of a sudden I was seeing through the eyes of the dragon! Relief from the nausea was almost instantaneous.

One of the first things I spotted with my new vision were the dark clouds that we were heading directly at.

"We're in for some bad weather," Lloyd confirmed *"Cotopaxi and Hera'sha'i, speed is your friend when flying in inclement weather. We will probably experience wind shears. When you do, don't panic. You'll drop, but if you're maintaining forward speed, you'll fly out of it. If you need to, nose down into a dive to build speed. You'll be fine."*

Swell. Bad weather on an adolescent dragon with no flying experience.

In no time at all, I began to get pelted with large rain drops. The drops seemed enormous compared to the raindrops on earth. In seconds, I was wet from head to toe. To make matters worse, we were hit with swirling winds that buffeted us hither and thither. I could tell that Cotopaxi was struggling to maintain level flying.

Without any warning, Lloyd yelled, *"Dive!"* and nosed down to gain airspeed, and then we were dropping out of the sky. Cotopaxi, being a young flier, tried to fly out of it rather than nose down into a dive. At the last minute, Cotopaxi nosed down only several hundred feet above the forest. I was busy trying to stay on Cotopaxi's back. I hadn't realized what an experienced flier Vesuvius was until I was falling out of the sky on my new dragon.

"Pull up! Pull up, Paxi!" cried Selena.

Straining, Cotopaxi tried to level out. Eventually we did, but by then we were already in the trees. Several small trees were snapped in half, but Cotopaxi was forced to weave in and out of the larger trees. Even with the enhanced vision, this was just too much. I got sick on the already sickified shirt.

I thought we had made it, when a branch violently swept me from my perch. One minute I was sitting on the back of a dragon hurtling through the trees, the next minute I was laying on my back, the wind completely knocked out of me, gasping for air like a fish out of water.

I was mentally taking inventory of my body parts, when a large dragon head came nose to nose with me. Cotopaxi's large eyes showed fear that I had been badly hurt.

"It's alright," I said. *"I'll be fine."*

I didn't feel fine, but I wouldn't have been surprised should the dragon burst into tears had I been hurt.

Gingerly I sat up, just as Abi and Sabryyna appeared.

"Are you hurt?" asked Abi. *"Here, let me help you."*

"No!" shouted Alan as he and Lloyd landed several feet away. *"Let me look at him first."*

Inch by inch, Alan pressed and prodded my body. In more than one place that he prodded, I let out a gasp of pain. Each time I did, Cotopaxi would cringe.

"You'll have to come up with some excuse to explain the scratches on your face, but otherwise you seem to be just bruised," explained Alan.

I realized that my face felt wet. When I placed my hand to the wetness, it came away bloody. With all the other sore spots, I hadn't realized that my face had been cut. One of my eyes started to swell shut, too.

Cotopaxi, when he realized that I wasn't mortally wounded, had slipped off by himself, his head drooping, his nose almost touching the ground.

"Hey, buddy," I said, coming up beside him. He wouldn't look me in the eyes, his head still hanging low.

"Listen, we're both going to make mistakes," I said. *"The main thing is that we're both unhurt. Let's just learn from this and move on."*

Cotopaxi still wouldn't look up, but he did send me a mental image for the very first time. It was a memory of him learning to fly with the other dragons. The rest of the dragons were easily able to master the flying techniques, while Cotopaxi struggled with everything. It didn't help that some of the other dragons began to pick on my dragon whenever he fell behind. The meaning was clear; Cotopaxi saw himself as a misfit.

I chuckled, which surprised the dragon. The look of despair that he gave me was heartbreaking. He thought I was making fun of him, too.

"No! No!" I quickly said, *"Don't you see? We're so much the same."*

Dredging up some uncomfortable memories, I let Cotopaxi see some of my embarrassing moments. The times I had gotten sick on myself and been chosen as a rider in front of all the clans, and the horrible stir that caused. The times I had been picked on by Eldon and his crew. Becky smacking me right in the face during class.

"We have more in common than you can imagine, Paxi," I said soothingly. *"When nobody believes in us, we'll need to be strong for each other."*

"Count me in too," chimed in Alan. *"We've got each others' backs through thick and thin."*

"Don't forget us," said Abi. She then showed Cotopaxi how the clans had reacted to her becoming a rider.

"We're kind of all misfits here, Paxi, so we've got to be our own clan. We're going to look out for each other," she said.

"Let's make things a little easier," said Lloyd. *"Marcus, you're a little too heavy for Cotopaxi at this time. Let's have Alan ride Cotopaxi, and you and I will fly together. Once we cross to the other side, Cotopaxi should be able to hold your weight better with the lighter gravity."*

There was wisdom in this. Alan couldn't hide his delight at riding Cotopaxi. Those two were already fast friends, and Lloyd was right. When we took off again, Cotopaxi seemed to be more comfortable flying with Alan's minimal weight. I could hear Alan laugh with delight as Cotopaxi used his unusual style of "porpoising" through the air. A surge of jealousy shot through me.

"Marcus, you can't blame Alan for being excited," Selena said, sensing my emotions.

"It seems Alan is more equipped to be a rider than I am. He can shoot lethal fireballs, use his crystal, and ride Cotopaxi like he was born for it, not me." I said.

"It just takes more time for you," said Selena. *"You'll pick those skills up. Don't worry about it."*

We rode in silence until we came upon the alternate wormhole.

"Watch me and follow," said Llyod.

Climbing higher in the air, Lloyd suddenly dove into a narrow canyon, his great wings nearly touching the sides of the canyon walls. Winding through the canyon was a stream. As we proceeded further up the canyon, I started to hear the unmistakable sound of a waterfall. I braced myself to either climb or dive, but instead we kept level, heading directly at the waterfall.

Lloyd began to soar lower until we were gliding just above the stream. We were going to climb then. I was bracing myself to shoot up into the air, but instead we kept flying directly at the waterfall.

"Uh, Lloyd," I began uneasily. *"We're heading directly at the waterfall."*

"Yes," he said, and kept flying.

Closer and closer.

"We're going to get a little wet," warned Lloyd.

At the base of the waterfall, Lloyd landed in the water. The spray from the waterfall quickly drenched me, and what wasn't wet, instantly became wet as we stepped into the waterfall itself. Several feet beyond the falls was an area that had been carved out by thousands of years of water erosion. Lloyd breathed fire for some light, and there it was. Up against the back wall was our swirling vortex. Without hesitation, Lloyd walked into the wormhole. Again I felt the immediate change in the gravity and atmosphere. Rather than wait for the others, Lloyd took to the air and circled the area from above.

"It's important to see if anyone is watching the wormholes, because it is the easiest way to launch an attack. They are fixed places in which we are required to use in order to travel from one world to the other," he said.

The others all came through the wormhole without incident. I knew about where we were from landmarks. Across the Columbia River is the state of Washington. It just so happens that the pacific northwest has a series of Volcanoes, one being Mt. Hood, near our town of Mt. View, and another is Mt. Adams in Washington. We were across the river in some woods near Mt. Adams.

After scouting around for a few more minutes, we landed next to the others. All of us were soaking wet, and with the onset of darkness, the weather was cooling off. Cotopaxi started a fire for us puny humans to warm ourselves by.

"When it gets dark and you have a chance to dry off and warm up, we'll be able to fly the rest of the way. We'll need to pick up your vehicle and get your grandmother. We'll get Alan to your home as promised," said Lloyd.

I learned something new that night. After we had dried off and warmed up, I learned that we couldn't just fly as-the-crow-flies directly to our car.

"In your world, radar is everywhere," said Lloyd. *"Because of our size and speed, we would show as an anomaly on your radar.*

The way to defeat radar is to fly low, hugging the contours of the land."

Flying without getting sick was hard enough, but flying in the dark, following the ups and downs, and ins and outs of the earth's surface was too much. When I finally stepped down from Lloyd, I made it a point to kneel down and kiss the ground. I will not elaborate on the state of my clothing, but yeah.

On the way home, we picked up Grandma who was very happy to leave. She had been cooped up the entire time, and for someone as independent as Grandma Torrey was, that was particularly trying. The Malloys had found a decent rental to live in and were no longer at Grandma's house.

Before Alan was dropped off at his parents new residence, we made sure to load him down with brochures and other items that one would normally accumulate while visiting a university. Fortunately, I had a spare jacket in the car that I was able to wear so as to not draw notice to my Jackson Pollock inspired shirt.

I might have been able to cover up the sight of my shirt, but the smell was another thing. I noticed that the others discretely cracked their windows, even though the fall weather got chilly at night.

....

The training began immediately. Cotopaxi was able to bear my weight better in our reduced gravity. We still struggled more than Abi, Sabryyna and Hera'sha'i, but at least we were moving in the right direction. Truth be told, Cotopaxi seemed to do better when just Alan was riding him. They connected on a level I didn't seem to be able to.

Our combat skills training was focusing on hand-to-hand combat using the enhanced striking skills. The idea was that if we were forced to fight in close quarters, we could magnify the strength of our striking, using the powers of the crystals. The timing was complicated. In order to project force, it was necessary to throw the punch or kick, and at the same time, project power while being connected to the crystal. To explain it, it might not seem that complicated, but to actually put it to practice... It was also a skill that Alan was struggling with as much as I was. Abi and Sabryyna had grown up practicing the skill. It was impressive to watch them spar.

There were several times in which I was able to get the timing. When I did, the punching dummy we were using fairly flew across the room from the force of the punch.

After a week of training, Lloyd brought us together.

"We have not seen any indication that the Gonosz are about, but that doesn't mean that they are not around. I think it would be wise of us to find an additional stable wormhole so that we are not using the same predictable sources. It will also be a chance for me to train our dragons in some dragon-specific skills. As you know, dragons are able to search out wormholes, but it is not an easy skill to master," said Lloyd.

It was decided that Lloyd would take the two young dragons to search for a stable alternative wormhole. Abi, Sabryyna and the rest of their "family" would patrol the area in the absence of the dragons.

The training had been strenuous to say the least. I was constantly tired, battered, and bruised. It was all I could do to stay awake and complete my homework, then off to sleep like a dead man.

"Hey," said Paul at school the next day. The football season had just wrapped up. Our team had lost some key players to injuries, and we had just missed the playoffs. Paul and Brent were sort of down in the dumps because of the high hopes of having a championship team. Although they were supportive of me not wanting to play, they were also confused because I had loved football so much over the years. It was a difficult thing to explain, even to Selena.

Alan and I had found ourselves at the fall school dance, despite the fact that neither one of us were in the least bit interested in being there. I went because Paul and Brent were my friends and were mourning a close game that determined whether our team went to the playoffs. Paul had been doing extremely well defending one of the best wide receivers in the state of Oregon, when he had slipped and sprained his ankle. After that, our opponents threw the ball almost exclusively to their star player. Even on the ankle, Paul made a huge effort, but on one play they went long, and Paul was not able to keep up. The score ended twenty one to twenty after our failed two-point conversion attempt to win.

I was at the dance to support my friends, and of course, Becky was there.

It had been quite some time since I was a wallflower, but here I was hanging out with Alan.

"Cutest date you have ever had," said Eldon to me in passing. His date was a stunning girl from a different school.

Alan and I had been unofficially elected by Paul and Brent to be the "watchers of everything coats and purses," while they and their dates danced. Alan was cool with the whole thing, having never had a girlfriend, but for me it was embarrassing to be dateless.

Selena was electing more and more to hibernate. I think she mourned the loss of Vesuvius more than she let on.

"Uh, oh," warned Alan. "Idiot at two o'clock."

Eldon had decided to circle back, apparently to show off for his date and hoodlum chums.

"Ladies," said the unmistakable voice of Eldon as he came back towards us, "Why didn't you tell me that you were having some troubles finding dates? I could have set you up with some of my entourage. Of course the only ones that would agree to go with you would be some of the fatties, but beggars can't be choosers."

"What do you want, Eldon?" I asked. "We're not causing you any trouble."

Leaning across the table, Eldon got face to face with me. I could smell alcohol on his breath.

"I don't like you, or your little boy-toy here. Why don't you just leave and spare me the agony of seeing your ugly faces?" he said.

"Back it up, Eldon," came a voice behind us.

"Hey, Mr. Cornwall," said Eldon as he leaned back. "We were just talking."

"Let's keep you two across the room from each other, OK?" said Mr. Cornwall.

Eldon stood and came to attention. Making a mock salute he said, "Yes sir, Mr. Cornwall, sir!" and goose-step marched off to join his admirers.

"Let's stay out of trouble, Mr. Harmon," he said.

"Glad to," I replied. Alan grabbed his glass of punch and downed it in one shot.

"I hate that guy," he said.

I ate a pile of cookies that I had grabbed off the snack table as I watched Paul and Brent laugh and dance with their dates.

I ate the last cookie and took a sip of punch to wash it down. The punch had a nasty after taste. Cheap party punch at its finest.

"Man, I don't feel good," said Alan.

"How so?" I asked.

"I'm gonna hurl," he said and sprinted off to the bathrooms.

I forgot about the nasty after taste of the punch and took another sip.

"Yuck," I said to myself.

It wasn't long before I too began to feel a little queasy. Not as bad as Alan, but I did feel a little nauseous. Maybe splashing a little water on my face would calm my stomach.

I walked into the restroom to find it empty. That was a little weird since Alan had just made a beeline here.

Bending over the sink to splash some cold water on my face, I was surprised to find Cowboy, Eldon's roping friend, standing behind me smiling. Before I could react, he had reached around my neck and put me in a headlock. I felt a foul-smelling rag placed over my face and nose. I instinctively tried to hold my breath, but Cowboy anticipated that and punched me in the gut, knocking the wind out of me. When I could breathe again, I naturally inhaled and fought to get my breath back only to inhale the contents of the foul-smelling rag.

Seconds later, I felt darkness closing in and I sank to my knees.

It seemed like I was only out for a moment, when I woke up to find myself bound and gagged, riding in the bed of a pickup. Alan was also bound and gagged, but was furiously working at the ropes that bound his hands. He had just freed his hands and was working on the ropes that bound his feet when the driver of the pickup slammed on the brakes. Both of us slid painfully, banging into the pickup cab.

"Nice try, Alan," said Cowboy. "Let's just tighten those knots a little better this time."

Throwing Alan on his stomach, Cowboy placed a knee in the middle of Alan's back, then painfully wrenched Alan's arms behind him. The knots were tied so tight that Alan's hands started to turn purple.

"Hey, sweetheart," Cowboy said as he came up to me. Grabbing my right elbow, he flipped me over on my stomach and examined the knots that bound my hands. Satisfied that they were tight enough, he got back in the pickup and we raced off.

"*What's going on?*" I asked Alan, grateful that we were still able to communicate.

"*I think Eldon dropped something in our drinks as he leaned over the table. This was all a setup. I've been working on my ropes for five minutes. You were out pretty good. Tried to wake you up the entire time,*" explained Alan.

"*You should fireball him again,*" I said.

"*Don't think that wasn't part of my plan, but they grabbed our crystals. They are in the cab with Cowboy, along with our wallets,*" he answered.

Fear went through me. Not fear of losing any of the powers, but to lose Selena.

"Selena, are you with us?" I asked.

"No good, Marcus. Been trying that too," said Alan.

"Any ideas of what their plans are?"

"No. But it's sure to be painful and humiliating," Alan's voice sounded grim.

It was obvious when the truck went from highway to dirt road. We were painfully thrown into the air as Cowboy took the bumps at full speed. A fine coating of dust soon covered us as it billowed into the back of the truck.

Both of us fought the knots that bound us, but Cowboy had been more careful this time.

After about fifteen minutes, we slowed down and turned onto a more primitive road. Alan and I were slammed around pretty good, despite the slower speed. After a minute or two, we saw what could only be the glow of a bonfire on the surrounding trees. We were greeted with hoots and hollers and the ignition was turned off.

Cowboy exited the cab and came around to drop the tail-gate, an evil grin on his face.

"I don't know how you made me catch on fire, Alan, but I know you were behind it somehow. Today is payback, son. Man-to-man style to be sure, but still payback," Cowboy said.

We were literally kicked out of the bed of the pickup, landing in a bundle to the ground.

I looked up to see about fifteen people standing around, most holding beer cans. This could get out of hand quickly. Eldon had removed the rear bench seat off his jacked-up Jeep and was sitting on it like a throne, beer can resting on his knee, a different girl than the one he took to the dance sitting on his right. She was practically draped across him. His dance date was standing behind them, the tear stains on her face telling a part of the story.

"Welcome to 'Fight Club'!" yelled a drunk Eldon, his face very red. I was determined to shelter Alan from as much of this as I could, but how?

"What's the first rule of fight club?" Eldon yelled.

"You do not talk about fight club!" yelled everyone back, all in different stages of drunkenness.

The girl sitting next to Eldon stood and walked to the center of the circle that had formed around the bonfire.

"Ladies and gentlemen, fight fans everywhere!" she yelled through a bullhorn, "It's time for our main event. Tonight, a mixed weight class fight between our two gladiators. Well, one gladiator, and one nerd that is. In the black corner, coming off a championship round of steer wrestling and undefeated against nerds, our man Cowboy," loud cheers went up as Cowboy stepped forward, shirt off and wearing Wranglers and boots.

"And in the white corner," boos erupted from the crowd. "Hey guys, shut up! Let me finish. And in the white corner, the nerdiest of nerds, Captain Underpants!"

"Who?" yelled someone from the crowd. "Which one is Captain Underpants? They're both nerds."

"You're right, Albert. We can't tell which one is which. Let's fix that shall we. Our nerd needs to be in costume," the girl said.

Two of Eldon's goons came over. I was determined to make a fight of it, but they left me alone and grabbed Alan.

Throwing him to the ground, they began to remove his shirt and pants.

"NOOOOOO," I screamed through my gag, and struggled to get up. A boot to the small of my back was an effective way to lessen my struggles, although I continued to try to get my hands loose.

Soon, Alan was stood up to his feet, wearing only his tighty-whitey's and sneakers. The embarrassment would be worse for Alan than any kind of beating. To add to the embarrassment, one of the goons stepped forward and gave Alan an Atomic wedgie to end all wedgies, before untying his hands and feet. As quick as lightning, Alan spun and punched the giver of the Atomic Wedgie square in the face. It didn't affect the goon, but it did make him mad and he cocked his hand to punch Alan back.

"Save it!" was Eldon's sharp command.

The goon desperately wanted to slam Alan, but no one disobeyed Eldon.

Grudgingly, the goon stepped back.

Alan spun around, looking for an opening in the crowd in which to escape. Several times he sprinted to the edge of the circle, only to be pushed back by the laughing and jeering crowd. This was going to be bad. This crowd was cruel enough, but fueled with alcohol, there was no telling what was going to happen tonight. I was a little ashamed to wish that Abi and Sabryyna were here. They could easily whoop everyone present, including Eldon.

I needed to get free and help Alan.

"If you get a chance to run, don't worry about me. Just get free," I said to Alan.

"Is there any way you can get my crystal?" he asked.

"Sorry. I'm still tied up with Eldon's goons watching me. Just try to get away," I said again.

"No," he said quietly.

"What? Alan, don't be stupid," I said in desperation. *"Just get away. Worry about me later."*

"No," he said again. *"I'm tired of running. I'm going to fight as best as I can. I'm going to try and get my crystal."*

"I'll fight, but I want my necklace back. It was given to me from my mother. As you know she was burned in the fire, and this is the only thing that she gave me that didn't go up in flames," he said.

"You get it back when you've been taught a lesson," said Cowboy.

"It's the only thing I have from my mother," he said again quietly.

"Hey, Cowboy!" yelled one of the girls "just give the baby his binky. It's not going to hurt to give it back to him."

She had obviously fallen for Alan's lie.

Surprisingly, Cowboy did as she requested. Must have

had a crush on her to give in so soon.

He jogged over to his truck and grabbed the crystals off the seat.

"I don't know which one is which, they were both wearing them. I think Marcus had two. Matching BFF necklaces, maybe?" Cowboy asked.

"Mine has the reddish stone," said Alan.

Cowboy sorted out Alan's crystal and held it out to Alan. Just as Alan reached for it, Cowboy dropped it in the dirt. Keeping his eyes on Cowboy, he reached down and grabbed the crystal, then placed it around his neck. Having a second thought, he removed the crystal and placed it in his right sock. Smart. Less likely to fall out.

Cowboy looked at the other crystals, then tossed them at me. They landed several feet from me, so I scooted on my side towards them.

A stiff kick to my back halted my progress.

"Just leave them there, Lover Boy," said the goon behind me. I needed to get in physical contact with the crystals, but how?

Again the girl with the bullhorn stepped forward.

"You've both been informed about the rules of the fight," she said.

"No I haven't..." began Alan.

"Yes you have. Everyone! Help Captain Underpants out. What is the first rule of 'Fight Club'?" she asked again.

"You do not talk about fight club!" yelled everyone once again.

"And there you have it. Those are the rules of the fight," she said and the crowd cheered.

"Stupidest rules ever," said Alan.

"The two fighters will come to the center of the ring," yelled the girl, thoroughly enjoying her role in tonight's festivities.

"You will fight until you are told not to," she said.

"Alan, run when you have a chance," I pleaded again.

"No."

"Black corner, are you ready?" asked the girl.

"Always," Cowboy said, and a cheer went up from the crowd.

"White corner, are you ready?"

"Ready," said Alan. Although he was visibly scared, he also appeared determined.

"Then....FIGHT!" she yelled and moved quickly to the surrounding circle.

"*Stay out of his reach,*" I said, trying to be as much help as I could.

Alan did just that. He darted around as Cowboy tried to close on him. Time and time, Cowboy would be within inches of grabbing Alan, but Alan was able to use his quickness to escape Cowboy. After a few moments of this, the crowd became tired of watching a game of tag. They wanted blood.

Alan had just escaped Cowboy and backed up against the crowd. but it was too late. I saw that one of the goons had stuck his leg out to trip Alan.

"*Watch behind you!*" I yelled, but by then, Alan had tripped and was scrambling to get to his feet. It was just enough time for Cowboy to get into reach and clobber Alan in the ribs with a meaty right hand.

Alan gasped and reached for his ribs. He was gasping for air. The air had been knocked from him.

"*You got to stay out of reach!*" I commanded.

"*What do you think I'm trying to do?*" he asked me, taking time to give me a dirty look.

The blow had slowed Alan down. One hand continually clutched his injured side, and once in a while a punch would get to him. After several minutes, he had a bloody nose and a visibly swollen eye.

"*Ok,*" Alan said, "*Here goes nothing.*"

"*Alan, just run. He's going to hurt you,*" I plead again.

"*If you haven't noticed, he's hurting me now. I'm fighting back,*" said Alan.

Alan stopped retreating and now stood his ground.

Cowboy had been waiting for this. He now stepped forward with a smile on his face. It was sickening to watch this group of people take so much pleasure in hurting someone like Alan.

Throwing a punch that looked like it would knock out a moose, Alan stepped under the punch and delivered one of his own to the ribs of Cowboy. Although it surprised Cowboy, Alan's timing was off. It had none of the additional force from the crystal.

Cowboy stepped back in surprise, but the punch didn't have much of an effect on him.

"That better not be the best you've got, son," he said to Alan.

"It's not," Alan replied back.

"Ooooh," went the crowd.

"I can't duck and throw a punch with force," Alan said, *"I'm going to have to take a couple of punches."*

"He'll kill you, Alan. Just dodge and wear him out," I said.

But Alan was beyond listening to me.

I was scooting slowly forward each time I felt that no one was paying attention to me. I was now only a couple of inches from Larzi, the other one several inches beyond that. If I could just reach the other crystal, I could communicate with Cotopaxi and tell him at least where to find our bodies.

Alan was trying desperately to get a solid punch in. He would bob and weave, but he was also taking a brutal beating.

After ducking a huge overhand right by Cowboy, Alan finally landed a solid punch right to Cowboy's solar plexus. With an audible "oof," Cowboy was knocked back several feet, the surprise at the strength of Alan's punch undisguised.

Cowboy was hurt, but didn't want to show it.

"Alan, he's going to try to take you down. You hurt him with that punch, and he's a wrestler," I warned.

"Ok," said Alan. Even his thoughts sounded tired and hurt.

I scooted an inch forward. Just a little bit to go.

Cowboy circled, and I figured that he was just stalling to get his breath back.

"Here it comes, Alan," I warned. *"Be ready!"*

As if Cowboy were reading my mind, he shot towards Alan and faked a swing at his head. Alan was ready for that, brought his knee up, and caught Cowboy right in the jaw. There was no force behind it, but it surprised Cowboy who now took a step back. Rather than also step back like he had been, Alan stepped forward and went on the attack.

His hand speed was amazing. Each time he struck, he caught Cowboy. Most of the blows seemed to have no effect on the brute, but once in a while, a punch would practically spin Cowboy around. Fear began to creep into his face after one of the shots knocked him back several feet.

"I think I'm getting the hang of this," said Alan.

Once again, he stepped into Cowboy rather than away. Cowboy had raised his hands to protect his face, so Alan slammed several fists into Cowboy's gut. Each blow appeared to have the added force of the crystal.

This time, Cowboy couldn't fake that the blows didn't hurt.

"Ahhh," he cried out loud. He took a step back and went down to one knee.

Up until then, the crowd had been raucous and cheering loudly, but something was going horribly wrong and everyone knew it.

I rolled a couple more inches forward. I could now feel Larzi and the other crystal beneath me. With my mind, I sang out my strange little melody. Instantly I was connected.

"Paxi," I called, *"we're in trouble."*

Trying to explain our trouble to a dragon that didn't have developed language skills wouldn't work, so I sent him an image of Alan fighting, and also an image of what the area looked like.

I *felt* Cotopaxi's anger after I flashed him images. It was fearsome.

A thought came to me. Maybe I could see through Cotopaxi's eyes and direct them to where we were at. Concentrating, I focused on the crystal and Cotopaxi. I was now seeing through his eyes. He was flying at a tremendous rate of speed. Lloyd was on his right, flying slightly behind Cotopaxi with Sabryyna on his back. Abi and Hera'sha'i flying on his left. I directed them to follow the highway I thought we had traveled on. When I was satisfied that they were heading in the right direction, I shut off the enhanced vision so I could focus on helping Alan.

If only I could shoot a fireball.

"Hey!" shouted the goon behind me. Grabbing me by my shirt collar, he dragged me back away from the crystals. It was only several feet away, but it might as well have been a mile.

Cowboy had gotten up, and now was circling Alan again. This time there was unmistakable fear in his face. The others saw it, too. Eldon actually had a disgusted look on his face as he watched Cowboy.

Alan was now the aggressor. He would slip in and out of Cowboy's reach, but not before delivering some very well-timed punches.

Many of the punches now had a devastating effect on Cowboy. Very soon, his nose was dripping blood, and his sides were heaving as he tried to catch his breath.

Up until now, Alan had been darting in and out. This time, he ducked in and delivered several blows to Cowboy's ribs, but instead of jumping back, he threw combinations to the face, each blow having some force. Raring back, he delivered an uppercut that knocked Cowboy off his feet. Cowboy crumpled to the ground, completely knocked out.

For the first time, the crowd was completely silent. They couldn't believe what had just happened.

A couple of goons stepped forward to help Cowboy.

"Leave him!" was Eldon's command.

Walking up to Cowboy, he stood above him, a look of

total disgust on his face. He squatted down and sat on his haunches.

"You always were weak, Cowboy," and emptied the contents of his can into Cowboy's unconscious face.

Cowboy sputtered awake at having the beer poured on him, only to see Eldon's face inches away from his. Cowboy's expression was confused.

"Well, at least you still have your steers," said Eldon.

Eldon got up and grabbed the Jeep bench seat that he had been sitting on, like a king on his throne, and started towards his vehicle. Cowboy also scrambled to his feet and started to follow everyone else towards the vehicles.

Eldon turned and looked at him.

"I'm sorry. Where did you think you were going?" he asked with fake confusion in his voice.

"I, uh, was just coming with you guys," said Cowboy. He looked very alone. His now ex-friends all standing with Eldon.

"No, I think that won't do," said Eldon. "You might not want to show up to school, either. You are an embarrassment to us, now, Cowboy. No one can associate with you now, Cowboy. You're weak. You disgust me," he said and spit in Cowboys face.

Cowboy just stood there as his friends drove off. His truck, the only vehicle in the clearing.

He turned and looked at us, fear and confusion in his face.

"I..." he began. "It's just...."

Then he got in his pickup and drove off slowly, leaving me and Alan alone with a very angry dragon circling overhead.

CHAPTER EIGHTEEN

SURPRISE ATTACK

I was surprised to see both Alan and Cowboy at school the next day. Both had taken a fearful beating, albeit that Alan ultimately triumphed, his face telling the story of several hard shots from the larger and stronger Cowboy.

Cowboy was a lost man that day. Not even a day before, he had been one of the mighty, a part of the ruling class. Today, he had nothing. He was now unclean, someone that everyone shunned.

I confess that I felt that he deserved it. His lassoing me still stung, and I had gotten more than a little satisfaction watching Alan destroy the bully.

Word had gotten around that it was Alan who had beaten Cowboy. He was greeted with respectful nods throughout the entire day. As he walked down the hallways, there was more than one group that would point and whisper. It wasn't difficult to figure out what people were talking about. "Hey, that's Alan, the kid who whooped Cowboy last night."

You would think that after all these years of being picked on, Alan would revel in his newly acquired notoriety, but he had something else on his mind. He thoughtfully had been watching Cowboy all day.

At lunch, Cowboy walked into the cafeteria, a room in which he used to rule, but today, he was as good as a leper. No one would dare allow Cowboy to sit next to them for fear of incurring the wrath of Eldon. With a long look around the room, he hoped to find at least one friendly face. There was none, and

Alan had noticed. Cowboy turned to leave when Alan got up and tapped Cowboy on the shoulder. Cowboy spun around, no doubt thinking round two was about to commence. Instantly all eyes were on the two.

"You might as well come sit with us, since Eldon hates us, too," Alan said, his hand offered in friendship.

For a long moment, I could see the wheels in Cowboys head turning. If he were to fight Alan again and win, he might earn his way back into the king's grace, but there was something strangely noble about Alan in that minute.

You could hear a pin drop as the cafeteria watched what was unfolding.

"Don't even think about it, Cowboy," It was an order from king Eldon who was watching from his kingly table, surrounded by his court.

Cowboy turned to look at Eldon. A long moment passed, and a decision needed to be made.

Cowboy turned back to Alan. It took another moment before he took Alan's hand.

"You and I both know that there is no coming back when you get on Eldon's bad side," said Cowboy with a shy smile to Alan.

Alan chuckled, and the two sat down next to me. I confess that I was not as forgiving as Alan.

The room was still hushed. Someone had directly disobeyed the king's order and was now sitting with the enemy.

"You know that you're a dead man walking," I said.

"I was anyway," said Cowboy. "You know how Eldon is. There are no second chances."

Abi and Sabryyna walked up, and after a couple of strange looks at Alan and Cowboy sitting together, they seemed to accept the situation and sat down next to us.

"Looks like you found religion, Cowboy," said Sabryyna.

"Yeah, I got baptized last night," he said with a chuckle.

And that was the end of that. Cowboy was now officially one of us. Weird how stuff like that happens. Cowboy's real name was Eugene Miller, but everyone called him Cowboy, even the teachers.

It just so happened that Cowboy was in two of my classes, was in one of Alan's, two of Abi's, and one of Sabryyna's. There was only one class where Cowboy was alone. Although I was not as charitable as the others about forgiving Cowboy, I still felt sorry for him. Brent and Paul raised eyebrows as Cowboy accompanied us to class, but refrained from saying anything.

It was the class that Cowboy was in alone that trouble arose.

Taking advantage of none of us being in Cowboy's PE class, Eldon and some of his goons pinned Cowboy outside the gym and gave him a beating.

It was me who found him. He was sitting outside of the gym with blood pouring from his nose and pulverized lips. Both eyes were starting to swell shut.

Looking up at me, I could see the relief in his eyes.

"I wouldn't blame you if you hate me," he said.

"I don't hate you. I hate bullies," I said.

"Yeah, I understand that now. I can stand taking a beating, but everyone that used to be my friend now won't even look at me. That's worse than any beating," he said.

We stopped at the restroom to wash the blood from his face and grab a couple of handfuls of paper towels.

"Man, where did Alan learn to punch?" he asked. "A couple of those felt like getting kicked by a horse."

"His dad taught him to box," I lied.

"That was inhuman," he replied. If he only knew that truth...

The training with our respective dragons began in earnest. Fortunately, the lesser gravity of earth gave me a chance to ride Cotopaxi. Compared to Vesuvius, Cotopaxi was less nimble. It's like driving a tank compared to a sports car. Abi's dragon, Hera'sha'i, had a quickness that bordered on unbelievable. What was even more remarkable was that both Abi and

Sabryyna were able to ride Hera'sha'i while she maneuvered through the air.

I, on the other hand, was in constant fear of falling off the back of Cotopaxi, even when he was flying low and straight. We were both awkward with each other while flying. I was constantly misjudging which direction he was going to take, something that Abi mastered effortlessly with her dragon.

"It's all about the mental connection that you have with Paxi," said Selena. *"Once you have established that connection, those things are second nature. You won't even think about it."*

Even though Alan and I were now able to access the crystal, we were both still having trouble finding the properties that it housed. Whenever I had spare time, I would try to explore the crystal. It just seemed empty, but Vesuvius had been vehement that it held great power. Lloyd also confirmed that it held great power.

"It's something I haven't experienced before," he said as Lloyd pondered it. *"It appears that you must unlock each of the properties, but I'm not sure how you are to accomplish that."*

Great.

One of the side effects of Alan and Cowboy's fight was that Eldon seemed to take a step back from antagonizing us. Alan had fought back and won. That was unthinkable in the world of Eldon.

"Maybe Eldon has learned his lesson?" asked Alan Hopefully.

Cowboy snorted in dark amusement.

"You don't know Eldon, then. You've seen the physical bullying, but you might not have experienced the mental torment when he turns it on full-force. I'd rather get beat up than endure that mental torment. He's a sadist, for sure."

It was funny how Cowboy had become a member of our group. We had all agreed to not tell anyone about some of the more unusual aspects about our life, including Cowboy, but he naturally fit in with us during the school day. Having a common enemy is a unifying event.

"It's a guy thing," said Abi. "You can't talk about personal issues to save your lives, but punch a guy in the face, and you are all best friends?"

It was becoming increasingly difficult to hide our activities from Cowboy. We were naturally tight with Cowboy, especially Sabryyna. Apparently, her family were farmers and also raised "cattle" on Vocce. She had told us that the cattle were very much like our bison, so she had some natural commonality with Cowboy, whose family had a ranch.

Cowboy was becoming suspicious because we had to constantly make excuses about our after school activities.

"We need to plan an activity with Cowboy," said Sabryyna. *"He keeps asking what we're doing all the time, and we're running out of excuses to keep him satisfied."*

The weather was getting cold, so we decided to get in one last weekend trip before the oncoming winter. Fortunately, the weekend forecast was sunny skies and seventy five degree weather. It was decided that we would head to the mountains for the weekend. Cowboy's family had a cabin situated in the foothills of Mt. Hood. The only access was with a couple of side-by-side off-road vehicles, also owned by Cowboy's family.

It was fun getting away. I had always loved camping, starting with my parents, but then Grandma and Grandpa Torrey had spent every moment they could outdoors, something that they passed onto us.

The dragons were also accompanying us, but discreetly. Of course, we were able to stay in constant contact with them telepathically. They were there for protection, and we needed to find another stable wormhole.

"It's not much, but we have plenty of firewood split. We don't have electricity or cell service, but it's clean and next to a private lake that we stock with trout. You'll love the view of Mt. Hood!" Cowboy said enthusiastically.

The trip was fun riding in the side-by-side vehicles after

we had parked our cars near one of several barns owned by Cowboy's family. We had to open and close several barbed-wire fence gates before we arrived in the clearing with the cabin.

It was a real log cabin, not a modern house that some people called a cabin, and it was big. Cowboy's family included several aunts and uncles with families, and the cabin was built with the intent that all the extended families could enjoy it all at once. The view of Mt. Hood was as good as Cowboy had promised. We arrived at dusk, and the fish were feasting on the various bugs that were attracted to the lake at that time of night. Ripples appeared now and again as the trout worked hard for their nightly snack.

I had brought Grandpa Torrey's ancient bamboo fly pole and intended to reduce the population of the lake by as many trout as possible.

I let the others situate themselves in the cabin. I could hear Abi and Sabryyna argue with Alan over a room that had it's own bathroom and solar-heated shower. I couldn't care less where I slept. I would crash on a couch or on the floor somewhere. I wasn't picky, and I was more interested in the fish that were obviously biting.

"I wish I could smell the forest," said Selena wistfully.

"I've noticed that you've spent a lot of time hibernating. Is everything all right?" I asked.

"It's becoming more and more difficult to remain," she said.

It was hard for me to listen to Selena talk about leaving. It terrified me, actually. I had already lost her once.

"Marcus, the crystal was never meant to be permanent. It is used to pass along information and training, then we move along. It is the natural progression of things," she said, sensing that I was uncomfortable with the subject.

"So, is there life after death?" I asked

"Sure. I'm not positive what it is or how it works, but something pulls me now and again, Marcus. Pulls me," she emphasized. *"Soon I will be ready, and we must prepare."*

By "we," I knew she meant me. She was only holding on

because of her love for me.

I had chosen a "Black Gnat" and tied it to my line. Line through the eye of the hook, wind the line around itself five times, then back through the top loop in the line before pulling tight. Then clip the extra line with fingernail clippers. It was Grandpa Torrey's "fail-proof" way of tying on a fly.

There is something almost spiritual about fly fishing.

"It's almost like dancing," said Selena as she watched my casting motions.

I took pride in my accuracy and my touch, the fly gently landing on the mirror-still water. Before long, I felt the strike of my first trout. It was medium-sized, but a fighter. I loved the play that Grandpa's bamboo pole gave when I had a fish on the line.

We fished in silence for another half an hour. I couldn't see Selena, but felt her presence, both of us enjoying a "normal activity."

Soon it was too dark to fish, but we remained by the lake, watching as the stars started to appear in the pitch black sky.

I felt his presence before his large head gently rested on my shoulder. I reached up and scratched the dragon's ears, the same contented rumbling issuing from deep within him.

"You have got to be careful, Paxi, Cowboy can't see you," I said.

....

Sometime in the night, I woke up with the chills. I had fallen asleep petting Cotopaxi next to the lake. Mostly, all we had done is train together. We never had just quiet time together, so this was a lovely change of pace. He had silently disappeared into the night, after I had fallen asleep.

"I'm going to miss this," said Selena. I suspected that she had been awake the entire time, enjoying the quiet.

I got up, my cold body moving slow. I should have brought a flashlight because it was very dark. Rookie mistake....

With a "whump," Lloyd landed with Cotopaxi and Hera'sha'i.

"Wake the others! They're watching the road," he commanded. I didn't need further clarification about who "they" were. But how did "they" find us? We hadn't discussed our plans with anyone, and we hadn't been followed, that we knew of. The dragons had flown out the night before to scout around and make certain that "they" were nowhere around the cabin.

"What do we tell Cowboy?" I asked.

Lloyd's voice sounded grim.

"He's about to get the surprise of a lifetime," he said. *"Get the others up and moving."*

"They're up," said Selena. *"I just told Abi the situation."*

As if on cue, a gas lantern was lit inside the house, and appeared to be moving from room to room as Abi awoke the others.

I trotted up to the house to hear a very confused and sleepy Cowboy.

"What...what's going on? What do you mean we have to go?" he asked, clearly groggy.

"I can't explain...someone is after us. A bad someone," she said.

"Is it Eldon? We can lock the doors..." he began but was surprised as Abi physically lifted him off the ground and pulled him out of bed wearing only his briefs.

"Hey! What are you doing? HOW are you doing..." he asked.

"Just get dressed," she said.

Alan had heard the commotion and came out of his room, already dressed for the night's chilly air. He was carrying his knapsack already packed.

"Just listen to her," said Alan as he started throwing clothes at an incredulous Cowboy. It was a strange enough situation that he realized that he needed to move fast, and in a moment he was ready.

"I'm glad I gassed up the side-by-sides before..." he began.

"Yeah, we're not taking the side-by-sides," said Sabryyna who had just come in from the outside. "Uh, you'll be riding with me."

"Riding...?" he asked.

Having grabbed our belongings, we gathered at the door.

"Cowboy, there is no good way to explain what you're going to see, believe me," said Alan, and he swung open the door to reveal three dragons peering anxiously into the doorway.

"Aaaahhh! WHAT THE..." said an astonished Cowboy. He had been walking through the doorway, but stumbled as he saw the dragons. He tumbled as he backpedaled out of the way.

"WHAT? DINOSAURS? Are those DINOSAURS?" he yelled.

Later it would be amusing to recount Cowboy's reaction, but we were too familiar with the enemy to let a second be wasted in getting away.

We all ran to our respective dragons, Sabryyna mounting Lloyd.

"Climb on behind me," she called to Cowboy.

To his credit, once he saw that he wasn't to become a meal for hungry dragons, he climbed up behind Sabryyna with a dexterity of a person who has rode horses his entire life.

"*Cotopaxi,*" said Lloyd, "*will have to carry two. We want Abi and Hera'sha'i to be free to fight, if needed.*"

Cotopaxi had already braced himself against a tree so that he wouldn't topple over because of his withered paw.

"*You got this Paxi!*" said Alan as he scrambled onto the dragon's back.

I took a short run and jumped onto Cotopaxi's back, worried that our combined weight would be too much.

Although Cotopaxi was a little unstable, he seemed to be able to withstand our weight. He didn't climb as fast as the other dragons, but there was a marked difference from the first time we tried to fly. He was getting stronger each day, although he wasn't nearly as nimble in the air as Hera'sha'i or even the elder, Lloyd.

I instantly connected to the crystals and got my enhanced vision going. I was amazed at how clearly I was able to see, even with how dark it was.

Scanning the ground, I looked for the enemy.

"I'll watch our six o'clock," said Selena.

Our first contact with the enemy came as a surprise. We were again flying as low as possible to avoid radar. Lloyd, who was leading, dived between two small hills, a natural place to hide from the radar, but our enemy had guessed that we would take this route. It was conveniently also the most direct route home, so the enemy had positioned two fireball shooters on each hill, effectively trapping us in a crossfire.

The first fireball struck Lloyd on his right hind quarter. He tumbled several times in the air, both Sabryyna and Cowboy demonstrating fantastic riding skill by remaining seated.

The second fireball missed Abi and Hera'sha'i, but the third fireball hit Hera'sha'i's tail, spinning her around, but not tumbling like Lloyd. She quickly righted herself and Sabryyna had the presence of mind to return fire to the same area from which the fireballs came from. A startled yelp indicated that she at least had alarmed the shooter.

The fourth fireball struck Cotopaxi's unarmored underbelly. The third shooter had also been positioned on the valley floor.

The fireball was a powerful one, and it knocked us out of the sky. Cotopaxi tried to right himself, but toppled to the ground. We would have been crushed, except that at the very last moment, Cotopaxi shifted his weight and we slammed into some saplings. They somewhat cushioned our landing. Even so, we hit hard, and Alan and I flew off of Cotopaxi and landed on the ground. Both of us had the air knocked out of us, so it took a moment to steady ourselves.

Cotopaxi was hurt. The fireball had scorched his under-belly, and he was dazed. He tried several times to rise, only to topple over.

"Stay still, Paxi!" called Alan.

With the enhanced vision still going, I peered around the area, watching for any movement. We had crashed several hundred yards beyond where we were hit, so it might be a few minutes before they showed up. Alan and I ran to where Coto-paxi was writhing in pain. He was making mewling sounds of a hurt animal, but he was also trying to rise to defend us.

With my vision, I spotted movement in the forest. I recognized the figure when he stepped into the clearing. It was Randolph's rider. He must have also had enhanced vision, be-cause he spotted us immediately and began to run towards us, that inhuman speed covering the distance, well...inhumanly.

I tried to shoot a fireball, but it fizzled out at about fifty feet, only giving the enemy a better idea of exactly where we were.

Alan, who didn't have enhanced vision, was handi-capped. He began to shoot off fireballs in the general direction of where I had fired my useless fireball, but many didn't come close, and the few that did, the rider used his incredible quick-ness and speed to avoid them. We only had a moment or two, and the rider would be upon us, my dragon helpless to defend himself.

Focusing like I never had before, I sang my little melody. Cotopaxi, realizing that I was trying to connect to the crystal, sang the counter-melody. On our third time through, we con-nected.

It was a desperate move of someone who had no other options, because once connected, I had no idea of what to do next.

The only thought was a fireball. Summoning all my focus, I fired at the charging rider. The fireball I produced wasn't the typical red fireball that I had seen. Mine was a blue fireball. It sped towards the rider, who dodged out of the way of the fireball, or at least he tried to dodge out of the way. The fireball had changed direction to follow the rider! It was like a homing weapon! The only thing that saved the rider was that he dived behind a large tree that splintered into a million pieces when my fireball hit it.

Alan, who watched the direction I was shooting, shot a fireball to both the left and right of where my fireball had exploded, correctly guessing that the rider would try to quickly find another cover. The fireball that he shot to the right, caught the rider square in the chest as he tried to dodge behind a larger tree. He dropped like a sack of potatoes.

And then the rest of them were upon us. We had been so intent on the charging rider, we had failed to scan other directions. Alan was shooting a wall of fireballs, some of which connected with two of the enemies. I tried to shoot another fireball, but was knocked to the ground by a rock that had been levitated at me. I was struggling to get up when I felt Cotopaxi's neck drape over me. I could hear a horrible roar within him, then a massive fireball, larger than I had ever seen, exploded from his mouth. Instantly, the night was lit up like it was daylight. Although the enemy was still too far away to get seriously burned, the fireball was large enough to stop them in their tracks, shocked looks on their faces.

Cotopaxi tried to position himself to defend us better, but struggled to move even a little bit. When the enemy saw that Cotopaxi was hurt, they split up with the intention of coming at us from multiple directions. Cotopaxi wouldn't be able to maneuver fast enough to protect all sides.

"I've got our six. You and Alan watch our sides," Selena instructed.

Again, Alan sent a wall of fireballs that the enemy was forced to dodge. I tried to shoot my blue fireball, but could only manage a couple of feeble red ones.

The enemy had seemed to disappear when Selena yelled out, *"Behind you!"*

I spun around to see a large warrior in mid-jump. When

he landed, he struck Alan in a serious blow that knocked him to the ground. Turning, he leaped into the air with a drawn sword, intent on skewering me like a shish kabob. Just at the top of his jump, Cotopaxi knocked him out of the air with his tail. The blow was devastating. The warrior was thrown against a tree, and he fell limp and lifeless.

Glancing around, I saw that there were too many of them.

"*Good boy, Paxi,*" I called. If we were going to die, I wanted my dragon to know he had done well in his final moments.

Cotopaxi was breathing fire in as many directions as he could, but it would only be a matter of time. Alan had been briefly knocked out, but now was up and firing in earnest. I wondered where Abi and the others were. We needed their help.

"*Abi, Lloyd, we're under attack,*" I called.

"*So are we,*" was Lloyd's reply. "*We are working our way towards you, but there are more than I expected.*"

An all out attack came on Alan's side. Alan's accuracy was uncanny, but without enhanced vision, he could only hit what he could see.

Cotopaxi seemed to recognize the problem. With a large intake of air, he let a fire-stream go that lit up the night. Alan was able to drop three attackers as Cotopaxi lit up the darkness.

Dropping another two other warriors stopped the attack in it's tracks. Unfortunately I had been paying so much attention to the attack on Alan's side, that I hadn't been paying attention to my area. A singed shoulder from a small fireball brought me back to my area of concern.

Several warriors charged into our area. One with a raised sword came straight at me. I had nothing with which to defend myself, and at the last minute fired off a fireball from point blank range. It wasn't a very big fireball, but it did stop the charge long enough for Cotopaxi to also swipe the warrior with his tail. The warrior was thrown to the ground, tried to get up, but another tail swipe hurled the warrior even further, and he got up no more.

I don't know how long we repelled attacks. Cotopaxi was our only saving grace. His armored hide shielded us from fireballs and levitated items. His large fire-streams both lit up the night for me and Alan to be effective, and also stopped the attackers from entering our perimeter. And heaven help someone who did get close. Cotopaxi's tail dispatched them with ease. One idiot tried a frontal attack. I wasn't sure what dragons fed on, but Gonosz warrior was on the menu tonight. A couple of gulps, and the warriors disappeared down Cotopaxi's gullet.

A fake attack was our undoing. When we knew the direction an attack was coming, it was very difficult to keep our attention on our assigned areas. Alan's side was attacked heavily, and naturally mine and Cotopaxi's attention was drawn to that direction. Selena had saved us several times by warning us of a rear attack.

Alan seemed to be getting more than his fair share of attacks, and they seemed to be getting heavier. Alan's marksmanship was uncanny. Combined with Cotopaxi's heavy fire-streams, they were able to repel attack after attack. There was less coverage for the enemy to hide on my side, and with my enhanced vision, I was able to shoot my fireballs at a greater distance. Fortunately, the strength of my fireballs seemed to be getting stronger, but I wasn't able to duplicate the blue fireball that seemed to have tracking abilities.

The attack on Alan's side was building. We could see multiple warriors dodging and ducking, but getting closer and closer. My attention was drawn to that side of the action because I was able to see our attackers better than Alan. It was when I had spied several warriors charging, that they mounted the surprise attack on my area. I was completely unprepared.

"Marcus, behind you!" was Selena's shout.

Spinning, I found myself facing a dozen warriors charging with swords and battle axes. Cotopaxi turned his head and fire spewed from his mouth, the only thing that saved us were several of the warriors got caught in the stream and went down screaming. It was repulsive to me to watch, even if they were intent on killing us.

I was firing as fast as I could, but wasn't as quick or accurate as Alan. Still, I managed to shoot the first couple of warriors to enter into our little perimeter, but there were too many for me to hold them all off. A couple of unlucky ones caught a face full of Cotopaxi's tail, but one particularly muscular warrior dealt a nasty blow to Cotopaxi's stunted foreleg. Blood began to ooze from the wound.

With a roar, Cotopaxi shot a stream of fire at point-blank range, the warrior bursting horribly into flames. The warrior screamed and dropped his sword. Grabbing the sword, I ran it through the warrior, who immediately stopped screaming. I looked down at the sword that now had blood on it. Blood because of my actions. Death because of my actions.

"Marcus, he was going to kill you. His death isn't your fault. You were defending yourself," said Selena, obviously reading my shock.

"Still doesn't make it better," I said bitterly.

"I know," said my sister quietly.

But I had little time to contemplate the meaning of death because the Gonosz attacked all at once from multiple sides.

I found myself facing a female warrior who jumped into the little open area that we occupied. Before I had a chance to defend myself, she levitated a rock the size of a cannonball at me. I ducked too late and the rock glanced off of my right temple, knocking me to the ground. My last conscious thought was that I had failed my friends, my dragon, and my sister.

CHAPTER NINETEEN

CHAOS AMONGST THE CLANS

I was surprised to be alive when I came to. I was positioned on a travois that was being pulled by several warriors. Struggling, I raised myself on my elbow, preparing to shoot as many fireballs before I would certainly be killed for good.

"Stop!" cried Selena. *"They are from the clans. They are on our side."*

I also realized that we must be in Vocce. My movements were sluggish, and my breathing was labored.

I saw movement to my right and saw that Cowboy and Alan were riding Lloyd, who had obvious damage to his right wing, which was probably the reason he wasn't circling the air above with Hera'sha'i, Abi, and Sabryyna. I was surprised to see Chayl with his dragon, Sjer-berha, and Marle astride Loem'na. They seemed to be flying formation above us, staying even with our progress, obviously protecting us from further attacks.

Turning around, I was able to spot Vesuvius's parents both pulling an enormous travois with a very wounded Cotopaxi laying on it. He didn't seem to be conscious, his head lolling as they dragged the dragon over the ground, a large swath appeared behind the wounded dragon as his weight gouged the ground as the two larger dragons pulled him.

"What happened?" I asked Selena.

"You were knocked unconscious," said Selena. *"Fortunately, I'm still able to see and react even when you are out, so I was able to warn Abi that we were desperate. Cotopaxi was ferocious*

after you were knocked out. Even though he was hurt, he draped himself over you and fought off several waves of attacks. Alan fought until he, too, was knocked out. Cotopaxi saved him, too. The same woman warrior that got you, had levitated a stump at Alan. Cotopaxi partially blocked it, but it still hurt Alan. A couple of warriors got in and were hacking at Cotopaxi, when the dragons showed up. Marle and Loem'na dropped out of the sky and took the attacking warriors out. The remaining Gonosz realized they were outmatched and fled. We learned later that Chayl and Sjerberha found and helped defeat more of the Gonosz who had a wild dragon, which is why Abi and Lloyd weren't able to come to our aid."

There was more that she wanted to tell me, but was hesitating.

"Marcus, Cotopaxi is hurt pretty bad. He fought bravely to save you and Alan. We're moving as fast as we can to get him to our healers. Alan saved his life with some healing herbs, but Paxi needs expert help now," she said.

As if on cue, a large dragon that I recognized from the previous times I had been here, landed. She had two women astride her. As soon as he touched down, the two women bailed off and ran straight to Cotopaxi, both carrying large backpacks. Alan also dropped down off of Lloyd, and for the first time, I saw the sling on his right arm. Alan staggered from the effort, but also made his way to Cotopaxi.

The three of them worked as a team on the unconscious dragon.

"You saved his life, attendant," said one of the women to Alan after they had done all they could for Cotopaxi. "Well done. He would have died without your saving herbs."

Alan just nodded his head at the praise, but dropped to his knees from the effort. He was escorted back to Lloyd and Cowboy. I noticed that Cowboy was trying to take it all in, but it was obviously a shock to him. It would have been humorous, had the situation been different.

With Cotopaxi stabilized, we continued our journey.

This time, I was able to spot landmarks that signaled that we were close to the Amphitheater. There was a great deal of activity from both clan and dragon. I detected an uneasiness from all.

"This attack was an ambush," said Selena when I expressed my uneasy feeling. *"Someone sold us out, and probably delivered the location of one of our wormholes. The Gonosz haven't had access to our wormholes that allow larger amounts of people through. They are very rare, and we are careful to keep them hidden. Up until now, they've been able to send one or two through a smaller wormhole, but this was a large-scale attack."*

We attracted everyone's attention as we neared the meeting place. People stopped what they were doing to stare at our processional. Of particular attention was the wounded Cotopaxi.

It was nearing mid-morning, when we halted at the meeting place. A large tent had been erected and the smell of food wafted from within. Alan and Cowboy dismounted and came over to me.

"How are you feeling, Marcus?" asked Alan.

"Got a major headache, but nothing serious," I said while Alan was peering into my eyes.

"How's your vision?" he asked.

"Little blurry, I guess," I said.

"Yeah, your eyes are slightly dilated. You probably have a small concussion," he said with some worry in his voice.

"I'll be fine. Good thing I was hit in the head, rather than somewhere vital," I said.

Cowboy was looking around at the spectacle.

"So, what do you think, Cowboy?" I asked, chuckling darkly.

"I keep thinking I'm going to wake up, but I hurt too bad to believe I'm asleep," he said. He was sporting some bruises on his arms and face from levitated items that had struck him. Seems as though most the attackers had levitation skills, and not fireball skills.

Abi and Sabryyna came trotting up.

"You're alive, at least," Abi said, looking down at me. I must have looked pathetic, but as usual, Abi and Sabryyna looked like they could have just stepped off the runway. It didn't seem fair.

"We're to gather in the amphitheater in about half an hour. Let's get some food so we can get some strength in you. You three stay here, Abi and I will bring some food back," she said as they both walked off.

"Gee," said Alan thoughtfully. "We've never really eaten here. We've always had our own supplies. Wonder what the food tastes like?"

Dinner consisted of a stew with what was obviously potatoes, but had other tuber-like vegetables that weren't as recognizable. The meat tasted like venison. One vegetable tasted like carrots, but was bright purple.

"*From the type of soil they grow in,*" said Selena.

"Oh," said both Alan and I at the same time.

Cowboy had a funny look on his face.

"*Has anyone told Cowboy about me, or our telepathic communication?*" asked Selena.

If Cowboy was incredulous about this information, he took it better than expected. Perhaps this whole thing overloaded his system, because when we filled in the details all he said was, "So, that's why the crystals are so important to ya'll. You might want to protect them better. They weren't that hard to take away from both of you," and he had a point.

I was feeling better, and the last thing I wanted was to be carried into the meeting. My previous visits had been disastrous to engender any kind of trust with the clans, and I wanted to at least stand tall next to the other riders.

As we entered the amphitheater, I noticed that I was receiving a great deal of attention. There were some faces that appeared to just be curious, but there were some actively hostile stares. Even some of the dragons gave me disapproving looks.

I noticed that Orthu, the dragon, and Kalam, leader of clan Reylor, were deep in conversation, often pausing to look over at us and the other dragons. It appeared that Kal was translating for them.

Qurum was conversing with Lowry and Sharry. I could almost swear that some kind of line was being drawn in the sand between those in their separate conversations.

"I think your instincts serve you well, young Jedi," said Selena when I brought my observation up to her.

"With Vesuvius out of the picture, there is no clear line of succession. I wasn't expecting a problem so soon, but with an active war, events seem to be spinning out of control."

Qurum strode to the front, and both dragon and clansmen took their respective places in the amphitheater. The riders and attendants were assembled next to the dragons, rather than with the clans. Cotopaxi had been left with the two female healers. Only Alan and I were alone.

Cowboy stood behind us. We had explained that he wouldn't be able to hear the proceedings because it would all be conducted with telepathy. Plus, he didn't have a crystal to translate the Vocce language, even if he could hear the conversation. He looked a little lost. I felt sorry for him.

The conversation died down as Qurum took the front.

"Clans, we are gathered in an emergency council to address recent events regarding the Gonosz. I will again act as translator for dragon and the clans. As many of you have heard, the Gonosz have crossed to Earth to make attacks on our trainees. The Gonosz crossed in numbers..."

A conversation roar went up at that revelation. It seemed that this detail was a big deal to the clans.

"...nearly seventy five warriors to our figures attacked our trainees, and if it weren't for the dragons, would have surely killed each candidate and their attendant. Cotopaxi was gravely wounded in the attack, with some of our other dragons also suffering from lesser wounds."

Kalam rose slowly from his position with his clan.

Qurum translating flawlessly for the sake of the dragons.

"It would seem that sending the trainees back to Earth was a mistake," a roar of agreement went up from Kalam's clan. I noticed that several of the neighboring clans also voiced agreement, while an equal amount remained stoic. The dragons remained quiet, but I saw Orthu nod slightly at Kalam's words.

"At this critical time, we cannot afford mistakes. Not only did the trainees get attacked, but it is obvious that Marcus, although from a warrior bloodline, was ill equipped to handle the situation. This resulted in nearly losing a valuable dragon," he said, directing his last comments in my direction. I wanted to sink into the ground, as all eyes turned to me.

"With all due respect," said Lowry, leader of the dragons, *"Marcus demonstrated skill, even though inexperienced..."*

Kalam's clan roared their disapproval at Lowry's words. It took several moments for the roar to die down.

"But a rider chosen from one of the clans would surely have been a better choice," said Orthu as he stepped forward. *"Even the climate and gravity defeats the rider Marcus, and we all have seen evidence that he doesn't have the stomach for any tactical flying."*

"What are you suggesting, Orthu?" asked Sharry, *"that our rider selection is flawed?"*

"Yes," was Orthu's blunt reply. This time it was the dragons that voiced their disapproval, but not all.

"You know that we choose candidates by the properties in which the crystals manifest. The crystals often choose the rider," said Sharry.

"I realize that is how we've done things in the past, but maybe it should be the other way around. We find the strongest, most able candidates and assign them to the crystal. They can make the crystals work for them," replied Orthu.

"That would violate the laws set down from the time that dragons were given the responsibility of choosing riders," she said.

"And the evidence of this being an unfit way in which to choose riders is the dragon Cotopaxi. His rider was unready in al-

most all ways to fill the role and now we have a dragon who is gravely wounded. If the rider and his attendant had been more capable, the dragon might not have been injured," he said, his voice raising in emotion.

"The crystal clearly indicated..." began Sharry.

"I don't care what you say the crystal indicated. We have an unfit rider who chose an unfit attendant, who both chose an unfit dragon," Orthu looked around at the stir his words were causing among the clans. All eyes had returned to me.

"I, Orthu, second in command of the dragon clan, do hereby propose that the rider, Marcus be given a vote of no-confidence. That he be stripped of his rights of rider, stripped of his valuable dragon, and be stripped of both crystals!" said Orthu.

The commotion that his words caused was frightening. Many of the clans clapped and shouted in agreement, their faces hostile, especially when they looked at me and Alan.

"We've NEVER rescinded the rights of a rider after the selection? Never!" said Lowry who had stepped out and was now eye to eye with Orthu. Although Orthu was younger and stronger, Lowry still commanded great presence. Several of the dragons had nodded in agreement at Lowry's words. I did, however, notice that it was the older generation of dragons that seemed to agree with Lowry and Sharry.

"We are in danger of being enslaved by the Gonosz, and you are worried about tradition?" asked Orthu, not backing down to Lowry's authority. "Maybe it's also time for the reigns of authority to be passed within the dragon clan, old friend?"

This caused the greatest commotion of all. It was several minutes before order was restored and Qurum was able to continue.

"We ask all the leaders of each clan to stay and go into emergency council. The clans will retire to their respective camps. We will reconvene this general meeting tomorrow at dawn," he said, his face weary and haggard.

....

It was only several hours until dawn, when we left the meeting. Hostility was the name of the game as we walked away. Abi and Sabryyna stayed close to us, with Hera'sha'i trailing closely, hissing at those who got too close.

"That wasn't what I expected," said Selena. *"This is a time of great danger. The clans should be pulling together, not fighting among ourselves."*

We had just begun to set up an overnight camp, when a cry went up. This was followed by more and more cries.

Abi and Sabryyna sprinted off to see what the commotion was. Alan and I needed to conserve strength in the heavier gravity.

Instead of the cries dying down, they in fact increased as each of the clans took up the cry. After several minutes, Abi came running back, her face white.

"We need to return to the amphitheater. Quickly, Alan, Cowboy and Marcus, mount Hera'sha'i. We must hurry," she said. By her actions and tone of her voice, we knew just to follow Abi's orders without questions.

With us mounted, Abi led off sprinting towards the amphitheater, Hera'sha'i loping behind. What we found was chaotic. Each clan was positioned in or near their designated areas, but there was conflict between the clans. Arguments, yelling, and an occasional brawl were occurring amongst them. The hostility was high.

"What's going on?" I asked Abi who was watching the chaos closely.

In answer to my question, Lowry strode to the front, followed by Qurum. Over and over the two tried to gain the attention of the audience, but it was of no use. It seemed to me that the uproar escalated.

As if on cue, the other dragons stepped forward, raised their snouts into the air in unison, and let go an enormous fire-stream into the air, accompanied with a bellow that I had never heard before. The fire-streams were terrifying, but the combined bellow of a clan of dragons was beyond terrifying. Immediately, a hush fell upon the crowd as we all stood in awe at the spectacle. I did notice, however, that not all the dragons were participants in this act. Orthu and many of the younger, stronger dragons stood off to the side. Alongside the dragons were Kalam, and some of the other leaders of various clans.

Once the uneasy peace was restored, Qurum began. He looked haggard and weary, his face betraying the fear he felt.

"Clans, we are now gathered in an emergency general session. Due to the nature and importance of this session, clans will be voting on decisions that will forever affect us going forward. To this end, I turn the time over to Orthu, second in command of the dragon clan. I will function as interpreter."

Even without knowing the governing structure of the clans, I could see that there was a shift in power among the clans and dragons. As Orthu came forward, he was flanked by Kalam and the leaders of several of the clans, who all now faced the audience.

"Fellow dragons and clan-members. The time to act is upon us. We can no longer follow foolish traditions and obey orders from wise, but out-of-touch leaders who no longer can foresee what is best for our clans."

Orthu's speech was interrupted by an uproar. Qurum, who had raised his hands in a gesture of silence, stood silently, waiting for the commotion to subside.

"Please, fellow clansmen and dragons. We will hear Orthu to completion. There will be time for discussion when he has completed his statement," he said.

Slowly, the commotion died, and Orthu was able to continue.

"Our course of action is clear. We must prepare and fight the Gonosz while we have the strength and power of the dragons behind us. As of now, they can capture and force wild dragons to fight, but we have sole access to the crystals that allow us communication with the riders and enhance our abilities to control certain elements."

Unfortunately," he said, looking directly at me and Alan, "*we have squandered these valuable crystals, with which our dragon ancestors imbued with power. The art of bestowing power to crystals has been lost, so the crystals that remain should be used and assigned to worthy caretakers, not wasted on unproven, weak strangers, no matter what their bloodline is.*"

"Gee, whoever could he be talking about?" asked Alan, his fists clenched tight.

"*We now have a chance,*" continued Orthu, "*for us to fix those mistakes.*"

Orthu now straightened himself. He was an impressively large dragon, towering over many of the other dragons.

"*I propose that the time of transferring power has come. With the death of Vesuvius, there is no longer a direct line of secession. As second in command, I submit to you that the current dragon elders are unfit for leadership...*"

Pandemonium erupted, prompting Qurum to raise his arms in silence once again.

"*...that our leadership is unfit for leadership,*" continued Orthu, "*and that the dragons put to vote which dragon is suited for the role as leader of the dragon clan. We value and respect the service in which Lowry and Sharry have rendered, but these times are perilous and require a different kind of leadership. A strong form of leadership based on the needs of our current situation, not useless traditions.*"

"*Furthermore, we must strip the valuable crystals from unworthy caretakers,*" again, he looked in mine and Alan's direction, "*even though some of the crystals have been bestowed to be passed down within a family.*"

This time, clans stood on their feet. Some in protest, but others obviously cheering the pronouncement.

"*Riders will be chosen from within the ranks of the clans, but riders will be required to demonstrate worthiness, or be stripped of such an honor,*" Orthu explained, scanning the audience as he gauged the effects of his words. "*We will tolerate the 'Rider for Life' mentality no more!*"

He paused for effect.

"*Our survival hinges on us taking this action immediately,*" he said.

"*Our STRENGTH has always been to value the words of our knowledgeable elders. Some of our elders have several lifetimes worth of knowledge. We would be rash not to listen to their wise words...*" began Lowry.

"*We would continue to seek their counsel,*" interrupted Orthu.

"*Please, old friend. I gave you the courtesy of uninterrupted speech. Please give me the same respect,*" Lowry drew himself tall at the rebuke. I could tell that the admonishment struck a nerve with Orthu, who nodded and backed down. Good. The old boy still had some respect and clout.

"*The ancient ones were the creators of the crystals and imbued them with power. Sadly, that skill has been long lost, and there are limited crystals remaining. Do you not think that the use of crystals was not well thought out? It is known that the clan family possess different skills, just as certain dragons have stronger skills than others. The ancient dragons knew this, and tailored the crystal traits to magnify the existing skills of the families. Other crystals were created to give enhanced gifts. These additional crystals were created to work in cooperation with the family crystals. By transferring the family crystal to another rider, many of the enhanced skills would be inaccessible to the new rider. It is the will of the elders to have the family crystals remain with the families. The same for all other crystals bestowed on the attendants, and others who have been given crystals from the dragons,*" he said, again standing tall and regal, reminding all present of his position and authority among the dragons.

Kalam stepped forward at the end of Lowry's speech. It was obvious that the ancient dragon had made vital points.

"*Clansmen and dragons. I Kalam, leader of Clan Reylor and mouthpiece of many of these clans, do place our support behind Orthu and his wise counsel. Our history is fraught with times of war. It was only by taking drastic action that the clans survive today. Again, we are faced with difficult decisions. Our survival demands drastic action. I propose that the crystals be given to those warriors and dragons, strong enough to win this battle against the Gonosz. They can always be returned after the defeat of our common enemy."*

Kalam's words were met with approval. "Borrowing" the crystals and dragons was more palpable than forcefully taking the crystals and assigning them to others. I could see the wisdom in this, especially because I felt useless as a rider. I looked at my small group to see their reactions to what I thought was a wise decision. Their faces told the story. They were solidly behind Lowry and the elders.

"I would speak," said Selena who was now projecting herself to be seen by all. It had to be vitally important. She had told me that the energy needed to project, dangerously drained her crystal to the point of running the energy dry, causing her to pass beyond with no chance of returning.

A gasp went out as Selena stepped forward. I could hear Cowboy's surprised intake of air.

"Is that really her," he whispered in my ear.

"Oh, yeah. That's Selena," I said.

"You need to join me up front, Marcus," Selena told me. I hesitatingly stepped in front of the gathered audience. It was the last place in either world that I wanted to be, but Selena needed me to be in proximity.

"I must object to Selena addressing the clans," said Kalam angrily. *"We must make decisions of great importance. We do not have the time to hear every point of view, even if it is from a fallen rider."*

"On the contrary, Kalam," said Lowry, *"I believe that Selena has earned the right to speak to this gathering. She has proven herself in battle numerous times, and I don't need to remind you that Kal owes his very life to Selena and Vesuvius, unless you have conveniently forgotten?"*

Wait, what?

Chastened, Kalam stepped back, but the rebuke appeared to have hit home. This was a story someone needed to tell me, and this was the first time that I had heard about Selena actually fighting battles. For some reason I had assumed that she was just going through training, and was readying herself for battle. Not a seasoned warrior.

Standing tall, and projecting herself wearing the battle armor of a dragon rider, my sister began.

"Clans, as you know, my brother and I are the remainder of what is the Musi clan. As you recall, the majority of Musi clan members have had enhanced abilities to utilize crystals, which was why we were actively sought and killed by the enemy. You've witnessed my skill, combined with my dragon, Vesuvius, in defense of the clans. Many of the crystals were imprinted with the blood of certain family lines as a defense against the crystals being stolen by the enemy and used against us. The crystals are passed from one family member to another through a blood trial, which enables the new owner to be able to access the secrets of the crystal. Without the blood trial, the one in possession of the crystal can only utilize the basic powers infused within the crystal. Those powers are for-midable, but nothing compared to what is stored in the crystals. Even I, who have been training in the use of the crystals my entire life, still do not know the vast potential the crystals store."

Selena shifted positions. Instead of addressing all of the audience, she turned slightly away from Kalam and Orthu and addressed the other clans. Her appeal was directly at the other clans.

"As Orthu and Kalam have mentioned, this is a great time of peril, but rash decisions are not the answer. The ancient dragons had this very situation in mind to create the safe-guards that they did. Keep that in mind as we come to vote."

I could feel that Selena was dangerously using the crystal power. She must have sensed it, too, because she immediately disappeared out of our sight to conserve energy.

Qurum stepped forward.

"We will vote," he said. *"Clan leaders will vote for their individual clans. They will respond to the entire gathering."*

"*Omner, leader of clan Wyr,*" called out Qurum.

"*We honor the wisdom of the ancients. Our vote is for the status quo.*"

"*Evyn of Clan Imor, state your vote.*"

"*These are tumultuous times. We vote in favor of the plan presented by Orthu and Kalam,*" said Evyn. Apparently, this was not a unanimous decision within the clan, as a cry of protest went out. Even Chayl looked shocked and surprised at the announcement from his clan leader. I saw him look questioningly at Abi who just shrugged.

"*Kalam, of clan Reylor.*"

"*We support the wisdom of Orthu,*" he said, no surprise there. "*Give us the tools in which to defeat our enemy once and for all!*"

A cheer went up from his clan.

"*Erom of clan Tyrm,*" called out Qurum.

"*Clan Tyrm will place its trust in strength and might. We follow Orthu,*" he said.

"*By my count, that makes one vote in favor of the status quo, three against,*" said Qurum.

"*Lowry, of the dragon clan.*"

"*Status quo,*" he said simply.

"*Two clans left,*" said Abi, her face anxious.

"*Cally, clan Malla.*"

A very striking lady stepped forward.

"*Malla votes status quo,*" she said.

"*Calla, clan Lemil,* " Qurum said as he looked around the crowd. Calla was Cally's sister, and there was no love lost with the two sisters.

There was no answer.

"*Calla, clan Lemil*" Qurum called out again.

A murmur went up throughout the audience as, again, no one answered from clan Lemil.

Cally stepped forward again.

"*I am sorry to inform the clans that clan Lemil is no more. My treacherous sister and her clan tried to overpower clan Malla*" *last night. A fight ensued, and my sister was killed. The remaining members of clan Lemil were given a choice to join Clan Malla, or die. Some chose unwisely."*

This news was met with a large uproar from the crowd. It wasn't unheard of that the clans would war to resolve disputes, but most clans had resolved their differences peacefully, once united against a common enemy. The implications of the news was apparent to everybody.

Three to three. Stalemate.

Orthu strode to the front. His swagger was that of triumph. He was a handsome dragon, and his physical strength was visible as the muscles rippled under his thick, armored skin. He was imposing, and I could see why the clans might rally behind such a dragon, and not the aged leadership of Lowry.

"As per tradition in the event of a tie," he began importantly, *"we call for the final vote to be cast by a commission of dragons. Also as tradition, the second dragon in command will head that commission."*

Well, that was that. It was obvious that Orthu and Kalam had planned in advance and were using the traditions in their favor. On the other hand, I would no longer be forced to embarrass myself in front of the clans, or fight, and certainly die in a war I knew little about.

"As head of the commission, I choose Verik, Crandl, ..." said Orthu.

"The voting is not yet concluded," said Qurum quietly.

"...Sali.." continued Orthu.

"The voting is not yet concluded," said Qurum again. This time Orthu turned, visibly confused at the interruption.

"I'm sorry. What do you mean? All six of the attending clans have voted. As we are in a voting stalemate, we will continue forward with a commission of dragons to determine our future," said Orthu.

"The voting is not yet concluded," said Lowry. Orthu turned in surprise to the leader of the dragon clan.

"*What kind of trick is this?*" asked Orthu. "*Stand aside, old friend. I know it is a hard thing to face, but you must accept these changes gracefully. We are ready to proceed...*"

"*The voting is not yet concluded,*" said Lowry, standing tall and majestic. "*There is a final clan vote. Marcus, leader of clan Musi,what is your vote?*"

CHAPTER TWENTY

BETRAYAL

The word for what came next is pandemonium.

Pandemonium – (noun) wild and noisy disorder. Similar words: bedlam, chaos, or mayhem. Example: "Pandemonium broke out when it was announced that Captain Barf-Shirt was the leader of clan Musi."

Actual swords were drawn, and I wouldn't have been surprised if one of the clansmen ran me through with his weapon. Several warriors appeared to think just that, as they jumped up and ran towards me.

The only deterrent were two wounded dragons who appeared by my side. Although both Lloyd and Cotopaxi were badly injured, their presence caused angry warriors to step back in haste. Cotopaxi looked especially fierce, as he draped his neck over my shoulder in a very protective stance. If a warrior was to get to me, he would have to get past both teeth and fire to do so.

"What is the meaning of this? You would try to steal away the will of the clans by giving voting rights to this...this..." began Kalam.

The uproar didn't seem to faze either Qurum or Lowry.

"How have we stolen away the will of the clans?" asked Lowry calmly. *"We have one more clan leader in attendance, and he has not yet cast his vote."*

"Clan Musi is no longer a functioning clan! It has been decimated to one member!" said an angry Kalam.

"Yet it does exist, and Marcus, who is the lone survivor, has been the leader of that clan ever since the death of his sister. Sel-

ena, as you all remember, had clan leader voting rights prior to her death. Marcus is, by all rights, leader of clan Musi," said Lowry.

"You will regret this decision, old friend," said Orthu. There was something sinister about the way Orthu said that, as if he knew something we did not.

There was a sadness in Lowry. I hadn't seen it until he turned and met Orthu's gaze.

"I regret many decisions, Orthu. It is the burden of a leader. However, it is you who will regret this nights' decisions."

He paused and looked deep into Orthu's eyes, like he was staring into Orthu's soul.

"The one thing I will never regret, is my loyalty to the clans, Orthu. I have spent my entire life in service to the clans, fighting the evil that is the Gonosz. I will go to my grave with a clear conscience on that particular matter," he said quietly.   *"Is your conscience clear, old friend?"*

"What are you insinuating?" asked Orthu, his eyes narrowed to slits. He looked very, very dangerous. Frightenedly dangerous.

"The Gonosz have possession of a wormhole large enough to send many warriors through. We have guarded all the known wormholes diligently. The wormhole in question is guarded by your clan, Kalam," said Qurum.

"Lies!" shouted Kalam, his face turning very red.

"I wish that this wasn't true, but it is," said Lowry. *"Unfortunately, this has been confirmed by Verbane."*

At the mention of her name, Verbane stepped forward.

"It's true," she said. *"I had my scouts fly to known wormholes immediately after the attack. We found the retreating Gonosz exiting the wormhole guarded by clan Reylor."*

To reinforce the point, Verbane showed us just what the scouts had seen. We could tell that the scouts were viewing this from a great distance, but with the enhanced vision of the dragons, it was still very clear. We saw the Gonosz soldiers emerging through the wormhole, to be greeted by none other than Kalam and Orthu.

I was watching Orthu throughout this exchange, and something changed in his demeanor as the truth came out.

Those with Orthu and Kalam must have silently communicated an order, because in a rush, several of the tribes that were aligned with each other drew their weapons and formed into a fighting unit. There were many of the younger, fitter dragons among them. They stood facing the rest of the audience who were in too much shock to move.

"I will not deny what Verbane has shown us," said Orthu.

An audible gasp went out from the audience.

"Our current leadership is blinded by the fact that we will soon be wiped out, regardless of how well we fight. It is only a matter of time," said Orthu calmly. *"I have taken steps to ensure our freedom. The Gonosz are not interested in taking over this part of the land. If we align ourselves with their government, we can remain free."*

A cheer went up from many clan members. Some people who had been sitting in the audience jumped up to join Kalam and Orthu.

"Since when do we trust promises from the Gonosz?" asked Lowry. *"Have you forgotten that they have attacked and conquered our villages, enslaved our people? I do not believe that they will simply let us be, if we join them. What do we owe the Gonosz in exchange for this freedom?"*

It was Selena who gave us the warning.

"We're being surrounded," she said to our small group. Sure enough, I could see movement in the treeline. Someone was moving out in the surrounding forest.

"Marcus, is there anyone behind us?" Selena asked. I knew she wanted me to scan the area with my enhanced vision.

It seemed clear, but I could see increased movement. We would quickly be sealed off if we didn't move immediately.

"Marcus, take us to the front," ordered Selena.

"The rest of you come with me," said Lloyd, who began to move slowly towards the dragons that were backing Lowry and Qurum.

Selena once again appeared.

"Clans, we have been betrayed. Even as we speak, we are being surrounded by the Gonosz." At Selena's statement, several dragons took to the air.

Verbane discovered the truth immediately.

"It's true," she said from the air. *"Clans, you are being surrounded."*

At the announcement of being surrounded, Orthu and Kalam had started to back away from the amphitheater. Those with them followed. I estimated that more than half of the audience followed them. The rest of the clans arranged themselves in defensive positions, weapons drawn.

"You that stay, are fools!" roared Orthu, all pretense of being aligned with the Gonosz gone. *"I've brought you freedom from war, freedom from annihilation. This is your last chance to align yourselves with us! If you stay, you will be considered our enemy."*

At his statement, even more of the clans rushed to join Orthu and Kalam. While the majority of the dragons stayed, they were the older dragons. Most of the younger, stronger dragons could be seen with the retreating clans.

It was terrible to watch the clans divide and choose their alliances. Friends, clans and families were split.

Of course, Kalam and most of his clan, including Kal and Kylor, chose to align with the Gonosz. The two sisters, Calla and Cally, were seen arguing in the center of the commotion. They ultimately chose different allegiances, Calla with Orthu and Kalam, Cally remaining with us.

Evyn, leader of Clan Imor, turned his back on us and headed towards the retreating army. Turning, he caught eye contact with Chayl and Marrle, who had remained at the front with the rest of the riders. Evyn jerked his head, motioning towards Orthu and Kalam, his meaning clear, but Chayl and Marrle remained firm. Chayl's attendant, Leor, was standing next to Evyn. He had made a decision to stay with his clan, although it seemed to me that he was being forced to remain with them.

"I Evyn, leader of Clan Imor, order you to follow!" he shouted, but Chayl and Marrle stood firm, their dragons at their side.

"I cannot," Chayl said simply. "This is wrong."

"You are dead to clan Imor! Dead! We recognize you no more! You have disgraced your clan, and your families," shouted Evyn. There were tears in the two riders' eyes as they watched their families and clan leave, but there was no hesitation. Both remained.

The battle lines were drawn, and it was bleak for us. Less than half of the clans had decided to remain. As I have said before, most of the remaining dragons were older, the younger and stronger dragons choosing to go with the Gonosz.

Eyes now turned to Lowry and Qurum.

Lowry said what we all knew was coming.

"*We must run.*"

"*Where?*" asked Cally. "*The clans all know the hiding places.*"

"*There are other... places,*" replied Lowry. "*Ancient places that only the dragons know. Ones that are only known to the Elders. We will retreat to those, and make preparations for war.*"

"*It's unfortunate, but we've felt the need to plan for such an event. Orthu and Kalam were always a threat,*" added Qurum. "*But while we are running, I think that we need all of the riders and their attendants to return to Earth. While we were at the gathering, Verbane had several of her loyal scouts return and seal off the wormhole controlled by the Gonosz. It was fairly unstable, and it didn't take much to seal it off permanently. They are without a reliable wormhole, so Earth might once again, be the safest place for you as you continue to train. Added to the fact that Marcus still hasn't gained the strength to train in our climate.*"

I wondered if I would ever be able to get used to this world. I shuddered to think of the cardio training necessary to function properly on Vocce. I was not, in any sense of the word, a runner.

"We will need to run immediately," said Lowry. *"And you, new dragons and riders, will need to also leave shortly. Lloyd will again accompany you, along with several other dragons who will serve as both trainers and protectors. Lloyd will know how to find us when the time comes to meet again."*

Cotopaxi hadn't left my side for the entire time. Amazingly, he seemed to be getting better and better right in front of our eyes, as was Lloyd.

"It's both the healing herbs that we administered, and the natural healing power of dragons. You would be amazed at the healing properties of some of the herbs here on Vocce. Puts our meds on Earth to shame," said Alan.

"Are you going to be able to travel, Paxi?" I asked.

In answer to my question, Cotopaxi stretched his wings and launched into the air. He moved slowly, and I could tell that he was still feeling pain, but he looked stronger than I would have ever imagined after being wounded so badly.

He landed with a "whump," and leaned up against a tree so that I could scramble on.

Cowboy had been quiet the entire time. I realized for the first time that this had all been thrown at him, and not yet being able to communicate telepathically, he had no idea what was going on.

"I'm sorry, Cowboy. You must have a thousand questions..." I began.

"Actually, Sabryyna has been filling me in," he said. "I can hear her in my head. She has been keeping me informed."

"It's a gift that I recently discovered with my crystal," said Sabryyna. "I can communicate directly with almost anyone, even if they haven't learned telepathy yet."

"Prepare for flight," instructed Lloyd. He amazingly looked like he was fit enough for flight himself.

"Just a moment," said Chayl. *"I believe Leor left us a gift."*

We watched as Chayl walked over to where Leor had been standing, before retreating with his clan. Reaching down, he picked up the dragon crystal that Leor had left.

"Leor was being forced to abandon us," said Chayl. *"He wanted to stay and finish his training, but…"*

Chayl returned to us, bouncing the crystal in his hand, a thoughtful expression on his face.

"I don't know you, and I don't know how well this crystal will work for you, but you seem loyal to Marcus and Selena," he said to Cowboy, "and it appears that I'm in need of an attendant. Would you consider being my attendant?" he asked a surprised Cowboy.

"I'm not sure what that means exactly, but I want to help, so sure," he said, accepting the crystal.

And with that, we mounted up, our small team of riders, attendants, and dragons to return to earth.

....

"Lloyd, where will the clans go? Why didn't the Gonosz attack when the clans defected? It seemed like we were outnumbered," I asked as we were flying back to the wormhole.

"We chose the amphitheater for a reason. It was easily defended. Did you notice that there weren't any Gonosz behind us? There is basically only one way into the amphitheater, and Verbane makes sure to post dragons to defend our escape routes. Orthu and Kalam of course know this, so they didn't press an attack," he replied.

He was thoughtful for a moment.

"As to where they will go? We have been anticipating that we would eventually have to confront Orthu. He and his mate have been vocal for some time about our Elders being out of touch. It was only a matter of time before he tried to take over. The hiding place is only known to a few of our Elders. It is a very hidden wormhole, that even if the Gonosz find its location, they won't be able to access it. It takes a special signal to open it. It leads to a very remote area of Vocce. We've been stocking the area for months, and it has shelters enough for the clans. It will buy us some time, but because it is remote, we are dependent on supplies. It is a short-term solu-

tion, but for the time being, the clans will be safe. They will have to travel quickly for several days, so there is still danger of being overtaken by the Gonosz, but I feel confident that they should escape. The old ones have some surprises that should discourage the enemy," he said with a dark chuckle.

Cowboy was mounted behind Chayl. I saw him give Sabryyna a wink and a smile. It appeared that there were some fireworks happening between those two. It was weird, because it was only a couple of weeks that Cowboy was a full-on enemy. Stranger still was the friendship that had built up between Alan and Cowboy. With them both being dragon attendants now, it was easy to see that they would have even more in common.

The trip back was uneventful, and it was always a relief for me to return to normal gravity and air supply.

Cowboy was also relieved.

"Man, I'm one tired buckaroo," he said. "And boy-howdy, do I have some questions for y'all." The tension of the previous days was momentarily broken as we broke into laughter. We were learning that Cowboy would revert to slang for comic relief in these situations.

We had gathered at the cabin where we had left the side by sides, and it was several minutes of laughter before we regained our composure. Alan and I had a pretty good idea of what he was going through, since we had gone through the same type of thing, making it that much more funny for us.

"We only have a couple hours of rest before Marcus, Alan, Cowboy, Sabrynna, and Abi need to get back to civilization," said Lloyd.

"Whoa, I totally heard that!" said Cowboy. It appears that Chayl had taught Cowboy how to connect to his newly acquired crystal, and like Alan, was able to utilize some of its properties immediately. Apparently, I was the only idiot in our group that struggled with everything.

CHAPTER TWENTY-ONE

COWBOY'S LOSS

The weather was getting colder, and the holidays were nearing.

One of the highlights was that Alan's family was all home now. Their insurance didn't pay for all of the damages to their home, but paid enough for them to purchase a pre-fabricated home that was set up in a matter of weeks. It was sparsely furnished, but at least all the family was alive and well. The community was generous and provided beds, clothing, and some of the little things that we take for granted. Grandma had been more than generous and had given them Grandpa Torrey's truck, theirs having been destroyed in the fire. I knew that it was the right thing to do, but I loved that truck and always hoped that someday it would be mine.

Selena had withdrawn more and more. Only the training that we had daily would pull her out of hibernation.

I deliberately didn't broach the subject, because in my heart of hearts, I knew that she was struggling with living within the confines of the crystal.

"I feel the pull to cross more and more each day," she confided in me. *"I just need to know that you and Grandma are going to be OK."*

School went strangely smooth for the next couple of weeks. Eldon had stopped actively tormenting us, although he did have a snide remark anytime any of us passed. He just didn't actively beat the daylights out of us anymore.

"*It's only a matter of time,*" Cowboy told us telepathically. It was a new talent that he had learned and used often. "*That one is a hater, and when opportunity arises...*"

He didn't have to finish his sentence for us all to understand.

Abi had taken to walking with me from class to class. Sabryyna, Alan, and Cowboy were often inseparable, having similar class schedules. Each time we would come upon Eldon or one of his cronies, she would either slip her hand into mine, or drop her arm around my waist.

I admit, I had fallen hopelessly in love with her, but there was something distant about her that kept me from pursuing her further. Couldn't put my finger on what it was, just something that kept her at a distance, despite our obvious friendship. There was a sadness in her that I could sense. I assumed because of the loss of her family. Whatever kept her at a distance, seemed impenetrable. I wanted to ask Selena's opinion, but never could broach the subject.

The strange thing about being on Earth, is that the events on Vocce seemed so distant. It was easy to forget that we were training for war. Lloyd kept us informed of what was happening with the clans. He would occasionally disappear for a few days while others would take over our training. When he would return, he would report on the clans, families, friends, and so on.

"*The clans arrived at the hiding place, and they are safe and well for the time being. Qurum and Lowry have instructed that we get battle-ready as quickly as possible,*" he reported.

Training was difficult, and it seemed that Cotopaxi and I were making little progress, while the other teams were turning into amazing fighting units. Cowboy ended up being an amazing rider. He was able to stay on the back of Sjer-berha, Chayl's dragon, even when Sjer-berha was doing fantastic aerobatics. Cowboy was also a natural with fireballs and levitation. Way better than I was.

I really couldn't understand how I was chosen to be a rider. I was awkward and uneasy on the back of Cotopaxi. It didn't help that the other young dragons were picking up communication skills. Cotopaxi would send images, but was not communicating with words.

"His father was a wild dragon. The wild ones never developed verbal communication, so Paxi might need some time," Selena informed me one evening when I had voiced my concerns with the training.

"Figures. I feel like I'm disadvantaged at every turn. I'm sure we'll be the first team to be killed," I said.

It was difficult to concentrate on school for many reasons. The obvious was this double life that we were living, and the other was that it was the beginning of the holiday season. Thanksgiving was only a week away, then of course Christmas was not far behind after that. The entire school was looking forward to the time off the holidays afforded us.

One perk about having new-found skills is that I no longer panicked about classwork and tests. It was like having the internet during test time.

"Alan, stuck on a test question," I said.

Telepathy has distance restraints, but within the school area, our communication was as clear as a bell. We had measured the range, and five miles was the magic number. The dragons were a different story. They were able to communicate at remarkable distances, just not with us. Between themselves, it appeared to be several hundred miles. They could receive information from us, but we weren't able to receive back from them, from a distance of over five miles.

"Sure. I bet you're not letting Selena hear our conversation," he said, chuckling telepathically.

"Nope! What she doesn't know won't hurt her," I said. Selena was strangely puritanical about me not cheating, or "using my newly-acquired resources," as I liked to put it.

"What's the question? Chemistry test, right?" he asked. Alan loved Chemistry. What a freak.

"*This noble gas also has the lowest boiling point of all the elements,*" I said.

"*That's easy,*" he said, "*what is the first noble gas?*"

"*This isn't 'Jeopardy'. I don't think I have to answer in the form of a question.*"

"*No, idiot! I was asking you what the first noble gas is,*" I could hear his telepathic sigh.

"*Hydrogen?*" I asked hopefully.

"*Not even a noble gas, but a close guess.*"

"*Boron?*" I guessed again.

"*You're the Boron. Boron is a metalloid, genius. But the answer you're looking for, but will never guess, is 'Helium'. Helium is also the first noble gas...never mind. You might as well just read the rest of the test to me. You're just going to ask the answer to every question anyhow,*" Alan said. "*But you're going to get a 'C' grade on this test. Because NOBODY would believe...*"

We had taken to doing our training on Cowboys property. It was secluded enough for us to practice using the dragons without the prying eyes of neighbors. Still, we had scouts, both human and dragon, running the perimeter to make sure that we weren't discovered.

Thanksgiving had been fairly uneventful. It was good to spend some time with grandma, just one on one. With the upcoming Christmas break, we were trying to get permission from Alan and Cowboy's parents to get away for three or four days during the break to visit the clans in their new hiding place. Cowboys parents were on board, but Alan's family was getting more and more concerned with how much time he was spending away from his family.

"We just don't see you anymore, and we want Christmas vacation to be about the family," said Alan's mom.

"It's only a couple days out of a two-week vacation," he complained.

"We'll see," was the non-committal reply.

Grandma was concerned, too. Things got real with her when we informed her of some of the events that were transpiring.

"Why don't the dragons choose grown warriors, rather than kids to be riders?" she asked. "What can kids possibly do better than grown-ups?"

"It's due to the connection that the young dragon and young rider make at that age," said Abi. "Our abilities to communicate and bond are better at a young age rather than full-blown adults, both dragon and human. When an older rider and dragon are paired, it is often too late for either to bond properly."

"Still, that's a lot of responsibility to put on the shoulders of kids...and dangerous on top of that. Selena is a good example of that," Grandam said, not at all convinced of Abi's argument.

It took some doing, but we were finally able to get permission to take four days to "get away as a group of friends" at Cowboy's family's cabin. We tried to find another destination, but there were those nagging things called "cell phones." The cabin was out of cell range, making it one of the only choices to really get away without being contacted daily by everyone and their dog.

Still, we began to worry about what to do when we needed to be gone for extended periods of time in the future. It was a real problem, and none of our solutions were good ones, or in any way full-proof. If only the Gonosz would agree to limit their shenanigans to weekends only.

Our trip back to Vocce and the clans was going to be difficult. We would have to travel fast in order to make the round trip in under four days. The wormhole that we were using was about one days' travel away from the wormhole that would take us to the hiding spot for the clans. We would burn two of the four days just traveling.

Cowboy and Alan were both giddy with excitement. Each day was a new adventure, and returning to Vocce was always interesting. I was not excited to return. Cotopaxi and I were still struggling, while each of the other teams were learning new skills every day. Paxi and I just couldn't seem to work on the same page. I wanted to zig while he zagged and vice versa. He couldn't communicate very well, and I could tell that he was frustrated with me.

Alan was sitting behind me, both of us astride Cotopaxi, who had started to grow into his awkward body. His strong wings now could withstand both of our weight, even when we crossed into the heavier gravity. At least there was that.

"We're going to need to find a backup wormhole," Alan was saying. "It's probably only a matter of time before Orthu or one of the other dragons find our current wormhole, and just camp out on it and wait for us to appear."

We were flying in our battle formation. Chayl and Cowboy were the scouts and were flying ahead. Their job was to alert the rest of us if there was any danger. Lloyd had remarked that Chayl and Cowboy were one of the best scout teams that he had ever trained.

Abi and Sabryyna were the rear guard, but their responsibilities were much the same as the scouts. If there was an attack from behind, it would be their job to alert us to the danger. Again, Lloyd was mightily impressed with their abilities.

"No one would believe that those girls were deadly warriors," said Lloyd.

We rode in the middle of the pack. Our jobs were to provide support to either the scouts, or the rear guard, in the event we were attacked.

We were joined by Lloyd and two other dragons, Crymyr and Shylo, who had aided in our training. They also flew with us in the middle of the pack, and would also provide support if attacked. Though older, and not in their fighting prime, the three were formidable, having years of experience. All three had been rider and dragon teams, their riders having died of old age long ago. They were a wealth of knowledge, just not to me and Cotopaxi. They didn't know what to do about us, it seemed.

"We're coming upon the wormhole to the clans," said Lloyd.

"Chayl, if you could please scout the area around for activity. The clans should have someone about to guard the wormhole."

Chayl sped ahead and began a circling pattern above an alpine lake. He started his circle wide, and then began to narrow his circling, until he was satisfied with what he saw. Taking one more circle, he belly-rolled and dived to the lake. It amazed me to see Cowboy and Chayl laugh at the death-defying flying. They seemed glued to the back of Sjer-berha. If Cotopaxi had tried that maneuver, I have no doubt that I would have been the belly-flop champion of both worlds, having fallen off into the lake below.

He was greeted by two dragons and some warriors who had emerged from their hiding places to greet us.

"I've provided the password," Chayl informed us. *"You can land in safety."*

Dropping to the ground, we were greeted by Qurum, who stepped out from the treeline.

"We need to travel fast. Our clans are relatively safe right now, but we need to plan for our next course of action," he said.

The wormhole was unremarkable. There is a small canyon with a stream that feeds the lake. As we entered the canyon, the walls of the canyon quickly became sheer cliffs on either side of the creek. Qurum was leading, and after walking for about five minutes, he turned right and walked into what looked like an eroded area dug out from the water.

"Lloyd, if you please," he said.

Lloyd's side heaved as he took a large breath, and then blasted the wall with fire. The heat was intense. After a few seconds, a familiar vortex appeared. One after another, we walked through the wormhole, led by Chayl and Cowboy.

When it was my turn, I stepped through with Alan and Cotopaxi right behind. The Vocce I knew was way different than the Vocce I stepped in to. What had been forested areas, lush with water and greenery, was now what I would call barren grassland. No trees. Old growth sage bush towered ten feet around us, affording us some concealment, but not much. It was easy to see why this area of Vocce might not be inhabited. It would be much more difficult to survive with less resources.

Qurum stepped up beside me.

"We are currently located on the far side of our planet, away from the Gonosz. Our old home was along the equator of Vocce. We're thousands of miles south of the equator, which is one of the reasons that there is little to no rainfall. Fortunately, we're days away from monsoon season, which only lasts a few weeks, and provides for the majority of the water for the remainder of the year. Only the very hardy survive in areas like this. We're fortunate, indeed, to have some clan members that were trained to survive these areas," he said.

We all took to the air after Chayl and Cowboy had a quick scout around. We needed to fly fast and long to get to the clans. They were camped on the only water source available to support a large group of people.

It took almost six hours of some of the most monotonous flying ever. This was mile after mile of grasslands and sage brush, unlike flying over the heavily forested areas of Vocce. Not a river in sight. Very little animal life. With my enhanced vision, I spotted the occasional field mouse and some funky reptiles that hunted the mice, but little else. Once I saw a large raptor-like bird that nabbed a mouse, only to be surprised to find out that it was actually a type of flying lizard.

I don't know if you have ever ridden a horse for an extended period of time, but if you have, you get saddle-sore pretty quickly if you are not accustomed to it. Riding while straddling something is never a fun thing for a newbie. When we actually landed and I was able to slide off Cotopaxi's back, I was hardly able to stand. For once, Alan seemed worse off than I was. He was feeling the effects of riding a dragon for an extended period of time pretty hard.

"Ahhhhh," he breathed a sigh of relief as he slid to the ground.

"No offense, Paxi, but I would rather fight Cowboy again in my tighty whities than endure that for another hour," he said

while massaging his inner thighs.

Cotopaxi reacted with a slobbery face licking, showing his concern.

"Stop, stop! I take it back! Yuck! Knock it off, you big silly lizard!" said a laughing Alan, as he tried to ward off Cotopaxi's attempts to console his diminutive friend. The licking didn't abate until Alan had wrapped his arms around the neck of my dragon and patted his head, letting Cotopaxi know that he had been forgiven.

We were met by Lowry who had been circling the area when we had landed. He was accompanied by several of the scout dragons.

"You will want to eat something and get ready for our strategy meeting. We have food ready, and you can wash up from your travels," he said. *"We don't have much time, so we will meet in an hour."*

The food was way different from what we had eaten before. As I suspected, there was little protein in the way of meat. The clans were subsisting on mostly a grain diet, as grain was most suited for cultivation. There were some other food items, but there was little of that. I recalled that most of the supplies had to be brought here. Our meal was bread made from an unrecognizable grain that had a peppery taste to it, and it was a bright orange color.

"The grain is amazingly nutritious," said Abi, between bites of the bread. "It has high protein content."

The dragons had grouped together and were in some sort of conversation.

Lloyd broke from the group and returned to us.

"The dragons have it worse here, as far as food goes. We will need to leave you for a while, as we fly a good distance away to a food source."

And with that, the dragons launched into the air to go hunting. I had hunted with Cotopaxi several times on earth, and it's a lot like how you would expect a dragon would hunt and feed. We would fly silently over an area until we found prey large enough to feed a dragon, usually a deer or elk. We had to have a discussion with the dragons about feeding on cattle. Cotopaxi especially liked a good rare beef steak. Bones, intestines, hooves, horns, and all.

"Isn't that what hotdogs are made of?" asked Alan as we watched Cotopaxi wolf down the guts of a cow elk.

The dragons were gone for almost the entire hour before they returned. Cotopaxi was excited. He tried to communicate, but couldn't, so he showed me and Alan what they had eaten. It was an enormous lizard, much like a monitor lizard, but one that weighed around eight hundred pounds. The dragons hunted the lizards with care, the lizards being very strong and agile. Great powerful jaws and sharp claws were formidable weapons, even against a dragon. In the end, the dragons brought down several large adult lizards, and had fed well. Cotopaxi was excited because one of the kills was his.

"*Good boy, Paxi!*" I said and gave him a scratch behind the ears. A contented rumble emanated from his massive chest at the praise.

The meeting ended up being between the clan leaders, the dragon council, the riders and attendants, along with their dragons.

The meeting itself was mostly about training issues, how we were to communicate, and how to resupply the clans with goods. I was tired already from the extended trip, and I was never good at logistics, so I found myself nodding off.

"*Marcus, you need to pay attention. This is all important stuff,*" Selena chastised me over and over. She had been "asleep" for several days, but had come to when the meeting started.

"*I've got you to remember all this logistics stuff. What's the big deal if I catch a wink or two?*" I asked.

"*Marcus, I've been trying to warn you, I won't always be here to back you up. One of the first things you learn about fighting is that the more knowledge you have, the better off you are in making battlefield decisions. That includes logistics,*" she said, but I was already nodding off.

Several hours later, we were shown to our temporary quarters for some shut eye.

"Tomorrow will be a downer," said Alan, as we were getting ready for bed.

"Why? It's just more meetings, right?" I asked.

"Dude, didn't you listen to anything?" he asked in exasperation. "Each of us is demonstrating our training. The others are miles and miles ahead of where we are. This is going to be humiliating."

Crud. I was able to shoot a fireball, sometimes. And I could levitate a stick if one end dragged the ground. I don't want to get into how foolish I would look if we were to be tested on our dragon riding skills.

Needless to say, I had a very bad night of sleep.

....

All of my fears were realized the next day. The other rider teams highly impressed the council with their developed skills. They were very impressed with Alan and his display of medical knowledge and the fighting skills he had developed.

Then they came to me and Cotopaxi. My first fireball was too weak to make the sagebrush burst into flame, but it was hot enough to scald one of the council members after it bounced harmlessly off the bush and landed square in his lap, requiring Alan to again show off his newly found knowledge about fireball scalds to sensitive areas of the human body.

Cotopaxi, to his credit, was able to perform his aerial maneuvers for the most part, but not with me as a rider. Twice I fell off and had to be caught by Chayl and Cowboy, who knew my skill level and had flown below us during the test. I could hear the mutters of disappointment from the council as we landed, me sitting between Chayl and Cowboy, both having a tight grip on me, should I fall again with nothing below to catch me.

Alan, of course, had been able to remain seated on Cotopaxi during the trial.

"The attendant is more of an able rider than the rider," I overheard a council member tell another.

With the trial over, I just wanted to be alone. I felt humiliated. Not only was I the weakest link, but I was the weakest link by miles. The dragons had been wrong to choose me.

"*Maybe they should just give Cotopaxi to Alan, and let's call it good,*" I said to Selena in private.

"*I wish I knew what was holding you back,*" she said. "*It was instinctual when I was learning. It just felt right.*"

"*Nothing feels right. I have to fight to do the simplest things. All the other riders and attendants can access their crystals with ease. I have two, and can't use either,*" rubbing my throbbing temples.

"*Well, once the decision has been made with the dragon council, there is no going back. In case you haven't noticed, Paxi loves you. It annoys you, but that is the reason he bumps his nose on you all the time. He wants your attention and he wants you to be proud of him,*" she said.

Lloyd came ambling over.

"*I wouldn't worry about the trials, rider,*" he said reassuringly. "*It takes time. You'll come around. Just be patient.*"

"*I just think I'm wasting everyone's time, and heaven forbid I need to actually fight. I would be as much of a danger to my friends, as my enemies,*" I said.

"*That's what the training is for. We'll be leaving soon. Eat, take a nap. We leave in two hours,*" he said.

Two hours later, we were back in the air. I thought we would stay an additional day, but apparently the council had seen everything that they needed to. In other words, their worst fears had come to pass, and I was even worse than they had guessed.

Cowboy and Alan were especially animated as we flew over the miles and miles of grasslands. They had both been praised for their skills. They were recounting the various skill tests, and analyzing how they could improve.

"Leave me at home. That would improve the teams' score tremendously," I muttered to myself.

As we neared the wormhole, Lloyd flew up alongside us.

"*Marcus, we are going to do some cross-training on each position that we have in our unit. I want you to take lead as we go through the wormhole. Fly over the area, and when you are certain that the way is safe, land and give the password,*" without waiting for an answer he flew off.

Panic struck me.

"*Alan, I don't remember the password,*" I said frantically.

He sighed audibly behind me.

"*You have to take these things more seriously, Marcus. What if this had been the real thing and I was unable to respond. Security is really important,*" he said forcefully.

"*Ok, ok. Enough of the lecture Selena, I mean, Alan. What is the password,*" I asked.

"*The guard will flash you an image of a yellow vase. Once you have received that, you will need to send an image of a bowl of porridge served in a blue bowl,*" with another audible sigh.

Cotopaxi understood his role as lead scout, and shot off toward the wormhole. I naturally had my enhanced vision going, one of the few things I knew how to do well to be effective. We carefully scanned the area and circled lower and lower. Finally I received an image of a red vase.

"*It's a test,*" said Alan. "*Do you remember the real color of the vase?*"

"*Yellow, right?*" I replied.

"*What's the protocol for a wrong question?*"

"*Just tell me what to do! You know I don't remember that stuff,*" I said angrily.

"*Reverse course and return back to your original circling distance. That warns our riders to be alert, that something is wrong.*"

I steered Cotopaxi to reverse course, and we sped away to our widest circling pattern. Instantly, I noticed that our riders went on alert and formed up on each other, in case of an attack. I had forgotten the drill, but it made sense now that I saw it in action.

"You need to send the image of the red vase back. Repeating the signal means that you are requesting that the question be sent again."

I did as Alan said, and sent the image of the red vase back.

I immediately got the correct image of the yellow vase. Focusing, I sent the image of the bowl of porridge.

"Welcome rider, please land," was the reply.

"You were slow in reversing course," Lloyd chastised me after we had all landed. *"The faster we know something is amiss, the faster that we can react. Since you were lead scout, you would have been in the most peril. We would have been able to give you backup quicker. A single second can be the difference between life and death."*

I was sore and tired from the long flight. I just nodded, sulking. It had been another test, and I had failed in front of everyone. Again.

"We will give you another chance, rider. Please lead us home," he said.

The flight to the wormhole home was uneventful. I rather suspected that the way had been pre-scouted before I was given the chance to be lead scout. I was especially careful to follow protocol as best as I could when coming upon the wormhole.

This wormhole was unguarded. The fewer there were who knew where the stable wormholes were, the better. The obvious downside was that if it was compromised, we would need to deal with the situation on our own.

Circling, it was obvious that no one was in the area. With my vision, I took longer than I usually would to scour around visually before landing. Minutes later the others landed.

"We're almost there," said Lloyd. *"Nice job following protocol, rider. Take us through the wormhole and to the cabin."*

It was always a relief to get back to the familiarity of Earth's atmosphere and gravity. Although I was getting acclimated more and more, it was still a shock to my system when we crossed over to Vocce.

We were greeted with some good old-fashioned Oregon rainy weather. It was a regular downpour, but with my enhanced vision, I was able to see my way around with amazing clarity.

The lights from Portland and Gresham were calming, somehow. Familiarity in a world that had been turned upside down for me, I guess.

We would fly at night to obscure the dragons from the casual observer, so the routine of returning to the cabin was also familiar. I took a deep breath and filled my lungs with the Oregon night air. The wind from the storm buffeted us around, which made flying on the back of a dragon even more scary, if that was possible.

To display that I had learned my lesson, I circled the area above and around the cabin, even though I knew that there was nothing to fear. I had vowed on the way home to start taking the training more seriously. It had been a slap in the face to realize that my actions affected the entire team.

Circling, I made a great show of scanning the area, being extra cautious. Nothing was out of order, and we had left the training team to guard Grandma and Alan's family, so there was no need for the password. We could always find another training area in the vast mountain range around Mt. Hood. We couldn't replace family.

I was about to land when I saw something with my enhanced vision. We had brought several side-by-sides to the cabin, but there was an extra vehicle that had been parked behind an out-shed that stored tools and equipment. Not one of ours, and a body laid next to it.

Immediately I reversed course. and urged Cotopaxi to climb as fast as possible. The maneuver likely saved our lives. On signal, the Gonosz stepped from behind their hiding places and fired fireballs at us. We must have been up against the varsity, because the accuracy was amazing, and the fireballs seemed to have more power than normal. We felt the heat of several that sizzled past us. If we had landed, I'm sure we would have been cooked.

Our first task was to get away, then the training was that we would return and form up with the team.

Cotopaxi was flying like he had never flown before. Amazingly, I was able to anticipate what he was going to do, and I remained seated firmly. Alan was scanning around finding targets and returning fire. Yelps of pain told me that he was successfully engaging the targets.

"*Chayl, take the lead,*" commanded Lloyd. I wasn't offended that he wanted someone else to take the lead. Those several seconds had been terrifying, and this was real, not a training exercise.

Selena had come to, once she sensed that we were in danger.

"*We've been betrayed,*" she said simply. "*Their wormhole was sealed. Someone showed them ours I bet.*"

Her words were confirmed when I spotted movement to our nine o'clock position. Turning my head, I was able to easily pick out three dragons, one of which was Verbane, the head scout dragon. Her rider was Kalam, and she was wearing the controlling harness that we had seen when we were attacked by the wild dragon. Her eyes were round and terrified. She seemed to be in a great deal of pain.

They closed on us quickly, but found us in fighting formation ready to defend. Their plans depended on us being caught unaware. Rather than attack, they flew off because even if we were young and inexperienced, we still outnumbered them.

As fast as the attack had happened, it was just as quickly over. Lloyd's training had saved our lives.

"*This isn't going to be good,*" said Alan. I knew he was talking about the body, but who could...

An anguished cry went out, the unmistakable voice of Cowboy.

Since Chayl had taken the lead back from me, it was his responsibility to check for danger at the landing zone.

Chayl uncharacteristically ignored protocol and dove for the ground.

"Come riders," said Lloyd. *"Land quickly and form a parameter. Cowboy needs us."*

Abi and Sabryyna had shot forward before Lloyd had even finished his sentence. They landed hard, but Sabryyna was already running toward the out-shed where Cowboy had headed to. We landed shortly.

All of us started towards the structure, but were stopped by an angry Lloyd.

"My order was to form a parameter!" he said angrily. *"Now!"*

Following our training, Abi and Hera'sha'I launched into the air. Chayl and Cowboy had both run to the shed, so Sjerberha took to the air without a rider to patrol with Abi and Hera'sha'i.

We remained on Cotopaxi's back, and he circled the area on foot. It was frightening riding the back of a dragon on the ground. Even as awkward as Cotopaxi was, he still was faster than a galloping horse. We had started with a small parameter pass, but we expanded it when we found no immediate threats near the cabin.

It was a good forty five minutes before Lloyd called us back.

When we returned back to the cabin, Cowboy was sitting on the porch steps, his head in his hands, his shoulders heaving as he sobbed. Sabryyna had draped her arms around him, her head resting on his shoulders, tears streaming down her cheeks.

"Cowboys parents must have come to the cabin while we were away," was all Lloyd said.

Alan hopped off, and ran to the shed, obviously in hopes that he could do something with his new training. He stepped out shaking his head, looking miserable.

Cotopaxi nudged me with his nose.

"Not now, Paxi!" I said angrily.

But Cotopaxi was insistent. Stepping in front of me, he looked intently into my eyes, then turned and walked purposely towards a dense thicket of wild rhododendron, his nose testing the air.

Nosing around, he snorted and turned to look at me intently.

Running up to where he was, I looked down where Cotopaxi had been nosing. It was Cowboys older sister, Peggy, but she was in bad shape. Her hair was normally blond, but now it was singed and bloody. Her face and chest were also horribly burned. Next to her was a smoldering side by side. It looked like it had been blasted by a dragon.

"Alan, I need you right now!" I yelled, and Cotopaxi let out a fireball to guide him to us.

Alan and Cowboy arrived at the same time.

"Peggy," said Cowboy breathlessly. "Can you help her, Alan?"

Alan was examining Peggy quickly and expertly.

"She...she's in bad shape, Cowboy. We have two choices. Someone flies until they can get cell service and call for an airlift, or..." he hesitated.

"What?" Cowboy yelled.

"It would be better for us to fly her back through the wormhole. There are herbs on Vocce that treat burns better than anything we have here on earth. The herbs we are looking for are just on the other side of the wormhole, and we don't know how long it would take for a rescue with this weather. I... I really think that is our best choice to save her," he said.

"Then let's leave now!" yelled Cowboy.

It took us a bit to figure out how to transport Peggy. She was unconscious and couldn't sit on the back of a dragon. Alan again came to the rescue. Rushing into the yard, he came back with a hammock that had been strung between two large pine trees. He tied one end around the neck of Sjer-berha, and the other end to the base of his tail. The hammock hung a couple of feet below his belly.

"Do you think you can maneuver with this on?" he asked the dragon. The dragon nodded and jumped into the air, to fly around a bit to make sure. Landing, he lowered his belly so that we could load Peggy into the hammock. She moaned loudly, even though she was unconscious.

Again, we took to the air.

"Marcus, take the lead scout position. Sjer-berha will need to concentrate on flying with the hammock," commanded Lloyd. *"Fly fast and safe. I am too old and will slow you down. I will stay with Cowboy's... family."*

"Thank you, Lloyd," said Cowboy softly.

"Worry about your sister, young one. I will see to things on this end," said the dragon.

CHAPTER
TWENTY-TWO

ALAN'S DILEMMA

Cotopaxi flew with surprising speed. His strong wings driving us into the buffeting wind and rain.

"Taking Peggy to Vocce is the right decision," said Selena, *"but also presents a bit of a problem. How are we going to explain everything?"*

None of us had an answer to that. Our thoughts were to save Peggy first.

As we neared the wormhole, I flew ahead to scout the area. I took special care to make sure the way was clear. Once I was satisfied that we were free from danger, we dove to the ground. Moments later, everyone was on the ground and I led the way through the wormhole.

Instantly, I could feel the pull of the extra gravity and thin air of Vocce. Following protocol, Paxi launched into the air to patrol the area as the others came through. We remained in the air as we watched the team set up a parameter and get to work on saving Peggy. Abi had remained on Hera'sha'i, and they now patrolled the area on foot. Hera'sha'i was much faster than Cotopaxi, and circled the area with frightening speed.

I could see Alan working steadily on Peggy. He had applied some of the herbs to the burned areas of her body. Every so often, he or one of the others would sprint off into the surrounding woods to gather additional herbs. A fire had been started, and I could see some of the herbs being added to boiling water.

I lost track of time as we circled. It felt like several hours before Abi flew up alongside us.

"*She's awake and stable,*" she reported. "*I've just eaten. Why don't you let me patrol, and you two get something to eat and some rest?*"

Gratefully, we dropped to the ground. It had been a long day, all of which had been in the air astride a flying dragon. I slid off Cotopaxi with a groan.

Peggy was awake and alert.

Sjer-berha was sitting next to Peggy, along with Cowboy and Chayl. Peggy couldn't keep from looking at Sjer-berha, but who wouldn't?

"I was following mom and dad, and was about five minutes behind them," said Peggy, whose face was almost concealed with loose bandages. A thick paste of some sort was smeared on the exposed areas of skin.

"I heard screams and commotion, so I sped up. When I got there, dad was standing over mom, who was laying on the ground. Both were badly burned. He was trying to defend her, but he was attacked by several men. He didn't stand a chance," she said with a sob. Cowboy's eyes were red, and I could tell that he wanted to hold her, but the burns kept him from doing so. He held her right hand, which didn't seem to have been injured.

"One man shot a ball of fire that knocked dad down. He didn't move after that. I couldn't believe how quick they were, and how obviously strong. I knew I couldn't survive, so I tried to hide. Then the dragon landed. It smelled me immediately. I was in the side by side, so I tried to outrun them. That's when it shot fire out of its mouth, like something from a movie," she said, visibly shaking now. She still wasn't looking away from Sjer-berha. It must have been a huge shock to see her brother with a dragon.

"The last thing I remember is the tremendous heat, and the pain." she said. "Where are we? This doesn't feel... right, somehow."

"This is the world that the dragons and the Gonosz come from. We crossed over to find you the curing herbs for your burns and other wounds. Alan is a doctor of sorts in this world," Cowboy said.

"We better let her rest," said Alan. "Peggy is stable, but not out of the woods. She can still develop some serious infections with her skin barrier removed. We'll need to take care of her here for some time. I'm not sure what our game plan is. We're just responding to whatever crisis is most important."

"We're going to need to come up with an explanation for Alan's absence to tell his family. He's the only one who can give Peggy the attention she needs. Let's brainstorm an excuse..." began Selena.

"No," said Alan.

"Alan, we have to explain your absence. An excuse of some sort..." began Selena again.

"No," said Alan firmly.

"I don't understand, Alan," said Selena. *"We have to cover for your absence in some way."*

"We tell them the truth," said Alan more firmly. *"They deserve the truth. I think that what we've all discovered these last couple of days, is that this is not a joke. It's very possible that one of us can get killed. In fact, it's very likely. We tell them the truth. Let them see Paxi."*

Alan looked over at me. *"Your grandma knows the truth already. It is only fair that my family knows the truth, too. Part of the strategy of the Gonosz is to go after our families. It's only fair that our families know the danger, and to be prepared as best as they can."*

Cowboy nodded in agreement. Maybe if his family had known...

We were all silent after what Alan had said. The fact that we were actually going into battle was a thought that we all had, but was becoming more and more of a reality.

Now that Peggy was stable, Cowboy naturally wanted to

get back to take care of his parents' remains. Peggy was fifteen years older than Cowboy, and there was also another sister named Melissa who was five years older than him. She was currently attending Eastern Oregon University, several hundred miles away on the other side of the state. Of course, she would need to be informed of the fate of her parents and sister.

Leaving Abi, Alan along with Sjer-berha for protection, Cowboy mounted up behind me. It was a long ride back, or so it seemed. Cowboy was crying silently as we rode home. Having lost Selena before I knew that she was still attached to the crystal, I knew how he felt. Some people liked to be consoled. Others, like Cowboy and myself, we just wanted to be alone without people prying into our lives. So I remained silent for the remainder of the trip, out of respect.

I learned my lessons about protocol, so I was careful on our ride home, but we encountered nothing out of the ordinary.

Circling the cabin, we could see Lloyd on the ground. We had signaled ahead to let him know we were landing, so he was scanning the skies for us. As we circled, he gave us the "all-safe" signal and we dropped to the ground.

"Your sister, attendant?" he asked Cowboy.

"She will carry the scars for life...severe ones according to Alan, but she is alive and stable," Cowboy reported.

"That is good. I...I took some liberties to hide the nature of the attack on your family," explained Lloyd. *"They were certainly killed by either a fireball from the Gonosz or a dragon, but I think I arranged it to appear that they were killed from the vehicle they were riding, catching on fire. The less questions from the authorities, the better. Marcus and Selena, I'm not familiar with the workings of your authorities. Perhaps you can examine my work?"*

I only nodded at the grisly request. I walked over to where their bodies lay. They were situated by two off-road vehicles that were now badly singed, both visibly smoking. The area around the vehicles was also badly burned and smoking. I was no expert, but it seemed like Lloyd had done a good job.

"I heated the fuel tanks until they exploded. It should appear that they were killed by the ensuing explosion, resulting in fire," said Lloyd.

"Marcus, let's get the fire extinguisher from inside the cabin. Make it appear that they were trying to put out the fire. It would explain why they were close by when the tanks exploded, instead of retreating to a safe distance," Selena said. It seemed like a good idea, so I retrieved the extinguisher.

"We've got another problem," said Selena. "We're going to have to bring Peggy back. She will need to be accounted for. Cowboy, this is a big ask, but can we wait for a couple of days before we call the authorities? I wouldn't ask, but…"

"I understand," his face a hard mask now. He had had some time to deal with his grief, and I could see that the grief was turning to anger. I understood him and the process he was going through.

"We'll bring her back and she can confirm the story," said Selena.

Cowboy just nodded. Turning, he entered the cabin, leaving us.

....

"Alan has the gift," said Lowry as he inspected Peggy. Lowry had been informed of the attack and had insisted on coming to inspect for himself. We had crossed back into Vocce and were discussing our plans with members of the council.

"Our healers said that if she feels up to it, she can manage the trip. I don't envy you having to explain to your officials what happened. Do you feel comfortable with your cover story?" Lowry asked.

"As good as possible. Having Peggy willing to tell the story will go a long way, we're thinking," said Selena.

"The story is simple, and if she is asked something that she can't answer, she can always fall back on that she doesn't remember because she was very hurt and fading in and out of consciousness. We think that will work in our favor," added Abi.

"*Please fill me in again on the cover story,*" commanded Lowry.

"*We're keeping it as simple as possible, with very little possibility of explanation. Peggy will report that she was riding several miles behind her parents to visit the cabin, which is true. She will report that when she arrived, her parents were already in the process of trying to put out a fire on the side by side. As soon as she arrives, the fire spreads and the tank explodes. That is the last thing she remembers until we show up almost a day later. We, of course, nurse her as best as we can, and send Marcus back to call for help, which he will as soon as we return. Most likely they will send a helicopter to fly her out. If we return today, the timing of the story will work almost perfectly. We're hoping that Peggy will feel up to flying,*" answered Selena.

"*The more simple the plan, the better,*" agreed Lowry.

We were now just waiting for Peggy to feel up to returning.

Alan knelt down next to Peggy.

"It is completely up to you. When you feel ready to…" he began.

"I'm ready now. It hurts, but I feel strong enough to be moved," she said.

"We don't want to rush things," said Alan.

"Alan, if we don't return now, it will become increasingly difficult to explain ourselves. I can manage. Cowboy says that you know what you are doing, and I trust you," Peggy said.

"We're going to have to remove the bandages and herbs that I've applied. We don't have the same herbs on Earth, so that would be suspicious to say the least. It's going to hurt," he warned.

Peggy's laugh was short and without humor.

"I'm guessing that will be the story for the rest of my life," she said, bitterness in her voice. I couldn't blame her. I would be bitter, too.

Cowboy came up to Peggy's side. He had been by her side constantly after returning, and he had changed. He seemed more determined and focused. I had noticed that when Peggy was asleep or resting, he would slip into the woods and practice his skills. His fireballs were particularly impressive. He was deadly with his aim, and he had discovered that he could cause his fireballs to explode on impact. Trees and boulders showed the scars of his new-found skill, and he no longer smiled. His eyes smoldered with hatred whenever someone mentioned the Gonosz. Again, it was difficult to blame him.

The trip was uneventful back to the cabin. Peggy was tough as they come. Although she was in obvious pain, she didn't complain a single time. Arriving at the cabin, the plan was to give her some time to recover before calling for help, but she refused.

"It is more realistic that I would be tired and in bad shape," she said, the weariness sounding in her voice. "It's going to be difficult enough to explain how I healed as well as I did."

"That's true," chimed in Alan. "Peggy responded very well to the treatment, and someone with training and experience with burns will notice that she is healing better than someone who has been without treatment for a couple of days."

Our plan had holes in it, but it was the best we could come up with. Our hope was that our story was simple and straightforward enough to avoid in depth questioning.

My job was to drive one of the off-road vehicles back to where we usually get phone reception, and make an emergency call. I would then wait for the emergency responders to show up. We figured either two things could happen. 1) That they would send a helicopter in for an emergency rescue, or 2) Send an emergency team in, then determine if a helicopter was needed.

Truth is that none of us really knew the answer to that one. We planned on both scenarios, but anything could happen.

Reaching an area that we knew had cell reception, I

made the call.

"911, what is your emergency?" a voice asked.

"Uh, we've had an accident. Two people are dead, and one person was burned badly. We need help as soon as possible," I said.

"What's your location?" asked the operator.

"Well, that's kind of a problem. We're at a log cabin in a remote location in the Mt. Hood National Forest. It's located off of highway forty-six. I am next to mile marker twenty-six, if that's helpful," I said. Even though I could give accurate directions and even exact GPS coordinates, we figured that it was more realistic if I were vague.

"OK, can you give me a name of a road or a nearby town?" asked the operator.

"Uh, not really. Sorry, I'm a friend of the family, so I don't have an address or anything. Sorry. I didn't think of that when I drove off. We needed help fast," I said.

"I understand. What is your name, please?" she asked.

"Marcus. Marcus Harmon," I replied.

"Good, Marcus. Please stay on the line while I look up your location," she said.

Moments later she was back on the line.

"You said mile marker twenty-six on highway forty-six?" she asked.

"Yes, yes that is correct. I can stay here until help comes, and I can guide them to the cabin."

"Can you tell me again the nature of the injuries? How many people are in need of assistance?"

"Well, just one now. The parents were killed when a gas tank exploded. Peggy, the daughter, was burned horribly on the face, shoulders and arms. She is in pain, and she had to spend a day or two alone, before me and my friends found her. There's no phone service where the cabin is located," I said, trying to stay to the story without any deviation. I was never good at improvising.

"Is the victim conscious?" was the question.

"Yes. She is in a great deal of pain, but seems to be alert," I said.

"And she was alone for several days before she was found."

"Yes. That is correct. She had water, but no food. We found her lying just inside the cabin door. She walked in, and collapsed. That's where we found her."

After several minutes of more questions, it was determined that a rescue from the ground would be better. There were meadows around the cabin, but not large enough for an air rescue.

I waited for about a half hour before the emergency vehicles showed up. There was an ambulance that was obviously a 4-wheel drive vehicle, designed for rugged roads, and two other emergency-like vehicles.

There were two law enforcement officers accompanying the emergency workers. One of them jumped in the seat next to me.

"You're Marcus, right?" he asked.

"Yes."

"Officer Matt Jansen," he shook my hand. "Go ahead and lead off. The others will follow. He wore a walkie talkie, in which he kept communication with the other vehicles.

During the ride, he questioned me about the accident. I remained true to the cover story, and didn't offer more than I already had.

Arriving at the scene, the only ones there were Cowboy, Abi, Sabryyna, and Alan. And, of course, Peggy. She had been moved to one of the couches. Her bandages had been removed, and her burns were visible. It was raw and ugly, blisters and all. She looked tired and in pain.

The paramedics got right to work, asking her questions about the accident and what treatment we had given.

I felt a nudge from behind, to find officer Jansen and his partner.

"We'd like to see where this happened," he said.

"Sure," I led them out to the area where Cowboy's parents were, and the burned vehicles.

They spent several minutes walking around, examining the area.

"I smell gas," said officer Jansen.

"Don't say anything. Don't offer additional information," Selena warned.

"I'm officer Walker," said the other officer. He removed the sunglasses he had been wearing and was looking intently at me.

"Do you want to tell me what happened?" he asked.

"We came up to the cabin as a group of friends. Our friend Cowboy, er...Eugene, his family owns the cabin. and we came up for a couple of days. This is what we found," I said.

They both pried and poked questions at me, but with several warnings from Selena, I just kept to the story.

"Why do you figure there is a smell of strong gasoline?" asked officer Walker.

"I really couldn't tell you," I answered. Gas had spilled during the attack on Cowboy's parents. They were probably in the process of refueling, when the attack came and the gas can was dropped.

After about forty five minutes of them examining the area, we were informed that Peggy was ready to be transported.

"I will ride with the injured woman," officer Walker informed his partner.

"We'll need your contact information," said officer Jansen, addressing our group. Cowboy and officer Walker followed, as Peggy was being loaded into the ambulance. Cowboy's parents had been placed in body bags and stored in one of the other emergency vehicles. The two vehicles took off, leaving officer Jansen alone with us.

"I'm very sorry for your loss. We'll of course autopsy the bodies. If we need anything else, we will be in contact with you," he said and left.

Alan let out an audible breath of air.

"I guess that's a good sign," he said. "They didn't caution tape the area. Maybe we caught a break."

We were a somber group riding home. We had gathered Cowboy and Peggy's belongings and returned to Earth.

Grandma sat silent as we rehearsed the events of the past several days.

"We're worried about your welfare, Grandma," I said. "The Gonosz have shown that they will go after families, and you are an obvious target."

She nodded.

"I have known this from when your parents first informed me of this Vocce world of yours," she said.

"Alan wants to tell his family," I said, looking over at Alan who was deep in thought. Worried about his patient, no doubt.

Grandma was silent again. After a few minutes she nodded.

"They are in danger. They need to be able to make choices to protect themselves. If you think that it's the best thing, Alan, then you better do it," she said.

CHAPTER TWENTY-THREE

BIG NEWS FOR THE MALLOY'S

Peggy ended up with severe burns and scars that would never heal. She spent nearly a full month in the hospital, and she would require multiple operations over the years. Like Cowboy, she took the discovery of a new world filled with dragons in stride. And also like Cowboy, her focus on defeating the Gonosz was strong. The death of Cowboy and Peggy's parents had been tough on the family. Focus on getting stronger to fight the Gonosz gave them direction and a purpose. Peggy became part of our small team and would attend our training sessions as often as possible. Peggy had a keen sense for tactics, Lloyd in particular was impressed with her abilities.

Christmas and New Years had come and went, as we continued training. Soon it was spring, with the prospect of summer vacation looming. Alan decided that he needed to tell his parents our secret, as we would need to go back to Vocce for most of the summer to train in earnest. I, in particular, still needed to acclimate better to the gravity and less oxygen. For the time being, it seemed that the clans were safe and that their hiding place was secure, but they remained hyper vigilant regardless.

Cotopaxi and I continued to struggle. All the other teams were working well together. The young dragons learned communication skills, but not Cotopaxi. We still couldn't communicate very well. He could understand us, sometimes, but couldn't speak back with us.

It made things very difficult when working with the other teams. They all functioned well in their roles. We were definitely the weak team, except Alan. He continued to progress and grow. He was the only saving grace. When Cotopaxi or I made a mistake, he was often able to set things straight with his quick thinking. Although he wasn't able to communicate with Cotopaxi, he was better at judging him and anticipating his movements and thinking.

Selena was hibernating more and more. She was having a difficult time staying with us. I dreaded the time she would leave for good, but understood her pain. I could feel it sometimes, and it was dreadful.

One bright spot was that Eldon seemed to have lost interest in us. Maybe the fight between Cowboy and Alan made him think twice.

"You don't know Eldon, if you think he's done with any of us," said Cowboy. "He's just biding his time. Keep alert, is my recommendation. He'll try to catch us when we least expect it."

I could tell there was something on Alan's mind as the rest of us talked. We were sitting just outside the music building at our school, right where Eldon had jumped me and Alan the first time. Some picnic tables with a gazebo were situated in the grassy area between buildings. It was our usual hangout. Even in bad weather, we preferred sitting under the gazebo rather than staying indoors.

"It's time to tell my parents," he said. "They love you guys, but it's getting harder and harder to get away."

"*What if they forbid you to continue with the training?*" asked Selena.

"Not sure, to be honest. I guess I need to show them that I'm needed by the team, and that I'm good at what I do. They were amazed that I was able to treat my mom and Allie. Their burns and scars are minimized from the treatment. Even the doctors were curious about what I did. Had to do a quick bit of thinking to explain that I had 'researched stuff on the internet' to find a treatment. I'm sure that the doctors figure it was a fluke."

Alan's plan was to bring his parents to the cabin to introduce them to Cotopaxi. He was nervous, and so was I. I didn't particularly like the idea of telling them. They could just forbid Alan from participating, and that would be it. Alan was the only thing that made Cotopaxi and I at least functional. No, I didn't like the idea of telling his parents at all.

When we told Grandma our plans, she nodded.

"I guess I better come, too. I might be able to smooth some things over with them. This is going to be the shock of their lives, and I might lend some credibility to this whole thing," she said. She was a wise woman.

It wasn't difficult to persuade Alan's parents to come to the cabin. They had asked over and over what we did each time we were there. We were pretty vague.

"We like to get away. Build a fire, make s'mores," was the usual response. As an explanation, it was getting less and less valid.

Lloyd was also on the fence as to the validity of telling Alan's parents, but left it up to Alan to decide what was best for his family. He would be on patrol as we introduced Paxi to the Malloy's. One dragon was overpowering. Two would cause cardiac arrest.

The ride to the cabin was now as familiar as driving around the block. We knew every twist and turn of the dirt road by heart. The Malloy's enjoyed the ride up. They had brought Allie and Tim, who giggled as we slid around the corners. They had brought all the fixin's for S'mores. They were in for the surprise of their lives, as to how we planned to start the fire.

We were all nervous. It was a sure thing that the Malloy's were going to be shocked. How they would react, was anyone's guess.

The entire gang was there, minus the dragons who were patrolling the area. Abi and Sabryyna had been part of the gang for the entire school year, and Alan's family loved both of them. Chayl was old enough that he didn't need to attend school, so he would be meeting the Malloy's for the first time. And, of course, Cowboy and Peggy. We hadn't told Alan's parents about "the fight," as we called it.

"Thanks for bringing us up here, Eugene," said Mrs. Malloy. "I can see why you all want to come up here so often. It's beautiful. The cabin, the pond, the view of Mt. Hood. Just beautiful."

"Wait until dark," said Peggy. Allie had taken a real liking to Peggy and followed her around constantly. Probably because they both had scars from fire, but Allie hadn't been burned nearly as bad. Some scarring, but not as bad as Peggy. They were fast friends who were constantly giggling about something or another. "There is absolutely no light pollution. It looks like you can just reach out and touch the stars, they are so clear."

It was decided that Peggy would watch the kids when Alan decided to tell his parents. We would tell them when it got dark.

The afternoon went quickly, and it soon was getting dusk. Alan was more and more nervous, and his mom in particular had started watching him, a concerned look on her face, but she remained silent.

The first stars began to appear in the sky when Peggy walked up with both Allie and Tim.

"Would you mind if I took the kids to the pond and watched the fish jump? We'll just be on the other side of the pond. We'll be careful," she said.

"That sounds fun!" said Alan's dad. "Maybe I'll come, too."

"If you can stay, I have something to tell you," said Alan.

Mr. Malloy looked over at Alan, realizing that they had been brought here for a reason. I chuckled to myself. They could guess for a thousand years straight, and never come close to what we were about to tell them.

As soon as Peggy left with the kids, Alan faced his parents.

"You'll want to sit down," he said, indicating some lawn chairs that were situated in the yard.

A look of concern was exchanged between the Malloy's, and we all sat down in a circle with Alan across from his parents.

"Ahh, there is no easy way to explain this...." began Alan, then stopped. A loss for words.

"Son, whatever you have to tell us, we're here for you. You can tell us anything," said Mr. Malloy.

Alan chuckled. "You are not going to believe what I've got to tell you."

Alan's mom cocked her head and looked quizzically at Alan.

"Does it have anything to do with how you knew how to treat me and Allie?" she asked. Her intuition must have been off the charts.

We must have all had amazed expressions on our faces.

"We, and Allie in particular, responded to your treatment extremely well. Better than the treatment given by the doctors," she said.

"Uh...yeah. Yeah, it has something to do with that. But that's not even close to the whole story we need to tell you," he said.

"Jan, you and Arthur are about to hear a weird, strange story," said Grandma. She had positioned herself next to the Malloy's, and she now reached and grasped Mrs. Malloy's hand. "But what they have to tell you is true and real. Maybe a demonstration would be a better way to explain things."

The Malloys looked concerned, like Alan had joined a cult or something. After this, I'm sure that they would wish it was just a cult that Alan had joined. I just didn't see this as going well.

"Yeah, well, here goes," said Alan, and he stood and faced the firepit that was situated twenty feet away.

Several fireballs from Alan ignited the firewood stacked in the pit.

Alan's parents both gasped. They had plainly seen that the fireballs emanated from Alan.

Alan slowly sat down and looked over at his parents, who just sat with their mouths hanging open.

"And that's not all," Alan said and proceeded to levitate a spare lawn chair sitting next to Mr. Malloy. Mr. Malloy did the most natural thing when seeing something that he didn't understand. He waved his hands above and below the chair to see if there were wires or something lifting the chair.

Sitting back in his chair, his eyes were wide.

"Whoa," was all he said.

"I don't understand," said Alan's mom.

"Well, these are some of the things I can now do, along with the medicine stuff that I now know," said Alan.

Alan paused, allowing things to sink in.

Alan's mom was the first to recover and ask the first question.

"There's more, isn't there," she said, staring intently into Alan's face. Her intuition was disconcerting.

"Oh, yeah. A lot more," replied Alan.

Alan's dad was still in disbelief, staring at the hovering chair which Alan set on the ground again. Mr. Malloy then turned his attention to the fire, which was crackling merrily away.

Alan let out a large breath of air.

"I guess showing you the next part will be easier, too. Good luck with this one, and don't scream," he warned.

"Scream?" Mrs. Malloy asked.

"Paxi, come here boy," called Alan.

Alan's parents were looking around them, perhaps hoping for a dog or a monkey to come out of the woods. What did come out of the darkness, came from the sky and landed with a ground-shaking thump.

It was Mr. Malloy who screamed.

"Shhh!" shushed Alan.

"WHAT THE...?" yelled Mr. Malloy. He had stood and was backing away, shielding Alan's mom from Cotopaxi.

Alan ran to Cotopaxi and wrapped his arms around the dragon's neck. Cotopaxi loved Alan, and began to lick his face. Despite the seriousness of the situation, Alan laughed at the attention from the dragon.

"Yucky, Paxi, yucky! No licks! Bad dragon, bad!" he said, but Cotopaxi continued to lick Alan's face, until he pulled away. One last lick to the back of his head, and Alan turned and faced his parents. He had a grin on his face.

"So," he said. "We have a dragon."

Alan's parents were staring at Cotopaxi in awe and fear. Again, it was Mrs. Malloy who seemed to recover first.

"The dragon is not from this world, is it?" she asked. Ok, that confirmed it. Mrs. Malloy was a Jedi. Nobody could convince me otherwise. I wondered if she knew that I thought she was hot. I would need to watch my thoughts around her. The Force was strong with that one.

"Good guess mom. Nope Paxi is not from this world. Neither is Abi, Sabrynna, or Chayl. Nor either is Marcus."

Both of Alan's parents turned and stared at me. They were shocked.

"They all come from a world called Vocce. It's a parallel world to ours. It's a really cool place. Beautiful," said Alan.

"So, you've been there?" It was more of a statement than a question.

"Multiple times," Alan confirmed. "And it's also the reason..."

"Our home was attacked," finished Mrs. Malloy. "By a dragon with a rider on it."

"You...you saw it?" asked Alan.

"I thought it was just shock, that I was imagining things, but...it really happened," she said looking back at Cotopaxi. "It was the dragon that started the fire, wasn't it?"

"Probably," I said. "But we all can manage fire, including

the Gonosz. They are the ones that attacked your family."

I also aimed a fireball at the pit. Missed by a mile, but at least I produced a fireball. It fizzled out, after striking the pond.

Cotopaxi had inched up next to Mrs. Malloy. Now he rested his head on her shoulder. Reaching up, she scratched his ears. Contented rumbling sounds issued from deep inside Cotopaxi's chest, and he half closed his eyes at the attention.

"What are you not telling me, Alan? There's more to the story," asked Mrs. Malloy.

"Well, there *is* more to the story. Marcus and I, along with Paxi are a team. You know, a fighting team. Do you remember Selena, Marcus' sister who was killed?" asked Alan.

His mom just nodded.

"She was also a dragon rider. A pretty great warrior, from all accounts. I guess riders run in their family, and Abi and Sabryyna are a team. They ride a dragon named Hera'sha'i. Chayl and Cowboy are also a team. Their dragon is named Sjerberha," explained Alan.

"And you're fighting the Go-nose...Go-nosey?" asked Mr. Malloy who hadn't blinked in a while, his eyes wide.

"Training to fight, but yes. We are to fight against the Gonosz once we are fully trained," said Alan.

"No! No way!" said Alan's dad, shaking his head. "You're not fighting. We can move. We'll run and hide. Go somewhere they can't find us. It's not our fight."

Alan stepped up to his mom.

"Mom, I have to do this. I'm really good at doing my job. I ride Paxi and keep Marcus and Paxi safe. And I'm also learning to be...a...a... I guess Medicine Man is the best description. The entire team depends on me to keep them healthy and treat wounds, if needed."

Alan grabbed both of his mom's hands. He looked her straight in the eyes.

"I came to you to be honest with you. No more hiding who I am. I've always been an outsider, not many friends. Not only are these my friends, but I am good at what I do. I've found my place, finally, where I fit in," he said.

"Asking if this is dangerous is probably a stupid question?" asked Mrs. Malloy.

"Very stupid," said Alan with a smile, which disappeared quickly. "I won't lie. There are very few of us, and we're fighting an army, but it's the right thing to do. I don't expect you to understand, but perhaps you'll respect my decision? I need to do this."

"No," said Alan's father again. "It's not our fight, dragons or no dragons."

Alan again looked into his mother's eyes.

"You understand me, right? That I need to do this?" he asked.

"You know that I don't like this?" she asked.

"Mrs. Malloy," said Abi. "Alan is very good at being an attendant. Maybe the best that I have ever seen. Not to pressure you, but he is a very necessary part of our team. We rely on him and his abilities. Marcus and Paxi would be lost without him."

Mrs. Malloy shook her head.

"This is a whole lot to dump on someone," she said with a wan smile.

"A whole lot to dump," confirmed Mr. Malloy, shaking his head.

"You should do it then," said Mrs. Malloy.

"What?" asked Alan, surprised.

"What?" asked Alan's dad, even more surprised.

"You would probably hop on your dragon and go anyway," she said.

"Not gonna lie. It's who I am now, and it's how I keep you all safe, too. I take the fight to them," he said.

"I hate the thought of you doing this, Alan. But I guess you are old enough to make decisions for yourself. You'll look after him, Marcus?" Mrs. Malloy asked, her eyes moist.

"We all will," I answered. Abi, Sabryyna, Chayl, and Cowboy all nodded in agreement.

"There is nothing that we wouldn't do to keep Alan safe.

We've got his back," said Cowboy.

Cotopaxi must have understood, too, because he stepped back and let loose a giant fireball into the air.

....

It is amazing how much of a weight came off of our shoulders, now that Alan's parents were in on our secret. We no longer had to make excuses, or tell cover stories about our activities. Mr. Malloy was still vocal about not wanting Alan involved, but at the same time, I think he was secretly proud of Alan. Often, the Malloys would come to our training sessions. They were careful to let Allie and Tim know that it was important that we kept everything a secret.

"Loose lips sink ships," was a phrase that we used with them, so that they understood that talking about dragons and such could put their brother in danger. The Malloy kids all were mature for their age, and they readily agreed to keep our secret.

That, and the fact that Cotopaxi became their huge scaly pet. When we weren't training, he could be found playing hide-n-seek, giving the giggling children rides, or his favorite, receiving scratches behind the ears or a good belly rub.

Allie, in particular, loved Cotopaxi and had a special name for him.

"Paxi-Loxi," she would call out whenever she saw him.

And "Paxi-Loxi" would joyfully fly to her to give her nozzles and licks. She, out of everyone, seemed to communicate best with him. I, in particular, struggled still with that.

We were gearing up to spend several weeks of training with the clans. I needed to develop my endurance so that I could handle the climate and gravity. The others were affected, but not nearly as bad as I. I just seemed to be the weakest link in just about every aspect.

The others were all excited to return to Vocce, but I didn't have very good memories of the world. Every time we went there, I either was made to look like a chump, or something bad happened. It certainly was interesting going to another world, but I didn't have the same feelings of excitement as the others.

Our extended stay required more planning than usual. We would be learning some survival skills, along with tactics and fighting skills. We would be training with other dragons and former riders. Our hope was to have a trained fighting unit before the clans were discovered by the Gonosz.

Alan was constantly collecting herbs and other chemicals and such. It was his medical supply. He also supplemented his supply with store-bought over-the-counter drugs.

"Vocce has an amazing amount of plants and herbs that have medicinal properties. Combined with a few of our drugs, I should be able to plan for most medical emergencies," he explained.

Allie was distraught at the thought that "Paxi-Loxi" was going to forget her.

"You'll think of me every day, right?" at which Cotopaxi would lick her face ferociously, Allie giggling the entire time.

We had assembled gear for the trip. We discussed our options, and we decided that part of our "war kit" would be tents made on earth. They were much more convenient than the cloth tents used on Vocce. The Vocce tents were effective, but not really convenient. The cloth was soaked in the liquid from a plant that secreted a latex-like sap. While effective at weather-proofing the cloth, it was necessary to constantly apply the mixture to be most effective. The cloth was also more prone to tear, requiring patching. The synthetic tents made on earth required less work and were easily set up and broken down.

We also decided to carry a supply of MRE's.

"Meals ready to Eat," said Cowboy, making a face, after downing something called meatloaf. "That's three lies for the price of one."

The MRE's would also be a time-saver, as we could quickly eat the contents without preparation.

Selena was very quiet during the week prior to our departure. I could feel that she wanted to talk with me, but was having difficulty in doing so. I didn't have to be a genius to know what was on her mind, and I couldn't bear the thought. She was just waiting for the right timing.

For the first time, I discovered that fighting dragons had special packs made that they wore on their backs that stored all of our gear. What was even more surprising, was that the pack extended to fasten under the neck of the dragon. It was like a built-in saddle for the riders and attendants.

"How come nobody told me this?" I asked as Alan and I settled into the seats.

"All riders learn to ride without the saddles first. During war, the packs can become damaged, and it is necessary to ride without," said Alan. "Most riders hate them, actually. They claim it's more effective to ride without the packs. Plus, they slow down the dragons."

But for me, the packs were a God-send. I was able to more effectively use my legs to remain seated on Cotopaxi. It just seemed more stable for me.

I had some worry that the additional weight would be too much of a burden for Cotopaxi, but although he hadn't grown much larger, he had filled out and it was easy to see the developing muscles ripple under his tough hide.

Taking a couple of running hops, we launched into the air without much more effort than usual, but it was a long trip, most of which would occur on a planet with more gravity and less air. Training on earth was both a benefit and a curse for both of us.

We had decided to fly under the cover of darkness. After some tearful goodbyes, we loaded up for nearly three weeks of training. We would then return for a couple of weeks to recover, then back again for the remaining part of summer. The plan for the clans was to remain hidden for as many years as possible. All the while, our little band of warriors would continue to develop and train to meet the armies of the Gonosz. Battle was the last thing that we wanted. We were outnumbered, although we had more dragons than the Gonosz.

After we had taken off, we formed into our flight formation. As was usual, I stayed in the middle of the pack. Chayl and Cowboy lead the way with Abi and Sabryyna bringing up the rear. We were all a little jumpy as we approached the wormhole. It was here that we were most likely to become sitting ducks. If the Gonosz ever discovered our wormholes, they would just need to camp out there and attack us either coming or going through the hole.

Chayl and Cowboy began their circling action as we approached the wormhole. Lower and lower they circled, until they felt that it was safe. Once down, we approached and landed. Our job was to touch down and run the perimeter of our landing zone. As soon as Cotopaxi's feet were down, he began to sprint and we began our perimeter run. It was awkward riding the dragon when he ran, because of the shriveled front paw. It was slower than the other dragons, and his gait was definitely less smooth. I never particularly like to run perimeters because I constantly felt like I was going to fall off. The pack made it easier to stay on, however, and we were able to run the perimeter effectively.

Once everyone was down, we were called back into the area.

"All's quiet," reported Lloyd, "Lead off Chayl."

This is where I was nervous. Passing through the wormhole was a danger. We didn't know what was on the other side, and therein lay the peril.

Chayl passed through without incident, and the rest followed after, Abi and Sabryyna bringing up the rear.

Once on the other side, I felt the now familiar heaviness and lack of air. Cotopaxi seemed to take it in stride. Maybe it was a dragon thing. He seemed happy to return to his world.

I let out a breath of relief as we found the wormhole clear. We had decided that it was more likely that the wormhole be discovered if we kept an active guard on it, so having nobody on the other side was actually a good sign.

The rest of the trip to the clans went without mishap. It was very stressful, however. The possibility that there was a spy within the clans was always a consideration, so we were on high alert for an ambush.

I was pretty tuckered out when we did land on the outskirts of the camp. Cotopaxi was also tired from carrying the extra gear, but he seemed excited to be home.

Our first order of business was to set up camp, even though we were all tired from the long flight. Fortunately, we had practiced setting up the tents on earth, so it was only a matter of a half an hour before we had our shelters up and we were digging into our MRE's. Mine was spaghetti-something-or-other. I didn't even bother heating it. The MRE's were made to drop into boiling water to heat, but I was far too tired and hungry to wait.

"You'll need to get water at the cistern we built. I will show you the way," said Qurum.

Following Qurum, we made our way to an entrance into the ground. A set of steps led down into the dark cavern. The heat of the dry desert air was replaced by cool fresh air, as we descended. Qurum had lit a torch prior to our descent and we were soon enveloped in darkness. At the bottom of the stairs was a flat area. Qurum raised his torch and what was illuminated was a good-sized underground lake.

"I wondered how the clans had enough water to support a small town in the middle of a desert," said Alan, his voice filled with awe as he looked around.

Bending down, I scooped a handful of water to my mouth. It was cold and clear, and possibly the best drink of water I have had.

"The dragons will need to have water hauled up the steps as they are too large to descend the steps," said Qurum.

"Wonder how much water a dragon requires?" I asked Alan out of the side of my mouth.

"Have you seen Paxi drink?" he asked "He sticks his whole head in the water. Dude likes his liquid refreshments."

That's what I was afraid of.

I knew that Cotopaxi was probably thirsty, so I grabbed one of the buckets of water and filled it. Alan handed me another and I filled that, too. Alan also filled two buckets and we spent the next ten minutes carrying bucket after bucket of water to the surface for our thirsty lizard. Alan wasn't kidding. He gustily guzzled bucket after bucket of water. Of course, he had flown the whole way with extra gear, so of course he was thirsty. After watering our dragons, they all flew off to hunt and eat.

Returning to camp, I struggled to keep my eyes open. I decided that I would go ahead and go to bed. The others were too wound up to go to bed, but I had the feeling that the training was going to be difficult for me, so sleep would be good.

"I'm going to miss all of this," said Selena as I settled into my sleeping bag. The desert was hot as Hades during the day, but cooled off surprisingly quickly after the sun went down. My tent had a weather fly that draped over it, but I had left it off so that I could see the star-filled sky. Qurum had assured us that there would be no rain for several months.

"Look straight up," she commanded.

I looked straight up.

"What am I looking for?" I asked. None of the familiar constellations were in the sky. On earth, I could look into the sky and name many of the familiar constellations, but not here. If we shared the same solar system, it was definitely from a different angle. None of the stars were familiar.

"See the bright red star?"

"Yes," I replied.

"We call that Primus. It is distinctive. Not real helpful in determining direction, but if you can find it, you can find some directional stars," she said.

"That's cool. I'm tired. Let's do this tomorrow night."

Selena was quiet for a moment. I thought maybe she saw the wisdom in getting some shuteye.

"I can feel it, Marcus," said Selena. *"It's real close now."*

I didn't know what to say when she talked this way.

"I've got a limited amount of time to teach you some important lessons, then I need to leave. Need to leave, Marcus," she reiterated.

Staring up into the unfamiliar sky, I suddenly felt alone. Without Selena, I was on my own. When we were training, the only reason I didn't ruin everything was because Selena and Alan were constantly in my head, making up for my mistakes.

Selena was also able to read Cotopaxi well. She could sense what he was trying to tell me, and she was more aware of his fighting and flying style.

I knew the others were frustrated with me. They were all learning their roles well. They also had developed skill using their crystals. I was still a one trick pony with a feeble fireball, and the dragon vision. I was able to use that well, but nothing else, and I had two crystals. The others were also communicating with their dragons better each day. The other dragons were able to talk with Cotopaxi fairly well, and they would relay messages to and from him, but it was a tedious Jr. High School process. But they also confirmed his communication skills were undeveloped, even between dragons.

"So, Primus is directly above us?" I prompted.

"Tonight it is, but it will be in different locations at different times of the year and throughout the night. It is so distinctive, that regardless of its location, you should be able to find it."

"Cool."

"Vocce also has a North Star. If you can locate Primus, then you can find Necoma, Vocce's north star. So, locate Primus."

"Got it."

"Just to the right of Primus, about at the two o'clock position is a bright white star. Do you see it?" she asked.

"Yes. It really is bright white. Really bright."

"Good. That's Drac, the dragon constellation. With those two points, you can find Necoma. Trace an imaginary line between the two, and follow the line all the way up and right. On the horizon, what distinctive star do you see?" she asked.

"*Red star?*" I asked.

"*Yep. That's Necoma, the north star,*" she said.

"*I just hope that where I'm going is always going to be to the north,*" I joked, poorly.

"*A point of reference can be the difference between life and death. Since you are a dragon rider, you will be required to fight at night,*" there was disapproval in her voice.

"*I'm sorry. You know me. I sometimes just don't get stuff as quick as everyone else,*" I said.

She was silent for a moment.

"*Maybe. But maybe you need to take some of these things more seriously. Marcus, this isn't a joke. In a very short amount of time, your team is going to be placing their lives into your hands. I know you sense their frustration with you, but you have to see it from their perspective. They can't be watching you, and do their own jobs at the same time. You have to be able to step up and add value to the team.*"

It was a lecture that stung. I was feeling a little alone, and the one person that always made me feel like I had someone to turn to, that fully understood me, was Selena. It hurt what she had to say.

To cover my hurt feelings, I turned over in my sleeping bag.

"*I'm pretty tired. I'll talk to you in the morning,*" I said.

CHAPTER TWENTY-FOUR

BROKEN-HEARTED DRAGON

Training began as I expected. As hard as I tried, I wasn't able to master many of the things that we were training for. The other team members had mastered many of the uses of their crystals. The dragons had been thorough in giving us crystals whose properties matched our needs.

Alan's medical knowledge wasn't the only special skill. Chayl had discovered navigation aids. Within his crystal was a list of important landmarks for both Vocce, and to a limited extent, Earth. He explained that he was able to see images of various landmarks for water, wormholes, food sources, and various other things that might be useful to us. He also explained that some landmarks had no explanation, so we were clueless as to why they were included.

Cowboy was learning that he had some measure of control over electricity. He was constantly making electricity jump from hand to hand.

"I can't create anything strong enough to use as a weapon, but I feel my control getting better and better," he said.

"*That's pretty rare,*" said Selena. "*The good thing about that particular skill is that I've seen it used to immobilize multiple fighters at a time. Fireballs are more pinpoint. Electricity can have more of a grenade-like effect.*"

"*Good,*" Cowboy said, a scary look in his eyes. "*The more

the better."

Abi and Sabryyna's skills were surprising. They had discovered that they were both able to levitate in the air. They couldn't propel themselves forward or backward, but they were able to levitate up and down.

"We haven't seen that skill in a lifetime," said Lloyd. "It is a skill with very practical applications."

And I was able to shoot a lame fireball with so-so accuracy.

"When I had Larzi, I was able to master several skills," Selena said. *"It is a pretty special crystal with capacities that are still undiscovered. Each person who inherits a crystal can more easily use certain skills easier than others. I could access things that mom and dad couldn't. You will just need to discover what works for you."*

"What skills were you using?" I asked.

"I had a detailed map, much the same as what Cowboy has now, but with more information, I suspect. It would be a great benefit if you had that. You can also add stuff to it, which I did. I had some limited medical information. Stuff like that. I'm sure you will find your own skills. It will just take time," she said. I was dubious.

Training was physically and mentally challenging, and not just for me. I noticed that the other dragons were starting to treat Cotopaxi differently. His shriveled paw was pretty noticeable, but his limited communication skills made things even worse. When training was over, the other dragons would often hunt together, and while Cotopaxi would go with them, when Lloyd wasn't along, he would often come back without having been fed, because none of the other dragons would team up with him to hunt. He would then make due with the small game around camp, for a limited meal. I could sense that he was lonely. Rather than hang out with the other dragons, he was usually with me or Alan.

Alan noticed it, too.

"Abi, why don't the other dragons like Paxi? Have you

noticed that they avoid him?" he asked one evening.

She sighed.

"*I love Paxi, but...*" she hesitated, trying to choose her words. "*He seems to have limited abilities. The other dragons see him as a liability. When they are working with him, they have to look out for him, rather than focus on their responsibilities. It makes things very difficult for them to do their jobs and watch out for Paxi, too.*"

Alan nodded, as if that was what he expected. I had a feeling that she wasn't just talking about Cotopaxi. I noticed that my team was frustrated with me when I didn't master a skill as fast as they did.

Cotopaxi and I weren't jelling either. For whatever reason, we just thought differently. We would see a situation differently, and act accordingly.

Lloyd had told us that one of the things that made a dragon and rider a formidable force, was that they both could instantly sense and anticipate what the other was going to do. The other teams were doing amazing things. I would watch as Chayl and Cowboy would cling effortlessly to the back of Sjer-berha with ease, even when Sjer-berha did aerobatics that seemed to defy physics.

I, on the other hand, routinely had to cling to a leather strap that I had fastened around Cotopaxi's neck, so that I wouldn't fall off while we were flying in formation. Alan had a better sense than I as to what Cotopaxi would do, but he some-times was surprised at Cotopaxi's maneuvers, too. Our connection and ability to communicate with the dragon wasn't even close to what the other teams were achieving.

At least Alan was achieving praise from the trainers and other team members. He was easily the best at many of the skills we were learning.

I was growing increasingly frustrated every day. I was always dead tired. The extra gravity and lack of oxygen had its toll on me every second of every minute of every hour of every day. That, and I couldn't do anything right.

And then the bad thing happened.

One of the things that Alan, Cotopaxi, and I struggled with, was our landings. Part of our training was that in a battle situation, we never would land and remain stationary. Because of the natural speed of the dragons, we landed "on-the-fly," meaning that we would touch down, but the dragons would retain their forward speed and either sweep the perimeter, or rendezvous at a predesignated landmark.

It was terrifying because the places that we landed weren't large, flat areas with lots of clearance. Those were too exposed and we were targets in wide open areas like large meadows.

Instead, the dragons would touch down in areas not much larger than themselves. The problem being that they would immediately need to dodge and weave between obstacles directly in their path. In the desert, this meant between cactus, or a type of scrub tree that had thorns just as terrible as the cactus. Plus, there was an abundance of sage brush that could easily trip a galloping dragon.

Cotopaxi also had his own way of thinking in those situations, because of his shriveled paw. What would seem like a logical route for either Alan or I to follow, wasn't the same route that Cotopaxi would choose because he wasn't able to pivot or plant his bad paw like his good one.

The result was that I would take a tumble just about every day as we practiced those maneuvers. Alan had spilled once or twice, but I was the all-time record-holder of eating dirt while traveling at the speed of a galloping dragon, and I had the bumps and bruises to show for it. Alongside of being tired all of the time, I also limped around like a geriatric widower.

It was on one of these maneuvers, when everything came to a head.

We had been training all day, and I was dead tired. We were actually repeating the maneuver because the previous one had been unsuccessful, because I misjudged what Cotopaxi was going to do. I had taken a fairly painful fall on rocky ground and into one of the scrub trees. Several thorns had pierced my skin, and a couple of the thorns had broken off, the tips remaining buried in my skin. It had taken Alan thirty minutes to dig out the painful thorns, and I was long ready to just curl up in my sleeping bag and forget the days' events.

Instead, we were trying the maneuver again.

"Perfect practice makes perfect. Let's do that again people," said Cowboy who was beginning to lose patience with me. He did little to hide his annoyance that I couldn't do the simple stuff.

We had chosen a wider area for us to land so that we could more easily complete the maneuver. All went well as we initially touched down, and we had a clear area in front of us to maintain speed without dodging between obstacles. But instead of proceeding straight ahead, Cotopaxi had dodged left for some inexplicable reason, and I had toppled to the ground. I landed directly onto one of the thorny trees, hundreds of thorns piercing my skin.

A painful side effect of having that many thorns piercing my skin and clothes is that I went into a terrific rate of speed, to a dead stop very quickly, the thorns now tearing my skin and clothes. I couldn't help but let out a cry of pain.

Cotopaxi and Alan immediately slowed and circled back to me, Alan sliding off the back of the dragon and running to me.

"Dude, you alright?" he asked.

Cotopaxi came up behind him, and laid his long neck over Alan's body, the dragon's face directly looking into my bloody face. I couldn't communicate with the dragon, but I could read his face fairly accurately. His face was full of concern for me. He began to lick my bloody face, letting me know he was sorry, but I had had enough.

"You stupid flying lizard!" I shouted out loud, pushing Cotopaxi's face away.

"Just leave me alone! I wish I was never chosen to be a

rider!" I shouted as the team filtered to the area to see if I was hurt, again.

Even though I was sure that Cotopaxi did not understand what I said, the meaning was fairly clear.

His large eyes opened even larger as he stared at me, and I could see into his soul.

I had hurt him worse than any physical wound could. When the other dragons had ignored him, he knew that he could always turn to me. Out of all the young dragons, I had chosen him, but now I had done the thing he had feared most. I had rejected him because of his short-comings.

He took several steps backward, still maintaining eye contact with me. Dropping his gaze, he looked for a moment at the ground, then with a mighty whoosh of his great wings, he launched into the sky. With speed I had never seen before from him, he flapped away and disappeared over the horizon.

Abi and Sabryyna had landed, but knew something had happened and immediately began to follow Cotopaxi, but at a much slower speed because of the load of the two riders, he had easily outdistanced them.

One of the side effects of the thorns was that they carried a small amount of poison in each of its barbs. Not enough to kill with one or two pricking the skin, but enough to make a guy pretty sick for a day or two when large amounts were involved. Because of the large amounts of thorns, I developed a pretty serious fever fairly quickly, as the poison entered my bloodstream.

The heat of the day was starting to clear to be replaced by the cold night air. I began to shiver uncontrollably.

"We need to get you back to camp," said Alan.

Rather than place me on a dragon and risk the danger of my falling off again, a travois was rigged and Sjer-berha pulled me back to camp.

Cowboy couldn't hide his annoyance, or maybe he had stopped trying.

"You know that Paxi made the right decision?" he asked.

"Chayl and I were on the ground acting as Gonosz. Had he run straight through the clearing, you would have all been "killed" in our mock ambush. He recognized the trap and acted correctly. It was you who failed today."

That was on my mind as I slipped into delirium.

I don't remember much of what happened that night, but I do remember Alan was there administering a poultice to my wounds, and giving me sips of a nasty-tasting drink. It was not until the next day that my fever finally broke and I was able to sleep more fitfully.

I woke to the feel of the cool night air. My mind was still foggy, but not bad. Alan was there napping on a camp chair. My stirring woke me up.

"How do you feel?" he asked.

"Thirsty," I said.

"That's normal. You'll want to sip water as much as possible throughout the day. You lost a lot of fluids, due to the fever and the heat these past days," he said, sounding very much the professional.

"How long have I been out?" I asked. I had caught that he had said "days."

"This is your third day of being sick. It could have been serious, but fortunately we had the right herbs and medication to combat the fever," he said, handing over a canteen of cold water.

I was thirsty, but did as the doctor said and took little sips rather than guzzling the whole thing.

Alan paused as he watched me sip my water.

"Paxi is still missing," he said. There was emotion in his voice. He loved that dragon.

"You know I didn't mean what I said. I'm just tired of being the weak link," I said.

"How do you think Paxi feels? You are the person who should be defending him, and you rejected him in just about the worst way imaginable. You hurt him bad, Marcus."

And there wasn't much if anything I could say to refute

Alan's accusation, and I knew it.

"Well, since you're better, I'm going to get some sleep. Haven't slept well with you in and out of a raging fever," he said as he got up and moved to the tent flap.

"We need to go find Paxi as soon as possible," he said and left.

"It's going to be up to you to make things right with Paxi," said Selena.

"I know," I said. "But I'm not sure what to do. I can't really communicate with him like the other teams can with their dragons."

"Communication with dragons is more than verbal. Vesuvius and I had a silent language that we developed. We just knew what the other was thinking. If you can't have verbal communication, then you have to figure out another way," she said.

"You know I'm not fit for this. The team is better with Alan and Paxi alone than me. Alan should be the rider. I should just go home and watch after Grandma," I said, and I meant it. It would be a relief to walk away from all of this. I wasn't just ineffective, I was a hazard to the team.

"I'm not sure why you haven't been able to develop certain skills, but you mustn't give up. You were selected to be a rider. The dragons sensed that you would be most suited to utilize the crystals, so we have to trust that," she said.

I snorted. "A lot of good that did. I can't even access the same things that you did. I think they were wrong this time."

"You'll feel better when we find Paxi and patch things up with him. Get some rest. We need to get you up, and search for him as soon as we can," she said.

With the help of Alan's treatment, I healed faster than we all figured. After a day of rest, the remainder of the fuzziness disappeared, and I felt up to joining in the search for Cotopaxi. The others had been relentlessly looking for him, but he seemed to have vanished. Not even a trace of him could be found. I had really made a mess of things. Instead of using this time for valuable training, we were looking for my dragon. I wasn't earning any points with my team, or trainers. Things were getting worse and worse, not better. More the reason that I should just bow out after we found Cotopaxi.

"We've searched all the water holes and places that a dragon would naturally feed, but we have found no trace of any dragon activity whatsoever," reported Abi. Out of everybody, she was the most understanding towards me. She always was encouraging me, and the first to praise me, if I did manage to get something right.

We searched the entire day with no success. I rode with Abi the entire time. Cowboy and Chayl made up the other team. Lloyd and some of the other dragons also joined in the search, but we found nothing again.

Returning to camp, I was pretty dejected.

"We'll find him. Just be patient," said Selena.

The others had such a connection with their dragons, that it would have been relatively easy for them to find each other, they were so connected. Not me, and I didn't know what to do about it.

We had tried everything. In desperation, I whistled my silly melody to connect to the crystal that had been given to me by the dragons. Larzi had been limited help, but my new crystal had been no help whatsoever. It may as well have been a piece of jewelry.

Having connected, I had Alan also connect. We had no idea what we were looking for, just that we needed to do something. We spent several hours searching. Neither of us sensing anything.

Alan got tired of searching the nothingness of the crystal, so he disengaged and went to his tent, still tired from watching over me the last several days. But I was determined to find something useful about the crystal. Other than chucking it at an enemy's head, it had no value to me.

With my mind, I searched what I thought was every inch of the crystal. Why didn't it respond the same as the others? I pulled the crystal out of its pouch and examined it for the hundredth time. It was so ordinary. Nothing remarkable. Sure, it had a small imperfection, an impurity that ran through the crystal, bisecting it. Maybe the imperfection made it unusable. I explored the imperfection with my mind. It just seemed to end there...or did it? Was there something beyond the imperfection? I explored it, but found nothing of interest.

Something was nagging my mind. Where would Cotopaxi go? He had grown up at the dragon hatchery, where he became my dragon. Where would he hide? He was as unfamiliar with Vocce as I was...

Earth. He had returned to Earth. That's where Allie and Tim were. They loved him and he loved them. That's where he would have gone. That was his safe place.

I walked out into the night and found Abi sitting at the campfire.

"I think I need a ride back to Earth," I said.

"Back to Earth? Why back to....oh," she said. "That makes sense. Paxi returned to where he feels loved."

My face must have dropped.

"Sorry. I know you didn't mean to hurt him. You've had a difficult time with all of this," she said.

"Yeah, I am not fit to be a rider. I know it. Everyone knows it," I said.

She contemplated that for a moment.

"Selena was a natural, you know. Maybe the best natural rider ever. We had high hopes that she would help us defeat the Gonosz once and for all, she and Vesuvius were that good together," she said. If she was trying to make me feel better, she was failing horribly. There was no way I could live up to that.

"Did you hear what I said? They were that good TO-GETHER," she said. "You will never succeed without Paxi. You've got to find a way to work with him."

"But..." I began but was cut off.

"...regardless of his or your short-comings. Yes, I realize there are some real issues to overcome, but we don't know either of your capacities yet. The dragons saw something in you, and you saw something in Paxi. Find him, bond with him, and make it work. End of lecture," she said with a smile. I loved her. Beautiful and smart. Just the kind of girl that shouldn't be seen with someone as dumb as me.

"Let's talk with Lloyd," Abi said. "He'll give us more direction of what we should do."

We walked to where the dragons had bedded down for the night. Part of our training was to always be informed where our team was located. We knew exactly where he was resting.

He heard us walk up, and he raised his head.

"I'm pretty sure he returned to Earth. That's where Allie and Tim are. He returned to Earth," I said.

"I guess that makes sense," said Lloyd. "What do you have in mind?"

"This is my mess. I need to do this alone, make things right with Paxi," I replied.

"Agreed," said Lloyd. There was rebuke in his voice and it hurt. I loved and respected Lloyd so much that I hated to disappoint him. Up until now, even my most stupid mistakes had been met with encouragement and praise, but hurting Cotopaxi had been the deal-breaker, and I had to make it right.

"We would like permission to take Hera'sha'I and return alone. We know that it is dangerous, but we feel that is Marcus' best chance of making up with Paxi," said Abi.

"It is dangerous indeed, but if that is what you think will make this right, then you need to do it. You have my blessing. I suggest you leave as soon as you can," Lloyd said, laying down his head, ending the conversation.

When I told Alan the plan, he was a little disappointed that he couldn't return, but quickly conceded that it was for the best.

"We're not exactly sure he's back on Earth, so I can continue our search on this side." Alan always found the best in every situation.

Abi and I quickly packed to travel. Since we were planning on returning, we packed light. This was going to be the first time that we were to be alone for any extended period of time. Not gonna lie, I was looking forward to that.

As we launched into the air, I couldn't help but feel the difference in how Cotopaxi and Hera'sha'I flew. It wasn't noticeable from the ground, but once on the back of another dragon, I could feel the difference. I was also able to take my cues as to what Hera'sha'I was going to do, because Abi would change and adapt to what Hera'sha'I was doing. It was remarkably easier this way.

It was also surprisingly tense riding without the other team members. We were so accustomed to having our various assignments, that going solo was a little intimidating. If we got into trouble, we would have to figure it out by ourselves.

Despite the tension, we made excellent time. Or perhaps the time just passed quicker because Abi and I were able to talk about things other than training. I found out that she had wanted to be a musician before her family was driven from their forest home. She was surprised to learn that I also loved music.

"Do you like the Beatles?" she asked.

"How do you know about the Beatles?" I asked back, surprised.

"When I escaped the Gonosz, I was found by a family that belonged to the clans. The Elders had no idea what to do with me, so it was decided that they would send me to Earth to learn the language, and become a fighter. We initially saw Earth as a place to escape to, but only as a last resort. The clans needed someone who knew the language and customs of Earth. That's where I came in, and it is how I got to know Selena. She taught me English and the customs. When she was chosen as a rider, it was an honor to be chosen as her attendant. Anyway, Selena figured out that I loved to sing, so she taught me English by teaching me some songs in English," she said.

"Cool. Mom and dad raised us on the Beatles, Jim Croce,

all the long-haired 80's rock, but the Beatles are what we listened to the most," I replied.

"What's your favorite Beatles song?" Abi asked.

"Something," I said. It had been my dad's favorite, and he would often sing it to my mom as he played the guitar.

"Oh, that's such a lovely song! Sing it to me," she said. What?

"What? Oh, no. My voice sucks," I said.

"Don't let him fool you, Abi," Selena said. Great. She was sure to comment on my lack of game when we were in private. Sisters.

"You hibernate all day, but wake up when there's an opportunity to make a fool out of me?" I asked.

"It's the sole reason for my existence right now," she replied.

"Please Marcus, sing it for me?" Abi said.

I sighed. I was sure that I would regret doing this until my dying day, but I was in love, and men do stupid, stupid things when a pretty girl is present.

"Something in the way she moves..." I began. There was no stopping now, so I continued, pouring my heart into the song. It was do or die. I knew the song well. It was the first song dad had taught me on the guitar.

To my surprise, Abi seemed to like it. She swayed softly as I sang through the verses, and when I got to the bridge, I was stunned when Abi joined in and sang the harmony.

"You're asking me, will my love grow? I don't know, I don't know..."

Finishing the song, we rode in silence for a few minutes. It had been magical singing with this beautiful girl, and I think she enjoyed singing with me, maybe...

. I was going to do it. I was going to pour my heart out to her. Let her know how much I had feelings for her.

"Abi, I just want you to know..." I began.

Abi quickly interrupted me.

"Please don't say anything more, Marcus," she said, hurt

sounding in her voice.

"But I thought…"

"It will never work, you and me. It can't work between you and me. Please?" she said.

And that was that. Of course, a pretty, smart girl like Abi wouldn't be attracted to a big doofus like me. What was I thinking?

Stupid, stupid doofus!

The rest of the ride commenced in awkward silence. I even faked being asleep so that Abi wouldn't feel obligated to make small talk with me.

At last we arrived at the wormhole. It had been a long ride after putting my foot in my mouth.

The tension had returned because this is where we would be the most exposed, the easiest place for an ambush. After scouting the area carefully, we determined that it was safe, at least on this side.

Our fears were for naught. We passed through the wormhole without incident, and we were able to head home.

We were dead tired when we got to the cabin, so instead of returning to our homes, we decided to stay the night there. We were pretty sure that Cotopaxi would return here, if he decided to return. This was what he was familiar with. Hera'sha'I promised to keep an eye out for Cotopaxi while we rested.

Finding an empty bed, I fell into it without taking off my clothes. I just wanted to sleep and forget ever falling in love with Abi.

"Just focus on getting your dragon back, King Dufus," I whispered to myself.

....

"He's here," said Hera'sha'i through Abi. It seemed like I had just closed my eyes to be awakened by the dragon.

"Go to him," said Selena.

"What do I say? More importantly, how do I tell him I'm

sorry?" I asked.

"*That's up to you, now. Nobody else can do it for you.*" Although Selena was of no help, I knew she was right. This was my burden and no one else's.

I walked outside. Cotopaxi was down by the pond. It was still dark out. He turned to see me, and prepared to take flight.

"Paxi, stop! Wait!" I called.

Cotopaxi turned and looked at me. There was fear in his eyes. He wasn't physically scared of me, it was worse. He no longer trusted me to always be on his side.

I still didn't know what to say. We stared at each other, as I tried to figure out a way to communicate with my dragon.

I must have stood there for several minutes, not knowing what to do. Cotopaxi again got ready to take flight. Instinctually, I stepped forward and wrapped my arms around his neck. He just stood there stiffly, not responding to me in the slightest.

"I'm sorry Paxi, so, so sorry!" I said. And with a rush of emotion, I began to sob. All the emotions of failing as a team member, the thought of Selena leaving me again, getting turned down by the girl I loved, and most of all from hurting my big, loveable dragon.

And it was ugly crying. Great huge sobs as I just let it out.

Cotopaxi's stance softened, and he draped his great neck across my shoulders. A loud, contented rumbling issued from his mighty chest, and we stood there for many minutes, dragon and rider.

Taking his head in both my hands I looked directly into his eyes.

"I'm sorry, Paxi. I will not hurt you again. I wish you could understand that," I said with great emotion.

Cotopaxi responded with a slobbery lick to the face, which almost toppled me over.

The tension was broken, and I laughed as he continued

to lick me again and again.

"That's a step in the right direction, I would say," said Abi as she came down the steps of the cabin. "Paxi might not understand spoken language right now, but he does seem to have a great capacity to recognize emotion and tone of voice. I would start just talking to him every day. You might be surprised at the results."

We were all tired from the flight, so we decided to sleep through the day and leave again that night. I spent nearly the entire time with Cotopaxi, just talking to him, reassuring him. I found that he was a good listener, even though he had no idea what I was saying, which is just as well, because I talked about Abi. A lot.

We were both napping by the pond when we were awakened by Abi and Hera'sha'I, who had walked up to us.

"We need to leave as soon as you are ready," said Abi.

"Sure. Give me a minute to wake up," I said as I stood up. We had been resting on the dock and I was near the edge when I stood up.

Without any warning, Cotopaxi knocked me off the dock with his tail. I sputtered to the surface of the water, to be met face to face with what could only be called a "grinning dragon." Grabbing the back of my jacket with his teeth, he hauled me out of the water where I was met by a peel of laughter from Abi.

"Paxi was just helping you wake up!" she said. "Good boy, Paxi!"

CHAPTER TWENTY-FIVE

WORMHOLE DISCOVERED

After I had changed and ate a quick meal, we headed out.

We had protocol for flying with two dragons. Abi and Hera'sha'I would lead and would function as the scouts. Cotopaxi and I were to continuously watch behind us. Sometimes, we would inform Abi and Hera'sha'I that we were going to circle back. This would allow us to see if we were being followed. It was good to have Selena with us, because she was able to see behind us easier. I reflected on the fact that I needed to stop relying on her so much. I could feel that she was very near her tolerance of remaining within the confines of the crystal.

I had learned my lesson in regards to protocol, and took my job seriously now. One mistake could be our last mistake.

Coming upon the wormhole, Abi and Hera'sha'I began their circle while scanning the area. They took longer than usual.

"What is it?" I asked.

"Hera'sha'I thought he smelled something unusual," she said. Hera'sha'I had an uncommonly good sense of smell, even for a dragon.

"What did he smell?" I asked.

"He can't really identify it. He says the smell of the area is just different than before," she reported.

Circling for several minutes more didn't reveal anything new, so we made the decision to go through.

Abi and Hera'sha'I led off and went through the wormhole. Moments later, Cotopaxi and I went through, at the ready to fight if needed. We found nothing out of the ordinary, but I felt kind of spooky, like something wasn't right.

Cotopaxi turned his head to look at me. There was concern in his eyes.

"Yeah, I feel it too," I said and patted his neck.

"Hera'sha'I doesn't like the feel of this. I don't either," said Abi.

"Then it's unanimous. We all don't feel right," I said.

We figured speed was our best friend in this situation. We had two strong-flying dragons who could cover distance if needed.

"Let's kick it into gear!" I encouraged Cotopaxi.

Cotopaxi must have understood, because his wing beats became more powerful, propelling at a tremendous speed through the air. Naturally, I felt the effects of passing through the wormhole. Would I ever acclimate to this weird world?

After a while of flying, we reduced our speed to save the strength of the dragons.

"I guess it was nothing," said Abi. *"It's just weird that we all felt something was wrong."*

"We'll just remain careful the rest of the way, but yeah. It seems to have been nothing," I replied, but I couldn't shake the feeling that something was out of whack. Turning around often, I would scan behind us with my enhanced vision. Cotopaxi must have felt my unease, because he would take unplanned turns so that he could also scan behind.

It was on one of these turns that we both caught movement along the horizon.

"Abi, I think we're being followed," I said. *"Paxi and I both saw movement several miles back."*

"Nice job spotting the danger. We need to take them on a wild goose chase to make sure they don't locate the wormhole to the clans," she said.

Up to this point, we had tried to remain hidden, but

now we needed to be seen so that we could lead whoever was following us to some harmless area. Abi had been adept at this very scenario when we had trained for it on Earth. She would lead the chaser to an area of her choosing, then seemingly disappear. The chaser would spend hours in the area trying to find her, while she was laughing at home base with Lloyd.

"Alright, here's the plan. You see that clump of trees off at two o'clock?" she asked.

"Yes," I said.

"We're going to land, but keep up your speed. We're going to show whoever is following us that we've landed, but we're going to circle back this way and let them pass overhead. We need to see who is following us. They will land and realize that we've backtracked. As soon as they touch down, we launch and fly hard back this way. There are several places that I saw that we will be able to lose them," she said.

It was a dangerous move, but I agreed that we needed to know who was following us. I trusted Abi that she knew how to lose our followers. Like I said, she was the grand champ at disappearing when she wanted to.

I was a little afraid of landing at full speed, since that is where Cotopaxi and I had troubles. Cotopaxi also seemed a little concerned, because he looked back at me with a quizzical glance.

"We'll be alright," I said, patting Cotopaxi's neck. "Just land and keep your speed up. Follow what Hera'sha'I does."

I hoped he understood.

We landed at a fantastic rate of speed. The fastest we had ever done before. I'm convinced that had I fallen off at that speed, it would have been death. Fortunately, we had Hera'sha'I to follow, and it made a difference. Hera'sha'I touched down in a large meadow, something that we would never do normally, but we actually wanted to be detected this time.

Heading straight, he quickly was in the tree-line again after several bounds. We followed about fifty yards behind. As Hera'sha'I charged into the trees, it appeared that he was going to remain heading straight for a small ridge that appeared before us.

"*Just do as we do,*" said Abi.

Hera'sha'I began to unfurl his wings and began to glide just over the tops of the tree tops. Cotopaxi followed exactly, and soon we were also skimming the tree tops. Without warning, Hera'sha'I made a right-angle turn. We followed, both me and Cotopaxi letting out a sigh of relief when we made the maneuver, but we shouldn't have been relieved.

After a couple of miles, another right-angle turn had us returning the direction we had come. This time we landed in a narrow spot, just wide enough for a dragon. We retained our speed. Now we had the canopy of trees above us as we charged through the forest. Slowing, Hera'sha'I found the perfect viewpoint to watch our pursuers. With my enhanced vision, I was able to see the meadow we had landed in very clearly. I could also detect the paw prints of both dragons, albeit that Cotopaxi's were distinctive because of its one shriveled paw. Instead of putting full weight on the paw, he would occasionally let it drag just to steady himself, but otherwise, there were only three paw prints.

It seemed that we waited a very long time before we got eyes on who was following us. It came as no surprise that it was Orthu with a Gonosz rider, but a very different Orthu. Orthu was now decked out in the same type of harness that the Gonosz controlled the wild dragons with. He looked haggard, but still retained his size and strength.

"*I feel bad for those who chose the Gonosz,*" said Selena. "*Enslaving both people and dragons is their way. Orthu and the others should have known better.*"

I was less charitable.

"*They got what they earned,*" I said.

"*You would think differently, had you ever been enslaved by the Gonosz,*" said Abi. Her face showed anguish and fear as she watched another enslaved dragon land not too far apart from Orthu and his rider.

"Your every move is controlled and monitored. It is a fate far worse than death. Many would choose death if they could," she said.

"How did you manage to get away?" I asked, remembering the imagery of Abi attacking her own people riding an enslaved dragon.

"The story is too long to tell now, but one that you need to hear, having never lived on Vocce," she said. She shuddered visibly at the thought.

Several other enslaved dragons landed, and now the hunt for the "wormhole" began in earnest. We waited and watched as their frustration mounted. When it became dark, we quickly sped away, back to the real wormhole.

We were met with concern when we returned to the clans. Because of our run-in with the Gonosz, we were late.

"It is only a matter of time until we are discovered," said Lloyd after we had reported the events of the day.

"Fortunately, Abi and Hera'sha'I were able to give them a false target," Selena said. *"They will spend a great deal of time searching through nooks and crannies. From what I saw of the area, the canyons and mountain areas will take days, if not weeks to explore. Really good choice by Abi and Hera'sha'I."*

"Never-the-less," said Lowry, *"Lloyd is right. It would be wise to increase our vigilance and prepare to leave at a moment's notice. We've been exploring different areas that we can move to and defend more easily,"* he said.

"And we need to be prepared to fight," added Cowboy with grim determination.

"Unfortunately, Cowboy, you are correct. We should be ready to fight. The time has come for the clans to train with the dragons and riders. We'll begin training in the morning," said Lowry.

Oh goody. Now I would get to train in front of even a larger crowd.

Hello Humiliation, my name is Marcus. I believe we've met. By-the-way, nicely played with adding even more people to watch and judge. Nicely played, indeed, Mr. Humiliation.

My exaggeration wasn't much off course. I knew that dragons and riders were vital to a successful battle, but didn't realize how much the clans relied on dragons and riders. There had to be real trust between everyone, each doing their vital role to attack, defend, and protect.

For instance, warriors on Vocce still fought with swords, spears, and ranged weapons such as bow, arrows, and slings. And of course, those with crystals were able to manage fireballs, levitation and such. Close quarter fighting was inevitable. As dragon and rider, we had been training on strafing runs. This was extremely effective in breaking up advancing enemy troops. Not many things more terrifying than a huge dragon bearing down on you, breathing fire. If the dragon missed you with fire, there were always claws, mouth, and tail to take a swipe at you.

Accuracy was paramount. Burning your own team is apparently frowned upon.

As riders, we were the sharp-shooters. On the strafing, both Alan and I needed to target the most dangerous threat, and take it out with a fireball. Alan, of course, was a natural. He was able to target the threats with amazing skill. The scary team was Abi and Sabryyna. Hera'sha'I was able to produce pinpoint fireballs that could singe an enemy merely feet away from our warriors. In our live training sessions, the clan warriors didn't even look up from their assignments as Hera'sha'I passed above them.

When we passed, everyone stopped what they were doing and covered up with their shields towards us, not the enemy. Cotopaxi had a tremendously powerful fireball, but little control. Although Alan was expert with his marksmanship, my fireballs tended to meander off course. Fortunately, they weren't that powerful to hurt anyone seriously, including the enemy, unfortunately.

Because of this, we were assigned to attack beyond the front line of the advancing army. There, our willy-nilly attacks could do maximum damage to only the enemy, but also more dangerous to us because we wouldn't be under the cover of our archer teams or fire-throwers. Cowboy, Chayl and Sjer-berha would be our cover. This seemed like a fine arrangement to Cowboy who seemed anxious to fight.

Peggy also seemed to notice Cowboy's enthusiasm for a fight.

"It's not worth getting yourself killed, or one of your team hurt," she chided him after he had made a critical error and had electrocuted some of our own warriors. The electricity was only strong enough to give them a powerful jolt, but could have been serious. Cowboy's control was getting better and better, and more powerful, but he had used it too close to our line, and the electricity had traveled through the ground and knocked a few of the clan warriors off their feet.

"Now we have to watch out for two bloody dragon teams," I overheard one of the warriors mutter savagely. He saw that I overheard, but wasn't going to back down.

"We heard the Gonosz were working on a secret weapon," he said, making sure I was listening. "It's you, isn't it, Marcus?"

Apparently, this passed as high humor on this planet as his squad laughed at my expense.

A sharp growl from Cotopaxi shortened the laughter as the warriors hurried off, but the damage was done. They had only voiced what I already knew everyone thought.

We had picked up our patrols around the wormhole on both sides. We wanted to know if anyone was close to discovering where it was. So far, nobody had even ventured close to the wormhole. It seemed secure, but we weren't going to risk things.

Teams of dragons were tasked to patrol the other side of the wormhole. This way we could fly through and not disturb the ground around the openings, thereby alerting the Gonosz to the location. Alan and I were teamed up with Cowboy and Chayl to patrol the other side that night. After a long day of training, I was pretty tired when we arrived at the portal. Our procedure was to cross to the other side, and move off to a distant location. While one team was in the air, the other would stay on the ground and sleep for a couple of hours before switching. In the event of an attack, the ground crew would go into action and provide support.

Chayl could tell that I was about to fall asleep on my feet, so he offered to patrol first. I was grateful for the offer, and immediately climbed into my sleeping bag and promptly went to sleep. Cotopaxi curled himself around both Alan and I, a protective measure that also served as a windbreak.

It seemed minutes before Cowboy was shaking me awake.

"You're up, Sport. Y'all got the patrol for a couple of hours. Wake us at daybreak, and we'll all head home," he said.

"Some movement to the North, but when we inspected the area, it was just migrating birds roosting for the night. Pretty quiet, otherwise," said Chayl.

Taking to the night air, I immediately utilized the enhanced vision. Nothing like being able to see in the dark.

The night air was brisk, to say the least. It was cool anyway, but to be on the back of a dragon flying through the air, it was chilly. I was wearing appropriate clothing to protect my body from the night air, but my face and hands always got cold and stiff.

Most of what we did was glide around the area, both looking and listening in the night for something that just did not fit.

"*I suggest we widen our search,*" said Selena.

We glided wider and wider. Cotopaxi had caught a thermal that kept us in flight without much flapping of his massive wings. As we were making a turn, I noticed some movement from the same area that Chayl had mentioned. Focusing with my enhanced vision, I soon saw the same birds roosting for the night.

Occasionally, the birds would flap, and it would attract

our attention… no. That wasn't right. The birds were actually being spooked by something. They weren't just randomly flapping, they were being disturbed and taking to flight and re-positioning themselves in other trees or flying off altogether. Something was fishy. This wasn't normal roosting behavior.

"Alan, Selena. To the north. Something is disturbing the birds," I said.

Alan turned his attention to the same area. He had brought night vision binoculars from earth, and he now brought them to his eyes.

"I'm not picking up anything. Wait, you're right. Something is disturbing the birds," he confirmed.

"*Marcus, move in slowly,*" instructed Selena. "*We need to identify what that is.*"

Following protocol, I informed a groggy Chayl and Cowboy what we were doing.

"*Copy that,*" said Cowboy. "*If it's the Boogie Man, give us a call.*"

Cotopaxi seemed to know what his mission was, because he drifted closer and closer to the disturbance with very little wing action. We were as silent as the night, as we neared our destination.

"*I'm not seeing anything,*" I said. "*I can see the area pretty clear now…*"

"*CHECK YOUR SIX!*" shouted Cowboy.

We had become so fixated on the birds, that we had foolishly forgotten to be aware of our surroundings. Cowboy's frantic message had saved us from the initial attack.

As we spun around, Orthu with his new rider nearly de-capitated us with his spread wings. As they sped by, Orthu let out a shrill, unworldly scream.

Instinctively, Cotopaxi dove straight for the earth. Alan and I both were able to remain seated, and we leveled off and Cotopaxi began to return to where we had left Chayl and Cowboy, wings flapping furiously. As we neared the temporary camp, we heard the unmistakable sounds of a fight. Each dragon has a distinctive war scream, and we were easily able to hear and recognize Sjer-berha's cries. Cotopaxi responded with his own cry as we joined the fight.

Coming in as low we were, we found ourselves below the fight. Sjer-berha was being hounded by two captured dragons with riders. The riders of the captured dragons were having trouble guiding their dragons, so they weren't effective in their efforts.

Alan joined the fight with a well-placed fireball shot that knocked one of the riders off his mount. The rider screamed as he pinwheeled to the ground. The fall was too high for anyone to survive. The captured dragon, finding itself no longer controlled by the rider, wheeled and broke for freedom, only to explode mid-air. It was the same as the other captured dragon we had fought against before. If their rider died, it appears that they died, too.

Alan's fireball had attracted attention. While the remaining dragon and rider pursued Sjer-berha, two others dropped from the sky to form up on us. Cotopaxi had seen this scenario before, and rather than run, he attacked the nearest dragon, surprising both dragon and rider. Before they could react, Cotopaxi had decapitated the rider with his tail. The terrified dragon seemed to know what was coming, because his shrill scream pierced the sky before being silenced in a very horrific way.

Cotopaxi turned to meet the other threat.

It was Kal with Kylor riding astride 'Elu'ali'aq'.

But it was a different Kal and 'Elu'ali'aq'. Both had filled out. Kal had always been huge, but now he was terrifying, wielding a sword and fully armored. And 'Elu'ali'aq' was larger than most adult dragons now. Kylor was also decked out in armor, but looked ill at ease riding behind his brother. He looked like he was on the verge of being sick. I knew that feeling all too well.

There are times to attack and times to run. Our first attack had been the right decision. Cotopaxi made the second correct decision when he bolted in the same direction that Sjer-berha had flown.

'Elu'ali'aq' screamed in rage as we flew off. Alan had spun around and was now shooting fireballs for all his worth. Each fireball placed with the same pinpoint accuracy he normally exhibited, but with no effect to Kal as the fireballs ricocheted off his armor. A well-placed fireball should have knocked 'Elu'ali'aq' off course, but he too, seemed unfazed.

Although Cotopaxi was flying for all he was worth, 'Elu'ali'aq' easily caught up with us and was now tailing us.

"I see that no amount of training has helped you, Marcus. Your dead sister was ten times the rider that you are," he taunted.

Kal wasn't someone who would be satisfied with just a kill. He needed to torture and terrorize his victim.

"Just so that you know," he said. *"'Elu'ali'aq' hasn't fed yet. We're going to clip your poor, crippled dragons' wings and let 'Elu'ali'aq' have his fun with him. It won't be a fair fight, by any means. I just want to hear the squeals as a helpless dragon gets torn to bits. You will both then be fed to 'Elu'ali'aq'. He likes his food to be warm and wiggling as it slides down his gullet,"* said Kal with a chuckle.

Cotopaxi was trying his best to outfly 'Elu'ali'aq', but the large dragon was merely playing with my dragon. He easily kept up, matching each zig and zag with bored ease. Alan tried everything in the book to get 'Elu'ali'aq' off our tail, but nothing worked. That armor was something we had never encountered or trained for.

"It's something new," Selena confirmed. *"Just bounces off without any damage what-so-ever."*

With no effort at all, 'Elu'ali'aq' reached out with his long wings and knocked Cotopaxi spinning. We crashed to the ground. The only reason Alan and I weren't crushed from the initial fall was that Cotopaxi righted himself at the last second and made a running landing. It was pretty amazing for my dragon, but 'Elu'ali'aq' remained firmly behind us.

He was so close that he was able to nip at Cotopaxi's hind

legs. Soon Cotopaxi was bleeding from numerous bites to his hindquarters and tail. One vicious bite did some real damage and Cotopaxi slowed to a limp. Knowing he now couldn't outrun the dragon, Cotopaxi turned to fight. All three of us sent fireballs in the direction of the huge dragon, but to no avail. We might as well have been shooting marshmallows at them. At least the marshmallows would melt and become sticky. Our fireballs did nothing.

'Elu'ali'aq' was clearly enjoying himself. He would slip in and out of Cotopaxi's guard, and give him a gash here and there. My poor dragon was now losing great amounts of blood and was becoming weaker and weaker.

One particular bite mangled Cotopaxi's one good front leg, causing us all to topple over.

Seeing his chance, 'Elu'ali'aq' struck for Cotopaxi's exposed neck.

"Nooooo!" I shouted as the large dragon went in for the kill.

Just as the dragon was about to strike Cotopaxi down, 'Elu'ali'aq' went into convulsions. It only lasted a second or two, but it was enough for Cotopaxi to spring back. With a mighty scream, Sjer-berha flew overhead and I saw sparks emanating from Cowboys hands. He must have mustered enough power to shock the big dragon.

"Make a run for the wormhole," commanded Selena.

Jumping on the back of Cotopaxi, he leaped into the air once again, but at a much slower speed because of his exhaustion.

We were to hide the wormhole as best as we could, but saving our dragons was more important. Without the dragons and riders, the clans were sitting ducks the moment they were discovered. And that, everyone agreed, was only a matter of time. Not "if" but "when."

With Sjer-berha flying behind us, we headed to the wormhole. Cowboys' ability to command electricity seemed to be wreaking havoc on 'Elu'ali'aq'. That big dragon did not like what Cowboy was dishing out. Instead of matching our moves and speed, he was holding back out of Cowboys' range.

"*We've got to get to the wormhole. The Gonosz will discover where it is, but we have no choice,*" said Selena.

Cotopaxi was tired, but trying his best. Alan was still shooting fireballs without success. The only thing that seemed to hold them at bay was the electric shock that Cowboy was doling out. He seemed to be getting better control, and the charge was powerful enough to make the enemy wary.

Nearing the wormhole location, Chayl ordered us through first.

"*Get through the hole and make a beeline for the clans. We might be able to hold them off because they will need to go through one at a time. Now that we know Cowboy can penetrate their armor, we can defend the entrance. You need to get Paxi back and treated, and let the clans know of the danger,*" said Chayl.

Flying through the wormhole, we were greeted by Abi, which was a surprise. She had been on patrol and had come to the wormhole to check things out.

"*We're under attack, Abi. The Gonosz will find the wormhole. You need to fly and warn the clans. Paxi is hurt, but can still fly,*" said Selena.

"We can go together," said Abi.

"*We're fine. The more time the clans have to prepare, the better. Mere minutes of preparation can be the difference between success and failure in matters of war. Go! We are fine! Go!*" she said.

Abi immediately turned and headed back to the clans at a tremendous speed. Cotopaxi remained at a steady pace, exhausted from the skirmish.

We landed just outside of the camp. Several of the healers from the clans were on hand to treat Cotopaxi. They came running as we dropped off of the dragons back. Cotopaxi was so tired that he flopped to his side once we were clear of his large body.

"It's alright, Paxi," said Alan. "You are going to be alright."

Alan started going over his patient, accessing his wounds.

"He's got some deep wounds, but they should be fine if treated. He's just lost lots of blood and the flight tired him out," Alan said.

"Say what you want about Paxi," said Selena *"but his heart and courage are huge, Marcus. You two will become a great team in time."*

The team of healers all began to treat Cotopaxi with their various treatments. For the first time, I saw that they all deferred to Alan.

"Is that because Paxi is his dragon?" I asked Selena.

"No. Alan really knows what he is doing. He has taken his role of healer very seriously, and the clans recognize that he has great knowledge, despite his young age. The information that his crystal holds must be vast and very complete," she explained.

The camp was a buzz of activity. We were camped in an area that was open and not easy to defend. The camp was located in this area because of the water source and because it was in an isolated area. Our defensive camp was located about fifteen miles away. It was an area that held limited water, so we would need to pack as much as we could to supplement the small amount. Water rationing would be required if we were to stay for any period of time.

The good thing was that the Gonosz would have the same limitation. Part of our plan was that we hoped that the Gonosz wouldn't be carrying enough water to sustain a long campaign. They would need to spend time finding a water source, and from our scouting reports, there just wasn't any large amounts of water on this part of Vocce. If we could hold them off for several days, they would be forced to call off the attack for lack of water.

My concern was Cotopaxi. My dragon was exhausted and wounded.

"More than anything, Paxi needs rest and fluids. Flying,

he can make that distance in a matter of minutes. We will stay here while the camp moves. On foot, the camp will need most of the night, and into the morning before they arrive. When Paxi is ready, we'll fly to the defensive camp and he can recuperate more then," said Alan.

Cotopaxi had promptly fallen asleep, his great chest heaving with every breath. Dropping down beside him, I laid my head resting on his belly. A rumbling issued deep within his chest, and he licked my face before falling back to sleep.

"Good boy, Paxi. Good dragon," I said with sincerity.

Abi and Sabryyna had offered to patrol while we rested. We were all concerned about Chayl and Cowboy. They were alone, trying to guard the wormhole. Lloyd and some of the older dragons flew off to assist them if needed.

"It's doubtful that they will attempt to come through right now. They know that they don't have the force to overcome someone guarding the wormhole. My prediction is that they flew back to their camp when they got an exact location for the wormhole," Lloyd had said.

We all must have been pretty tired. It was full daylight when I finally opened my eyes. Alan was up attending Cotopaxi's wounds, and the dragon looked far better than he had when we first landed.

"Are you going to be able to travel?" I asked.

Cotopaxi must have known what I said, because he got up and shook out his wings. He moved a little stiffly, but otherwise seemed good. A testament to Alan's new-found medical skills.

Abi and Sabryyna had returned, accompanied by Chayl and Cowboy. Fortunately, Chayl and Cowboy had not been forced to fight.

"The Gonosz definitely know the exact location of the wormhole," said Chayl. "Kal's dragon, 'Elu'ali'aq', must have a tremendous sense of smell. He tracked us through the air and landed fifty feet from the wormhole. Cowboy was just outside the hole, watching. When they landed, Cowboy slipped through the wormhole and we took up position to defend against them trying to come through, but they must have gone back to the Gonosz camps rather than risk an attack under-manned."

Gathering our gear, we distributed our equipment be-tween the other dragons so that Cotopaxi wouldn't have any additional burden. Alan rode behind Cowboy and Chayl, and I hitched a ride behind Sabryyna and Abi. The dragons had be-come stronger since the pairing. Although they were burdened more than usual, they seemed to manage fine.

We took the lead with Cotopaxi second and Chayl and Cowboy brought up the rear. By air, we were able to cover the distance in no time at all. Because we were at war, protocol was paramount. To land, we had to respond with the correct password.

The camp was set up on top of a rocky hilltop. Fortifica-tions were set up to block an advancing ground army, but we also had prepared for an air attack of dragons.

The hilltop was incredibly rocky, providing shelter from dragon fire and arrows. We had built several fortifications that had several feet of rock and dirt roofing that were able to stop the fireballs from both dragon and human. Only a direct frontal attack would allow damage to the occupants, but the idea was to have so much firepower issuing from the fortifica-tions, that it would be suicide for anyone attacking from the front.

There was a large cave that functioned as a living quar-ter. It was heavily fortified and had defensive structures that the enemy would have to pass through in order to get to the occupants. The entrance was small, only allowing one or two people to enter at one time, and dragons were out of the ques-tion. A person entering the cave would need to pass through nearly one hundred yards of narrow cave, before it opened up into a large cavern. They would also have to pass by nearly ten attack points and two gates before they could get to the cavern. It was a practically impenetrable entrance that could be readily defended by the occupants.

This was also where the water source, albeit a small amount, was located. We were rationed about two quarts per day, which is fine for drinking, but that didn't include cooking, washing, or a number of other things that we depend on water for. This was survival amounts of water only. The dragons had an outside source that was considered too alkali for humans to drink, but didn't seem to bother the dragons much.

There was also an escape tunnel that few knew of. Our fear was that if we had an informant in our midst, the enemy could use this against us and block off all escape routes. Then it would only be a matter of us running out of supplies. As we figured it, we had enough supplies to last about three months. With no water to even shower with, we were going to be pretty stinky.

Meanwhile, the enemy would have to bring their own supplies, including water. They would surely find the water source in the abandoned camp, but it was still a days' hike away to get to it. We intended to make their life as miserable as possible for the next two months, then escape through the hidden tunnel where we would either mount a surprise attack, or make another run for it.

In return, we would defend and launch counter-attacks against the enemy. The enemy should suffer significant losses and hopefully become demoralized, but as Mike Tyson famously said, "Everybody has a plan until they get punched in the mouth."

With this plan, the dragons and riders were on the sharp end of the stick. It would be us who went out to wreak as much havoc as possible. Cowboy was giddy with excitement at the prospect of getting back at the Gonosz. His sister was constantly on him about not getting too emotional and doing stupid things that might jeopardize the rest of the teams.

Peggy had also proved her worth to the clans. Her strategies were unique, and she was able to think out of the box. Having a common enemy seemed to allow the clans to accept

Peggy quickly into the fold.

"We want to make things as difficult as possible for them," she said. "They will need water and supplies. We need to figure out how to stop their supply chain."

It was decided that much of our patrol time would be dedicated to discover how to disrupt the Gonosz camp life as much as possible. A tired, thirsty, and hungry soldier was a disheartened soldier.

In addition to our strategy meetings, we were constantly on patrol so that we were prepared for the Gonosz. We would go in dragon team pairs. It took about a week of healing before Alan allowed Cotopaxi to start doing abbreviated patrols. His wounds were healing well, but he was still weak from the ordeal.

"They found the old camp," reported Abi after one of her more extensive patrols. "They've set up their own camp there, and they are sending patrols to find us. It's only a matter of time now. We'll remain under cover as long as we can, but we'll be fighting soon."

Our time was spent building further fortifications and training our warriors how to defend our camp.

It was while I was on patrol with Cotopaxi and Alan when we found out that we had been discovered. We were night flying, which was an advantage for us because of my enhanced vision. The enemy had been good at keeping their patrols under cover, but at night under the cover of darkness, they got sloppy. Two of their patrols were out riding their captured wild dragons.

We spotted them flying towards us, so we dove for the ground to remain undetected. We were a long distance from the defensive camp, but the dragons weren't just looking willy-nilly. They definitely had a destination. We were able to drop in behind them several miles away without detection. Had the dragon been guided to turn around, it is possible that they might have detected us with their dragon vision, but instead, the Gonosz riders kept them straight forward towards our camp. It was a mistake.

Once within several miles of our defensive camp, they split up and began scouting our camp. They stayed far enough away to not be detected by us, but it was too late. We had found them. So now we knew we were being watched.

"They know our location," I told our leaders after landing. "They are currently scouting us."

"*It's only a matter of time then,*" said Lowry. "*Our patrols and outposts should give us ample warning of their advance.*"

"I suggest that we don't show our hand," said Peggy. "We might be able to lure them into a trap, if they think they have the element of surprise."

"*Agreed,*" said Lowry. "*A surprise counter-attack can cause panic and disrupt any plans the enemy has made. Peggy, you have proven yourself valuable for planning and logistics. We would like to invite you to join our strategy team as a permanent member. What say you?*"

"Of course," said Peggy. "You all know that I have a special interest in defeating the Gonosz. I will be happy to offer my assistance."

"*That's quite an honor,*" Selena told me. "*I'm not sure when someone outside of the clans was ever invited to join their strategy team.*"

Our first order of business was to set up our patrols to look intentionally ineffective. We would leave holes in our patrol patterns. We were sure that we were being watched, so we gave the Gonosz predictable patrol patterns that we rarely strayed from.

I was chosen to fly most of these patrols. The enemy had seen me as a bumbling puke-shirt nothing. Naturally I wouldn't be effective at patrolling in their eyes.

Not going to lie. Kind of hurt my feelings, that this was the perception that the clans had of me. It troubled me even further that it was true.

The other teams used their dragons on the ground from viewpoints to watch the enemy, and the enemy moved fast.

The wormhole was too small for more than a few people at a time, or one dragon with a rider to come through. The Gonosz spent several days just getting their army through the wormhole and situated.

Fortunately, they did as we expected. They found the old clan camp with a water source and used it as their base camp. Naturally, my patrols didn't include searching the old camp, but rather, I would have Cotopaxi fly in large circles around the defensive camp. Each turn highly predictable, and mightily boring for all involved.

"If we make this same circle again, I'm jumping to my death," grumbled Alan.

Cotopaxi must have understood Alan's mood because he shook his head and snorted in agreement.

"Patrol team, please report back at camp," said Lloyd from several miles away. We always stayed within telepathy range when on these boring patrols. The range seemed to be around what Alan figured was about ten miles. It seems like a great distance, but when you're riding a dragon, it only takes a few minutes to get out of range.

It was a relief to land after such a long time in the air.

"You were being watched very carefully," said Lloyd.

"We know. I was keeping an eye on them with my enhanced vision," I said. It was the only unique ability I had. Truthfully, it was the only thing that made me useful. The other teams didn't share the ability, which surprised me somewhat.

"It is a unique gift," said Selena. *"Not many crystals have that particular capability."*

A woman approached us.

"If you will please follow me, we're planning our first attack," she said.

This was somewhat of a surprise. We had our counterattack planned out, and it seemed to be a strong plan.

All of our dragon riders and teams were present. Some of the older dragons were on patrol so that we could all be in attendance.

We were escorted to one of our large tents that we used for training and various meetings. Lowry was already positioned at the front, and we appeared to be the last to arrive. The other teams were in place along with various other leaders.

Once situated, Lowry began.

"After some contemplation, we've decided to attack first," said Lowry, much to our surprise.

"With that, I will now turn the time over to Peggy who has developed a plan that we've all accepted, and now will implement," he said, with a chuckle. It seemed an odd time to find humor, but whatever.

Peggy, too, had an amused look on her face.

"I call it 'Operation Upchuck'" she said with her own chuckle. Only a few people actually laughed. The rest of us were still in shock at the announcement.

"The enemy out-numbers us, so we will need to think unconventionally if we are to win. Our plan to make them carry water over a great distance to fight is a good plan. They are experiencing some struggle with how to transport water to the battlefield, just as expected. But we can make the water situation even more of a burden," she said with the same smile.

With a gesture from Peggy, several people came forward carrying a large hand-drawn map. They pinned the map to the front of the tent for all to see. It was easy to recognize the location the map depicted. I had seen it many times from the air as I flew over it. It was plainly a map of the old camp.

Central to the map was the area of the water cistern highlighted in blue.

"As you all know, the cistern is the only water source large enough to support an army the size of the Gonosz. It is vital to their success. It will be guarded with every resource that they have. Entrances will be impossible to enter. They will be heavily fortified and guarded twenty four hours a day," she said.

"But we have a little surprise for them," she continued

as she walked to the map with a pointer. "As most of you know, the cistern is fed by a single underground stream. The source of the stream is the small mountains located just north of the camp. The stream remains underground the entire route to the cistern, but there is a small cavern closer to the mountains that leads to the stream. As of this morning, the cavern has been undiscovered by the Gonosz."

With the pointer, she showed us where the cavern was located. It was only a mile or two upstream from the camp.

"This," Peggy said, pointing at an area colored black, "is an old lake bed. It has been dry for hundreds of years. It once was an alkali lake. The water is long gone, but the alkali content remains in the lake bed and is highly concentrated."

A pause.

"Our plan is simple. We need to place as much of the alkali material into the stream, so that it contaminates the cistern water. Our team doesn't believe that we will be able to contaminate the water enough to kill, but it will certainly be enough to cause severe nausea and vomiting to anyone drinking the water. This will make it unusable to any human. It doesn't seem to affect dragons, however. Even so," Peggy said with a chuckle, "Anyone desperate enough to drink the alkali water is in for an unpleasant couple of hours. This should damage any attack plans that the Gonosz have for the near future. They will need to solve their water problem before they can concentrate on us. That will give us time to plan other such attacks that will be of minimal risk for us, but cause real problems for the Gonosz."

Peggy then outlined the plan. It was rather simple. The dragon teams would take a few hours to rest this afternoon, then fly in a wide loop avoiding any patrols that the Gonosz sent out. Once on the far side of the small mountain range, we would land and the dragons would cover the remaining distance by foot. Fortunately, there were ravines and small hills that would hide our approach. Once at the dry lake bed, we would have old growth sage brush to hide our actions, but we would have to be careful of any Gonosz patrols.

That's where I came in. With my enhanced vision, I would sneak through the sage brush to a vantage point in which I could see the Gonosz camp.

I had been patrolling all day, so I was bushed. After departing from the meeting, I went to scratch Cotopaxi on the snout, then headed directly to bed. In a few moments, I was asleep, not having even taken the time to eat. I was getting used to the gravity, but it still took a toll out of me.

CHAPTER TWENTY-SIX

A PREEMPTIVE STRIKE

"Shake it loose," said Cowboy, as he tussled my hair. "We got us some live action against the enemy!"

Cowboy was very excited about the prospect of getting back at the Gonosz. He had been looking forward to retaliatory action the entire time since his family was attacked, and this was our first planned strike.

I was nervous about the strike. The team was relying on me to be their eyes. If I was too late in recognizing a patrol, we would be discovered. Discovery that close to the camp of the enemy was a sure way for us to all be killed or captured.

"It's worth the risk," said Selena. *"We can cause a lot of damage to the plans of the Gonosz, with a relatively small amount of work."*

Some of the older dragons had been on patrol as we rested.

"You are clear to head out," said Lloyd. *"Their patrols are mainly toward the south. They assume that we might try to make a break for the wormhole, so they are patrolling the most likely routes heavily. You should be free of patrols to the North, but that doesn't mean we could have missed something. You need to remain vigilant and never break protocol."*

Chayl and Cowboy led off as the scouting team, followed by me and Alan, then Abi and Sabryyna followed last.

As soon as we were in the air, I swept the area with my

enhanced vision to make sure that we were indeed alone and free to fly the mission. It appeared that Lloyd had been correct. There were no visible enemy patrols. In the great distance, I could recognize some of the older dragons of our camp, flying patrol missions in our absence.

We kept low to the earth, just skimming the bare ground and following any canyon or hill that would conceal our movements. It was nerve-wracking. Even though we had practiced formation flying, that had always been in training. This was our first mission, and it was terrifying knowing that this was the real thing.

In order for us to remain safe, we had to fly wide of the camp, head north, then make our way back to the small mountains from which the spring water was found. It took several hours of careful flying, but we eventually were able to land on the North side of the mountains.

Now would come the most dangerous part. The mountains would be a natural lookout for the camp. If the enemy was smart, they would have a scouting team watching over the camp. Surprisingly, as we carefully made our way through the mountains, we found no evidence of such a team. Had we found one, our instructions were to evade and return to camp, or kill the lookout team, then return before they were missed. In either case, that would mean the end of the mission.

Won't lie. I had hoped to find a patrol. I was frightened of the whole thing. Great dragon rider I was turning out to be.

"*Clear,*" said Chayl as he circled back to us from scouting the two peaks that would be the most obvious spot for a patrol to be.

"*Abi, you're better on the ground. You lead off, we'll bring up the rear. Marcus, just follow Abi at a safe distance and provide instant backup, should they run into a surprise attack,*" said Chayl who had been assigned as the mission leader.

We made our way through ravines and low spots slowly. Soon, we were on the edge of the dry lake bed. We took several minutes to make sure there were no others about before we entered the open area. Abi led off towards the landmark rock that indicated where the cavern entrance was. It was barely large enough for Hera'sha'I to enter, and she was the smallest dragon.

"Cowboy, Sjer-berha, and I will move the alkali material to the entrance of the cavern. Hera'sha'I is the only dragon that will fit, so she will work inside the cavern with Abi, Sabryyna and Alan. Marcus and Paxi will need to head out and be our lookout," said Chayl.

We had brought several large sacks that could be draped over the backs of the dragons. We also had several shoves to fill the sacks.

Cotopaxi and I headed off for our predetermined lookout destination. We made our way slowly, Cotopaxi routinely looking back at me for reassurance. I tried to look calm and collected for the sake of my dragon, but I'm sure he could tell I was scared.

Ten minutes later, we settled into a position that we could watch the camp and most likely routes the patrols would take.

"Trust your training," Selena said to both me and Cotopaxi. *"You've done something like this hundreds of times during training. Stay focused. It is when you lose focus that bad things tend to happen."*

We had chosen a position close enough that we were able to communicate telepathically with the team.

"We have eyes on the camp. All quiet. Some activity within the camp, but no patrols or movement in the near vicinity," I said with more confidence than I felt. *"Continue mission."*

"Copy that," replied Cowboy.

Our plan had a time frame. It would be dark for about five hours. At the four hour mark, we wanted to be in the air, heading back in the cover of darkness. We only had a few hours to do some damage.

Soon, the camp began to wind down for the night. Token patrols were out and about, but they didn't even scan the hillside. They weren't expecting an attack, and it appeared that everything was pretty lax in camp. If we were successful, that would all change.

Sooner than I expected, Chayl called us back to the cavern. My team was all laughing quietly as I rode up.

"What's up?" I asked with some surprise. We still had an hour of moving dirt.

"Alan needs to tell you," said Sabryyna.

Alan was grinning ear to ear.

"You won't believe what I found," he said, holding up a brown weed of some sort.

"You guys were smoking wacky weed, right?" I asked. "What's the weed for?"

"This, my friend, is what the locals use when they are feeling a little constipated. It's like prunes on steroids and energy drinks. It will clean your pipes fast," he said with a small chortle.

"Fortunately for us, it can be concentrated by boiling the plant and extracting the liquids. We just dumped enough of the stuff in the water to unblock twenty elephants. Along with the alkali, this is going to be one sick camp. The thing is, the alkali will have an immediate effect on the system, whereas this will take several hours to take effect. I wish we could stay and watch the festivities," he said wistfully, the smile still on his face.

"Spewing at both ends!" said Cowboy with an audible chuckle. "This we gotta see!"

"Well," said Selena. "It will take all day for the contaminated water to travel to the cistern. Maybe we can convince the council to send us on another mission."

"Our work is done here," said Chayl. "Let's mount up and head home."

Our return home was also without incident. After this attack, we couldn't expect the enemy to be so lax. We had just kicked the hornet's nest.

"We might indeed need to see what effect our attack had

on the camp," said Lowry after Chayl had made his report. *"And Alan, that was quick thinking on your part. The amount of alkali might not have affected everyone, but with your added ingredients, the entire camp is bound to be sick. Well done."*

Alan beamed with the deserved praise.

"Marcus, with your enhanced vision, you will be vital on this next mission," said Lowry.

After the debriefing, and a quick breakfast of an MRE that the package said was an omelet (we'll agree to disagree on that one), we headed to our various sleeping quarters. The dragons headed off for a quick hunt, then they too, slept throughout the day.

After we had rested for the day, we reported to the briefing tent. The same map was hung at the front of the tent.

"This briefing will be quick. You have already scouted the area, and know your way around. Peggy, please continue," said Lowry.

"We need eyes on the ground to confirm the effectiveness of last nights' mission. You will return, but this mission is purely fact-finding. Avoid conflict at all costs and don't be afraid to call off the mission if it becomes too dangerous. Any questions?" asked Peggy.

Chayl was once again the team leader, and truth is, he was born for this type of job. He readily interpreted situations correctly, and had the temperament to not get rattled under any circumstance. He was smart and capable.

We took the same general direction as the day before, but varied our route, just in case we had been spotted. We didn't want any kind of ambush.

The return trip went without a hitch. We landed in approximately the same place as the day before, and started making our way through the ravines and hills that lead to our observation area.

"Paxi and I positioned ourselves just over on that ridge," I said, pointing at the ridge.

"Good position, but we will need to choose another in case

your tracks were spotted. They will know they were being observed," said Chayl.

We moved at a snail's pace as we approached another vantage point. It was well-concealed and looked over the camp without obstruction.

"Marcus, you take the lead. Get situated and scan around for movement, or any nearby human activity," ordered Chayl.

I stealthily made my way to the vantage point where I laid down and started to scan the area. It was a good ten minutes before I felt it was safe enough to bring the rest of the team forward. Chayl remained with the dragons in a small ravine that hid their presence.

The others had brought binoculars that we had brought from Earth as part of our gear. They were able to see shapes and figures in the dark, but nowhere close to the detail I was able to see with my enhanced vision.

At first it appeared that nothing was out of the ordinary, but I began to recognize some behavior that was out of the ordinary.

There appeared to be quite a line for the communal bathrooms that the clans had built. There wasn't such a thing as plumbing in the camp, so a communal latrine had been fashioned to take care of the "bodily needs" we all have.

The camp was made up of Gonosz warriors, not women and children. A great many had lined up waiting their turn, only to step out of line to vomit or retch.

A couple of unfortunate souls couldn't stand the wait and had to run off into the surrounding desert to squat behind any random bush large enough to conceal their actions.

Also, there wasn't actual toilet paper on Vocce. We all used a type of moss that actually worked wonders. However, it was one of the things that needed to be transported from the more humid side of the wormhole. There had been a covered storage bin that we left heaping with the moss as we evacuated camp, but it was now totally gone.

So, what were they using?

Let's just say, I saw a man go into the latrine with stockings, only to come out with none. They were down to using cloth, or pieces of their own clothing.

I laughed quietly at the scene.

"What's so funny?" asked Alan.

I realized I was the only one with vision good enough to see these details, so I sent a mental image of what I had observed.

Soon, we were all trying to stifle bursts of laughter as I sent image after image of similar scenes.

The camp was definitely in no shape to attack. Our strategy had worked, for the time being. Alan figured that it would take about two weeks before the water was usable again. This presented a problem for the Gonosz who couldn't survive without it.

"We need to take advantage of this," said Selena. *"If we have two weeks, then we should be able to make a major action of some sort to hurt the Gonosz again."*

After observing for an hour more, Chayl called it a night.

"Well team, we have seen enough. Return to the dragons and mount up. The council will want to hear our report," he said.

Upon our return, I showed the council the same images I had shown our team. Even though there was laughter and amusement, it was subdued. Our lives depended on making strong moves and correct decisions.

"Nice work, dragon teams," said Lowry, *"and I believe that Selena is correct in that we need to make the best of this successful attack, otherwise it will be in vain. The Gonosz will surely guard the cavern from further attacks, and they will know that we were responsible. Our ability to get this close to their camp will never be this easy again."*

"Just so you know dragon teams, we have other assets watching the camp, and they reported that there were several executions of high-ranking officers and various warriors within the Gonosz camp. This was a major disrupting attack, and they

should have been guarding their only water source with utmost care. It was a failure on their part, and we should never expect an easy attack like this one."

CHAPTER TWENTY-SEVEN

PAXI TO THE RESCUE

It was out on patrol the next day, that Cotopaxi began to act strangely. We were flying over a remote area that was the furthest away from the Gonosz camp. In order for the enemy to attack us from that direction, the enemy had to do as we had done, and make a wide circle that would take them far out of their way. We had learned from our own experience of attacking the enemy camp, that this was an area sometimes neglected for a serious patrol, therefore the easiest approach for an attacking army. So we upped our patrols so that we could cover that area better.

We were supposed to be making one more pass and then return to camp, but Cotopaxi refused to leave an area just above a narrow deep canyon. Every time I urged him to leave, he would turn his head and look at me.

Finally, I gave in and we dove between the narrow walls. Flying through the canyon was nerve-wracking, and Cotopaxi was bent on searching for something. Occasionally he would land, look around, only to return to his search.

We had just passed a wide spot in the canyon when he came to an abrupt stop, almost throwing both me and Alan off.

He immediately started toward a large crack in the canyon wall, and there it was. A wormhole. Alan slid off with me not too far behind.

"Where does this lead, I wonder?" I asked.

"No telling. Earth, Mars, Des Moines Iowa, forest filled with nude dancing Panda's. Your guess is as good as mine," Alan said.

"I guess we can always go through and then come right back," I said.

"*Not wise,*" answered Selena. "*How do we know that there is a return wormhole on the other side? We need to let the council know. They have more experience than we do with this kind of stuff.*"

"Good job, Paxi!" said Alan, scratching behind the dragon's ears. "That's a good dragon."

Cotopaxi beamed with pleasure at being praised. He might not have understood the words, but he certainly understood Alan's tone.

Upon our return, we reported directly to the council. They were excited to hear our news, but cautious.

"*Oftentimes the new wormholes do not pan out,*" said Lowry. "*We know of dozens of locations that lead to deadly areas. One we know of leads to the bottom of one of the oceans, several lead to solid rock. You were wise to return.*"

"*How do we verify new wormholes?*" asked Alan.

"*Some dragons are born with a sense for what is on the other side of a vortex, but they must be in close vicinity,*" answered Lloyd. "*My sense is good, but Sharry's is better. I suggest that we return with Sharry and myself to see if the way is viable.*"

The discovery must have been important, because within a few minutes of finding Sharry, we were back in the air to return to the portal.

We were tired from patrolling, but the council seemed anxious to find out what was beyond the wormhole.

Landing, we directed Sharry to the crack in the wall. It was barely tall enough for a dragon to squeeze through. For several minutes, she stared intently at the portal. Lloyd had also moved close to the wormhole and gave it the same intense stare.

Finally, Sharry backed off.

"*Unfortunately, I can't get a sense of the danger on the other side. What do you sense Lloyd?*" she asked.

"*Same as you, Sharry. I can't sense any danger, but I can't confirm that it is safe,*" he answered.

"*What is your suggestion, then?*" asked Lowry.

"*We typically send a dragon through first, but since we are so few in numbers, I don't believe we should risk it. Maybe if we find ourselves without any other options...*" said Sharry. Lloyd nodded his head in agreement.

"*Well, we need to follow your instincts on this matter. We won't jeopardize the life of a dragon or human recklessly. Perhaps if we have no other options, we will risk sending someone through,*" said Lowry.

And with that, the council turned to leave.

A bellow stopped them, and all eyes turned to Cotopaxi, who was staring back at them intently.

"*You did well, young one, to discover the wormhole, but it is too dangerous,*" said Lowry.

Cotopaxi looked at me for understanding.

"We can't go through, Paxi, we don't know if it's safe," I said soothingly.

The others turned to leave once again, but Cotopaxi ran and blocked their way.

"*I'm sorry, young one, my answer stands. We will not send someone through the wormhole,*" said Lowry, who was now getting angry. He was under a great amount of stress, and this was an open and shut case in his opinion. He angrily pushed past the smaller Cotopaxi.

A confused Cotopaxi came back to me, a pleading look on his face. The others waited impatiently for us to mount and follow.

Alan and I went to mount up, but Cotopaxi turned and faced the wormhole again. Turning his head, I could tell that he was pleading with me to go through the wormhole with him.

"Don't do it, Marcus," Alan warned.

One of the problems that Cotopaxi and I had was that we didn't trust each other. Cotopaxi obviously sensed that the wormhole was safe and wanted to cross over to show everyone that it was safe.

I am not one that makes rash decisions, but Cotopaxi seemed sure that we needed to go through the wormhole. I made my decision and hopped on the back of my dragon, hoping that he indeed was right.

I was surprised to feel Alan scramble up behind me.

"If you two die, my life won't have much meaning, so let's get this over with," he said.

We barely heard the shouts of the others, as a now gleeful Cotopaxi headed for the wormhole.

With a backwards look of assurance, Cotopaxi's head disappeared into the vortex. Moments later, I felt the now familiar sensation of traveling through a wormhole. As we emerged on the other side, we found ourselves in complete darkness. Cotopaxi soon rectified that with a sustained blast of fire.

We found ourselves in a large cavern. Alan and I slid off and began to explore. Right off, we knew that we were still on Vocce because of the gravity and lack of oxygen. What we found was running water that ran clear and cold. After further exploration, we found that it was a series of large caverns. What was exciting was that it was large enough to house all of the clans and dragons.

What we needed, though, was to find an exit. It took an hour of exploring before we found what we needed. We found an opening just large enough for a dragon to get through.

"Let me go out and explore," said Alan. "I am the more stealthy of us all. I will yell if I need help."

With that, he crossed through the opening and into the daylight.

We waited in the dark cave for what seemed an eternity, and I could tell that Cotopaxi was about to go looking for Alan when he returned, a large smile on his face.

"Gentlemen, oh, and Selena, follow me," he said.

What we walked into was like a dream. We exited the cave and found ourselves in a lush jungle, much the same as we traveled through on our first venture through a wormhole, but somehow, it had more abundance. I recognized several trees that grew edible fruit much like a banana. After all that time in the desert, this was indeed paradise.

"I think we've found our exit plan," said Alan with a smile.

Our return was met with a stern bunch of people and dragons.

"Our rules are not to be broken. They are in place for a reason," said a clearly angry Lowry.

"But..." I began, but was cut off.

"We will harbor no one who readily breaks our rules and orders, even if you are dragon riders," Lowry said. *"We have to know that you are not going to jeopardize our chances of survival, especially as we are in conflict with the Gonosz. We will bring this matter before the council..."*

"We found it," said Alan quietly. All eyes turned to him. Alan was well-respected by the council, unlike me. I seemed to be somewhat of an annoyance to the council, if I'm being honest.

"What do you mean?" asked Lloyd, who knew Alan better than most.

"We found it," repeated Alan. *"We've found a place for the clans. Water, food, shelter, large enough for all the clans, plus dragons. Paxi found it, that is."*

That got everyone's attention.

"What did you find?" asked Lowry.

"Directly on the other side of the wormhole is a large enough series of caverns to house the entire population of clans, plus their dragons. It appears to be a place on Vocce, not earth. Outside of the cavern is a lush jungle. We'll need further exploration, but it just might be our salvation," said Alan.

Lowry contemplated what Alan said.

"Let's take this before the council," he said finally.

The ride back was done in silence. I could tell that there was still anger towards us for disobeying orders, and at the same time excitement over the possibilities.

Once on the ground again, the council was assembled for an emergency meeting.

Alan was asked to explain exactly what we had seen. Council members were obviously communicating back and forth as Alan described the events of our adventure. After more questions, we were dismissed with the orders of getting rest.

"That was rash," said a disappointed Lloyd.

"But Paxi was right," I said.

"That is true, but we could have explored the wormhole in due time. Your actions were rash," he repeated.

I was too tired to argue. Nodding my head, I went to Cotopaxi who had just started to bed down for the night. I decided to forsake my comfortable bed, and laid down leaning up against my dragon.

"You were right, Paxi. Good boy Paxi," and promptly fell asleep, serenaded by the rumble of a contented dragon.

....

The next day was a flurry of activity. Several times that day, some of the older dragons would fly off towards the wormhole. Once, Chayl and Cowboy, riding Sjer-berha, flew with some of the older dragons towards the wormhole. Each group that came back appeared to be excited.

"Paxi did good," said a smiling Cowboy. "Apparently, the other dragons can't sense the location of the wormhole until they are within feet of it. Paxi must have a gift to be able to sense it from so far away, and he was able to sense that it was safe," he said with a friendly scratch to Cotopaxi's ears.

"Don't get me wrong," he added "they are still pissed at you for disobeying orders, but they are getting over it."

The council had been exploring the location, and they

figured that it was positioned on a known island off the main-land.

"Because of our twin moons, our tides can be very danger-ous. The stretch of water between the mainland and the island is treacherous because of tricky and ever-changing currents. The island has never been populated because of the lives lost trying to access it from the mainland," said Lloyd.

It was decided that we would move the clans as quickly as possible to the island. We would pack our camp and prepare to leave in five days. It would take approximately three days to move thousands of people to the wormhole, and possibly sev-eral days to move everyone through the wormhole.

A plan of action was formed. An advanced group of people, mainly young fit warriors, would be the first group to leave the next day. Their job was to break the trail that the rest of the clans would use, and make preparations for the clans once they got to the other side of the wormhole.

The next group that would leave would be the elderly and those families with small children. They would require more time to travel. The elderly dragons would also be a part of this group.

The remaining group would be the warriors guarding camp, along with the remaining families. We would be on high alert the entire time. The last thing we needed was word leak-ing out that we were on the move. That would put our people out in the open, subject to attack.

The dragons and riders would be the last to leave. Our presence flying scouting missions would surely be noticed if they suddenly stopped. It would put us in the most dangerous position, but the results of the clans being attacked in the open would be disastrous.

As part of our patrols, at least one team would fly over the traveling clans to make sure that they were safe and pro-vide whatever support was needed.

I was often used to patrol over the traveling clans, while the others had the more critical job of both flying the same type of missions that was expected of us and also gathering information about the Gonosz.

The Gonosz had to suspend their plans to sort out their water problem. They had actually pulled a large number of their army back through the wormhole in order to be able to have enough water. Water had to be brought in by captured wild dragons carrying large water skins. The cistern would probably flush itself out within the week, so that was what our timing was. We wanted everyone through our new wormhole in less than seven days.

The first group made it to the wormhole in record time. They quickly set up a guard on the wormhole, and got to work making preparations for everyone else.

The second group was taking longer than we figured. One large problem was the same problem that the Gonosz now had. If you were to have water, you needed to carry it. Water weighs a lot, so our second group was having trouble.

"We need to reroute our second group," Qurum told us dragon riders. "There is an easier route, but it will add two days."

"Our final group will arrive at the wormhole before group two," Alan said.

"That's our plan," said Qurum. "We can then send a healthy team after them to assist the weaker of group two. We feel this will give the clans the best chance to all get to safety. Marcus, we need you to fly to group two and give them this new route."

Grabbing a map out of Qurum's hand, I took a look at it. The way would be easier, but longer just as Qurum suggested.

"That will also leave group two without much of a patrol to guard them. They will also be out of telepathy range, so they can't call for help," Selena said after we had looked over the route.

"We feel that there is little risk of a Gonosz patrol to find their whereabouts. The dragon patrols need to give us information about the Gonosz camp actions. Marcus will be more useful with his enhanced vision, watching the enemy," said

Qurum.

For the next two days, the dragon teams resumed our regular patrols, with the exception of me, Alan and Cotopaxi. Because of my enhanced vision, we would fly in closer to the camp under the cover of night. Once in place, I would watch and report on anything unusual.

For the most part, the Gonosz were busy cleaning the cistern. Bucket after bucket of water was brought outside and dumped on the ground. After a while, there was a small pond of the contaminated water just outside of the cavern opening. I smiled at the thought of the chaos that we had caused.

The only thing that seemed a little odd was that their dragon teams weren't active. You would think that they would be out on patrols, like us, but we saw little of them.

"Anything new?" asked Alan, who was gazing through his almost useless binoculars.

"No. Unless you count the new military leaders to replace the ones that were beheaded. They are ruthless," I said with a shudder. I had unfortunately seen that particular event. There was no room for failure within the Gonosz military. If you fail, you usually die.

"Still no sign of Kal?" Alan asked.

"Nope. Not a sign of Kal," I answered.

"Well, that's all we need for tonight," said Abi as she came up behind us. She was assigned to patrol around us as we watched the enemy.

"Let's wrap everything up and head back," she said.

We mounted up and headed back in the direction of camp. Again, part of my job was to scan the area with my vision to make sure we had a clear course home.

Far off in the distance, I caught some movement. The movement was in a direction that we had no reason to suspect anyone would be, so I focused on the area with all my attention. There was definitely movement.

"Who do we have about twenty miles west of where we are?" I asked.

"No one," said Abi immediately. "Why? What do you see?"

"It's probably nothing. Just some movement," I said.

"*Until it is identified, it should be considered dangerous,*" said Selena.

"Let's close in and try to identify," ordered Abi.

We were out of range of telepathy with the camp, but it was within our training to take action when we deemed it necessary. Even though it would delay our return time, Abi thought it important enough to make that decision.

Instead of taking a direct route to where I saw the movement, we took our time and made sure that we weren't heading into an ambush, unlikely as it might be.

I had seen the movement up against a small mountain range that ran parallel to our route home. As we neared the range, we slowed our pace again, and we searched the area more thoroughly. We found nothing. I scanned the area again, broadening my view. It was there again, but further along the mountain range. Whatever it was, was following the range to remain out of view of our regular patrols.

"I think this is serious enough that I need to report it," said Abi. "I will fly back and warn the clans. You will need to follow and try to identify what or who it is."

I was still not convinced that the movement I saw was anything, so I wasn't particularly worried. I was pretty sure that we would find nocturnal birds or the huge, bright yellow bats that seemed to thrive on Vocce.

Flying along the mountain range, Abi suddenly broke for the east and headed back to the clan defensive camp, leaving me, Alan, and Cotopaxi to our own devices.

I scanned ahead and was not surprised to find no more movement. I was almost sorry that I had mentioned the movement at all.

I was looking for movement miles ahead, and it was almost our undoing. I had broken the cardinal rule of making sure our immediate area was safe. It was Selena who saved us.

"Paxi, dive!" she commanded.

I'm not sure if Cotopaxi understood, but he must have, because Alan and I had to hold on for dear life as Cotopaxi nosed over into a steep dive.

Leveling out, I looked around the area trying to find what Selena had seen.

Rounding a small mountain ahead of us was Kal and Kylor riding 'Elu'ali'aq'. They were making a circle to see if anyone was following them, and had it not been for Selena, 'Elu'ali'aq' would have surely seen us with his enhanced dragon vision and alerted Kal. We were now flying almost directly below and slightly behind 'Elu'ali'aq', making it difficult for him to spot us. Cotopaxi slowed his glide slightly to take us even further behind 'Elu'ali'aq'.

They must not have seen us or found anything out of the ordinary, because they finished their turn and headed back to their course along the mountain range, with us following at a healthy distance now.

We followed 'Elu'ali'aq' as he hugged the contours of the mountain. Several minutes later, he joined up with several other rider teams. The riders were all riding captured wild dragons who wore the deadly harnesses. Kal and 'Elu'ali'aq' took the lead with the other following.

We flew for many miles, following the enemy. Occasionally, Kal would circle back to see if he was being followed, but we were able to stay far enough back for him not to spot us easily. I don't particularly think he expected anyone, so he was careless and mostly pulled the maneuver as a routine action.

I could tell by their direction that they were trying to come up on our camp from an unexpected direction, much the same as we had done to them when we poisoned the cistern. As much as I hate to admit it, it might have worked had we not discovered them.

We continued to follow them until we came to the end of the small mountain range. It was here that things would get tricky. We wanted to, of course, continue to follow Kal and his team, but we would do so at incredible risk as we would no longer have the mountain range to hide behind. Our only option was to remain far enough back that we would be difficult to detect.

It was also getting dark. With my enhanced vision, this benefitted us. I could readily see what would be total darkness to Kal and his team. The dragons could see as well as I, but they were ahead of us, not really looking back as much as they should.

As we came to the end of the range, we slowed our advance. This would be a logical place for Kal to turn around, camp for the night, or change direction. We didn't want to come up on them if they happened to either turn around or camp.

Our carefulness was without merit. We came to the end of the mountain range, only to discover that the team had continued and were now a fair distance away. I could only detect movement, but no features of the dragons and riders, they were so far ahead. If we didn't speed up, we would lose them.

In doing so, I forgot about our own protocol of "checking our six."

We rounded the range, and at my urging, Cotopaxi opened it up, trying to catch the enemy in front of us.

"*The information that we have is that you are the weakest dragon team,*" said Kal accompanied by the unmistakable sound of the wing beats of a dragon. His message was punctuated with a terrifying scream from 'Elu'ali'aq'.

We had no time to react. 'Elu'ali'aq' had come up behind us, and with a swipe of his massive head, knocked Cotopaxi into a spin. We dropped out of the sky at a tremendous speed, and nearly crashed into the ground before Cotopaxi righted himself.

Alan was instantly firing fireballs, but because he couldn't see as well as I did, was just firing blindly.

I quickly scanned the sky and located 'Elu'ali'aq'. He was coming up directly behind us.

"Six o'clock!" I shouted.

Alan spun around and shot fireballs at a tremendous rate. We caught 'Elu'ali'aq' by surprise, because we knew his exact location. Two of the fireballs hit him square in the chest. Normally, that would be enough to cause a dragon some damage, but it mostly just surprised 'Elu'ali'aq', who veered off to the right to avoid any more fireballs.

Cotopaxi was now flying all out. When we trained, Abi and Hera'sha'I were usually the chasers due to their amazing speed and agility. We rarely escaped their "attacks," but the payoff from practicing with them was that we were able to keep 'Elu'ali'aq from landing another blow through Cotopaxi's evasive flying.

Time and time again, 'Elu'ali'aq' would close in for an attack, only for Cotopaxi to make an evasive move that would throw the larger dragon off momentarily.

We couldn't escape with straight speed, but neither could the larger dragon get close enough for a kill shot. Plus, with Alan's accuracy, he was now targeting the larger dragon's unprotected eyes with fireballs. Time and time again, the dragon had to move his head to avoid them.

With my vision, I could see that Kal was getting more and more frustrated with each furtive attack.

"His mistake was that he had to announce his presence. Had he attacked without warning, we might be dead. Don't ever become narcissistic, Marcus. It can kill you," said Selena.

"Yeah, well, if you haven't noticed, he's still on our tail. I'll let your lecture settle in when we're on the ground, back at camp," I said.

Cotopaxi was heading back to camp as fast as he could, but even though we were in a deadly escape situation, we still needed to protect the camp, and especially our second group of slow-moving clan members. Cotopaxi was taking a round-about way back to the safety of our patrols, when Kal pulled up unexpectedly.

"Well, well," he said, tauntingly. *"Our other riders seem*

to have found your clans trying to escape. Our war council will be excited to learn of this development. That information is more important than killing you right now. We were trying to figure out how to draw the clans out into the open, and you seem to have done it for us. This isn't over, Marcus. You're lucky to be alive. I won't make that mistake again."

With that, he was gone, and we were flying all out now for camp. Group two was now in mortal peril.

I'm not sure how long it took for us to get back to camp, but when we did, the camp had gone to bed for the night.

There was a large set of skin drums that were set up near a guard station that served as an attack warning for the camp. We alerted the night guards that we were coming in fast and hard. The camp was always in a state of alertness, but more so with the enemy so close. As we were landing, the guards were already alerting the camp using the drums.

Instantly, the camp came to life.

Warriors came running to find out where the attack was coming from.

Lowry, for all of his old age, was one of the first to greet us. We quickly reported the events of the night.

Lowry listened intently, asking only a few questions here and there. The council was quickly assembled, and we were asked to once more relay the events.

The second group was now fully exposed. Many warriors had either children or elderly parents, or in some cases, both, in that group. There was no question whether or not we would try to protect them. It was just how would we protect them?

"We will need to abandon camp tonight," said Lowry. "We'll need to bring every resource that we have for their protection. Send out word that we will leave camp at dawn. That's only a few hours away, but group two needs us now."

"It will take us several days to reach them. We won't make it in time," said Peggy.

"If you are suggesting that we don't try..." began

Qurum.

"Never," she said, cutting Qurum off. "But we need to create some time. I suggest that we send the dragons to group two camp tonight. Any dragon that can move fairly fast. If we load them with some of the slowest elderly and children…"

"They still won't make it to the wormhole in time," said Qurum.

"Which is why we reverse their course and bring them back towards us. Reversing the course might be unexpected for the Gonosz. If not, we still bring them closer to our warriors. If we have them reverse course and we leave at dawn, we can make contact with them in just two days, not three. It might be the difference. Remember, the Gonosz must make plans and then send their dragons. It is too far away for their foot soldiers to get here quickly."

So here it was. After all the training and preparation, we now had no choice but to fight, and I was scared. I was ill prepared to be a dragon rider. The others took to it like a duck to water. What was it about me that I couldn't even access the crystals? The crystals were the game changers, what made a dragon riding team formidable warriors. Not me, and not Cotopaxi.

Naturally, the dragons were dispatched immediately to protect the now vulnerable group two. We quickly grabbed our gear and left for their last known location.

Both us, and the enemy used an ingenious method of communication. By spacing scouts at about eight mile intervals between armies, we were able to communicate telepathically fairly quickly with each other through relaying messages. Part of our job was to take an additional warrior to drop off along the way. The scouts were vulnerable to attack, as one can imagine, because communication was key during battle.

We scouted locations that would give the scouts a good hiding place within range of each other. It was vital for us to have these lines of communication.

After dropping the scouts off, we flew the rest of the

way to group two. The camp was just waking up to the brisk dawn morning. The leader of the camp was a fierce-looking warrior named Hammand. He took one look at us, and sounded an alarm.

"He's signaling the danger warning," said Chayl, admiration in his voice. "Hammand is pretty shrewd. There is only one reason that the base camp would send all of the remaining dragons. He's already figured that his camp is in danger."

Landing, Hammand had his camp nearly ready to leave.

"We have everything packed and ready to go the night before," he explained. It was a good lesson.

Hammand was surprised at the plan to turn around, and he didn't agree.

"We're only three days' travel from the wormhole," he said. "The camp is full of elderly who have limited endurance. We should continue on."

But Hammand was a consummate soldier, who even though he didn't like the plan, was able to make the best of the situation. We had the entire camp on the move within the hour. Some of the more elderly, or the very young, rode on the backs of some of the dragons.

We had to push hard to reach our destination. It was a defendable area, made up of a rocky area, and was one of only two places that had a water supply. Again, we planned to use the lack of water to hamper the Gonosz. In this case, the water was from a spring that had the smell and taste of sulfur, but smelly water was better than no water.

The lack of water was also a problem for us. We had enough with us to make it back to our destination, but just barely. If something were to go wrong…

We traveled all day and I can tell you, I for one was looking forward to the cool evening and the prospect of getting some rest. It was all we could do to put one foot in front of the other, and the only thing that spurred us on was the fear of being caught in the open and having to defend ourselves without any support.

I had allowed several elderly women and one pregnant lady to ride Cotopaxi while I walked. I was glad to see that my endurance had improved enough for me to accomplish such a feat, but I was now exhausted.

Finally, the command to halt for the night came, and I collapsed to the ground. I felt like I couldn't take another step.

"Everyone prepare a meal and eat, but don't set up camp as of yet," was the message that was passed around.

I was just about to dig into an MRE when Lowry called all the dragon riders and their teams to his location.

"This isn't going to be our camping spot," he said. *"We're reversing course again. This was a ruse."*

My heart sank. I felt like I couldn't take another step.

"Why?" I asked. The others nodded in agreement.

"We've suspected a spy in our camp. Rather, a spy network of sorts. Actually, Marcus confirmed this with his last report," reported Lowry.

"What?" I asked incredulously.

"Oh, yeah. That makes sense," said Alan. "Remember? We reported that Kal said that their report was that we were the weakest dragon team? Someone is watching and reporting to the Gonosz."

Lowry grunted to confirm Alan's speculation.

"So now we turn around and head back to the wormhole?" I asked.

"It will be difficult to say the least, but Hammand was right. We just needed everyone, including each camp, to believe in this ruse. We've even gone through great lengths to move key scouts around, so that the communication chain is now broken. We truly are on our own now, but it might be our only chance. Our main army is now on a forced march that will take them the shortest route to the wormhole," said Lowry. "It is also a route that will put our army between us and the Gonosz, so they will take the brunt of the attacks."

"Our only hope to avoid an attack on group two is to move tonight, under the cover of darkness," Lowry paused.

"It will be difficult...and unexpected. Everyone would expect us to stop for the night."

And that everyone included me.

Heading back to Cotopaxi, I was dead tired. I pulled my MRE out of my bag, but fell asleep chewing on a mouthful of freeze-dried spaghetti.

Alan nudged me awake.

"We're on the move again, buddy. Why don't you ride Paxi? One of the ladies wants to walk a while," he said.

I felt like a cad, letting an elderly woman walk while I rode, but I was too tired to argue. Climbing into my usual spot just ahead of Cotopaxi's wings, I soon fell asleep as we plodded through the night.

It was the cold night air that awoke me. We were still slowly making our way through the night. Cotopaxi, with all his strength and endurance, was now occasionally stumbling as we walked. It was a sure sign of exhaustion, but he wasn't alone. Even our strongest warriors and dragons were dragging, just able to put one foot in front of the other.

I quickly looked around. I was afraid that the elderly woman who had felt like walking was still on the ground, but she was also mounted behind me on Cotopaxi's back. No wonder my dragon was tired. He was carrying four people, plus all our gear. I marveled at the heart of my dragon.

Dropping to the ground, I jogged up to his drooping head.

"Good boy, Paxi! You're a good dragon, Paxi," I said with sincerity as I scratched behind his ears. His sunken eyes lit up briefly, and he gave me a tired lick to the face. I would remain by his head the rest of the night, offering words of encouragement as we trudged along.

When we did finally arrive at our destination, very few used the time to eat. All of us wanted to just sleep, but we had to follow protocol. It would be disastrous for the enemy to catch us in a surprise attack.

It was decided that we would conserve the dragon's

strength, since they were so vital in moving the camp. We were all assigned a two-hour watch. I was particularly needing to be a part of the watch because I could see much further than anyone. I had taken a nap on the back of Cotopaxi, so even though I was still deathly tired, I was in better shape than most.

I set out for a hilltop that would give me good vision of the area.

We had made good time, and we were now thirteen hours away from where the Gonosz thought we were.

It was now daylight, so I was able to see even further than I could in the dark. I knew the route we had followed, so I paid special attention for any movement that would indicate that we had been discovered. Fortunately, there was no such movement.

I was struggling dearly to keep my eyes open, when Alan relieved me.

"I've got the next couple of hours. Why don't you head back and get some sleep?" he asked.

"I think I'm going to curl up here. Too tired to walk back to camp," I said.

"Suit yourself. Nighty-night," he said with the sun high in the sky.

CHAPTER TWENTY-EIGHT

AMBUSHED

It seemed a matter of moments before Alan was shaking me awake.

"We're moving again," he said.

I groaned as I got to my feet. It felt like I had been beaten up by Elden several times over.

Back at camp, everybody was wrapping up their morning chores. Hammand had once again made everyone pack before turning in for the night, even though the camp was exhausted. The result was that we were ready to go at a moment's notice.

If we pushed hard, we were only two days of travel to the wormhole and safety. I vowed to sleep for a week when we arrived.

I could tell that Cotopaxi was tired, so I remained on the ground to walk alongside my dragon. Several dragon patrols had scouted the path ahead, and they had found a freshwater source about twelve hours of travel ahead, but the way was difficult. We were packing two days-worth of water, but as you can imagine, water in containers in the heat of the sun soon tasted stale. The prospect of fresh water was a motivator for our weary camp.

The way was difficult. We were traveling at night to avoid detection of the Gonosz scouts, and also for a practical reason. It was easier to travel in the cool of the night rather than walking along in the blazing sun. In this way, we were able to conserve our meager water rations. Had we traveled during the day, we would consume the water twice as fast in order to stay hydrated.

The way was rough. We were traveling through a particularly sandy area. Each step, we would sink several inches into the sand. Each step was agonizing. The dragons, for all their strength, were struggling, too. Their great weight caused them to sink even further into the sand. We stopped often, but for very short amounts of time.

I don't know how Hammand had the energy, but he would walk up and down the line of our camp, encouraging everyone.

It was towards the ten hour mark when several of the walkers sunk down to the ground. They were so weary that their muscles were cramping up. Alan checked them out.

"They are just too tired to go on," he reported to Hammand.

"Let us rig some travois for the dragons to pull," he said. Pulling a travois would be easier on the dragons, but the telltale drag marks would be a certain giveaway to our location if enemy scouts discovered them.

"The Gonosz scouts won't miss the tracks in the sand, anyhow," said Hammand. "We need to conserve the dragon's strength."

Most of the tents that the clans used had long poles of a wood similar to our lodgepole pine. We took these poles and lashed three at a time into a triangle with the two legs extending several feet past the base of the triangle. Blankets, or similar material was stretched over the frame to create a place for people to recline. Gear remained on the backs of the dragons, but at least the weight of the humans would be off the backs of the dragons.

Cotopaxi actually sighed in relief. With his shriveled paw, it had been even that more difficult than the other dragons.

It was still a difficult process, but our speed actually increased by using the travois, but the drag marks were unmistakable. Even in the dark, scouts would be able to easily track us down.

The sun had been up for several hours, when we arrived at our destination. The water source was another spring that flowed from a rocky hole in the ground. Hammand quickly organized the camp so that everyone got a turn at the water. We were each given a chance to drink deeply from the water, then move off for others to use it. When everyone's thirst was quenched, we were able to return to fill up our containers to use for our meals. The dragons were less prone to thirst, but when they did drink, it almost drained the remaining water from the spring. We would need to let it refill during the day, so that we had enough to replenish the waterhole.

The sun beat down on us mercilessly, and we were all thankful that our leaders had the sense to travel at night. We slept away the heat of the day with frequent sips of our fresh water. Too soon, the sun dipped behind the mountains. It was time to make our last push, but it would be another hard one.

Our last trek would take us about fourteen hours of travel. We wanted to make the entire trip in one shot, which would take us the entire night and into mid-morning just when the sun started beating down, but we would arrive at the wormhole and safety.

If we were careful, we could send the entire clan through the wormhole, then conceal the entrance. Cotopaxi had been able to locate it from a distance, but he was the only one who could do it. The wormhole was situated so as to not attract attention, and could be concealed with a little work, but we needed everyone on the other side before that could happen.

Worse case scenario would be that the Gonosz find the wormhole right away, then we would be no better off than we were now. We would have to flee or fight, and we weren't ready for an all-out fight.

We trekked through the night. The sandy ground

changed to rocky ground. It made the ground easier going for those walking, but harder on the people riding on the travois. They were constantly jostled, but it was better than the alternative.

It was in the early hours of the morning that a messenger from our scouts came rushing up to Hammand and Lowry.

She quickly delivered her message and then sprinted off into the night.

By the looks on Hammand's and Lowry's faces, the news was not good. That was confirmed as the dragon riders and several key warriors were called to Lowry's location.

"The third group is under attack from the Gonosz," reported Lowry, his face grave. "The Gonosz used captured dragons to carry many more warriors than we thought possible. The dragons were loaded down too heavy, and many of them died from the exertion, but the alternative was also certain death."

I was able to picture the exploding dragons that wore the harnesses. It was not a good memory.

"We're going to need to speed up our march," said Hammand.

We were already weary, but the news that group three had been attacked was not good. We needed to get to the wormhole as soon as possible.

Our speed increased, and our stops were less frequent. Several older dragons that couldn't carry a load were asked to patrol the skies around us. If we got caught in the open with the elderly, along with women and children, we would be as good as sitting ducks.

"Would the Gonosz really kill women, children, and the elderly?" I asked Selena.

"*Worse,*" she replied. "*They would be captured and have the explosive implant placed in them. They would essentially become slaves,*" she said.

"How did Abi escape?" I asked, remembering her story of being captured and the scar on the back of her neck.

Selena hesitated.

"That's a story for Abi to tell," she said.

As the sun rose in the sky, we were discovered by the Gonosz.

Several large dragons were spotted in the distance. Our elderly scouts dove for the ground to escape detection, but they were elderly dragons and didn't move as fast as the younger ones.

It didn't take long before several large dragons flew overhead, led by Kal.

"There you are! I was wondering where you had tucked your tails and ran to," he said as he flew over us. *"We'll be seeing you soon, Marcus. I suggest you learn to fight."*

With that, they reversed direction, and flew back as fast as they could. We were now in serious trouble. We were still several hours away from the wormhole. We had very few warriors, and all of our dragons and dragon riders were exhausted from the trek.

Our only hope was to make a run for it. It didn't seem possible, but we increased speed again, and again, Hammand wouldn't let up on his encouragement. Time after time he jogged to the end of the line, to encourage everyone. He was a bundle of energy, and we took his encouragement to heart.

We were now within two miles of our destination, but it might as well have been one hundred. We were so close, but even if we arrived at the wormhole soon, it takes time to go through wormholes one at a time.

"Take me to Lowry," said Selena.

I rallied what little strength I had, and jogged over to where Lowry was, encouraging everyone to move as fast as possible.

"I have a plan," said Selena.

Lowry listened patiently, then nodded his head in agreement.

"It is a good plan, and it might buy us some time," he said.

We needed time to get everyone through the wormhole

and to cover our tracks as best as we could. Selena's plan would help us do just that.

The canyon in which the wormhole was located had several very good places to hide. If we could get the clans into the canyon with cover, the Gonosz could fly over and not suspect that there were people hidden below.

An ancient stream had cut under the mountain in several places that couldn't be seen from the air. We needed to get our people hidden, then filter people through the wormhole as fast as we could, but it would be disastrous if we got caught in the canyon by the Gonosz.

Selena's plan was simple. We would get our people in the canyon and under cover. We would cover as many tracks as possible, but use deception to lead the Gonosz away.

This would be done with the dragons and travois loaded with rocks to simulate the weight of people and supplies. The ground we were on now was rocky and hard. Our tracks weren't as defined as when we were in the sand.

Our scouts had indicated that there was a large area of an old igneous rock, an old lava flow from eons ago. It was several miles wide, and hundreds of miles long. We would have the dragons drag their empty travois to the formation. It would be almost impossible to accurately track movement on the rock formation. To complete the ruse, the dragons would then fly to another location miles away, land, and drag the travois through dirt that would readily show their tracks. The Gonosz might be suspicious of our ability to move that fast, but by the time they discovered that the trail led to nowhere, it might give us just the right amount of time to get everyone through the wormhole.

We had to move now to make it happen. No rest for the weary, they say.

....

The dragons would need a rider to accompany them to

load and reassemble the travois during the time in the air.

Alan's skills as a healer were needed with the camp. Many of our camp had been driven to the point of exhaustion. When Cotopaxi and I left, he was going from one patient to another, administering to them as he saw fit. He was perfectly in his element.

Dragging the travois with the rocks wasn't any easier than real people. We needed the travois to weigh the same. Empty travois would have caused the tracks to be less defined.

Poor Cotopaxi was dead tired, but Selena was right. He had a big heart and wanted to prove his worth.

We completed the first part of the trip in record time. We came to the rock formation, and everyone dragged their load up onto the ancient lava flow.

Once there, all but several of the travois were disassembled and loaded onto the packs of the dragons. Several dragons volunteered to continue to drag their load along the old lava flow so that a casual observer would think that the entire camp had traveled the route. The rest of us flew miles ahead and landed. We quickly reassembled the travois and loaded the rocks back in.

Lowry came back chuckling.

"*Luck is finally on our side,*" he said, his eyes dancing with excitement.

We were instructed to follow him.

As we crested the hill we were on, Selena started laughing.

"*Perfect!*" she exalted.

Before us loomed a large opening to a cavern. Lowry led us all up to the cavern.

"*Quick!*" he said "*we need to build what would look to be protective barriers. It needs to appear that we've hidden within the cavern.*"

We quickly put up some makeshift barricades. Within minutes, it appeared that we had stopped to defend ourselves from within the cavern.

With that, we slipped back into the sky to return to the valley.

With any luck, the Gonosz would believe that we were within the cavern. It was a defensible position, and they would need time to find it, but also plan on how to attack it. Kinda wished I was a fly on the wall when they finally stormed the cavern to find it empty.

Once back at camp, we were slowly sending people through the wormhole. The advanced group had done a marvelous job in preparing the way. The dragons and riders were allowed to slip through to get some much-needed rest. We all knew that we would return to the remaining group now under attack to help them, but right now, we needed to water up and rest for a couple of hours.

Lloyd had been with the first group through the wormhole, and it was him that woke us up.

"The Gonosz found your tracks and followed them. As we speak, they are assembling troops to attack the cavern," he said with a chuckle. *"But we need to head out again. They have sent part of their army to the cavern, reducing the numbers that had been attacking our last group. Now is the best time to defend and drive off those attacking group three."*

Of course it made sense, but I wished we could have had a day or two of rest.

Some of the dragons were with our third group. A dragon alone is a formidable foe, but with a rider, their ability to fight is multiplied.

As riders and attendants, we were the eyes and ears of the dragon, allowing them to focus on fighting. With Alan's talent for fireballs and other tricks, we were able to defend the dragon and rain down destruction on an enemy. Having Selena was another bonus, because she could give us another set of eyes.

Like a fighter pilot, Alan and I had a checklist of things we did prior to flight. The first thing that we did was both connect to the crystals.

"Your enhanced vision really is a help to the team," said Alan. I figured he was just trying to make me feel good, because it was the only thing I felt I contributed to the group.

I would connect first, and then Alan would connect through our password system. When I sensed that he was trying to connect, I would ask the password question. We would change it up every few weeks even though there was virtually no way for anyone to know, but Lloyd was insistent that we did this.

"What is your favorite color?" I asked, enjoying the familiarity of our ritual.

"Blue...I mean yellow!" responded Alan and we both enjoyed the chuckle and I would allow Alan access to the crystals.

We would then check our gear, Alan having his medical pack, and I mostly carried food and cooking and eating utensils. We both had a leather canteen made from the hides of the large lizards that the dragons fed on. When cured, they were water-tight, and we could carry several liters of water apiece. The dragons could typically go all day without water, but by the end of the day, were pretty parched.

I looked around at my team. They were solemn, but didn't seem overly scared. Cowboy was clearly ready for the confrontation. Peggy was with the third group and he was anxious for her safety. The others were just going about their preparations without any excitement. Apparently, I was the only chicken in our group. I was terrified. I had no doubt that this was going to end in a horrible way for me.

Cotopaxi was nervous, too. Time and time again he would bump me with his nose anxiously.

"I know, Paxi," I said as soothingly as possible, "we're going to be alright."

But the dragon knew me well enough that he knew I was scared.

Cowboy appeared, and we all got quite a start. Cowboy's mom was from New Zealand, and he had painted his face in the manner of a Mauri warrior, and it was frightening.

"Normally, this would be a tattoo, but we'll make due with this face paint," he said as he placed a can of black paint before us.

Before she could argue, he sat in front of Sabryyna and began to apply the paint. As he did, he gave us instruction on how to properly put on the paint.

"This usually takes hours, or even days, but we don't have that kind of time," he said. We each spent a few moments applying the paint to our partner. It might seem a trivial thing, but it brought us together as a fighting unit, and my team truly looked formidable.

Cowboy went even further by performing a *haka*, a Mauri ceremonial dance. He told us that Mauri warriors would perform the dance in preparation for war. I didn't understand the meaning of the dance, but I knew it was Cowboy's way of imparting courage to us. I was grateful that he would share that tradition with us. It did give me a measure of solace knowing we were all on the same team.

And then it was time to leave.

We took to the sky just as it was getting dark. We would be flying the entire distance unguarded and alone. If a patrol of any size were to intercept us, we would need to fight our way out of the situation, and then continue to our small army. Our hope was to avoid any patrols so that we could render aid to our army as quickly as possible.

That's where I came in. I, along with the dragons, would need to scan ahead to spot any Gonosz patrols. I was finding that my enhanced vision was even slightly better than that of the dragons. As it became darker and darker, their vision would suffer more than mine.

I guess it was because I figured that my life was near the end, but for the first time, maybe ever, I realized the beauty of the world I had come to. The night was cool and clear, the only sounds were of the flapping of the huge wings of the dragons.

Unlike the night vision goggles which turned the night a weird green, my enhanced vision allowed me to see in full color, so in many measures my night vision was invaluable.

We flew in our familiar formation, with Chayl and Cowboy in the lead. I rode in the middle, but I was constantly scanning ahead to give Chayl and Cowboy information. I would have been better able to see ahead if we took the lead, but their team was so advanced with their skills, that it was still better if they were the scouts.

We were also flying with one of the younger dragons who served as a guide. The clans were utilizing his youthful speed as a courier between camps, so he knew the location of the clan camp. His name was Clemente. He was quiet and spoke little, unless one of us spoke to him, and then it was usually a one or two-word answer.

"*Bear east of the mountain range,*" he instructed Chayl. We all had a good idea of the location of group three, but to pinpoint in the dark could be tricky. Clemente's directions made sense. We would be able to keep the mountain range between us and the battle until the last few miles. We didn't want to be spotted, and we hoped that we would be able to implement a surprise counter-attack with our dragon team leading the charge.

Clemente was also flying in the middle of the formation right behind me.

Little by little, he was starting to fall back in our formation, which struck me as odd because he wasn't burdened with a rider or any gear.

"*You need to stay directly behind Paxi, Clemente,*" said Abi who was bringing up the rear.

Without a word, Clemente sped up right behind us, but immediately began to fall back again.

"*Clemente, increase your speed. You need to keep up with the team,*" Abi warned him again.

Again, Clemente sped up, but began to veer right of our formation. Something was up with that dragon. Cotopaxi sensed it too, and he turned his head to look at me. Paxi was worried about something.

Clemente's behavior was odd, and we were all now paying attention to his behavior.

"Marcus, you need to scan the area. I think Clemente is leading us into an ambush," warned Selena.

I pulled my eyes away from Clemente and scanned the area. Sure enough, I spotted movement ahead. and two dragons with riders on their backs appeared in the distance. All the dragons had the horrible harnesses on them.

"Dragons straight ahead, Chayl," I warned. Without further warning, Clemente veered sharply to the right and disappeared through the break in the mountain range. He was indeed leading us into a trap.

The dragons in front of us were closing fast.

"Dragons behind us!" Abi informed us.

"Here it is," said Chayl. *"This is for real. How many are behind us?"* he asked Abi.

"Two dragons with riders," she said.

"We don't want to take on four at a time. Reverse course and attack!" he ordered.

We had practiced reversing direction, and we did so flawlessly and with a speed that surprised the dragons following behind us. Since Abi was bringing up the rear, she actually continued forward until we were back to her before she reversed course, and by then it was too late for the dragons that were following us. They had been so intent on catching up with Abi and Sabryyna, that our maneuver caught them by surprise.

One of Alan's potent fireballs struck one of the riders directly in the chest and we watched as he fell screaming to the ground.

Not to be outdone, Cowboy sent a lightning bolt that struck the other dragon square. It wasn't enough to cause major damage to the dragon, but it had the same effect as Alan's fireball, and the second rider also fell to his death.

The now two rider-less dragons began to flee, but before they could fly very far, the harnesses they were wearing exploded just as before. It was a horrible sight, but we didn't have time to dwell on the thought.

"*Reverse and attack,*" came Chayl's orders.

Again, we reversed course, but the dragons and riders had seen our original maneuver and were ready for us to do just that. With two of their numbers down, we now outnumbered the riders. and they turned and sped away, following the same course in which Clemente had taken.

"*Good job spotting the attack, Marcus,*" said Cowboy.

"*It was Selena who figured out something was hinky with Clemente,*" I said.

"*Still, you did well to locate our attackers,*" he said. It was good to receive a compliment once in a while. I didn't receive many.

CHAPTER TWENTY-NINE

HEROIC ARAYN

Fortunately we were able to find the camp on our own, without Clemente's assistance. We had all been drilled on where the camp was located, but it was difficult finding things at night and in an unfamiliar area.

The camp was very happy to see us. They had been fighting off dragon attacks most of the day. The marathon-like pace that the camp had been keeping had accomplished what it was intended to do. The only fighting units to be able to attack the camp had been from Gonosz dragon riders. The Gonosz soldiers were practically running themselves to death trying to catch us, but it was a numbers game, and they didn't have the time to catch up before we disappeared into the wormhole.

"They will want to do something to stop our progress," said Peggy. It had been a joyful reunion between her and Cowboy.

"Their best chance to stop us will be when we pass through this valley through the mountain range," she said pointing at a spot in the large map.

The valley was the most direct path to the wormhole. Although the Gonosz didn't know for sure where we were heading, it was only a matter of time before they would know an approximate destination. We wanted to keep the wormhole hidden. We would only be buying a short amount of time if they knew the exact location of the wormhole. We would be in the exact trouble as we are now.

The trouble would come from any of their dragon teams.

"Kal has turned into a formidable foe," said Peggy. "He can fly like a veteran rider, and his brother, Kylor, is very skilled at both fireballs and lightning. His accuracy is uncanny. Their team has several of our dragons, both old and young."

They didn't have many dragon-rider teams, but they did have all the newer more physical teams, and we were also outnumbered.

Since we were so far ahead of the main army of the Gonosz, our mission was to move as fast as possible. We would provide scouting for group three, plus any protection from the enemy dragon teams.

For some reason the Gonosz were sending mostly captured wild dragon teams with their horrid harnesses. We knew from experience that those teams weren't very effective against us. Our dragons were free to instinctually fly and fight with us, providing support and eyes. A captured dragon needed to be guided much the same as one would a horse. It just wasn't as effective against a trained dragon rider team.

It was effective against a ground army that didn't have dragon rider support, however. The rider-less dragons were often targeted and double-teamed. They simply couldn't see in every direction, and a good dragon-hunter team could often kill them.

Our army had been taking some real abuse from the captured dragon attacks. They would come in waves and shower down dragon fire.

One of my football coaches had fought in the war in Viet Nam. He told us that the enemy would often set boobie traps that were designed to maim, rather than kill outright. The reasoning was that a wounded soldier needed to be cared for. The more wounded, the better.

"We think that is part of their strategy," said Peggy. "They are trying to wound as many as possible, so that we are slowed down. The dragon riders will help us maintain speed by limiting our injured, and if they can kill a few of those Gonosz dragon teams…"

Peggy didn't complete the sentence, but a look that passed between her and Cowboy was enough for us to infer the meaning. It wouldn't hurt their feelings much.

Before, we had flown in pairs mostly, but now we were flying as a complete team. Some of the other dragons would provide most of the scouting. We needed to be in the air around our army in case they needed to be defended against an attack.

We were tested immediately. Surely Clemente and the other dragon teams had reported that we had arrived at the camp. Rather than let us have time to plan and rest, they decided to attack that day.

We had just eaten and were going to take a few hours of rest, when a flare went up from the south end of our camp.

"To the air, riders! That flare means a dragon attack," said Peggy. It appears that she had earned even more authority because it was her that was giving the orders.

Pandemonium broke out throughout camp. People ran to the meager cover that the terrain offered, while others armed themselves with bow and arrow and other weapons. From what we gathered, they were mostly ineffective against dragon attacks.

Alan ran to Cotopaxi, who had just settled down to rest. He jumped to his feet so that we could strap on the riding harness and gear. We were the only team still using the riding harness, but I just couldn't seem to ride Cotopaxi without it.

In a few moments, we were ready. The rest of the team was already assembled and waiting for us. Cowboy was glaring at us. He wasn't particularly sympathetic that I still needed the riding harness.

I looked at my team. We all still sported the war paint on our faces. Everybody was too tired to have washed it off.

"You know your roles," said Chayl. "Everybody do your

jobs, and we'll be alright."

And with that, we all launched into the air. We had done so much night flying that it was almost strange flying during the day.

We hadn't had time to do our ritual, but Alan and I quickly exchanged the passwords, and Alan connected to the crystals. I accessed the enhanced vision and went to work scanning the skies, but in particular to the south. That is where the flare indicated the attack was coming from.

It wasn't long before we spotted the attack, and they were coming in numbers. I was able to count four dragon rider teams, all captured dragons wearing the harness. Accompanying the teams were three rider-less dragons. I scanned all around us to see if there were any other dragons attacking from another direction. I had learned a valuable lesson with the last attack. Don't get tunnel vision on the obvious danger.

We were outnumbered, but our training had been for this specific scenario because we knew that this is how we would end up fighting.

Our strategy was to engage the rider teams as fast as possible. They were the most dangerous, but we couldn't ignore the rider-less dragons either.

Cowboy was the most equipped to deal with the dragons. They absolutely did not like the lightning that he threw around. It was now strong enough that he could stun them. He was skilled at either pinpointing his lightning, or spreading it out to hit multiple targets. When he spread it out, it was weaker than if he pinpointed a single target, but it still carried a punch. Our fireballs seemed to have little effect as they were wearing the protective gear.

With Cowboy targeting the dragons, it was the rest of our responsibilities to target the riders. Abi had a nasty little trick that she now used. She had discovered that she could control her fireball even after they were shot. She rapidly shot two off, and let them travel slowly towards the riders. They were still several miles off, and closing fast. They easily dodged the fireballs which were burning out because of the distance, but they still carried some kick. As soon as they passed by the fireballs, the riders ignored them. That was a mistake. Abi reversed the direction of the fireballs, and we watched as the two hit one of the riders directly in the back. It wasn't enough to kill, but it did cause the rider to veer off to our right as she slapped at her now flaming clothing.

Abi's trick had the desired effect. The attacking riders and dragons now began dodging and diving, thinking that they were being attacked from the rear. Two of the riderless dragons reversed course and were now flying back from where they had come from.

Instead of a large attacking force, they were now scattering in various directions on the defensive.

Abi came even with us.

"We've got the three rider-teams on the left," she said. Cowboy and Chayl were better at independent fighting. They would act almost like snipers and pick off the individual enemy, while Abi and I would work in tandem targeting the riders.

Abi, Sabryyna, and Alan were all busy firing fireballs at the riders. Sabryyna scored first with an arrow to the neck of one of the riders. The rider clutched his neck, but slumped over and fell without any more movement. I was expecting the dragon to explode like the others, but it remained in formation with the two other dragons.

Abi and Alan were having more trouble hitting their targets. The dragons seemed to be trained to absorb the fireballs with their body. Time and time again, they would fire what should have been kill shots, only for the dragons to shield the rider with their bodies.

"We have to change tactics," said Abi. "Sabryyna and I are going to bows and arrows!"

The speed of the arrows would make it more difficult for the dragons to shield the riders. Abi and Sabryyna were almost wizards with the bow and arrow. The problem with those weapons was that we had to get in very close contact with the enemy. Alan and I would provide support for Abi and Sabryyna in this scenario.

Now rather than maintain our distance, we would get as close as possible. Alan and I would still use fireballs, but mostly to keep the enemy dragon teams distracted. We then would take the lead. Our hope was that we would shoot our fireballs, and when the enemy dragons reacted, it would give Abi and Sabryyna a window of opportunity to shoot one of the riders as they dodged the fireballs.

At least with this strategy, I was somewhat useful. I didn't need to be accurate, I just needed to be able to shoot a fireball that could be seen.

Closing in tight to the enemy riders, Alan and I let loose our fireballs. When Cotopaxi realized what we were doing, he let loose with his own fireball. To our amazement, his fireball directly hit one of the riders. With a scream, he burst into flame and fell off his dragon, cartwheeling to the ground.

"Good boy, Paxi!" I yelled.

He turned his head briefly and looked at me, his dragon eyes wide. He apparently was as surprised as we were.

The commotion was enough to give Abi and Sabryyna clear shots. Both sent their arrows true, one enemy rider falling, the other slumping over without any further movement. It was only after the final rider was incapacitate, that the detonator went off to kill the captured dragons.

"Form up on Chayl," said Selena.

We quickly looked around to find Chayl in a dogfight with two of the independent dragons. Cowboy was having trouble hitting the dragons with the lightning bolts.

"They figured out that I have limited range," he quickly explained. *"They are staying just out of reach."*

Our only hope now was to have our dragons physically attack their dragons, since our fireballs were ineffective. This was extremely dangerous, but our only chance against a dragon with armor.

I could tell that Cotopaxi was nervous about engaging the dragons.

"It's OK, Paxi," I said, trying to reassure my dragon with the tone of my voice.

Both Hera'sha'I and Sjer-berha were skilled flyers. When we changed tactics, they immediately went on the attack against the single dragons. Cotopaxi circled the fight, looking for a way in which to aid the other dragons.

Very quickly, the rider-less dragons realized that they were outnumbered, and it was now pointless to fight. On one of our passes, we closed in tight to one of the dragons. Its eyes were wide with terror. The smart move would be to disengage and escape, yet they both remained to fight.

"They are terrified to stop," said Selena. "I wonder if someone has to trigger the detonator? There may be a spotter some place to make sure the dragons fight."

"Good thinking," responded Chayl. "Break off and search. If we can confirm this, it will be valuable in future fights."

We didn't want to be too obvious about our tactics, so we continued to circle the fight, but now I was using my enhanced vision to scan the area.

"Whoever it is will need to have a clear view of the fighting. Since you're not seeing anyone in the air, my guess is that they are on the ground. They will need to be mobile. It's probably a dragon and rider," said Alan.

We were up against a mountain range, so the peaks and hillsides seemed to be the logical place to view the fighting.

I began to search the areas we thought might be the most likely places for a team to hide.

On the third pass over a particular peak, I spotted them. It was indeed a dragon and rider, but one of the captured dragons. They were neatly hidden in a small alpine valley near the top of the peak, and it offered a good view of the battle.

"Chayl, we have found the spotters. They don't know that we've seen them, I think. Do we attack them?" I asked.

"Let's not give away the fact that we know their tactics, yet.

Disengage and return to us," he said.

As we returned to the battle, Sjer-berha and Hera'sha'i had dispatched the rider-less dragons. It was sad to see.

"Just remember that that is two less dragons that we have to fight in the future," said Cowboy, his face grim.

....

We were only two days travel away from the wormhole, but we had a dilemma. We needed to hide our destination from the Gonosz. If we traveled directly to the wormhole, the enemy would just need to follow us through, and the other side of the wormhole was an Island. We would be trapped and killed.

The wormhole was fairly well disguised. Cotopaxi had been the only dragon to detect it, so we felt fairly confident that if we could get everyone through, it would be very difficult for the enemy to find it. Of course, if there was another dragon with Cotopaxi's skills...

Our initial ruse had worked better than we had hoped. Our spotters had reported that the fake cavern that we had led the Gonosz to, had kept their attention for better than two days before they felt comfortable attacking. They had been very surprised to find an empty cavern, and several of their commanders had been executed on the spot for the blunder.

They were now desperate to find our real hiding spot.

We were now spotting Gonosz patrols several times a day. They were definitely keeping tabs on our location and rate of travel.

"As you all know, the wormhole is located in this valley in this mountain range," said Peggy as she pointed at the location on the large map. This was a meeting for the dragon teams only. The other commanders would be briefed separately.

"As you also know, we need to disguise our destination first and foremost. We've sent out several of our patrols to discover some options, and we think that we've come up with a plan." She looked around at us.

"We have spies within our midst," she said calmly. "We are sure that spies within our camp are communicating with the enemy. We've actually confirmed at least two humans, and one dragon that are smuggling information. At this time, we're keeping their identities secret, because one of them is a double agent for us."

This information was delivered with a wide smile.

"We will be using these agents to our advantage. Very few of our numbers know the exact location of the wormhole, and we've been giving the camp information that the wormhole is actually located in the mountain range beyond the actual location. We're confident that the false information has been delivered to the Gonosz, and they are making preparations based on that information."

The plan was simple. It was all a timing thing. The Gonosz didn't have the resources for multiple battles. They had time to prepare for one battle. The same agent that was giving the enemy false information was also getting information for us. We learned that the Gonosz would use the captured dragons to haul groups of soldiers to a place in which they intended to ambush us.

The valley in which Cotopaxi had discovered the wormhole bisected the mountain range. We had entered the valley from the east side of the range. The fastest route was to keep to the right side of the range, then enter the valley. We were giving the enemy information that the mountain range to the northwest was our destination. In a few miles, if we took the east route, we would have a direct shot at the wormhole. If we took the west route, we would be traveling on the other side of the mountain range. Eventually we would come to the same valley that contained the wormhole, but from the other side of the mountain range.

It was much farther than the east route, but it would give the enemy the impression that we were indeed heading for the mountain range beyond. Once we got to the valley, a large part of our army would break off and enter. The rest would defend the mouth of the canyon, should we be discovered.

"We're counting on the Gonosz to set up an ambush here," Peggy said, pointing at the one water source found on the other side of the mountain range. It was an obvious destination for a thirsty army, and it was twenty miles past where our wormhole was. If we pulled this off, we could disappear without a fight in which we would lose.

"I'm going to have you meet our double agent so that you can all be on the same page," said Peggy.

She disappeared for a moment and reappeared with a young dragon that I had seen and recognized. Her name was Arayn.

"I have been informed of the plans. Tonight, I will meet with Kal, who is my commander on the Gonosz side. He will be given this false information. I will probably be told to return to the clans, but there is also a good chance that I will be ordered to go to the Gonosz camp and set up for the ambush. There is no way of determining what will happen for sure," she said.

"But if you go to the Gonosz camp, won't that mean that you can't join the clans through the wormhole?" asked Alan.

"There are sacrifices that need to be made," Arayn said coolly. *"If this can help the clans escape, then it is a small sacrifice. I'm sure you would all do the same."*

In order for the plan to work, we needed to physically move our camp as fast as we could. It would be another move that would take the Gonosz by surprise, and cause them to commit to a plan. Hopefully the wrong plan.

We would not be stopping for rest from here on out. We would be on a forced march the entire time. The dragon teams would be taxed to the extreme, flying scouting mission's day and night, only an hour or two break each day to eat and get additional orders. It was going to be brutal.

We waited until it got dark and quickly packed up the camp. Group three was mostly soldiers and the remaining dragons. In order to move faster than was anticipated by the

Gonosz, we would walk for fifteen minutes and trot for fifteen minutes. Each soldier wore armor and carried a weapon of some type. I figured that we would all be dropping like flies in no time.

We would be leaving behind all unnecessary equipment to speed up our journey. I learned that the food wagons and tents were some of the things deemed unnecessary.

I was on patrol when I spotted Arayn leave camp under the cover of darkness. What she was doing seemed incredibly brave. I hoped that she was, indeed, on our side. We had been burned a few times, and I was not becoming a trusting soul. I watched as she flew back towards the Gonosz camp. Soon she disappeared behind a mountain range. Our fate was now in her hands.

The dragon riders would remain in the air for most of the march. We would only land sparingly. When we did land, it was to eat, drink, report our findings, and receive additional orders. There was no time to rest.

We made very good time. Everyone knew that our march was a matter of life and death. We actually did better than we figured for the first day. Each step brought us closer and closer to safety. Our speed had the effect that we had hoped for. When the Gonosz scouts appeared in the sky, they were frantically searching for us. We weren't in the place that they expected. Once we were spotted, the Gonosz scouts quickly reversed course to report on their findings.

"*That will cause some mistakes, hopefully,*" said Chayl.

With my enhanced vision, I was very useful as a scout. It was my job to make sure that we didn't get attacked by surprise. I would circle wide of the traveling camp. Cotopaxi was getting bigger and stronger, but he was being used so often for the most tiring missions, that we were granted three hours of rest later that afternoon. Our current speed would put us at the canyon the following day. As we neared our destination, it would become more and more dangerous, and I would be needed at the danger. We were granted some rest in preparation for tomorrow's final push.

Alan and I ate an MRE, while Cotopaxi just dropped and slept. One of us would need to keep watch while the other two slept. Alan volunteered to take the first watch. I would sleep for an hour and a half, then Alan would sleep for an hour and a half. We determined that Cotopaxi could sleep the entire three hours.

It seemed like I had just laid down, when I felt Alan shaking me awake.

"All quiet," he reported. With that, he dropped to the ground and was instantly asleep.

In order to stay awake, I knew that I couldn't just sit and watch. I needed to be up and walking around, or I would fall back asleep. We were several miles in front of our army. Before we could sleep, we were ordered to scout the way ahead to make sure that there were no surprises.

The day had heated up, which was tiring in its own way. I was really struggling to keep awake. I would only sit down for a moment or two…

....

"Wake up, Marcus. It's about time for us to head back," said Selena.

"I'm so sorry! I am just so tired," I said.

"I know. That's why I didn't wake you. I was watching," she said.

How long had I been out? Checking the sky, I could tell that it had been over an hour. Even though I hadn't overslept, I was still embarrassed that I had fallen asleep at all. I jumped up and started jogging back to where Alan and Cotopaxi were.

A crashing noise stopped me in my tracks. We had landed in a small wooded area at the base of the mountain range. The trees were small and had thorns. They were more like the size of large bushes, but well-suited for the dry climate. The crashing had stopped, but I knew the direction it had come. I slowed my pace and crept back to investigate.

I could now hear ragged breathing. Afraid of being spotted, I knew I had to find out if this was a danger to us or not. Slipping slowly through the trees, I used all of my skills to move stealthily. I knew I was close. Slowly peeking around a tree, I was able to see a large form on the ground in front of me.

It was Arayn. She had been horribly mangled. Both wings shorn off completely, she was covered with deep claw and teeth marks. Her breathing was labored, and I doubted that she would last long.

Not knowing what to do, I slowly slipped backwards until I was out of sight. When I felt it was safe, I ran as fast as I could back to where Alan and Cotopaxi were sleeping.

"Paxi, Alan! We've got company!" I said, shaking both of them.

Alan was instantly awake. It took a shake or two more to wake the exhausted dragon.

Quickly, I explained the situation to Alan.

"What do we do? We don't want to expose our position," I said.

"I think the fact that she has been attacked is something that we need to investigate. We need to find out what the Gonosz now know," said Alan.

Alan and I returned to where Arayn was lying. We left Cotopaxi with the promise that we would be in range to call him if we needed him.

Her eyes were open, and she was staring right at us when we found her.

"Run!" she said. *"It was Kal and 'Elu'ali'aq'. They tortured me. They are close! Run!"*

We could now hear the unmistakable sound of dragon's wings.

"It's too late to run. Hide, and don't expose yourselves no matter what!" called Arayn.

We quickly ducked behind some of the trees. We could see Arayn's fallen body, but little else. We didn't need to see. We could hear it all.

"Well, you had more courage than I figured," came Kal's voice, somewhere beyond our vision. *"I underestimated you, but no matter. I will rectify that oversight now."*

"Don't you mean you will command 'Elu'ali'aq' to rectify your oversight?" asked Arayn. *"You personally couldn't do anything to hurt me, even in my current condition."*

We could hear footsteps as Kal climbed off of 'Elu'ali'aq'. Arayn's insult was exactly something that would enrage Kal to foolish action.

"Stop and think, brother," came Kylor's voice. "She is indeed dangerous to you right now. Control your impulses."

The footsteps stopped, but from the length of silence, Kal was having a deep internal struggle.

"I have to compliment you on your bravery, Arayn. Fighting to the very end. You almost goaded me into making a mistake," Kal said.

"Kill her!" he commanded 'Elu'ali'aq'.

Before she could fight back, 'Elu'ali'aq' had attacked and snapped her neck. That was one scary dragon. He was immense now, but he was also strong and surprisingly both quick and fast. I worried about Cotopaxi's fate, should he be forced to fight a dragon such as 'Elu'ali'aq'.

"You need to control your anger, brother," came Kylor's voice again. "It will get us in trouble sometime."

"When I want your opinion Kylor, I will beat it out of you," said Kal. He was trying to make a joke after almost making a serious mistake, but it fell flat. Kylor wasn't amused.

"A level head is needed in battle," said Kylor.

"Everything worked out," Kal said with a shrug of the shoulders.

"This time. We won't get many more chances," said Kylor. "We need to get back to camp and prepare for the ambush."

I felt movement behind me. Cotopaxi must have searched for us. Fortunately, he had the good sense to be stealthy and not give away our position.

We all listened silently as Kal mounted up and took to the sky.

After fifteen minutes, we crept out to see the carnage. Arayn's neck hung at an unnatural angle, her eyes now glassy and lifeless.

Cotopaxi let out a low howl of sorrow.

"They're preparing an ambush," Selena said. *"We need to let the camp know."*

Our flight back to the camp was silent, except for the unmistakable sound of the rhythmic beat of dragon wings. We were all on edge and watching for the enemy, knowing that they were close and ready to attack.

Landing, there was a briefing in progress.

"Welcome back," Peggy said from the front of the room as Alan and I slipped in. "Have you anything to report before we move on?"

"We just witnessed the killing of the dragon, Arayn," reported Selena. There was an audible murmur from those in the briefing. We had all desperately hoped that she would be safe, but somehow she had been betrayed.

"Kal and his unit had tortured her horribly. She managed to escape briefly. It was fortunate that we stumbled upon her and she warned us to hide. We were listening when Kal had 'Elu'ali'aq' kill her. They are planning an ambush. They are closer than we had supposed. We need to move quickly," said Selena.

One of the things that we had learned was that when we had information, we needed to act on it immediately. We knew that an ambush was in the making.

"Pack up," said Lowry, *"we will make a run for the wormhole within the hour."*

It was a testament to the readiness of the camp, that we were underway in about twenty minutes. As tired as we all were, a successful ambush might result in the defeat of group three. We suspected that our location was known.

CHAPTER THIRTY

SELENA'S LAST STAND

We took to the air with two objectives. First, to protect the camp from a surprise attack, and second, to locate the position of the enemy. This is where I was again useful. We would need to range far and wide, so that I could use my ability to find the enemy. Abi and Chayl would accompany me. The rider-less dragons would pick up the slack in patrolling around the immediate area of the traveling camp.

There were still several hours of daylight left. My greatest advantage was in the dark. We would patrol until night, and we would actively seek the Gonosz camp to determine their strength and readiness. My enhanced vision proved invaluable in situations like these.

We flew for several hours without any sighting of the enemy. We had remained fairly close to camp. Now it was time to expand our range. I was nervous. We were close to the wormhole, and it was going to get dangerous.

Our thought was to return to where Arayn was killed. She had been running away from what I thought was a south easterly direction. If that was true, that would be good news for us, because it placed the enemy on the south side of the mountain range. Our plan was to take the clans on the north side of the mountain range and access the wormhole from there.

The first thing was to confirm that the Gonosz were indeed camped to the south of the mountain range.

As soon as it was dark enough to give us a vision advantage, we began to make our way east, toward the mountain range that held the wormhole.

It was fairly slow-going. We had to be both meticulous and stealthy. I had a greater advantage over the dragons with my enhanced vision, but they could see fairly well in the dark. If we weren't careful, we could easily be seen. We would be flying closer to the ground in order to remain hidden.

For several hours, we zig-zagged back and forth, until we started to see signs of the enemy. Our first sighting of a Gonosz patrol indicated that we were getting close.

"We'll stay back, but try to follow them as best as possible," Chayl ordered me. *"We'll try to follow them back to their camp."*

I tracked the patrol for several hours before they suddenly changed direction. At first, I thought that we had been detected, but quickly it became apparent that it was a changing of the guard. Off in the distance, I could see another dragon team coming toward us. The two enemy teams appeared to greet each other, the new guard took up a patrol pattern, while the team we had been following headed further east in a beeline. It was in the same direction as the cave that we had fortified to mislead the enemy. The Gonosz must have assumed that our destination was somewhere around that area. That particular ruse was paying dividends.

In order to find the exact location of the camp, we would have to break off our visual contact with the patrol heading home. If we had tried to follow the patrol, the new patrol would have easily spotted us. We would have to circle wide of the patrol, and hopefully find the camp off of the direction that we had seen the returning patrol fly.

It took a good two hours to fly wide enough to avoid detection of the patrols. When we felt that we were beyond their detection, we started to slowly close in to where we thought the camp was.

It wasn't long before we found signs of a camp.

"Sjer-berha is smelling campfires and cooking," reported Chayl. *"Marcus, you will have to close in by yourself. Be careful, but proceed."*

We slowed our approach, but I very rapidly started to see the signs of a camp. I saw the glow of the cooking fires first. Urging Cotopaxi to climb a little, I was able to see over the tree line. The camp was huge. Larger than we expected by two times. Our little group three was grossly out-numbered. If caught in an open fight, we would easily be slaughtered.

I took a mental photo and sent it to my team members. Cowboy swore.

"How did they move such a large army in such a short amount of time?" he asked.

"Let's get out of here," said Chayl. *"Lowry will want this information."*

It took several hours to get back to our camp. We had to avoid several patrols along the way. The enemy would surely act soon.

Our report was received with more gravity than usual. We had supposed that the army that the Gonosz would send would be smaller in scale, but somehow they had transported hundreds of warriors to intercept us.

"We'll need to march without rest," said Lowry upon hearing our report. His demeanor more grave than I had ever experienced.

We were just a few miles from the point of the mountain range. We hoped that the enemy was planning on us taking the southern route. If they set up an ambush on that side of the mountain range, we stood a chance. We would be taking the northern route, but it was still dicey whether or not we would be detected in time for the Gonosz to set up another plan to destroy us.

Peggy was silent as she stared at the map. She turned to us, her face unable to hide the concern.

"Even if we move as fast as possible, the Gonosz have the ability to wipe us out. All they have to do is to send enough warriors to attack us and force us to fight. If we have to defend ourselves, that will give the remainder of their army a chance to catch up and finish us all off. If we have ever needed a diversion, we need

one now. *Any options?"* she asked, looking around the room.

"We attack," said Chayl quietly, but all eyes turned to him.

"Right now. We'll be wiped out if we make a run for it, and you just said that if they attack us and we have to defend ourselves, it will force us to fight. Why can't that work both ways?" he asked. Most looked at him in disbelief.

"What do you propose?" asked Lowry, his head cocked inquisitively as he looked at Chayl.

"The dragon rider team will need to launch a night attack. That's where we have the only advantage, because of Marcus. We will need some of the younger dragons to accompany us. We will fly strafing runs on the camp. If we attack at dusk and keep up an attack all night, that will give the clans the needed time to make it to the northern end of the valley and then to the wormhole," he said.

"That's a suicide mission," said one of the elder dragons.

"It's our only option," said Chayl cooley. *"If someone has a better plan..."*

The silence told that story.

"Tonight is the night, then," said Peggy. *"Chayl, if you will stay with our strategy planning team, your squad can go rest."*

So, this was it. No more running. We were taking the fight to the enemy.

I had no doubt that I was going to die.

The team was silent as we prepared for war. Cowboy had his war paint on again. Without asking, he went from person to person to reapply war paint of our own. Peggy entered the room, she too sporting the terrifying war paint.

In beautiful synchronicity, they performed a haka to prepare us for battle. After their dance, they touched foreheads, looking deeply into each other's eyes. There seemed to be no need for words, and Peggy turned and left the tent in silence.

We had our briefing, and there was nothing left for us to do than take to the air.

When you believe that you only have several hours left

before you die, you start to list all the things that you will miss. I felt the wind in my face as we flew towards the enemy camp. I smelled the desert below, I heard the steady flap from the wings of the dragons.

Abi was flying in her normal rearguard position. Chayl, our natural-born leader, was in front. I was in the middle of the pack with several of the younger, more fit dragons. In all, there were eight dragons and six humans on our way to attack a camp of hundreds. Right.

"Yesterday, all my troubles seemed so far away..." Abi sang.

The Beatles song seemed appropriate for the occasion.

Sabryyna chimed in with some beautiful harmony. Music might be the thing that I would miss most, so I added my voice to the cool night. Selena was never as musical as I was, but she hummed the melody along with Abi.

I hadn't known Alan to be musical, but he showed to have a hauntingly beautiful tenor voice as he joined us.

In what seemed an impossibly short amount of time, our song came to an end.

"Oh, I believe in yesterday."

Nobody felt like talking after that. It was the one last beautiful thing before we were sure to experience the horrors of war.

The sun dipped behind the horizon, and it was time for me to do my thing.

"Take the point," commanded Chayl.

I urged Cotopaxi forward, and I began to scan around us in earnest.

I was the eyes of our "army" of eight. They would have to trust me to direct our strafing runs and warn everyone of danger. My fear was that I would fall off the back of my dragon during one of the runs, and leave the team without any eyes. That wasn't out of the realm of possibility. Not by a long sight.

Part of our hope was that their dragons and dragon teams would be patrolling to find our group there, then we would be able to be somewhat effective in attacking their camp. They knew how many dragons and dragon teams we had, so an attack by us should come as a surprise. Mostly because what kind of idiots would attack an army with eight dragons and six kid humans?

We didn't have to kill to actually be effective. A wounded soldier was just as good as a dead soldier, in this case. I still didn't hold any hope that we would be effective, but we had to at least try.

Cotopaxi was just as nervous as I was. We had some familiar signals that we used to have rudimentary communication, but nothing like the other dragon teams. I knew that he was more nervous about screwing up than getting hurt himself. He wanted so badly to help our team. He kept turning his head to catch my eye. He needed reassurance.

"It's going to be fine, Paxi. You are doing so good. We'll be fine," I said.

My dragon turned to me with a snort.

When we found the camp, my job was to lead the strafing runs. The dragons would follow me, and we would make our pass. I would then find a safe route to retreat and re-form for another attack.

Our hope was that we could keep up an attack for several hours at least. Longer would obviously be better, but two hours would give our camp a real chance.

Several miles before the known location of the camp, we landed for one last briefing and a small meal.

"*You need to eat something,*" Selena chastised me. "*You will need the strength.*"

"My stomach has too many butterflies. I would rather not die as 'Captain Puke Shirt' if I can help it," I said.

"*At least drink some water. You will be surprised how dehydrated you're going to be,*" she said.

I complied.

"What are our chances?" I asked.

"*Well, not great, but if we can cause some real damage, that will save hundreds of our clans. Worth the sacrifice, I'm thinking,*" she said.

Alan and I made one last check to make sure that we were both accessing the crystals. Both having one last laugh at our absurd password exchange.

"Blue, no yellow..."

Then it was time.

We launched into the air and began to close in on the camp. We seemed to be fortunate, as there didn't seem to be any dragon rider teams about. I did spot one lone dragon circling the camp. At the moment, it was on the far side of the camp, so we could approach without being seen. Our first pass had to be the one that caused the most damage. After that, the camp would be alerted. We would be hard-pressed to have effective attacks.

I had Cotopaxi climb so that I could get a good view of where to attack. As was the tradition of our clan, the Gonosz camped in their distinctive clan units. Each area was marked with banners with that clan's colors. I was able to recognize most of the clan banners.

"Chayl, I'm seeing an area central to the camp that doesn't contain any of the banners but has the single banner of the Gonosz. Not sure what clan that is," I said.

"Describe the tent arrangement," he ordered.

"Tents are arranged in two circles, one outer circle with a smaller circle of tents in the interior," I reported.

Chayl actually laughed out loud at my report.

"They are overconfident," he said. *"Favor smiles on us. The Gonosz have arranged their tents after the manner of a clan gathering, rather than a warrior camp. Those central tents will be those of the clan leaders and their captains. They have foolishly placed their leaders in one convenient location! That's our target, Marcus. Does everyone understand our mission?"* asked Chayl.

Everyone responded back to Chayl, including the riderless dragons.

"Lead us in, Marcus," he said.

Pointing Cotopaxi in the direction of the camp, I guided

us. Cotopaxi took direction cues mostly from my knees. I would apply more pressure with the knee in which direction we needed to fly. Through trial and error, we had figured out what worked for us, but it wasn't nearly as effective as the other teams. They were well-oiled machines in the way they communicated and flew.

The first thing that we did was climb to a higher altitude. In that way, we could go into a shallow dive, and glide into the camp without giving away our location until the last second.

Our attack formation was with me in the lead, Chayl behind me, but offset twenty feet to my right, and Abi offset twenty feet to Chayl's right. That way we could strafe a wide swathe. The riderless dragons would follow behind, and also strafe the area as best as they could.

We had practiced this kind of approach many times before, but this was the first time that we had done it for real.

"You will probably have two, maybe three passes in formation, then all hell will break loose," Lloyd had said over and over. *"Make your first passes count, then you will need to adjust your attacks as needed. Most likely you will need to fight as individuals. That's where the dragon teams have the advantage over riderless dragons. Riders can offer great protection to their dragons by being additional eyes and ears, and of course, by using the gifts from their crystals to both fight and defend."*

I took a mental photo of what I saw and sent it to my team. They now knew what to look for, the two rings in the middle of the camp. Many of the campfires were still burning from the meal preparation, another bonus because it was a beacon of sorts for my squad.

Cotopaxi might have been nervous, but he hid it well. Alan was practical as usual.

"Big fire, Paxi. We want a big fire!" he said. I'm not sure if Cotopaxi understood, but this attack was familiar to him and he knew his role.

Closer and closer we glided. The camp was situated on the far side of a small hill, so I decided to use the hill as a shield until the very last second. I had Cotopaxi drop lower and the rest of the team followed. Minutes later, the hill and camp were right before us.

We coasted to the hill, and just before we crashed headlong into its side, I pulled Cotopaxi up so that we barely crested the top. The camp appeared directly below us with our targets directly in front of us.

Quiet time was now behind us. I let out a shout that Cotopaxi recognized as his signal to let out his own bloodcurdling scream. Heads popped out of tents as we swooped down. Alan started shooting fireballs at the tents that were arranged in circles in the center of camp. Cotopaxi joined in with a large fireball, the largest I had ever seen him form before. Tents burst into flames as his large swath of fire spewed from his lips. I, too, fired off fireballs as best as I could, but none hit their intended targets. I did hit one of their large water skins, which was great and all, but I had been aiming for a particularly large tent fifty yards to the right of the skins.

Looking back, I watched the attack from the rest of the team. Abi and Sabryyna had opted to use both their bow and arrows, and shoot fireballs at the same time. It was a new attack technique, and it was amazing how accurate they were. Chayl and Cowboy were effectively shooting fireballs at selected tents. I don't believe either one of them missed their targets. Each dragon was leaving huge patches of scorched ground and burning tents.

After we had made our first pass, I quickly led us up and away from the camp to come in from another direction. We wanted it to appear that there were more of us than there really were.

I guided Cotopaxi into the camp again. This time there were more warriors out of their tents, armed with bow and arrows. They were mostly staring in the direction that we had attacked from, fearful of more dragons. Our cross attack took them by surprise. Again, we effectively strafed the camp. I was just winging fireballs with abandon, no real hope of hitting my target, but hoping the fireballs caused confusion.

Our attack was going better than could be expected. By targeting their leadership, we had obviously caused massive confusion. They had been very unwise to congregate their leaders into one small area.

Pass after pass was made, arrows bouncing harmlessly off the underside of our dragons. We were able to come into the camp from unexpected angles, because I was able to see where they were concentrating their forces. I would easily avoid the areas of camp that seemed to be fortified. and enter into a weaker section. When forces were expended to reinforce that area, I would choose another weak point. I was finding that I had a knack for finding weak spots.

One of our riderless dragons, Gorban, had been assigned to patrol the perimeter of the camp, to warn us if reinforcements were coming.

We were making another pass when we were contacted by Gorban.

"Dragons from the east!" he warned.

Dragons were the real danger to us. I pulled up immediately, rather than to complete the run. The others followed. I wanted to climb up and away so that I could get a good look at the dragons.

My heart sank. There were at least ten dragon rider teams. Kal was leading the way, but I was sorry to see that Marrle, astride Loem'na, was also in their group. Jazmyne was also riding behind Marrle, in her customary place as attendant. We hadn't seen Marrle since the clans split, and I had genuinely liked her and Jazmyne. and now they were our enemies.

I took a mental photo and sent it to the rest of the team. We were silent for a moment while we took it all in. Chayl broke the silence.

"We still need to delay an attack on group three. It is too soon for us to break off now," he said.

"We can't take on ten dragon teams, even if most are captured dragons," Alan said. *"We wouldn't last a couple of minutes if*

we tried to take them all on."

"That's why we're going to do what we are never supposed to do. We're going to split up and force them to chase us. We will try to lead them away from the clans and their destination," said Chayl.

"I don't like that one bit," said Sabryyna. *"There is strength in numbers."*

"Yes," said Chayl *"but we need to cause as much confusion as possible. If we force them to chase after us, we stall them longer, and we are all going to meet and reform. We need to buy time without getting ourselves wiped out."*

We quickly formed a plan to split and hopefully take a portion of the oncoming dragons with each one of us. We agreed that if we were able, we would meet back at an old campsite that group two had stopped at.

To cause them to make a split-second decision, we waited to fly off until they were fully upon us. In unison, we turned and sped into the night together. Once we cleared the small mountain range, we split, each taking his or her own direction. Hopefully the chaos caused from such a drastic move would cause confusion with them.

And it worked...sort of. We did indeed confuse them, but in the course of making them make a split decision, I picked up five of the ten dragon teams following me. Kal and Kylor now followed our every move. Chayl and Cowboy got two of the captured dragon teams to follow them, and Abi and Sabryyna got the remaining three teams, one team being Marrle, Loem'na, and Jazmyne.

Cotopaxi, Alan, and I were now in trouble. I had no doubt that Chayl, Sjer-berha and Cowboy would make it out fine. Two captured dragon teams were no match for that team. Sjer-berha could often outfly any dragon, even carrying a burden of two humans and their gear. And Chayl and Cowboy must have used super glue on their rear-ends, because they could remain seated while Sjer-berha performed impossible acrobats in the air.

I was concerned with Abi's team, but Sabryyna immediately cut the odds down by shooting an arrow through the neck of one of the riders who slumped over his dragon's neck, then slid off into the darkness. They now had two very cautious dragon teams following them.

Cotopaxi had decent speed, but Kal's dragon, 'Elu'ali'aq', was much faster.

It came as no surprise to hear Kal's voice. He loved to taunt his prey.

"Do you smell that, Marcus?" he asked. *"That is the smell of your last minutes of being alive. What does it feel like to know you are going to die soon? Have you vomited on yourself yet?"*

In response, Alan fired a well-placed fireball that took Kal right in the chest. What should have been a deadly shot, ricocheted harmlessly away.

Kal chuckled.

"It's going to take more than that to save you. Fireballs hold no fear fo..." an arrow from Alan cut off the rest of Kal's sentence. Kal was forced to deflect the well-placed arrow with his shield. There was some good information, at least. Kal still feared arrows.

We were slowly being overtaken by the five dragon riders. Cotopaxi would need to take evasive action to save us. He looked back at me apprehensively. He was well-aware that I couldn't remain seated when he took any kind of evasive action.

"Alan, if I fall off, save yourself and Paxi. Don't do something stupid and try to come back for me. We'll all die if you come back for me," I said.

"Just don't fall off, moron. Then I won't have to come back for you," he replied.

Just then, a fireball sizzled through the air above us. They were now close enough to attack.

"Evade Paxi, evade!" I yelled.

Cotopaxi made a half-hearted dodge, but looked back to make sure I was still seated. He was worried that his evasive flying would cause me to fall. He was right, of course. I was still using the riding harness, and I desperately hung on to the straps.

"Paxi, you have to evade! Don't worry about me," I yelled.

A fireball sped towards us. Rather than dodge, Cotopaxi spun to take the full brunt of the fireball to his own chest, protecting me and Alan. We could feel his shudder at the impact. He then turned and continued to flee.

Time and time again, rather than risk knocking me off, he would absorb either an arrow or fireball. His speed began to lag. He was hurt. My dragon was going to kill himself for my sake.

"Paxi, you have to evade. Please Paxi, save yourself and Alan. Don't worry about me!" I yelled. My command was ignored.

"Selena, I'm going to bail. When Cotopaxi dives, I need to jump. I have to save my dragon and Alan. I'm just going to get them killed if I remain. I hope you understand," I said, making sure that I was speaking only to her without Cotopaxi or Alan hearing me.

Selena was quiet.

"Selena?" I asked. *"I have to save Paxi and Alan. Do you hear me?"*

I was now desperate. My dragon was taking too many hits and I could hear his labored breathing.

"Please Paxi, evade!" I begged again as another fireball sizzled past my ear.

"Marcus, I don't have time to explain, but Selena has a plan," Alan said as he sunk a needle into my shoulder. I felt a burning, then I went totally limp. I was still conscious, but without control of my body.

"Sorry Marcus," said Selena. *"We're desperate, and this is all I can come up with."*

My mind was going a thousand miles an hour. Why would they paralyze me? To make it easier to push me over? I would have gladly jumped.

Gradually, my limbs started to twitch. My left hand

grasped the flying harness without my guidance. I could also feel my legs clench Cotopaxi, again without my guidance.

"Give me entrance to Larzi. I need access to our crystal," commanded Selena.

I could feel her presence trying to gain entrance to the crystal. I let her in. I was instantly shut out of the crystal.

Selena's control over my body was getting stronger and stronger. She was now actively guiding Cotopaxi using the same knee signals, but her commands felt more natural. Cotopaxi easily interpreted her intention.

Feeling more secure, Cotopaxi tentatively started to evade. Selena remained solidly square on his back. He tried other things, Selena and Alan mirroring Cotopaxi's every move. Confident that he could fly unhindered, Cotopaxi began to evade shot after shot. He easily dodged both fireballs and arrows.

All this time, it was me that had been holding Cotopaxi back from flying well. He had been protecting Captain Puke Shirt this entire time. My dragon was actually born to dogfight. He belly-rolled, twisted and turned, dived and dodged.

Alan whooped with glee as one of the dragon's following us overshot us because of one of Cotopaxi's aerobatics. Now positioned behind the dragon, Cotopaxi let loose a tremendous fireball that enveloped both the rider, and the entire dragon. This time, the fireball overpowered whatever armor the rider was wearing. His screams announced that fact. An arrow from Alan put the rider out of his misery.

The change in Cotopaxi confused the chasing riders.

Cotopaxi had a plan. Rather than target Kal and 'Elu'ali'aq', he evaded them to single out one of the less dangerous captured dragon teams.

As good as Cotopaxi proved at evading, he was even better at mirroring the movements of the escaping dragon. No matter what the dragon did to lose Cotopaxi, it was unable to shake my dragon.

I was now getting a master class from my sister. She sat

effortlessly on the back of Cotopaxi. Each of her moves with my body was made to enhance Cotopaxi's movements. There was never a point where their movements fought against each other, the total opposite of how it felt when Cotopaxi and I flew.

I could feel her mastery over the crystal. I was shut out, but I could feel her working with the crystal. It was amazing!

"There you are, old friend," she said.

She then shot a fireball. It was the blue fireball that I had unwittingly managed at the cabin. The fireball went straight, and when the dragon dodged, rather than continue on a straight course, it followed the dragon. Our regular fireballs did some damage to the dragons, but they were rarely kill-shots. It was often the accumulation of shots that killed dragons.

A flash of light indicated that the dragon had been hit by the blue fireball, but the *crack* sounded louder than any of our regular fireballs. Instantly the dragon folded upon itself and fell to the ground.

The other dragons following us pulled up sharply, including Kal and 'Elu'ali'aq'. Selena's shot had come as a total surprise.

CHAPTER THIRTY-ONE

ESCAPE

We still were not out of the woods. Kal and 'Elu'ali'aq' were still very, very dangerous, and we remained outnumbered. There were still three dragons on our tail. They had been surprised, but were now using their heads. It had to be Kylor's doing. He was the only voice of reason. They started to hunt us systematically.

"Alan, we need to reduce their numbers. If we are to survive an attack by 'Elu'ali'aq', we will need to take out those other two dragons. Focus on them...but if you have a chance to get Kal..." Selena said.

The Gonosz were now wary of us. Cotopaxi was proving to be a worthy opponent. His natural flying instincts kept us out of trouble as he dodged both arrows and fireballs. They also had to be careful to stay out of range of Selena's blue fireball. They had figured out that it had a limited distance before it burned out.

"That's what I hope they think at least," said Selena. *"I can also control when it burns out. I'm luring them in for a cleaner shot."*

I was realizing just what a liability I was, while watching my sister fight. She was a natural. I had never felt as useless to my team as I did then. I saw the potential of what a great dragon rider was, and I wasn't even close. No wonder everyone was disappointed in me. Even if I was half as talented as Selena, that would have been quite a lot.

She had set the trap, and the Gonosz fell for it. Kal had fallen back behind the two captive dragon rider teams. They had been steadily pulling forward, as Selena allowed her blue fireball to burn out closer and closer to us. Soon all three were in range.

All of a sudden, she guided Cotopaxi to spin around on a dime, and charge the on-coming riders. It was such a surprise that none of them reacted in time. Selena had been firing single fireballs up to that point. Now she fired three, all tracking into the on-coming dragons. All three hit their targets. Both captured dragons crumpled and were dead before they hit the ground. 'Elu'ali'aq', although stunned, still managed to turn and flee.

Cotopaxi turned on the speed, and we tried to catch the massive dragon to finish him off, but Elu'ali'aq's larger wing span and some well-placed fireballs from Kylor, kept us from gaining on him.

Selena's movements were beginning to be sluggish, her movements not as sure. Soon, 'Elu'ali'aq' began to distance himself from us.

Cotopaxi looked back at us. It was weird that I could see everything, but had no control of my body what-so-ever.

"Alan, I think it's time to give Marcus the antidote. I..I'm exhausted," Selena said. I could hear the weariness in her voice.

I felt the same needle prick in my shoulder. My body began to tingle as I gained control, little by little over my body.

"Selena, that was amaz..." I began.

"Marcus, be quiet and listen," she said, cutting me off. *"I have little time, Marcus. I've used the energy reserves in the crystal. There's not enough to keep me around for long,"* she said.

Panic shot through me.

"We'll land. Paxi will recharge the crystal," I said. I wasn't ready to lose Selena.

"There's no time, Marcus. You need to get back to the clans. They will need you to hold back the Gonosz to safely enter the

wormhole."

"But…"

"*Shut up and listen, Marcus. Are you seriously going to let my last moments with you be an argument?*" she asked. "*It's time for me to go. I fought one last fight riding a magnificent dragon. Paxi really is a great dragon, Marcus. You will do great things, riding this dragon. You and Alan will be a force to be reckoned with, riding Paxi,*" Selena said, her voice getting weaker and weaker.

"I can't even properly stay on Paxi's back. I can't even speak with him. I hate to disappoint you, but I will never be a fraction of the rider you are," I replied.

"*About that,*" said Selena quietly. "*I have been speaking to Paxi throughout this fight. That is why we were so effective. I was able to easily communicate with him when I took over your body. His speech is less developed than other dragons his age, but that is because… the crystal still recognized me as the rightful owner. This entire time, the crystal wasn't allowing you full access, because I was still here. I didn't figure that out until I was able to access my blue fireball, but when I did, I came to a full realization as to why you couldn't do the same things I used to be able to do. I'm blocking you, Marcus. I've got a feeling that when I'm gone, you will be able to access the crystal and speak with Paxi.*"

I could feel her getting weaker and weaker.

"We could just have Alan give me the drug. I don't mind if you take over my body…"

"*That's not the way it works, Marcus. It takes too much energy to do that constantly. Besides, it's time. It's time Marcus, please understand that,*" she pleaded.

"I love you Selena," I said with a sob. I heard the pain in her voice. I was being selfish by wanting her to stay, but I was terrified to let her go.

"*Love you, too, Captain Puke Shirt,*" she said with a soft laugh.

I laughed, too, but it came out more as a sob.

"*So…weak. Say goodbye to Grandma Torrey for me,*" Selena asked.

"Do you have energy to appear to me again?" I asked.

"*One last time,*" and she appeared before me, a smile on her face.

I took a mental photo of her as she quickly faded away.

"*Goodbye, Marcus. And you Alan, take care of him, will you?*" she asked.

"*Always,*" was his reply.

And then she was gone.

....

Alan was kind enough to ride back to the rendezvous site in silence. I unashamedly shed tears over my sister as we rode back.

"*Selena gone?*" asked Cotopaxi.

"*Yes, Selena is gone, Paxi,*" I said, patting his neck, not even being surprised by being able to talk with my dragon finally.

"*Marcus loved Selena?*" he asked.

"*Very much, Paxi.*"

"*Paxi, too,*" he responded.

"*I know you did, Paxi. And Selena loved Paxi,*" I said.

The other two teams were already on the ground when we landed. One look at me, and Abi knew something was wrong.

Alan quickly and concisely explained what had happened. Tears ran down Abi's cheeks as she heard the news that Selena was indeed gone.

"I'm so sorry, Marcus," she said, laying her hand softly on my shoulder.

"She said that it was time," I said, "but I wish she could have stayed longer."

"Even before I met you, I knew all about you. She talked about you all the time, Marcus. She loved you more than anything," Abi said.

"Thank you. I know," I said. "And I loved her more than anything, too."

We didn't have time to sit and mourn. We needed to help the remaining clans make it to safety. Without us, they would surely be wiped out.

Taking to the air, we flew as fast and hard as we could to the place where the clans were making a forced march. Even from the air, we could tell that they were exhausted from being on the move for such a long time with very little rest, but they had been spared detection because of our actions. Now it was just a matter of time before we were discovered. We needed one last push to get to safety.

It took us longer than expected to find the clans. Peggy was again proving to be a genius at logistics and planning. They were miles ahead of where they were supposed to be.

"I figured that we were so close, that we no longer needed most of our supplies. The all-important thing is for us to reach the wormhole. If we don't, our gear isn't going to be of any help because we will just be wiped out by the Gonosz anyway," she explained.

I had hoped that we would have a few minutes of rest, but the dragon riders needed to take to the air to make sure that the clans weren't walking into an ambush.

"The clans should make the wormhole in about two hours. That puts us almost a day ahead of schedule. Peggy is a genius!" said Chayl as we started our air patrol. Once again, I was being counted on as the eyes. So far, I had seen nothing to suggest that we had been spotted, but that could change in an instant.

We were now just north of the mountain range that contained the valley with the wormhole. The other clans had entered from the south side of the mountain range, so our hope was that the Gonosz trackers would concentrate their efforts on that side of the range, and we would be able to slip into the valley undetected. The previous clans had done an excellent job in concealing the tracks of the clans within the valley. Several times, we had flown over the area to make sure that there were no Gonosz in and around the small valley.

"*Let's widen our patrol, but stay within telepathy distance. Marcus, you and Alan stay north of the mountain range and patrol the area there. Abi and Sabryyna, you will fly across the mountain range and patrol the south side. Cowboy and I will scout further ahead and try to find where the Gonosz are,*" said Chayl.

"*Let's be careful,*" said Alan. "*We need to hold off the Gonosz for only an hour or two, and then the clans should be safely through the wormhole.*"

With my enhanced vision and our patrol area being to the north of the mountain range, I was able to have my eyes on the clans as they made their way to the little canyon within the mountain range. Everyone knew that they were close, so it appeared that they had all had a burst of energy as they made their way closer and closer to safety.

We had been patrolling for about an hour when I spotted the movement.

"*Climb a little, Paxi,*" I said. It was so much easier getting the dragon to do what I needed, now that I could talk with him. I no longer needed my knees to guide Paxi, although I still wasn't secure enough to not need the riding harness.

My heart sank as I got a good look at what was causing the movement. It was Kal, along with at least fifteen other dragon teams, one being the team of Marrle, Jazmyne, and Loem'na, and they were heading directly towards us. There was no way that they wouldn't spot the clans now. With fifteen dragon rider teams, they would easily be able to attack the exposed clans, and it would be worse once the clans entered the valley. The walls would force the clans into a tight space in which the dragons could concentrate massive fireballs.

The canyon that was our source of escape was now a death trap.

"*Hey guys, we've got company. It's Kal and a whole bunch of dragon rider teams. They are coming from the northeast. There is no chance that they won't see the clans, unless we do something drastic,*" I called frantically.

The reason why Chayl was such a great leader was that he never seemed frazzled.

"*Remain steady, team,*" said Chayl, his voice icy-calm. "*I'm just east of the mountain range. All teams meet me here. And Marcus, make sure that Kal sees you and follows you. The closer he is to you, the better. We're going to try to lead them away.*"

By now, the clans were within telepathy range, so we quickly informed Peggy of our situation and what our tentative plan was. Peggy was now as adept at telepathy as a native of Vocce.

"*We're totally exposed,*" said Peggy. "*we will need to rely on you to lead them away.*"

Kal and his warriors had not seen us yet. Dropping lower, I had Cotopaxi speed towards Chayl. Once I felt sure that the clans were not in the sight-line of the attacking dragons, I had Cotopaxi pop up to expose us.

I cut it too close. Kal and his warriors were practically upon us already. I had mis-judged their speed.

We were very surprised at their appearance. If we looked startled, it was because we were. There was no need to act like we were shocked.

This time, Kal attacked without his normal threats. Maybe he was learning. Great. Kal was getting smart at the exact wrong time.

With a roar, 'Elu'ali'aq' was on us tearing at Cotopaxi's wings with his claws. It must have been one of his favorite moves, as I remembered the wounds that the dragon, Arayn, had received.

Cotopaxi took a bad tear in his left wing, but managed to roll away out of further damage. After that, it was a full-out sprint towards where Chayl and Abi were, and Cotopaxi flat out moved. I had trouble breathing as the wind rushed by us. Taking a quick look back, we started to edge away from the pursuing dragons. Selena had been right. Cotopaxi really was a magnificent dragon, despite the deformed claw.

"*How's your wing?*" asked Alan.

"*Paxi good. Don't worry about Paxi,*" said the speeding dragon.

"*Chayl, we're coming in hot,*" I said. "*And I mean they are right on our tail.*"

"*Good,*" said Chayl. "*We've got a little surprise for them. When you get to the mountain range, cut sharply behind the first peak and dive.*"

The peak appeared directly in front of us. Cotopaxi, once beyond the peak, cut and dove, just as Chayl had ordered. My stomach dropped as we pulled the maneuver. Kal and his dragons followed suit when they, too, cleared the peak. So intent were they on catching us, that they didn't see the attack from above. Chayl and Abi had been hiding in ambush. To be honest, it surprised me, too.

With bone-chilling screams, the dragons Sjer-berha and Hera'sha'I attacked two of the captured dragon teams. Within seconds, both of the captured dragon teams were either killed or wounded. The surprise attack pulled the attention off of us, and we were able to loop over and join with the attackers. Alan had already started shooting fireballs. Abi and Sabryyna were raining both fireballs and arrows down on the enemy. Not to be outdone, Cowboy had sent a bolt of lightning into the fray. Several dragon teams that had been close on our heels were now fighting for their lives.

Our attack was so unexpected and ferocious, that the enemy broke and ran. The escape route they chose took them right over our clans, as they made their way into the canyon. They now had a known location of the clans, and in the worst possible position. The narrow confines of a canyon.

It was too late to turn back now. The clans were committed to making it to the wormhole. Worse, the Gonosz would know the location of the wormhole. There would be no time to obscure the tracks of the clans. Even if they reached the wormhole, they were still in trouble.

We chased the enemy dragons, but it soon became apparent that word had gotten to the main body of the enemy.

On the horizon, we could see as many as fifty captured dragons heading toward us, each dragon carrying multiple warriors. They would be upon us in minutes.

Kal and the remaining dragon teams halted their retreat and reversed on us. Now that they had the numbers, staying to fight would be an annihilation. It would serve no purpose.

We were out of time. It was an all-out sprint by the clans now. We had let them know that they were discovered.

The first dragons to attack were Kal and his group, along with Marrle. It saddened me to see her and Jazmyne participate in the attack. I had sincerely liked both of them.

Kal led the attack. 'Elu'ali'aq' rained down fire as they passed over the clans. Screams of pain and fear could be heard from our position. Surprisingly, Marrle flew directly behind Kal, but Loem'na's fire caused no damage. In fact, it seemed to be directed into the walls of the canyon, and not at the clans.

"Follow me," said Chayl. *"We need to cover them as best as we can."*

Each time the enemy dragons started to make a strafing run, one of us would dive on them, causing them to pull up. Chayl's strategy was working. The dragons couldn't make a run with us diving on them. They were too exposed. Some of the clans were now able to enter the wormhole, with the vast majority still working their way through the canyon. If we could delay just fifteen minutes, but Kal changed strategies. Rather, I suspect that Kylor came up with the strategy. It wasn't necessary for the enemy to make strafing runs.

Instead, they landed the remaining dragons in front of the clans, blocking the path to the wormhole. From the air, I saw that the remainder of the Gonosz sealed off the other end of the canyon. The clans were about to be wiped out with both escape routes now sealed. My heart sank.

There were six dragon rider teams, with Kal blocking the way. Time and time again we attacked, but were driven off. Kal had focused two of the teams to hold the clans back, and believe me, two dragon teams were enough. The other four teams were tasked to fight us off. We couldn't get in close enough to effectively fight.

On one of my passes, Marrle caught eye contact with me.

"Be ready on your next pass," she told me telepathically, but her telepathic voice was weak. They were all wearing armor with an unusual helmet. I wondered if the helmet hampered the telepathic signal.

Not knowing if this was a trap, I relayed the message to the rest of the team.

"I always wondered why Marrle went with the Gonosz. This could be a trap, but Marrle's our only hope now. I guess we trust her," said Chayl.

We didn't know what to expect, so we made another dive. Normally, when we passed over, the dragon teams would concentrate fire at us, driving us off target. This time when we passed over Marrle's dragon, Loem'na, directed a fireball at Kal and 'Elu'ali'aq' who were facing away from Marrle. The surprise was complete as I heard Kal and Kylor yelp from the unexpected fireball. Unfortunately, 'Elu'ali'aq''s tail absorbed most of the fire, causing them little damage.

"Concentrate your fire at Kal," commanded Chayl. *"He's their leader!"*

All of us spun around and started firing on Kal. He had turned to fight Marrle, but we were now coming up behind him. Realizing that he was the focus of our attack, he ran. The other teams, seeing that their leader was running, also made a run for it. Abi and Sabryyna made short work of the two remaining captured dragon teams, who were keeping the clans at bay from entering the wormhole.

The clans now had a clear shot at the wormhole. Unfortunately, the main body of the Gonosz were hot on their tails. They might make it through the wormhole, but there was no reason why the Gonosz couldn't just follow them through, and finish everyone off. They now knew the location of the wormhole, but we would worry about that after we got everyone through.

"Let's get them as much time as possible," said Chayl.

The rear fighting was worse than we had thought. The rear guards were trying to hold off the main body of the Gonosz, but were paying a terrible price, and now we had another trained dragon rider team.

"Welcome back, Marrle and Jazmyne. You, too Loem'na," said Abi.

"It's a long story, but it is good to be back," said Marrle.

"Let us get back to work, then," said Chayl.

Peggy was with the main body of the clans, and she ordered us to the back to help with the fighting. The fighting had stopped the clans in their tracks, and we needed to get everyone moving again.

Flying through the canyon walls was a reminder of just how narrow the walls were. Cotopaxi's wings often brushed the narrower places within the canyon. Several times we resorted to landing and galloping several hundred yards until the canyon widened.

Reaching the battle, we realized just how bad it was. The captured dragon teams were charging forward breathing fire. The clans were getting mowed down.

With a roar, Sjer-berha rammed into the charging dragons. We followed suit and soon we were all in a ground battle, chaos everywhere. Alan proved himself once again, with deadly fire. I accessed Selena's crystal. I needed to help, even if my fireballs were largely ineffective. As I entered, I felt that this time was different. More powerful.

This time, when I shot the fireball, I felt real control over the placement. What I aimed at, I hit. For the first time, I felt that I was contributing to the team.

....

Our attack was giving the clans the time they needed to enter the wormhole. All that remained was the rear guard, tasked to keep the Gonosz off the main body of the clans. That, and us of course. The battle wasn't over. The Gonosz would just follow us through the wormhole, and we would be stuck trying to defend ourselves on an island with no escape.

"We'll need to get through the wormhole and set up to defend," said Alan. "They will need to come through one at a time. I hope that is enough of an advantage."

Only fifty warriors remained. We were going to make it through the wormhole. Peggy was ordering ten people through at a time.

Speedily, several more groups passed. All that remained were the dragon rider teams. Our training was enabling us to fight off the attacking enemy.

"Alright, riders. Break off your attack and come through the worm..." Peggy began.

A shadow passed over us. Looking up, I saw the largest dragon that I had ever seen. It was at least double the size of the largest dragons of either the clans or the Gonosz. It's mostly gray hide iridescent, alternating between gray and green.

When it landed in between us and the wormhole, the entire ground shook.

"Gyilkos!" breathed Chayl, and I could actually feel the fear in his voice.

It was the leader of the Gonosz, and he wasn't alone. His escort amounted to five dragon rider teams. Not captured dragons, but real dragon rider teams. Each dragon, a specimen in its own right. They had also landed and positioned themselves between us and the wormhole.

Kal was also with them, but a very different Kal. Kal was bloodied and bruised, with Kylor and 'Elu'ali'aq' not much better off. I knew that we hadn't caused such wounds, so it must have been Gylikos. Kal's head hung, sitting astride his dragon, not looking up.

Gylikos was well-muscled and had the lithe body of a warrior, but it was his eyes that held my attention.

His eyes were a bright sapphire blue. His skin and hair a

contrasting alabaster.

Without a word, he nodded towards us. The dragon teams that were with him instantly attacked. Up until now, our dragon rider team had done well. Our training had enabled us to do a match up against the Gonosz, but this was the varsity, and we were from a 2A school and they were from a 6A school.

As soon as we engaged, we knew we were outclassed. Cotopaxi was attacked by one of the smaller dragons, but she was fast and exceptionally quick. The rider and attendant were both smaller females, but battle-hardened and skilled. It was now a free-for-all. Each dragon rider doing what it took to stay alive.

Gylikos remained at the wormhole entrance, blocking the way to safety.

"We need Gylikos out of the way. Form up the best as you can, and let's attack him directly," Chayl ordered. Each time we shot fireballs or arrows, the projectile would fly straight at Gylikos, then with a wave of his hand, he would send them off harmlessly careening away. Even Cowboy's lightning bolts would ricochet away. Gylikos, sitting astride his dragon, a dispassionate look on his face as he effortlessly batted our fireballs, arrows, and lightning.

I hadn't taken the time to explore the crystals after the death of Selena, but we were desperate. Connecting with Larzi, I explored the familiar areas of the crystal. As far as I could tell, there was nothing new. It wasn't until I expanded my search, when I came upon what appeared to be Selena's blue fireball.

Accessing it, I could feel its power. It's several times more powerful than the fireball I had been shooting, and there was something else. I felt complete control over the fireball. I felt I could maneuver it however I needed to.

"Here goes nothing," I said to myself, as I turned and fired it at the small dragon that was attacking us.

The orb tracked straight until the small dragon easily dodged out of the way. Instead of continuing straight, the fireball followed my gaze, which was tracking the small dragon. With a spectacular flash of light, the blue fireball knocked the small dragon tumbling. Up until now, our fireballs had little effect on the dragons, but the blue fireball was much more powerful.

Turning my attention to Gylikos, I started firing my regular fireballs at him. I wanted to work my way as close as possible before I used my new weapon. My regular fireballs shot off harmlessly as Gylikos sent them harmlessly away, with as little effort as it takes to shoo a fly.

When I deemed we were close enough, I let loose the blue fireball. This time when Gylikos waved his hand, I could feel the tug on the fireball. Although it was knocked a little off course, I was able to quickly correct its flight path.

The fireball caught the massive dragon square in the chest, staggering the dragon.

For the first time, the expression on Gylikos changed. What had been an expressionless face, now showed genuine surprise.

Not allowing them time to recover, I shot another blue fireball, which took on the large dragon on his right side. This time the effect was pronounced.

With a roar, the dragon sagged to his knee upon contact. I shot several more fireballs, one after another, forcing the large dragon to take to the air to avoid being hit.

Our path was clear, but the rest of our team was still fighting for their lives.

Chayl was now flying directly towards us, a dragon team matching his every move.

"*Chayl, dive on the count of three!*" I said. On the count of three, Chayl dove, but not before a fireball glanced off of Cowboy. Cowboy instantly went slack, forcing Chayl to hold onto him as they nosed over into a dive.

Just as the dragon following them also nosed over, I fired a blue fireball that unseated both the rider and attendant. They both crashed to the ground as I sent more fireballs at the fleeing dragon, now riderless, flying for safety.

Abi and Sabryyna were flying with great skill. They had forced the dragon attacking them to make a mistake and overfly them. Dropping in behind the Gonosz dragon team, they easily dispatched the rider and attendant using arrows. Neither Gonosz rider was unseated, but as they flew off, they looked like pin cushions, arrows fairly bristling from their bodies.

Chayl was now making his way to the wormhole, Cowboy still slack and wrapped in Chayl's bearhug. They were followed by Marrle and Jazmyne, who were both bloodied and singed from fire.

"We're going to have to defend the wormhole," Alan said. "We can't let the Gonosz through it."

Landing, we eased over to the wormhole.

"Do we defend it from this side or the other side?" I asked.

Cotopaxi was staring intently at the wormhole.

"Probably this side," said Alan. "We can see when the attack is coming, and maybe we can hold them off in time for the others to prepare before we're overrun."

Cotopaxi was still staring at the wormhole intently.

"Hey Paxi, we're going to need your help now," I said.

The dragon wouldn't look away.

"Paxi we need you now."

"It seals," said Paxi.

He turned and looked at me.

"What?" I asked.

"Wormhole," he said. *"It seals."*

"Great! Let's go through and seal it up!" I said.

Cotopaxi shook his head.

"This side. This side seal," he said.

I instantly realized what the implications were. We were going to be able to protect the clans, but in doing so, we would be sacrificing ourselves.

Pushing the last of the surviving clans through the

portal, we turned to see Abi and Sabryyna land.

"*You first,*" I said. "*We'll follow.*"

I had no intention of following. Cotopaxi would gladly sacrifice himself for us by remaining alone, but I could never do that. I watched as Abi, Sabryyna, and Hera'sha'I charged through the hole, and I turned to Alan.

"Alan…" I began.

"Shut up, Marcus! I'm staying and that's final," he said.

Nodding, I took up a position in which to defend us while Cotopaxi started blowing fire on the portal. Alan gave me a crooked smile and did likewise. We had no illusions about our outcome, but at least the clans would be safe for the time being.

We knew that it would take several minutes before Cotopaxi would be able to seal the wormhole. We had to hold off the attacking Gonosz from getting to Cotopaxi for that entire duration, and they were coming in force.

Alan and I were now shooting fireballs at anything that moved, but without having the great and powerful flames of Cotopaxi, the enemy was able to get closer and closer. It was only a matter of time before we would be overwhelmed.

Several attacks were mounted that we were able to fend off, but finally there were just too many. Two large Gonosz got into our perimeter and started to attack Cotopaxi directly. In order to seal the wormhole, Cotopaxi needed to keep a steady stream of fire on it.

Alan had turned to fight the soldiers attacking Cotopaxi. My attention was with two dragon teams that suddenly materialized through the canyon.

One of the dragons started to breathe fire, but was just out of range. A blue fireball knocked him rolling, but the other dragon was right behind, and let loose with her own fireball. It knocked me over, my hair and skin singed. I turned in time to fire two more fireballs, but it wasn't enough. I was knocked down again as the dragon flew past, her tails lashing out to catch me in the chest. The wind was knocked from me, and I was sure that I now had a broken rib. I was an expert on broken ribs.

I had failed.

Cotopaxi had to break off his attention on the wormhole and was now standing over me and Alan, fighting off the enemy.

Another Gonosz dragon team had gotten by us and entered the wormhole. This was the beginning of the end. We couldn't keep them back now.

Just as the Gonosz dragon team entered the wormhole, it came back, each of its riders filled head to toe with arrows, and right behind them emerged Abi riding Hera'sha'i. A huge breath of fire from the dragon sent the enemy scrambling for cover.

"Why didn't you come through the wormhole?" Abi asked, her face angry.

I shrugged.

"The wormhole seals from this side," I said.

"Why didn't you tell me," she asked furiously.

"I wanted you to be safe."

"Idiot," she said, with a shake of her head. "We need to give Paxi time to seal the wormhole, at all cost."

Wave after wave of attacks were sent at us for the next few minutes. Each of us sustained injuries, but we continued to fight on.

Then with a "pop" the wormhole was sealed, no trace of the vortex.

And there we were. Two dragons and three riders, against an entire army.

In the distance, we could see Gylikos and his dragon riders. It was easy to see that they were going to attack with force.

"We can either stay here, defend ourselves, and die, or we can attack and die," Abi said with a ferocious grin.

When you are going to die in the next few minutes, and the girl you love suggests going out in a blaze of glory, you don't say "no," or argue.

In seconds, we were astride our dragons, charging Gylikos and his dragon riders who were bunched together within the narrow confines of the canyon. We had no plan, only to do as much damage as possible before we were killed.

Of all the things that Gylikos was expecting of us, an attack must not have been one of them. Before he could react, we were in the midst of the enemy dragon riders firing, fighting, and clawing. The momentum of our charge took us barreling through the surprised front line, the enemy scrambling for safety.

Cotopaxi had just spun to return to attack when Hera'sha'I came charging by.

"Scrap Plan A. Follow me!" yelled Abi.

Our charge had taken the enemy by surprise, and Abi had recognized the opening. The canyon was too narrow to fly where we were at, but there was an opening further ahead. We fairly mowed down any of the enemy in front of us.

The enemy dragon riders had re-grouped and were now hot on our tails. We could hear them crashing through the canyon behind us.

The opening in the canyon appeared before us, and Hera'sha'I sprang into the air, Cotopaxi not far behind.

When we got into the air, I began to scan around the area. Some of the captured dragons had been used as pack animals on the ground, but many of them were in the air patrolling.

We had the element of surprise. Before they could react, we were flying hard to the northwest, back toward the wormholes that would take us back to Earth.

If we were to survive, we needed to outdistance the enemy dragon riders, and Cotopaxi was showing signs of tiring. We had been flying and fighting for several days straight, and he was starting to labor in his breathing.

I could feel the riding harness strain each time he took a breath.

"Help me cut this thing off," I said to Alan.

"Are you sure?" he asked. I didn't have the most stellar record of being able to stay mounted without the riding harness, and the possibility that Cotopaxi would need to use evasive flying was pretty high.

"Paxi needs every advantage," I said.

Strap after strap was cut, and finally the harness fell free.

Now free of the harness, Cotopaxi could breath free and move without constriction.

"*Better, Marcus. Better.*" he said with gratitude. "*Don't fall off!*"

CHAPTER THIRTY TWO

CATCH YOU ON THE FLIP SIDE

Night was fast approaching, and it was the only advantage we had. We were now passing the fortress in the mountains that we had built to defend against the Gonosz. I wondered how long we would have lasted, had we stayed and defended ourselves there instead.

We decided that we would avoid the old clan camp and head straight north to the wormhole that would take us back to the original clan camp. It seemed like years ago that I had been in that amphitheater and chosen to be a dragon rider.

As darkness closed, I could see that we were outdistancing the trailing enemy riders. I watched as Gylikos directed small groups of riders to break off and search different areas. With my enhanced vision, I could tell that they had now lost sight of us because of the darkness, but the majority of the riders were on our tail because they knew our destination.

It took several hours, but we finally closed in on the wormhole. With my enhanced vision, I scanned the area. There was what looked like enough for two squads, guarding the wormhole. My heart sank. There were two captured dragons with them, but blocking the wormhole.

"There's about twenty warriors and two dragons," I reported to Alan and Abi. *"The dragons are directly in front of the wormhole."*

"Now isn't the time to play it safe. Follow me in," Abi said

and Hera'sha'I dove.

Cotopaxi didn't wait. He naturally followed the other dragon as we dove into the camp of the enemy. They were on alert, but we dropped in on them before they could react. Hitting the ground running, we didn't slow our charge. Ramming into the nearest dragon, Hera'sha'I knocked the surprised dragon out of the way, clearing the way to the wormhole.

Charging through the wormhole, we came out on the other side. We went from the dry desert climate, to lush rainforest. Without any guidance, Cotopaxi veered to the right and charged into a boulder field. Making his selection, he started to push a boulder the size of a large car towards the wormhole. Seeing what Cotopaxi had planned, Hera'sha'I joined in and pushed another boulder towards the vortex.

A warrior jumped through the wormhole and was rewarded with several arrows to his midsection, and a fireball to the chest for his efforts. Abi had anticipated his arrival. Cotopaxi rolled the boulder up close to the vortex, and Hera'sha'I fitted his in behind it. It would take some effort to move them out of the way.

The boulders shook from a large collision.

Cotopaxi snorted with amusement.

"Dragon has a bad headache," he said, his eyes sparkled with amusement.

Within a couple of hours, we came up to the wormhole that would take us back to Earth. Landing, the dragons flopped to the ground completely spent.

"Let's spend the night here and return home after the dragon's rest," Abi said.

The dragons weren't the only ones exhausted. We had been either on the run or fighting for several weeks. The physical strain was horrible, but the mental strain was nearly unbearable, and I hadn't had the opportunity to fully mourn the death of my sister. I suspected that Abi, in her great wisdom, knew that I needed time alone before returning home.

Leaving our camp, I slipped into the coolness of the

night. The change in climate was night and day. We never seemed to have enough water in the desert climate that we had come from, and now we were camped next to a stream brimming with water.

Without even removing my clothes, I stepped into the water. It felt amazing.

I let myself slip under the surface, and swam out into deeper water. When I felt that I was alone, I abandoned myself to grief.

It was several hours later when I returned to camp, soaking wet. Abi stirred when I came back.

"I miss her too," she said softly.

There was a small fire burning. I sat down next to it.

"I'll turn my back. Change into dry clothing and let your wet ones dry by the fire," she said as she turned her back to me.

I changed quickly and set my wet things by the fire. I had been beyond tired when we first landed, but now I was strangely unable to sleep.

Abi had fallen asleep, and I could hear the steady breathing from both her and Alan. Nobody could miss the deep breathing of the dragons. I was more alone than ever. For over a year, Selena had been a constant presence. I had felt her twenty four hours a day. Now there was nothing.

Not knowing what else to do, I connected to Selena's crystal, which was now my crystal. I had not explored it much because we had been on the constant move since Selena's death.

Exploring around, I found the blue fireball, but there was also something new. I accessed it with my mind.

Selena sprang up before me.

"*Before you get too excited, I must be dead if you are accessing this,*" said Selena. "*This is a stored memory. This takes up a fantastic amount of energy to store a memory, so this will be short. The crack in the crystal...there's something about it that I haven't been able to figure out, but my gut tells me that the crack is important. I'm guessing that it was purposely placed there by the dragons*" *that imbued the crystal with its powers. I know you don't want to hear this, but it's up to you to figure it out.*

I love you Marcus. I'm also guessing that you will need to inform Grandma of my death, so give her all my love. Catch you on the flip side, Captain Puke Shirt."

Over and over I played the message, just to see and hear Selena. Somewhere along the way, I fell into an exhausted sleep.

Epilogue

It had been two weeks since we had crossed through the wormhole to Earth. Telling Grandma about Selena was even more difficult than the first time I had had to do it.

Alan's reunion with his family was joyful, to say the least. They were awed at the changes in him. Both of us had gone through some serious physical changes, living in a world with heavier gravity and lesser oxygen, but Alan just carried himself differently. Even with his slight size, he had a confident aura about him that was undeniable.

Wynn and Maria had remained on earth when we had crossed over, and they were now living in the cabin owned by Cowboy and Peggy's family. Abi had returned to living with them. Several times Alan and I had traveled out to the cabin to give our report and to see Abi. She was missing Sabryyna who had stayed to watch after Cowboy, who had been hurt in our battle with the Gonosz.

It was strange going from war back to normality. I had nightmares every night that we were still back on Vocce, but I was slowly adapting regardless. Wynn and Maria had suggested that we slip back into our old lives. With the wormhole sealed, the clans were relatively safe, and there was nothing we could do to help them now.

I pulled up to the school to register for classes. I had parked in one of the lesser-used lots so that I could avoid as many people as possible, but in doing so, I would need to cut through the buildings.

"Hello, sweetheart!" said a familiar voice.

Turning, I found Eldon sitting at a gazebo with several of his friends.

"I thought you graduated. Why on earth are you still hanging around here?" I asked.

"Not that it's any of your business, but I'm working maintenance for the school district as a summer job before I go to college," said Eldon. "Where have you been? You haven't called, you haven't written, it's as if you don't love me anymore."

I knew what was coming. There was no use running from it. I just waited for it to happen, but then I felt a familiar presence. I couldn't see him, but I knew he was there.

"*Should Paxi eat chubby boy?*" asked the dragon.

"*No, Paxi. This is something I have to do on my own,*" I said, wondering where the dragon was hiding. He was amazingly stealthy and I had long since stopped trying to get him to not follow me everywhere.

"*Good. Him not shower much. Probably taste terrible. Paxi can't brush teeth like Marcus,*" said the dragon.

My laughter caught Eldon off guard. I wasn't acting the way he expected, and it bothered him.

"What have you been doing all summer? The last time I beat you up, you were all soft and doughy. Now you're all muscly and pretty. Not that it's going to help you at all," Eldon said.

I remained still, my hands hanging loose at my sides, my body relaxed. My attitude bothered Eldon, bad.

And then he punched me in the stomach...or rather he tried to punch me in the stomach. In every fight, the stomach had been his go-to move, and I was ready for it. Blocking his punch, I stepped out of arm's reach, my arms dropping to my side again. My body relaxed, but ready.

"I'm giving you a chance to save face in front of your friends, Eldon," I said softly, so that only he could hear. "I'm not the same scared boy you used to pick on."

"I'm going to hurt you one last time before I bless those hot college women with my presence," he said loudly, ignoring my offer. He had made his boast in front of his friends, and he couldn't back down now.

As quick as a cat, he struck. But again, I calmly blocked his punch.

"One last chance, Eldon," I said softly.

My reactions weren't what he was expecting, and it bothered him. I could tell that he didn't want to fight me now. I was too confident, and he liked to be the sure-thing bully. He might have backed away except...

"You've got this, big man!" shouted one of the girls that hung around Eldon and his friends. "Don't let this punk talk his way out of a spanking!"

There was no saving face now, and he was now committed.

Charging in, his fists were now flying in looping punches. Rather than back off, I stepped inside his punches and fired short body shots to his ribs. Each punch had the added force of weeks of training with Alan. He had taught me well how to throw the enhanced hits.

The look on Eldon's face might have been comical if it weren't so sad. Eldon's entire identity was that of the bully. In seconds, I had robbed that of him as he sank to the ground, the wind completely driven from him. His eyes wide at the surprise of being hurt.

I wasn't even breathing hard as I knelt next to him.

"I warned you. It didn't have to come to this," I said, and I turned my back on him and walked away.

Just as I got to the main door, Abi and Alan walked around the corner, smiles on both of their faces.

"You were there all along?" I asked Abi.

"Of course," she said.

"And you didn't come to save me?"

"You didn't need saving."

And three dragon riders walked arm and arm into Mountain View High School to register for fall classes.

Made in the USA
Monee, IL
15 April 2022

94779377R00266